Salad Days
Charles Romalotti

D1595867

Layman Books

Austin   New York   London   Sydney   Hong Kong

SALAD DAYS - LAYMAN BOOKS
ISBN: 0-9679235-0-6

All rights reserved.
Copyright © 2000

Edited by Marilyn LaMarsh and Daniel Smith
Cover art by Daniel Smith
Cover layout design by Daniel Smith and Dylan Muir
Photo of Romalotti by Andrew Ellis

Available direct-mail from Layman Press for $10

Layman Press
P. O. Box 4702
Austin, TX 78765-4702
www.flash.net/~layman
layman@flash.net

Writing began December 1995, completed January 1999

Release date: June 1, 2000

Printed in the United States by
Morris Publishing
3212 East Highway 30
Kearney, NE 68847
1-800-650-7888

ACKNOWLEDGMENTS

This book was only made possible by the overwhelming support of
Carolyn LaMarsh.

I am indebted to the following people for giving their time and generous comments to
help complete this novel:
Carolyn LaMarsh, Yancy Westgate, Ginger Stringer, Jan Fanette, Laura Gramly,
Marilyn LaMarsh, Molly Lambert, Heather Lambert, Amy Gilmore, Josh Muir, Cassie
Marshall, Jesse Casas, Christopher Bryant, Windy Boyd, and Connie Westgate

And to those who supported my creative efforts early on:
Roberta Smith, David Dutton, Dominick Haen, Donna Hauser, Leonard Smith, Cassie
Marshall, and Christopher Bryant.

Finally, I would like to thank my excellent parents—Bertie and Clarence. They raised
a good kid. I didn't turn out too bad, either.

for Charlie
who helped me keep the dream alive

Where It All Begins

My best friend died today. The truth I can tell you now, as plain as the black words that you read, yet the truth has not yet found its place amidst my rational comprehension. The news yanked me from a deep slumber. I was awakened minutes before the call stirred my quiet quarters. Somehow, I knew. My life would never be the same.

It is election day. November 3, 1998. The beginning of the rest of my life...

Before the sun had brought forth a new day, I had already finalized arrangements for a last-minute flight from Austin to Kansas, charging the trip to my final line of available credit. I am now officially broke. And my dead-end job—well, it will have to wait for my return.

The time is a little past eight o'clock, and the life of the city is slowly gaining its momentum. Outside, I can see the landscape of runways of the Houston Hobby airport. Inside, I wait patiently for a connecting flight in an overpriced airport diner. *Betty's World Famous Apple Pie*. There are no other occupants.

An adolescent girl with bad acne and an even less appealing sense of fashion is tending the counter, watching the *Jerry Springer Show*. Her face is drawn into a complacent scowl that lightens only when the transvestites come to blows. She finds comfort in their pain. It makes her feel normal, average. It makes her skin fit more comfortably. Most importantly, it strengthens her faith in mediocrity. Her transparent eyes give this away. I could imagine her thoughts as she stands at the career that saps her life: *this is as good as it gets...*

An empty foam cup sweats in my hand. I pick up a piece of ice—slightly browned from the Pepsi, and shove it into my mouth. The faint taste of soda quickly dissolves to the bite of frozen water slipping down my throat. I haven't got the money for a refill.

"What does your tattoo mean?" the young girl asks me between commercial breaks. She points down at my arm, at the words: *Committed For Life*.

I look up and smile politely. "Everything."

From the window, the world seems immense. It didn't look that way yesterday.

The Muzak version of Modern English's *I Melt With You* is playing softly from a nearby speaker. Warm memories surround the song. Memories of my dead friend. Memories of the way life once was. New Wave music was my life back then. It changed my way of being, and it changed the way I viewed what was once a simple and predictable world. My perspective wasn't shared in the farming community in which I was raised. Iola, Kansas. That small ripple of expression became something more substantial when I discovered the Dead Kennedys' latest release, *Plastic Surgery Disasters*. The flood followed soon after.

Everyone has a story to tell. And this one is mine...

Condoms Arise!

The wind ripped through the windows of my old 1965 Ford Falcon Ranchero, tossing my stiff dreadlocks like live snakes. The trail of my fate followed a barren, gravel road through endless fields of wheat. My thin white hands gripped tightly the steering wheel as the car swerved from side to side, floating over the gravel like a rudder through water. The road stretched outward to the level horizon, its destination and starting point both oblivion. I was stuck somewhere dead-center.

The setting sun casted a tremendous glare on my dusty windshield. It appeared as the head of a rusted nail driven into a copper sky. I raced toward it like a moth rushing to a lamp, driven by the hope and promise of a safe haven.

I knew better.

I glanced at the speedometer—seventy-five miles-per-hour over loose gravel. In my rearview mirror a glowing cloud of dust erupted from beneath the tires. The bright headlights of a truck rumbled through the haze, trailing me like a wolf set on killing and devouring its prey. I glared defiantly into the mirror, my foot a lead weight on the flattened gas pedal. The Ranchero roared into the sunset with the anthemic blast of Black Flag's *Rise Above* filling the solitude of the empty cab.

The identity of my pursuers was as much a mystery as I was to them. All I knew was the town they claimed as their own: Chanute, Kansas, home of the Fighting Cocks. Their intentions were pure, just a couple good ol' boys out for a Sunday lynching. It was the type of activity that'd make their daddies proud.

Over meat and potatoes they'd boast proudly:

"Hey, Pop! Almost caught that faggot from Iola today!"

"Well, son, I'm proud of you! You'll make a fine cop someday. Better luck next time, Junior. Don't forget your sister wants you to be her date to the Prom..."

The truck followed tightly. The headlights represented the eyes of seven thousand citizens watching my every move through clouded vision.

The sun edged closer to the sparse horizon. It would soon be dark, when all good lynchings take place. Unlike their fathers, these kids weren't wearing bed sheets, and they didn't have a cross to burn on my lawn. They were proud of their actions, and wanted their involvement in my destruction known. They'd brag about it at school all week. This day, they wouldn't have the honor.

Eventually, and in no record time, the lights began to fade behind me. I was safe to return home, to end another typical day.

For the record, let me state that my story is not an uncommon one. As with many others, teachers often shared with me their lack of faith in my future. Cops threatened violence after having chased me down lonely back roads for no apparent reason. My high school principal loathed my existence. I was banned from several restaurants and institutions in town. Occasionally, the locals would bleed me for my "cause." I had no friends, but all that changed my freshman year.

That's where I'll begin, on the upswing...

It was a cool autumn day, though I could only guess the weather from the window of my last afternoon class. At the end of the day, I had a race to run—a race any class geek was forced to endure. My opponents were a clan of farmboys following the leadership of two twins, Jack and Ben Dewie. They maintained sturdy, masculine frames and intolerant dispositions. Their matching reddish-orange crewcuts looked like the crowns of spring dandelions.

I stared blankly at the chalkboard over my instructor, Mr. Lippschitz's shoulder. Mr. Lippschitz could've been the leading man in any Russ Meyer film, all the way down to the 1970's styled mustache. His shiny brown hair was well managed, feathered and parted down the middle for the wind-blown effect. His silk shirts were always two buttons loose from the collar, revealing a thick covering of chest hair and shiny gold chains.

"...so as the Allies were preparing their big strike on the shores of Normandy, Hitler had—"

"I wonder if we would've beaten them at basketball..." Howard Feltersnatch, popular athlete pondered loudly to the class.

"Beaten who, Howard?" Lippschitz pried with a friendly chuckle.

"Hitler's team," Howard said as he ran his fingers through his own wind-blown, feathered hair. The length of his mullet hairstyle rested on the erect collar of his baby-blue Izod shirt.

"I don't think Hitler had a basketball team, Howard."

Lippschitz smiled awkwardly at Howard, a look that seemed to request permission to continue. The class laughed at Howard's attempt at humor to ensure their social standing. I laughed at this absurd political game-playing, wondering how many more seconds Howard would allow Lippschitz to discuss History before announcing to the class he was taking his sister to the Prom.

"Frank, are you finding something funny?!" Lippschitz asked sharply as the classroom roared with laughter.

"Well—"

"Stay after class," he growled fiercely. "Now, Hitler assumed the Commies—or, the Russians..."

As class came to a close, I stepped up to his desk and waited for our routine confrontation. He gave the popular kids a cheery farewell, ignoring the less fortunate, nerdy kids whom actually paid attention to every lecture.

"Frank, what's your problem?" he demanded.

I didn't reply, or if I did, it wasn't with any distinguishable words.

"Mind if I knock that chip off your shoulder about not making the basketball team?" he threatened, referring to the tryouts the previous week. "Still a little sour, are we? I honestly can't fathom that you wouldn't cut your hair in order to join the basketball team."

I weaved my fingers through the dreadlocks of my ratty mohawk. "Of course not."

"I always thought you loved to play. I'm really disappointed in you. You've spent your whole life playing this game, and now you're just throwing it away for a haircut? You understand you will never be able to make this choice again?"

I nodded.

"I can't believe your sissy hair means that much to you."

"It means nothing to me," I told him.

3

"Then, why? I don't understand you, Frank. If it were me, you can bet I would discipline myself and stop going against the grain, stop dressing like a faggot. I'd clean my act up, get a haircut, buy some decent clothes, act like the rest. That's what I'd do."

"That's what you'd do?"

"Yes, of course," he determined quickly.

"That's all the reason I need."

"You're a lost cause, Smith. You have a lot to learn about pride, about self-respect, and integrity..."

I smiled. I thought back a couple years when my brother was also cut from the roster. Pursuing basketball was his dream. He had the skill, but not the clout. Our house had a heavy air of silence for quite a while. I stood before the man who had decided our fate.

"I don't know why I bother trying to help you, Frank. You're a loser, like your brother. People like you disgust me...I feel my stomach churn when I think of your pathetic existence. You will never be *anything*, you will never amount to *anything*...get the *hell* out of here!"

I grabbed my books and strolled out the door, following the extension of his pointed finger into the quiet hallway.

Suddenly, I felt my body smash firmly against the cold metal lockers. I turned to the fiery hair of the Dewie brothers, backed by several of their comrades. They stared at me with hollow, reflective eyes.

Forcing myself free of their clutches, I scurried awkwardly down the hall and out the doors. Patches of mint and teal and peach clothing vibrated through my line of vision as I rushed to the gravel parking lot. I could tell by their quick steps that they weren't far behind me.

As I rounded the building, I spied another set of goons standing patiently by my Ranchero. They were getting good at this. They clearly had me this time.

An old pick-up truck filled with bales of hay pulled out of one of the stalls and headed toward me at a tremendous speed. It skidded next to me as a trail of dust rolled over the hood like a thunderstorm.

"Get in," rang a thin, high voice from the cab.

The duststorm quickly dispersed to reveal the stern face of Stanley Stockton—the short, chubby introvert from Biology class. We had never spoken. As far as I knew, he had never spoken to anyone. His green eyes beckoned me with reason and compassion.

Empty-handed and free of option, I heaved myself over the rail of the truck's bed onto the hay. I clung tightly to the bailing wire as the scavengers reached the tailgate. They clawed at my shoes while grabbing tightly to my ankles, pulling. The truck sped off through the parking lot with a shower of rocks pelting them from the wide snow tires. The cloud of dust consumed them, yanking them from my vision—and temporarily from my life.

My fleeting sense of safety became suffocated at the hands of reason as I looked over the cab to my unknown destination. The frigid wind blasted my pale face while the smell of mud and manure seeped from the bed of the truck. I clung tightly to the wires that encased the dull golden bails. My scrawny body rocked back and forth against the inertia of each turn.

I knew close to nothing about Stanley Stockton. Aside from his impeccable scholastic record, he was practically mute in a world that screamed around me. There was only one fact I could pull from common knowledge: he was heir to his family's

4

immense farming empire in nearby Woodson county. He would someday own a good portion of the county's land.

Mechanical parts and tools cluttered the cab of the filthy vehicle. A lead pipe was wedged between the seats with the words *The Enforcer* written in black ink down the shaft. A faded Harley-Davidson sticker clung loosely to the cracked dashboard— apparently keeping it intact like a bandage. Cassette tapes of Johnny Cash and Roger Miller lay amongst bolts and wingnuts on the oil-stained floorboard.

The truck skidded to the side of an alley by the town Square, giving me just enough time to roll off the bails onto the street. I landed awkwardly on my knees. As I stood, I could feel the burn of blood seeping from new wounds, staining my freshly ripped jeans.

"They get you every day, don't they?" His voice was sweet and honest—a strange mixture of country-boy and college professor. Thick strands of coarse, sandy-blond hair clung to the perspiration on his forehead. It hadn't been combed in days.

"They try now and then. You know...they aren't all that smart."

"Yeah," he mumbled as he checked his mirrors. "Like a rabbit in a foxhole. I have one of them in my Chemistry class."

I surveyed the quiet streets, revealing my calm as a facade. "They aren't going to be happy about this."

"Fuck 'em," he said with a smile. Blond whiskers covered his rugged face. "Need some excitement 'round these parts. So, what's that fucked-up music I hear you playing in that old Ford of yours? It's not from around *here*." There was a subtle bite of sarcasm supporting his comment. I respected the fact that he assumed I would catch it.

"No, it's not from *these parts*."

"Tell you what," he began, "you make me a tape of that music, and we'll consider ourselves square."

"Why?"

"Because I haven't heard it. What's it to you?"

"Okay, you got it," I promised.

"You can find your own way to your car, it's not that far. Hell, nothing's far in this town."

The next day after school, he waited in the parking lot next to the Ranchero. A faded pair of Big Smith overalls covered his stout body. He stood firm like a sentry, his stocky build passed down from a lineage of hard-working farmers.

"Do you still want it?" I asked, pulling the cassette from my pocket.

He looked at me with an insulted glare and snatched it from my hands. He nodded slowly, confidently before examining the cassette. He struggled to read my writing through the plastic case.

"The Fartz, huh? There's a band called the Fartz?" He wasn't so much asking as reveling in the absurdity. I knew at that moment he would like it. "The Circle Jerks! The Dicks! Where'd they get these names?!"

"Enjoy the tape," I told him as I stepped up to my car. "Thanks again. I guess this makes us even?"

"The Hard-Ons! Doggy Style!"

"I'll see you later..."

I jumped into my Ranchero and rushed out of the parking lot through a somber, quiet neighborhood scattered with fallen leaves. I smiled to myself as I raced home with M.I.A.'s *Boredom Is The Reason* blasting from the cab.

5

The shrill cry of the bell echoed through the hall as I rushed up the stairs to my first period class. The hallway cleared quickly as the seconds raced toward the threat of tardiness.

"Hey, Frank," a voice beckoned timidly over my shoulder.

I turned to Thik Toller, a classmate two years my senior—a professional high school student. His name, by the way, was pronounced *teak* rather than the obvious *thick*. He was a short guy of medium build with messy, thin black hair. He stood calmly before me with his limp hand resting passively inside the pocket of his faded, bleach-stained jeans. He propped himself casually against the wall. An old Kiss concert T-shirt hung loosely from his pale body like frozen waves of tar. A smile of comfort and pride lit his pasty, freckled face.

Thik was the drummer for a local hard rock cover band named Vengeance. His other claim to local notoriety was for his small-time thievery—a reputation he was proud to have acquired. He and a few of his friends were part of a "gang" called the Kleptos. Their only crime aside from spray-painting *Kleptos* on highway overpasses was their deep pockets for anything that could fit, regardless of value. The youngest of two siblings, Thik was the only one not viewing the world through bars.

"We're playing a gig this weekend," he told me. "Whitaker's garage. Think you could show?"

"What about Whitaker's parents?" I asked.

Thik laughed quickly, something he did quite often. He understood my point. Whitaker, the band's guitarist, was the oldest child of Whitaker MacGregor Senior, principal of one of the town's three elementary schools. The MacGregors were pillars of Iola society. They weren't fond of our notorious reputations.

"They'll be shopping in Kansas City over the weekend," Thik responded. "That's what people like them do."

"Okay, I'll be there."

"Right on." He scooted away with an awkward, untimely giggle.

Thik always held a great deal of respect for me. Not that he was aware of any reasons for which respect was due, but he did understand how I effortlessly ruffled so many feathers. That was all that mattered to him.

"If I'm going to make an impression on someone," he once told me, "it better be a bad one."

The tables of the school cafeteria were one of the most complex structures of territory I have yet to experience in my life. Once a table was claimed by a certain clique, it was their domain until graduation. In the center of the lunchroom was a group of old tables with chipped tops and loose, squeaky chairs. This was my territory, away from everyone else. Lunch was a time of quiet solitude for me. No one spoke to me, and I spoke to no one. Then, of course, as I had mentioned, all that was changing...

"Hey, man, I talked to Whitaker in the gifted class," Stanley said as he took a seat across from me. "He wants me to check out Vengeance. I was thinking maybe you'd want to go with me..."

I nodded politely. "Actually, Thik asked me to go. I was planning on it."

"I could drive," he offered. "My mother would let me use the car."

The Dewie brothers wandered into the cafeteria, cutting quickly to the front of the line.

"Sure," I said. "Sounds good."

6

"I like the tape," he told me. "I like it a lot. I listen to it every day."

I nodded politely. "I do, too."

The Dewie brothers strolled our direction after they gathered their food.

"Are you sucking this guy off now, Stanley?" Ben Dewie asked, staring at him as if he were a traitor.

His followers laughed on cue, stopping together on a dime.

"Yeah, are you a faggot, too?" Jack Dewie asked slowly.

Laughter to silence in unison again.

Stanley slowly took a sip of his chocolate milk as they stood behind him, scratching their balls.

"You gonna start dressing like a faggot?" Jack asked with a chorus of laughter to back him. He was clearly the thinker of the group.

"How does a 'faggot' dress, Jack, and how do you know this?" Stanley asked.

The chorus chuckled together until they realized Jack wasn't satisfied with that particular response. One of Jack's goons kept laughing by himself, his short attention still lingering on how to conquer that itch.

"I'll kick yer ass, you damn queer!!"

The cafeteria became deathly quiet, edged with anticipation to the next hormonal outburst. A nearby table of popular girls sat ogling his bravery as he and his mob towered over the two of us. Mr. Lippschitz, the "Security Man" of the cafeteria watched excitedly like an adolescent boy viewing his first porno. He would have some food for thought while masturbating later that night.

Suddenly, Jack smacked the back of Stanley's head. The shrill sound of it echoed over the diminishing buzz of conversations. Lippschitz approached at this point—his chest protruding from a tragic imbalance of testosterone.

"Jack, you and the boys need to mosey on over to your own stables before your fixin's get cold," Lippschitz said firmly, yet cautious to maintain their respect.

The Dewie boys strutted away with Jack saying something profoundly clever to the effect of: *"I'll get you sometime, faggot! At the bike rack—three o'clock!"*—his threat characteristically drawn from the previews of the World Wrestling Federation. He even had that slobbering, frothing-at-the-mouth effect that any given masked wrestler mastered in front of the bathroom mirror.

All the girls in the cafeteria were impressed. Maybe they'd request he do it again during a romantic moment in the back of his pick-up truck at the drive-in theater.

"Just one more time, you cuddly baboon," she'd whisper softly.

"Well," he'd return with a sultry, breathy voice while scratching his crotch for good measure. Moving in for the slow, passionate kiss, he'd scream: *"I'll get you, Faggot!"*

...and their lips met as a strand of drool swung from his chin onto her rosary.

"You're the greatest, Jack," she'd say as she began counting the hairs on his chest once again.

"Stanley," Mr. Lippschitz said as he took a seat at his side. "Why are you hanging out with this creep?" He gestured to me, eyeing me up and down. "Look at this waste of human life. Do you want to be like this? Do you want to be the laughing stalk of southeast Kansas, too? I mean, come on, Stanley. You aren't this much of a pathetic loser—you could be a doctor or lawyer, you could really be something someday. Why this?"

"Why what?" Stanley asked, a spoonful of mashed potatoes filling his mouth.

7

"Don't do this to me, Stanley," he said as he stood. "I worked really hard to give you the education you have."

Stanley rushed to finish his meal. His irritation stiffened his large frame.

"I look forward to the day you try crossing the street in front of my car, queer," Lippschitz warned me as he returned to his post.

Stanley quickly left, leaving me in silence as the whispers spread through the cafeteria like malaria.

"So, Frankie," the voluptuous brunette whispered in my ear.

I opened the passenger door of my Porsche 911 for her to slide into. Her beautiful brown eyes stared into mine with attention, and intention. Her full red lips seemed wet enough to stir. Liz Claiborne spoke my name without words, pressing me to act on every impulse exploding within my body. Black Flag's *Slip It In* hummed from the boxy Alpine speakers.

"What would you like to do now?" she asked. She ran her index finger from her neck, down her cleavage, to her slim waist. Her black satin dress blew in the gentle, soft breeze. Her long, claw-like nails were painted candy-apple red to match her succulent lips. Long, thin hoops of gold hung from each ear, tangling her permed locks. Her perfectly shaped legs drowned inside shiny, red leather pumps.

I wanted her now more than anything on earth.

"Well, Miss Canyon," I replied nervously, loosening the bow tie of my tuxedo. My cumberbun was suddenly strickening me. I felt hot and overdressed. I felt she must've been hot and overdressed as well. At least she appeared to be.

"Please, Frankie, call me Christy."

"Okay, Miss Canyon, I mean Christy...I guess we could go back to my suite at the Marriott and..."

"*Frank,*" Mr. Dalton, my drama teacher said to me, taking me far from my fantasy world into a much darker realm of my actual surroundings. "Could you meet me after class?"

I nodded apprehensively. Dalton had never given me trouble before. I could only imagine what he wanted.

He continued his lecture, cracking jokes to maintain attention while he over-enunciated every word. He was a small man with a receding hairline that cheated the appearance of a boyish face. His passion for dramatics appealed to me—the content of his lecture was a distant second.

When the bell rang a few minutes later, I remained seated as he shuffled papers and attended to small, pointless chores until the classroom was our sole domain.

"How are you, Frank?" He sat up comfortably on his desk in front of me. He loosened his cuffs and rolled up each sleeve. The ironed fabric folded unwillingly.

"Fine."

"Dead Kennedys, huh?" he groaned as he stared down at the various buttons of punk bands on my jacket. "That's atrocious."

"Yes, you've made that comment before."

"I'm sure I'll say it again." He smiled briefly before falling into a firm stare. "Why aren't you trying out for basketball?"

"Didn't know you were a fan."

"I can't imagine why you wouldn't try out," he said. "I've seen you play. Is there some truth to these rumors about drugs?"

I laughed. "To answer your question, I did try out."

"You got cut? Certainly not."

"I didn't get cut, I was...removed."

"How?" he asked, genuinely confused by my wording.

"My unruly appearance."

"What?" His face restricted with confusion. "It's a mess, I admit, but not a hindrance."

I shrugged my shoulders with calm indifference.

He shook his head and scratched his clean-shaven chin. "That's reason enough to keep someone off a basketball team? And Principal Small is aware of this?"

"Aware? Of course…"

His gaze landed somewhere between the desk and my feet. His forehead descended into a contemplative glare. I had never seen him at such a loss for words. It felt strangely improper for me to bare witness, as if we were sitting together in our birthday suits, talking anatomy.

He suddenly looked up at me with a stern, commanding expression. "Are you planning to audition for Forensics?"

The abrupt subject change threw me, though it was pleasantly received. "Honestly? No."

"I think you should."

"I don't know if it's really my thing," I confided with respect.

"Oh, but it *could* be. I wish you'd at least try out. You gave Lippschitz a try, didn't you?"

"Yeah, and look where that got me."

"I don't discriminate," he announced with conviction. "*Period.*"

"Well, I'll give it some thought."

"Okay," he said, smiling politely to cover the burden of a deeper thought. "That's all. Thank you for staying, Frank."

That weekend, Stanley and I made our way to the MacGregor's garage for an evening of regurgitated rock and roll. We sat timidly in the clean corner on the new John Deere lawnmower as Vengeance proceeded with their third rendition of Billy Squier's *My Kinda Lover.*

Vernon Gigger, the band's singer and bassist dominated our attention with his starry presence. He strutted back and forth in front of the microphone, his hips swinging loosely under electric-blue spandex. The Union Jack covered his sleeveless shirt. He had just enough hair to pull it into a tight, stubby "ponytail." Unbeknownst to him, his presence was like a vortex of independent thinking and creativity, as if his aura was so purely white and reflective of its surroundings that it scalded the naked eye. Ironically, he was all too aware of his *radical edge.* In certain circles, which I felt he was constantly surrounded, he was likely considered a boundless rebel, a loose cannon.

He existed in the warm environment of the rock and roll dream, of someday being catapulted into a world of easy women and high-grade cocaine. Without a single original song in his repertoire, his dream had the buying power of a sandcastle in Saudi Arabia. His job was temporary, as he saw it, working at Gates Rubber Co., making balls for candy machines in grocery store lobbies. His dream was so thoroughly planned that he even had a stage-name prepared: *Johnny Panther.* His bass guitar had a rough painting of a wild panther lying asleep on the pick guard—its tail the tassel of his graduating class of 1979.

9

When the performance ended, Panther left without muttering a word. This was how famous musicians handled the public, for which Panther found himself as no exception.

"Thanks for coming out," Thik said to us as he opened a beer. He kept his drums in the corner, resisting the task of disassembling them for another day.

"Yeah, really...thanks for coming," Whitaker added as he packed away the shiny new Gibson SG guitar his father had purchased a few weeks earlier. He wiped its smooth, white surface once more with a starchy handkerchief before gingerly closing the case.

"Want a beer?" Thik offered us.

"Sure," Stanley replied. "Only one. I'm driving."

"Frank?"

"No, thanks."

"What?!" Thik protested. "Come on, what kind of rebel are you?"

"Rebel? I've never rebelled against anything in my life," I said.

"What would you call it, then?" Whitaker asked as he refastened the buttons to his stiff collared shirt.

"Standing for what I believe in."

Thik delivered a goofy chuckle as he shoved a cold can into Whitaker's hands.

Whitaker sat down on the clean cement floor, filling the gap of our small huddle. His hair was short, reddish-brown, and straight. His face was attractive, but not exceptional. His plain facial features were free of character—his build large, but not muscular. He spoke loosely amongst peers with style and profanity—his way of rebelling against the weight of the family tree that constantly urged him to *do what's right*. He was known in Forensics for his ability to successfully debate any issue, any stance. He popped the top of the beer and poured a small portion on Thik's head after a quick swallow.

"It's cool to have an audience!" Whitaker said as he wiped the foam from his upper lip. "First time we've played for anybody. Now we know who to invite."

I nodded my head, tearing the rubber patch from the heel of my Chuck Taylors. "Yeah."

My casual reply came as soothing sounds of inspiration, although the comfort of dreaming outweighed the work required to achieve tangible, real success. They were a high school cover band with a watchful eye on the glory of others who had walked with stronger steps before them. Their audience never stretched beyond Stanley and me.

One day after school, I was scraping a thick layer of ice off my windshield, battling the quick accumulation of falling snowflakes—and losing. I circled the Ranchero, kicking through piles of snow that had engulfed it throughout the day. The wind blew effortlessly through every thread of clothing on my body, chilling my youthful bones to the degenerating throes of false aging. The parking lot was vacant and quiet with the exception of my hammering at the relentless sheet of ice.

"Frank!" a voice screamed from a distance, muffled as if my ears were stuffed with cotton.

I looked up to see Mr. Dalton leaning out a second-story window. He propped himself up with his hands stretched far apart in a pillow of snow. His thick, wool sweater—a very elegant color of burgundy wine—encompassed his small torso rather comfortably as his breath exhaled in a pale vapor.

10

"Why don't you stop fighting that windshield and come on up here. We're holding tryouts for Forensics."

I looked up at him and smiled, suddenly aware that my glove was somehow frozen to the dangling scraper. I succumbed easily to temptation, kicking through piles of snow as I headed back to the old brick building.

The glass double-doors reflected the icy street of a shallow town behind me. The snow covered the lawn like a bubblebath. Standing directly in front of me was an adolescent deviant with the eyes of fire. At least that's how I liked to see myself... Stern brown eyes absorbed the light that reflected off the snowbanks. Broad shoulders and firm forearms accented an impeccable posture. My body was otherwise long and thin. A cleffed chin and an up-turned nose were the more striking features to view. Large ears and thick eyebrows were the less striking ones. Soft, yet full lashes retained a child-like appearance. Thick coils of brown dreadlocks hung over the side of my face from a wide mohawk. The shaved sides of my head were pink from the lapping of the cold wind.

Chunks of snow fell from my soaking wet canvas shoes as I climbed to the second floor. The hallway was filled with at least half the entire student body, all rehearsing lines and doing whatever seemed pretentious enough to prepare themselves. I took a seat at the back of the line, away from the others. My bubble of personal space had a unique way of tripling its size in the presence of ignorance. My bubble of personal space was often tripled in size.

I yanked on the scraper. It ripped from the glove like new velcro.

Mr. Dalton peeked his head out the door as a popular student left the room with a proud, toothy grin. "Who's next?" he asked down the line. "Ah...Frank Smith."

I stood quickly, glancing at the long line before me. I could hear the breathy whispers of girls as they watched me pass. The maniacal skull drawn on the back of my jacket inflicted curiosity to their feeble minds. Mr. Dalton held the door like a courting gentleman. I nodded politely as I entered.

"All right, Frank," Dalton said as he stepped behind a bulky video camera. "Please stand where the X is taped on the floor."

"What am I to do?" I walked over to the bulky device that looked like a VCR with a stiffy. "Should I sing? *Hello, my baby, hello, my darling...*"

He handed me a sheet of paper. "We'll be reading from Oscar Wilde...you read the part of Algernon Moncrieff. I'll be Lane. Okay...begin."

I stared into the camera. The red light of the *Record* button was barely visible through the reflection on the window behind it. "Okay," I muttered. I glanced down at the paper. "Can I take off my jacket?"

"Of course."

I took my time and his to casually unload the heavy coat. Its chains and safety pins rattled as I gently folded it and placed it on a nearby desk.

"Okay," I said again, yanking uncomfortably on the collar of my Minor Threat T-shirt. I cleared my throat and began reading. "Did you hear what I was playing, Lane?" I asked in a different voice, one with exuberance and excitement. I made a point to maintain a steady, who-gives-a-fuck feel to the presentation. I didn't want to overact.

"I didn't think it polite to listen, sir..."

"I'm sorry for that, for your sake. I don't play accurately—anyone can play accurately—but I play with wonderful expression..." I read to the bottom of the page and looked up.

11

"That'll do, Mr. Smith. Thank you for showing." He hustled me out of the room and ushered in the next student.

The door slammed behind me and there I stood with half the student body staring. I shook my head with a condescending smirk. *If that wasn't a waste of time...*

The following week, the names of the new Forensics squad were posted in the school newspaper, *The Morning Wood*. At the very top of the One-Act Play cast was my name, followed by a good portion of the honor roll. My name would top that list through to graduation. Mr. Dalton's efforts for me was the first defense I had received in Iola from an unrelated adult, and it was an effort I would never forget.

The blur of lush green fields occupied my attention. In fact, I found my thoughts had numbed from the repetitive stimulation. It was as if my brain were stuck in a groove on a record. I kept visualizing the audience that sat before our performance not an hour ago. My involvement in the One-Act Play had brought forth a great deal of attention. My name and my legend had been spread like the plague. My Forensics travels supplied the more obscure villages in southeast Kansas the chance to witness a "freak" of current folklore. My presence alone would always pack the house. I was comfortable with my fame and reputation. It came with the territory of such adverse style.

The passing of a sign announced our entrance into Allen county. It stirred the putrid stench of my reality. We would soon be back in the town for which my performances ironically represented.

I glanced at Whitaker who stared forward with a robust smile pasted to his face. He bobbed slowly to the music generated in the headphones of his Walkman. Every trip, I supplied a new band for him to explore. This day was the Circle Jerks. His smile said little to me. For all I knew, he hated it. I really couldn't care less what he thought.

"I like it," he said.

"That's cool."

"We should form a band," he told me while shutting off the tape.

I laughed.

"I'm serious."

"I know," I told him. "That's why I'm laughing."

"Fuck you, then," he said swiftly. "No...I'm serious."

"You're serious, are you? And your dad would be all for it?"

"He doesn't mind Vengeance. He thinks it's good for me to get it out of my system. You know...while I'm young, before I go to college."

"I see. So, what would I do?" I asked. "I have absolutely no musical ability."

"You could sing!" he suggested.

"I can't sing. Have you ever heard me sing? Obviously not."

"Who cares? Do you think *these* guys can sing? Give me a break."

"One break...coming up."

"What would we call it?" he pondered.

I found Whitaker's naïve excitement to be cute. I kept quiet, allowing his adventurous mind to go wild. His desire to be some angry Simon and Garfunkel didn't interest me. I was far more intrigued to understand why the motion of buses always gave me erections...

"The Needledicks?" he asked with a laugh that echoed throughout the bus. "How about Kermit's Green Penis? The Crotch Rockets? The Barking Spiders? Thunderpussy? How about...um...how about The Fluorescent Condoms?"

I smiled politely.

"The Fluorescent Condoms!" he continued. "Just think of the album names! *Lubricated, For Her Pleasure.* Or, *Vibra-Ribbed.* How about *Only Dicks Can Get Into the Fluorescent Condoms*? That's it! That's awesome, man—we *have* to do this."

We had this conversation each trip, and each time he'd add onto the theme of our "band." Soon we had more concepts, more album cover designs, more titles, more T-shirt ideas than any band existing on the planet, except maybe Pink Floyd. Unlike Pink Floyd, we had no band, no songs, and no members.

"I've had it with this juvenile bullshit." Panther tossed his white leather jacket over his bony shoulder. "Fuck you and your faggot friends. I'll see you clowns at the top!"

He climbed inside his black Trans Am and pulled recklessly into the street. With screeching tires, he rounded the corner, never to be seen again—not even at the top.

Thik and Whitaker had already begun drinking the stolen beer.

"What happened?" Stanley asked.

"Thik kept calling him Vernon rather than Panther," Whitaker confessed.

"He doesn't call me Daddy, why should I call him Panther?" Thik asked.

Whitaker shook his head and laughed. "Sure, Daddy. Daddy-O, I mean. Geez, musicians are so damned temperamental."

A mischievous smile lit up Thik's freckled face. "He left his rig here, maybe I should sell it."

"Is he coming back?" Stanley asked.

"I don't think so," Thik said. "I think he quit. He wasn't happy that no one showed up again."

Whitaker shook his head with a sigh of resignation. "He should expect it by now. No one's going to listen to us in this town."

Thik crushed an empty beer can against his head. "Now what? I guess we get drunk."

"Let's jam, Frank," Whitaker suggested.

Thik stood lazily and seated himself behind the drums, staring at us with a silent curiosity. "Well...what else is there to do?"

Whitaker picked up his guitar. "Can you play bass, Stanley?"

"No, I don't know anything about it."

"You don't need to know. Anybody can play bass."

"What if I mess it up?" Stanley mumbled apprehensively. Despite his reserved pose, he took a curious step forward, tucking his thumbs inside the pocket of his old, faded Levi's. His green eyes studied the instrument as his large body remained still.

"Like we give a shit," Thik said, still chuckling.

Whitaker quickly turned and hurled a half-full can of beer at Thik's head, missing by half an inch. "Do you ever stop laughing?"

Thik's giggling deterred a better reply.

Stanley took a deep breath that conveyed enormous contemplation. "I'd hate to have to buy him a new one."

"Do you think I give a flying monkey fuck?" Whitaker asked irritably. "Grab that bass, Stanley."

Stanley took three momentous steps forward and timidly put the strap over his shoulder. His left hand clutched the neck of the bass, holding loosely the strings with his thick fingertips. He looked as awkward as he must've felt. Flicking switches and adjusting knobs, he waited until Whitaker brought the instrument to life.

"See my index finger?" Whitaker instructed. "That's the root note. When and where it moves, you play in the same place on the bass. If I play on the third dot, you play on the third dot. Got it?"

Stanley nodded as he banged the low string of the bass, releasing a tremendous rumble that shook the frame of the garage. It was the type of noise I'd expect from a guy his stature.

I stood hesitantly, yet strangely excited. I knew I couldn't carry a tune, had no concept of pitch. I was Johnny One Note, and had no intention of fooling myself into thinking otherwise. Yet, as Johnny One Note sang out with gusto and passion...I reached down and grabbed the microphone. Looking into the wire mesh of it, I thought: *Anybody can do this. That's what it's all about. I'm not just anybody.*

"Check," I whispered into it. Hearing my voice like thunder gave me an odd feeling of exhibitionism—a quality I never knew existed in me. "*Check!*"

Thik banged his snare while Whitaker played some loud, powerful chords. Stanley stood beside me, pounding on the bass, making awful noise.

"Finally!" Whitaker yelled over the chaos. "The Fluorescent *fucking* Condoms!!"

He began playing a song from a tape I had loaned him months earlier. It was a song by the Descendents called *I'm Not a Loser.*

As the guitar snarled with the slightest brush of the pick, I felt the bottled anger within me surface, forcing itself out my mouth in a vicious scream like the dry-heaves. I let out a guttural roar that climbed into the black coil of blinding darkness that consumed the town. The words erupted like a volcano spewing molten energy. The feeling was like no other—far beyond masturbation. The music must've sounded unbearably awful, but the intensity was maddening. I felt myself lose control. My body thrashed about, colliding with Stanley. I could feel their eyes watching me, studying me. It was a good feeling.

On that spring night, my first band, the Fluorescent Condoms was born out of à time-killing joke.

My parents reluctantly agreed to transform the garage into the Condom headquarters for the summer. It became our own hip version of a child's tree-fort. We met every day for rehearsal. Practice would always begin as soon as Thik arrived a few hours late.

Some two weeks after our fateful formation, Thik "found" a four-track recorder at the JuCo and the production of our *albums* began. The recordings consistently turned out atrocious—no better than the quality of the music, I might add.

Within the first month, we had expanded our rehearsal space into the driveway where our noise could be heard throughout the entire town. The police came often to shut down our practices. Sometimes they simply parked a block away and waited for all hell to break loose. It was nice having an audience.

Our name spread like dirty gossip. Everyone in town had heard of us, or had heard the music for themselves—given no other choice in the quiet town. The town's newspaper reporters came to our practice site twice that summer. We became their front page headline. The others in the band had never known such exposure. I couldn't claim the same.

Over coffee tables in nicer quarters, housewives traded mixed opinions. Although Thik and I had separately earned our bad reputations, eggshells surrounded Whitaker and Stanley. It was initially dismissed as a passing trend because any contrasting opinion faced a stronger, less satisfying jury.

"Here it is," Whitaker announced at practice one day, waving a cassette tape proudly in the air. "I stayed up until three in the morning mixing this on my parent's stereo. It's our *first* album—the *Lubricated* album!"

"Took all summer," Thik complained as he downed the first beer of the morning. "By the way, I can't practice tomorrow. I'm going to Lawrence to buy new heads for my drums."

"It's about time," Whitaker snapped.

Thik took a sip of beer as he formulated his counter-attack. A moment later, he looked up with a smile and gave his calculated response: "*Your mama.*"

"What are you going to do with the tape, Frank?" Stanley asked.

"Send it off to some publications."

Whitaker perked up immediately. "What publications? We're going to be in magazines?"

"Not really magazines. Fanzines. *Maximum RockNRoll, Hippycore, Flipside...*"

"How many people read them?" Thik asked.

"I don't know. A lot, I suppose," I said casually.

"Is it all over the country?" Whitaker asked.

"Hell, it's all over the *world*," I replied. "There are bands in them from Italy like Negazione and Raw Power, B.G.K. from Holland, the Hard-Ons from Australia...not to mention all the British bands."

"You're shitting me!" Whitaker exclaimed.

"It's nothing, really. Say we practice?" I asked.

That night I was up several hours past midnight, strategizing the band's debut release. By the week's end, Thik had "borrowed" fifty cassette tapes from the local TG&Y store to pull off the Condom invasion. With one fateful trip to the post office, we were ready to conquer North America.

My throat ached of a dry heat that burned like gasoline. I was parched with a thirst that water alone couldn't quench. I lowered the microphone from my dry lips and stared at the band that encircled me. "Practice over?"

Whitaker removed his guitar and placed it in the case. "Let's call it a night."

"Frank," Stanley said to me softly. "Hold it a minute."

I turned to him, giving my full attention.

"I wrote some music last night," he told me. "It's my first song."

"Cool, let's hear it."

He took a second to watch Whitaker pull his amplifier back inside the garage. He struck the thickest bass string forcefully, plowing through a groove with fierce intensity.

Whitaker stopped dead in his tracks.

The music was like nothing we had conceived. It was a perfect dictation of determination and accomplishment. There were no notes to be heard. Only passion.

When the song came to an end, he looked up at us with relaxed eyes. "That was kind of sketchy..."

"That was amazing," I told him.

Whitaker stood motionless, nodding slowly. "My God... We need to work with that one." He quickly pulled his amplifier back outside. "Show me that song."

15

The music came together in the time it took to hear it. It flowed like a perfect stream, like it was meant to be. I decided that the words would have to be equally potent—our doctrine of principle, our theme song. The lyrics revealed themselves on a piece of scratch paper before me. I simply had to color in the lines.

"*Persistence, Resistance*," I told them. "That's what I'm calling it. My life, my philosophy…it's all in this song."

"I like that," Stanley said. "Will you sing it through one time?"

I reached for my sore larynx. "Okay."

Together the band delivered the song once again, this time with me. With this one tune, we had stepped up to a higher level. Our jovial band suddenly had a reason to take itself more seriously. This song was the reason. It would change the way we wrote our music. The song became definition.

"Here, I almost forgot," Thik told me as he packed away his drums an hour later. "Check this out…I got this flier for you in Lawrence. Don't you listen to this band—Black Flag?"

"Black Flag are playing in Kansas?" I asked, flabbergasted. He handed me the flier and I couldn't believe my eyes. "At the Outhouse? What is that, I wonder…"

"How about these other bands?" he asked. "The Jerk Offs or the Pain Killers?"

"Never heard of either. Oh, man, I *have* to go. I couldn't miss something like this." It was my wildest dream. I had no idea a band such as Black Flag would play in Kansas. This had to be some rare occasion, I thought. How many Kansans had even heard of Black Flag? Not many, I assumed. "I *gotta* see this show."

Just then, a rusted Chevy Nova pulled up to my driveway with a rugged farmboy gripping tightly the wheel. His name was Tommy Thomas, and his neck was as red as his thumbs were green. He looked at me and nodded politely with agricultural distinction.

"That's some darned funny shit ya'll doing there," he said with a distinct twang. "The music, that is. I was down the road a ways listening with my cousin, Oscar." He removed his greasy hat and ran his greasy fingers through his greasy hair. The hat was once yellow with the logo of a company that manufactured auto parts or chicken feed. His thin, pathetic mustache glistened of sweat as he smiled briefly. His teeth were stained like tree bark from chewing tobacco. "I respect what you fellers are doing."

"Well, thanks," I replied smugly.

The passenger door swung open, and a short, blond fellow placed a firm, ragged Adidas onto the pavement. He took a couple steps forward, then stared with shifty eyes. His strut was swift and macho, though he couldn't have weighed more than ninety-five pounds. His jeans were about three inches too short and faded. Small holes were torn at the knees unnaturally. A plain white T-shirt outdated his own existence. His father had probably rolled a pack of Camels in the sleeve when it was new. His nipples poked through the thin material.

Tommy broke the silence with a polite introduction. "This is my cousin, Oscar Thomas."

Oscar jerked his head as if to greet us. It was a manly gesture, the type you receive exclusively from a guy his size.

"Hey, what's up? Is there anything to do in this little town? Where are the chicks? Are there chicks around here? What the hell is this place?" he asked with no breaths, no pauses, and no reserve.

Tommy butted in with a comparatively dim repose. "He just moved to town from southern California—"

16

"San Diego."

"Yeah, San Diego," Tommy continued. "He likes the same stuff ya'll—"

"Iggy Pop, ya know, the Stooges, man. The Stooges fucking rawk! Do you guys like the Stooges?"

I nodded apprehensively.

"Yeah, the Stooges totally rock hard, dude."

"And he's kind of high strung, so I figured I should show him ya'll," Tommy explained. "I've heard you guys act that-a-way, too, so—"

"Are there *any* chicks in this town? I can't believe I'm stuck in Kansas. The middle of nowhere—where's Dorothy and that little dog Toto? That little fucker..."

"His old man just retired from the military, so the whole family moved out here to live in these parts and—"

"Do you believe that shit? I'm stuck in Kansas. I can't believe this. I *hate* my old man..." He took a firm step forward. "Not bad punk rock for a bunch of cow farmers. I liked that last song. Are there any places to see bands? All-ages venues? I'm not as old as I probably look."

"I don't know," I told the little guy. "I've got this flier for a show in Lawrence—"

"Where's that?" he asked.

"One and a half hours north of here," Whitaker answered politely.

"One hour and fifteen minutes if you're driving with me," Thik boasted.

"About twenty minutes west of Kansas City, and twenty minutes east of Topeka," Whitaker clarified.

Oscar snatched the flier from my hands. "I'm going," he demanded flatly. "Who's driving? Are you driving?" He pointed a stiff finger to Thik. "You said you can get there faster. What's your name, hot-shot?"

"I'm Thik."

"I'm Whitaker and this is Frank."

Oscar stared directly into my eyes. "Nice dreadlocks, Frank."

"Thanks...uh...whatever your name was."

"That's Oscar, tough-guy. Don't forget it. White people shouldn't have dreadlocks. I've seen no chicks in this town. Oh, yeah—who's driving to this show?"

"There are no chicks here," Thik informed him. "None that'll give you the time of day, that is."

"So, what do you guys do, circle jerk or something? If that's what you guys are all about, you can count me out right now."

"No, we like girls," Thik said defensively.

"We'd *like* to like girls," Whitaker corrected.

"I don't have time for this shit—no time for small talk. I'll leave that up to my fucking Granny in the nursing home. I need action, not talk. Here's my number, are you ready to take my number?"

"What's this for?" I asked.

"You're taking me to Black Flag—what, are you stupid, or just deaf? Are you ready for the number or not?!"

"Go ahead, I can memorize it."

"It's easy. It's three-six-five..."

I repeated it once before he had made it back to Tommy's car, nothing else said.

"See ya'll later," Tommy told us politely.

"Hurry the hell up!" Oscar scorned. "Jesus Christ, my dead grandmother..."

*   *   *

17

Thik chauffeured us to the Black Flag show in his old, brown station wagon. The rear window revealed the scenery of vast fields in bloom stretched to each horizon under a blistering sun. As immense the landscape, it paled to the unproportional sprawl of Oscar's life, dictated almost from a third-person perspective. A Mexican soap opera would've seemed bland by comparison. After one and a half hours, I was still only certain about two things with him: his love for Cracker Jack candy and the size of his bladder.

The flatlands of the world I claimed as my own began to wrinkle and roll into hills and valleys as we approached the city limits of Lawrence. Descending down one of the largest hills in the eastern side of the state, the road tapered with a clean stretch to what appeared as another little town.

"That's Lawrence," Thik said. He pointed to a small Volkswagen rushing beside us, its occupants a couple of hippy kids with glum expression. "Slug bug green," he announced, landing a firm fist on Whitaker's shoulder.

Whitaker rubbed his arm defensively as he quickly scanned the highway for another Volkswagen from his passenger seat post. With a deep scowl, he resigned to attend the radio, tuning it through static. Voices from talk shows squeezed through as static turned to violins only to be lost. Bits and pieces of civilization surfaced with the slow turn of the dial. The furious rhythm of punk music slipped briefly through the noise.

"Hold on," I told him, feeling a bit surprised by his discovery. "There's a punk rock song in there...under the noise...listen."

He tuned it closer. The shrill guitar tore through the static as if fighting to overcome the weak reception. The vocalist snarled like a savage. It was intense enough to take the paint off the stereo. I had never heard the song before, but I knew I would have to hear it again.

"What is this?" I mumbled to myself. "On the radio, even. I can't believe it."

"Slug bug yellow," Thik said as he smashed his fist into Whitaker's arm once again.

Whitaker shook it loosely as if to release the pain.

The song abruptly ended, followed by a few seconds of unprofessional silence.

"Some local music," the announcer said eventually. "That was *Crack in the Wall* by the Jerk Offs, who will be at the Outhouse tonight with Black Flag. Don't forget, this is KJHK, the sound alternative in Lawrence and anything else you'll listen to is a waste of your time..."

I knew at that moment I would like Lawrence.

The sun had already sunk beneath the hilly horizon as we drove through the quaint little college village. On old wooden porches, groups of young people sporting Birkenstocks and tie-dyes sang simple songs about the color of grass, or something equally impertinent to daily living.

There was a strange aura about the town. An aura that made the air more breathable and alive. I inhaled its vitality with ease and comfort. It was an unusual feeling for my otherwise cautious senses.

Eventually, we made our way to the mysterious Outhouse. The directions to the venue took us four miles into the open country. The landscape was desolate, populated only by a scarecrow or two. Night consumed the quiet countryside as the lights of the city faded behind us. A tiny flame appeared in the distance—the only sign of life amidst the stretches of farmland. The flame slowly mutated into a huge bonfire off the road where hundreds of social outcasts stood in a mud lot. Beyond the fire was a small chicken shack that had been converted into one of the oldest existing punk rock venues in history.

This was the Outhouse.

We were greeted at a rusted gate by a man with a flashlight. He shoved the light through the station wagon's open window with complete disregard. "How many?"

"Five."

"Twenty-five bucks."

Whitaker collected our money in a pile and passed it through the window.

"Give me your wrists," the flashlight-man demanded. He used a felt pen to scratch the word *fags* on our wrists. "Go ahead."

Thik advanced down the gravel country road until we found an open space to park by the sloping ditch.

I could sense the excitement within our small group, but our pace was slow and resistant. We didn't quite know what to expect. Judging by the mile of cars parked by the roadside, it was clear that my expectations were already horribly inaccurate.

I walked up to the Outhouse slowly, brimming with wonder as we passed through the cliques of aggravated youths. I reached out and touched the cool brick where countless bands had spray-painted their logos on layers of graffiti. Minor Threat, Angry Samoans, Dead Kennedys, D.O.A., Millions of Dead Cops, Micronotz... Each lamppost bore thousands of old staples from fliers of shows past. Fumbling in disbelief, I took note of two different upcoming events: Toxic Reasons and Bad Brains.

I wandered to the entrance where two large, tattooed bald thugs guarded the door. They conversed with stiff gestures and rigid expressions. Their matching flight jackets had the initials L. A. S. H. embroidered on the breast under a patch of the American flag. The initials stood for Lawrence Area Skinheads.

In white cursive letters, the name *Vernon* was embroidered on the back of the stockier guy's jacket. His neck glistened with a bright new tattoo of a swallow.

Vernon looked down upon me with eyes like glass, cold and hard. "Let's see your wrists."

I nervously raised my hand to him, revealing the flashlight-man's train of thought. I awaited Vernon's next request fearfully. He gave a short nod. Without a second to spare, I grabbed the handle and pulled it like the door of a chocolate factory, more marvelous than any golden ticket could ever grant. A blast of heat struck me—foul, like sweat and beer. The stench soiled our clean, white faces, penetrating deep into our expanding minds.

Smells of an unknown origin flooded me. It was a varying combination of clove cigarettes, warm leather, marijuana, patchouli oil, and sweat. To my right was a large counter where the band was selling T-shirts, records, and stickers. To my left was a sea of people facing the stage in the far corner. A couple of people were setting up the first band on the short platform of a stage that may as well have been pieces of plywood supported by milk crates. *Stranglehold* by the U.K. Subs played over the poor speaker-system to give the atmosphere that final touch of finite detail to prove its authenticity.

The floor was slick with spilt beer that turned the dirt into a sticky mud. I could feel my forehead speckle with sweat as I anxiously examined the other occupants of the room. I couldn't help but wonder what stories could be told. I was in a room with family, I knew this. They had bitten the same bullet for the same reasons. Like me, they survived.

Silhouettes of shaggy heads and mohawks separated me from the stage. I was never too vain to believe I would become so close to something like this. Not in

Kansas. I slowly paced back and forth across the muddy floor, gazing happily at the various heads and haircuts, feeling a strange sense of belonging. I almost forgot the actual reason for my attendance, to see Black Flag.

As I stood soaking the atmosphere, a couple of average-looking youths took the stage. The music over the speakers faded as the crowd delivered their attention to the first act. The front of the low stage had an arrow spray-painted upward to the band with the words "Fucking Rock Stars" along the base.

The guitarist was a well-built skinhead, shirtless with a treasure trail of hair pouring down his flat stomach into a pair of Levi's stay-pressed jeans. Oxblood Doc Martens boots gave him the appearance of a hardworking tradesman. His upper body was firmly toned and tanned, covered with tattoos of American pride that flattered his roguish physique. He was an attractive guy with a chiseled jawline and the perfect five o'clock shadow. His dark hair was cut into a tight crewcut. His sideburns extended to the bottom of his pronounced jawbone. Two small silver loops hung from each ear.

The bassist gripped the neck of his instrument with both hands forcefully as he sized up the crowd with attentive eyes. His appearance was smaller in contrast to the guitarist. He was modest and scrappy. A pair of tropical-styled Ocean Pacific jams looked comically large on his compact frame. His thin, hairy legs sunk into a pair of Eastland boat shoes. A button-up white shirt with vertical black pin-stripes completed his haphazard, though presentable image. His skin was naturally dark without blemish. Curly brown hair flowed down his back like the pouring of hot fudge. It was well managed and clean. His massive nose casted a harsh shadow on his thin lips. He smiled politely into the crowd with pearly white teeth, though his dark brown eyes peered with disdain.

The drummer was a small girl who appeared to be twelve at best with loose cotton shorts like pajamas or men's underwear. Her black, sleeveless T-shirt had a pink triangle across the back with *Kansas* printed over the top in white. Long wavy locks with split-ends hung loosely over her cute, elliptically boyish face. Thick-rimmed glasses covered her hazel eyes, kept up by a tiny button nose.

The vocalist stood proudly at the edge of the stage, staring into the crowd with confidence and conviction. His attire was loose and fitting, lacking any pretense. He was older than the rest of the group and appeared to be at least half Native American. His black hair was average length, concealed under an old baseball cap turned backward. I wouldn't have guessed we shared a common denominator such as this music. His appearance was subtle and humble, like he either pumped gas for a living or mowed lawns in the suburbs.

He tipped a beer to the crowd and smiled with reserve as he finished it with one quick gulp. "I'd like to thank you all for coming out, but I know you don't give a shit about us, so you can all fuck off right now."

His hostile antagonism contrasted his childish, endearing charm. Apparently others hadn't felt the same. A black eye and swollen lip seemed relatively fresh.

"I'm Norman and we're the Jerk Offs from Lawrence, Kansas. This is our third show ever." He paused for another swallow of beer. "Tonight…is a night of your life."

The shrieking tone of the guitar rushed me with a sense of urgency and strength. I could feel the hair rise on my arm, charged by an electrical current down the spine of my back. It seemed predatorial, raw with passion. It crawled under my skin and to this day refuses to leave.

The avalanche of music that followed instantly catapulted Norman into animation, sending him in a furious wreck across the stage. The audience responded similarly as if churned by the pure force of the music.

Norman jumped up from the stage and grabbed one of the rusty rafters with a clenched left hand—the right clutching powerfully to the microphone. As he swung back and forth, people rushed the stage to quickly spring themselves back onto the swirling pit. He sang swiftly to the rhythm, the words indistinguishably choppy. Whatever he was saying, one thing I felt certain—he meant it.

The small drummer played viciously and competently, her hands practically blurred by the speed of the rhythm. The guitarist and bassist stood at opposite ends, sneering into the crowd as Norman writhed about, gargling in a guttural voice the slur of syllables. Within a minute, the first song had ended, sending the crowd into wild screams of praise as the pit unwillingly slowed to a halt.

"Yeah, suck my dick," Norman said. He turned to the drummer and pointed a stiff finger. "*Go.*"

An intense tribal beat churned the pit once again as the music snapped back into its vigorous wreckage. Within two minutes, the song was over and the crowd was once again in upheaval.

"*Your mother wears combat boots when she sucks my dick, Norman!*"

"Thank you," he replied. "This next song is on KJHK. *Crack In the Wall.* It's off our first seven-inch, which can be yours for three dollars."

"*Rock stars on the fucking radio! Get off the stage, rock stars!*"

The bassist began sawing at his bass as the band kicked in with their first moderately paced song. Norman plunged himself onto the swirling mass, allowing them to carry his thrashing body over the top of the pit. He suddenly fell into the whirlpool of limbs, yet the vocals continued. He resurfaced again some fifteen feet away, floating to the top of the chaos at once. They tossed him back on stage just before the song ended.

"*Harder! Faster!*"

"Yeah, that's what your mother tells me, too," Norman returned quickly as the music continued.

The energy was fast and ecstatic. The band only seemed part of it, as if they were just something to concentrate on as the crowd exuded electrical energy like a thunderstorm.

The rest of their set was equally enjoyable, the turbulence never relenting.

"That was our last song," Norman said as he put his cap back on his head. The band switched off their amplifiers and quickly left the stage. "We refuse to play anything else for you pussies." He tossed the microphone aside and walked casually through the rear door into the corn field.

There was a long line of hooligans at the back counter waiting to purchase their seven-inch single. I was one of them. The opinions of those standing in line were quite flattering. I agreed with them. The Jerk Offs were amazing—guilty as charged. I tossed three dollars on the beer-stained counter as a scowling skinhead shoved a record in my needy hands.

I took the record outside into cooler, cleaner air and situated myself under the lamppost. I pulled the vinyl disk out and examined the lyrics sheet like a well-versed veteran. Norman's words were deep and thoughtful—so concise with the emotional content of the music that it seemed almost too obvious. The foundation of all great art rested in my hands. The Jerk Offs had a new fan.

21

Stanley emerged from the crowd, smiling as he bounded up to me.

"Was that cool or what?" he exclaimed.

"They were great," I replied. "Especially for a local. Amazing."

"I overheard someone saying they've been together a year, they just never play shows. They're better than we are."

I nodded with a quick smile.

Oscar came stumbling up to us. "Have you seen all the girls here? You know, everything I say is a waste of my breath, a waste of my time, and a waste of your time. I love women. Everything else I say is horseshit."

In a split second he was off again, losing himself in crowds, imposing himself in conversations, and generally annoying whomever would give him their short attention.

"Will you make a tape of that for me?" Stanley asked, pointing to the record.

"Of course."

"You're a pal," he said. "You and me, man. Tighter than a gnat's ass."

A couple of New Wave girls passed slowly, their hair immaculately in place as the wind tossed their black skirts like Jolly Rogers. My inhibitions ceased the warnings.

"Not bad," Stanley said. "They could eat crackers in my bed. I wonder where they're going, who they're with?"

"Not us."

"I wonder their story, their lives," he speculated.

"Who knows…"

"Do you think we'll ever get laid?"

"I would hope so."

"Do you think I'll know what to do when the time comes?" he asked.

"Oh yeah, it's like riding a bike."

He shook his head. "How's it like riding a bike?"

"Hell, I don't know. You hear that kind of thing, and it sounded good, didn't it?"

"It did sound good," he confirmed. "Like riding a bike…where'd you get that?"

"From the *Penthouse Letters*."

"So someone said it's like riding a bike?" he asked.

I nodded quickly. "Anyway…tell me a story, Stanley. Any story…about your life."

"Does it have to be true?" he asked.

"Preferably. Who was the first person you felt you loved?"

"My mother," he said quickly.

"Okay, who was the first person who made you feel hatred?"

"Michael Corbett. Do you know him?"

I thought a moment, trying to place the name. "From elementary school? He was a year older than us?"

"Yes, and he moved away when he was in seventh grade, or so."

"What about him?" I asked.

"I took violin lessons from this lady who lived on Sycamore. She taught me on Wednesdays, right after school. I spent a half hour there, and was always passing by Michael's place at around four o'clock on my way home. Well, Michael found out what I was doing. Girls play violin, you know? That's what he told me, at least. Anyway, he would have his friends over, so when I passed by, he could confront me. He'd throw my violin case on the ground and beat the holy shit out of me. Beat me senseless. His friends would laugh and laugh. I imagine he looked pretty cool. I will never forget that feeling, with my nose numb, blood draining, dripping onto my hand

as I picked up my case. And I'd look up at them, all his friends pointing and laughing."
He shook his head uncomfortably. "What about you?"

"I used to be popular," I confessed boldly.

"Yeah, I remember."

"You know Veronica Staple? I used to go out with her."

"No way!" he exclaimed.

"It was only seventh grade, but she had the biggest crush on me."

He laughed. "She wouldn't talk to you now if you paid her. Man, you really did slide down the leeward side of the hill, didn't you? Now look at you...so, what do your parents think of all this rock and roll stuff?"

"They didn't think too highly of it at first. Once they finally understood what it's all about, they relaxed a bit. My parents are cool people. They respect me, and they respect my decisions."

"How did you ever find this music in the first place?" he asked.

"A few years ago I was really into New Wave music—which I still love. I remember quite well how it happened. Of course, you know there aren't any record stores in or around Iola. I had to order albums through the mail. A lot of the time the companies would request an alternate choice in case they were out of stock. I was ordering Tin Tin and Strawberry Switchblade, and neither were in stock. I ended up with my alternate choices—Dead Kennedys' *Plastic Surgery Disasters* and Bauhaus *In The Flat Fields*. My interest in this music was all a mishap, basically! But when I listened to that Dead Kennedys record, and read those potent lyrics...man, I was hooked! Their views and philosophies were my own. And the music was delivered with such power and so little pretense. It was the *real thing*. The more underground music I bought, the more I became hooked. I'm not sure if it shows, but I have a lot of self-respect. I get that from the music. The music means everything to me. Without it, I'd be lost."

Our conversation fell quickly to silence with the soothing sounds of insects and wind and everything wild. Looking up at the stars, I imagined a flying saucer descending from the far corners of space or sub-space to dispel gravely important information on the fate of mankind. Then we'd find ourselves on a mission to save our planet, to assassinate the anti-Christ before he released his treacherous scheme on the world. And, of course, the beautiful damsel in distress would sleep with both of us, making us alternate duties of holding the camera. Our parents would wonder where we went, and why we missed supper, and then we'd see our faces on milk cartons...

The explosive sound of a snare drum caught our attention, summoning us back for more. We raced to the door in a frenzy.

The next band to take the shanty Outhouse stage represented a different flavor of punk. Their music was influenced by the roots of British punk, falling between the cracks of Sham 69 and the Anti-Nowhere League.

The only member of the four-piece group with any hair was the vocalist—a scrawny, handsome guy with a crown of white-blond spiky hair. He had a prominent, distinguished brow that absorbed the lights of the stage and the attention of the audience. A large scar separated part of one eyebrow, splitting his eyebrows into thirds. He stared down his slender and pointed nose at the crowd with confidence. His large eyes were sunken in deep sockets over high cheekbones. His face appeared like a skull with watchful eyes. With every motion, the tall blossom of hair on his head would quake and tremble.

"We're the Pain Killers from Oklahoma City, who are you?" he asked the crowd.

23

"Fuck off, asshole!"

"Eat shit, albino Woody Woodpecker motherfucker!"

"All right, thank you very much," the singer returned kindly. "How about a joke? Do you people up here in Kansas like jokes?"

"Suck my dick, you Oklahoma bastard!"

"Go home to your red dirt, dickface! Oklahoma is for queers!"

"Okay," he said. "How many skinheads does it take to change a light bulb?"

"As many as it takes to screw your mother, Woody Woodpecker!"

"Hey now, let's not get fussy," he said. "One hundred. One to screw in the light bulb, and ninety-nine to get on the guest list. What do bananas and punk rock shows have in common? Both are only good once you get rid of the skins."

"You're a fucking asshole!"

"Play before I kick your ass, Woodpecker!"

"It seems we aren't quite ready yet," he said to the crowd. "How many punks does it take to change a light bulb?"

"Fuck you!"

"Punks aren't ever going to change anything." He paused for a response, yet received only silence. "Okay, this is a song off our latest EP..."

The band kicked in loud and strong, yet half the tempo of the Jerk Offs. Their set was short and intense. With the way the singer carried on, I almost sensed he had a second set-list, the other containing the timing for his humor and charm.

As the stage cleared, I stood perfectly still, waiting for Black Flag. The crowd slowly shuffled to the muddy lot as other small circles stood in their respective place, waiting like me.

The vocalist from the Pain Killers stepped forward from the stage, pawning his records with a devilish smirk. His swaggering gait brimmed with confidence. I wasn't sure if I respected him or considered him thoroughly annoying.

"Hey, man," he said as he greeted me with his box of records. "Cool hair."

"Thanks."

He held up a couple of records. "For a mere three bucks, you could take a load off my hands."

"Three bucks, huh," I said. "I can swing that."

"Where you from?" he asked as I exhausted my savings from shallow pockets.

"Iola, Kansas."

"Never heard of it."

"It's somewhat near the Oklahoma border," I said, handing him three dollars.

He placed a record in my hand and bowed his head respectfully. "My name's Merle."

"I'm Frank," I replied.

"I don't forget a name or a face—especially one attached to those dreadlocks. Thanks for buying the record. I'll see you around."

He took two steps to the next person and started his pitch again. I admired his perseverance, but that ego...

"Did you buy *another* record?" Whitaker asked, who seemed to appear from nowhere. "This place is really bizarre. I'm afraid to go into the bathroom."

"It's unisex, isn't it? Maybe you'll get lucky."

"That's okay, I'll find a tree."

24

We stood silently, watching the road crew load Black Flag's gear to the stage. Their entourage looked as rough as sandpaper and as weathered as a historical monument.

"Oscar's out by the fire, trying to convince girls to give it up," Whitaker told me. "Can you believe this guy? How much of his life story did you buy? Like all that karate stuff, being a brown belt in Shoto...whatever he called it. He can't bullshit me."

The crew made one last check of the tuning and volumes.

"I think they're about to start," Whitaker said as Stanley came to join us. "I'm going to go out and get a breath of fresh air. This place is too stuffy."

"Want a better view?" Stanley asked me as he pointed to the stage. He proceeded toward it, dragging me with him.

We pushed our way to the center of the hall about twenty feet from the stage. Within minutes, the entire venue had exceeded its capacity. There Stanley and I stood, just a couple faces amongst hundreds of others. It was the first time in years I had felt safely invisible, and I craved it. I had finally found a place, left astray and starving too long. Yet, at the same time, the occupants of the Outhouse practically rendered me immobile from intimidation.

The crowd went wild as the band took the stage. Henry Rollins, still with long hair at the time, stepped up to the microphone and stared into the crowd with the expression of a stone wall. His muscles seemed flexed even when motionless. A pair of black satin shorts scarcely concealed his manhood. The words *Search & Destroy* were tattooed across his back from shoulder to shoulder over an enormous red and orange sun. He epitomized the strength of will that the lyrics of Black Flag represented.

"I'd like to thank you for coming out," he told the crowd coldly as he paced back and forth.

The crowd didn't heckle Henry as they had the opening bands. I couldn't tell if it were out of respect or fear. I would've fallen in both categories.

Greg Ginn's trademark guitar-style sent the crowd into chaos as the band began with *My War*. The audience became a torrid frenzy with Stanley and I being tossed like limp ragdolls. We found our way to every corner of the club as bodies hung from the rafters overhead. Some made it to the stage where they launched themselves aimlessly atop the pit. It was a good time for all.

The Black Flag show was my first encounter with punk culture, and I knew it wouldn't be my last.

Sweat covered their firm, brown bodies. The summer sun reflected off their skin with a polished sheen from baby oil. They appeared as glazed hams tempting the hungry eyes of several secret spectators. Bottles of oil stood erect between them.

Children splashed wildly behind them, enjoying the final days of summer at the public pool.

"So, these are my classmates, huh?" Oscar asked as he clung to the chain links of the fence, his face mashed like a waffle iron.

We sat perfectly still watching them, pale and pathetic.

"Yup," Stanley said, slurping on a Jolly Rancher.

I glanced down at the park bench, at the peeling white paint and ancient etchings from couples past. "Don't make me late for practice, Oscar."

"Wouldn't you love to bite her on the ass?"

"Give it up, dork," Stanley said. "You'd be lucky if these chicks were to even laugh at you."

25

"Oh, they'll talk to me," he insisted, clinging to the fence. "Man, I love girls. Nothing else matters."

"I think he's talking to himself," I said, frustrated by the heat. I wiped my brow with the back of my hand.

"Yup," Stanley repeated.

"Oscar, let's go! *Now!*" I demanded.

"Leave me here, go on without me," he mumbled through the fence. "I've found my reason for living."

I pulled Stanley to my Ranchero as Oscar followed close behind, kicking rocks.

"I love girls," he whined as we piled inside the car. "Anything else I say is a total waste of breath."

"Yes, I know," I agreed as I steered through the park.

"Someday I'm going to win the lottery," Oscar told us. "I'll be totally rich and all the chicks will dig me because of my car..."

"Wake up, dreamer, you aren't going to win the lottery," Stanley groaned.

"That just shows how *stupid* you are," he said. "I'm leaving."

"Oh, you are, are you?" I eyed the speedometer. "Forty-five miles-per-hour—"

"Later." He climbed out the window and effortlessly scaled onto the hood.

I maintained speed, weaving through traffic on Iola's Main Street. He climbed onto the roof and out of sight. Suddenly, I felt a moist finger enter my left ear.

"Wet Willy! Wet Willy!" he shrieked.

"Get your finger out of my ear and get back in the car right now."

"I'll give you a buck to slam the brakes," Stanley said casually.

I could faintly hear Oscar screaming obscenities to other cars.

"Okay, a buck fifty and no more. He isn't worth any more than that."

"I'm going to climb under the car like Indiana Jones!" Oscar screamed wildly at us.

"Good luck," Stanley reassured him as we rounded the corner to my house.

He slithered down the hood, clinging desperately to the grill. Thik and Whitaker sat in the driveway waiting as we slowed to a stop. Oscar dropped safely to the ground.

"No room in the car?" Whitaker asked him.

"No," Oscar replied, wiping himself clean. "The disrespectful clods."

"Ready to practice?" I asked.

"Sure," Whitaker replied.

Thik tipped his beer at me, which was all the communication I expected or needed of him.

We pulled our equipment to the middle of the driveway, which at that point was standard procedure. The police arrived at the top of the hill as typical at the onset of rehearsals. I wished Thik had been as much a stickler to our schedule as they were. With our audience in attendance, we were ready to begin our destruction of tonality.

Practicing with the band had become my obsession. My future took shape in my eyes like droplets of water dripping from the roof turning to solid icicles. Each practice brought about more formation, more distinction.

My father pulled into the driveway halfway through our rehearsal that day. He always came home for lunch, usually when we were in the process of polluting his neighborhood with our noise. After he questioned Thik about the beer, he handed me some mail.

There were two letters addressed to the Fluorescent Condoms—one from Fayetteville, Arkansas, the other from Huntington Beach, California. Both letters

26

contained three dollars and a request for our tape, which we referred to as *The Album*. The girl from Huntington Beach mentioned she had read a review in *Maximum RockNRoll* and that she liked the name. She was purchasing a tape for no other reason.

We were flabbergasted. We had no idea anything had been printed. Whitaker couldn't believe our band's name was spread across the country in an international publication. Stanley was impressed someone actually wrote. Thik hoped the six dollars would be for beer.

"Maybe they'll want to interview us or something," Whitaker said.

"Oh, they don't do that—we do that," I told him. "We have someone such as Oscar ask us questions, then we send it to them."

"Let's do it," he said quickly. "You never told us this—let's do it! Let's do it *today*. Now."

"I'm not going to ask you guys questions," Oscar said flatly.

"Yes, you are," Stanley challenged.

"Okay...how come you guys never get laid?"

"Because we hang out with you," Stanley answered swiftly.

Whitaker ignored the casual comments as his imagination wandered to the trail of red carpet to the Grammy podium. "Come on, Oscar. My parents should be really impressed. Maybe they'll see the potential and stop fussing."

"Are your parents pissed that you're a Condom?" Thik asked.

"Well, they didn't like our picture in the paper *twice* this summer. Their friends are giving them a lot of trouble about it."

"Hang in there, man. There's potential," I said, concerned. "Oscar, will you do it...seriously?"

"Yeah, I'll do it."

"Hey, Frank," Thik said, crushing the empty can of beer against his forehead. "What are we going to do with the six dollars?"

The final weekend of summer, the five of us piled into Thik's station wagon to see the Bad Brains at the Outhouse.

Oscar monopolized the conversation as expected. He bounced quickly from heroic surfing tales to karate championship victories. I found myself fading in and out as he expounded upon his love for girls and Cracker Jack. I stared out the window, day-dreaming as we edged closer to my chosen reality.

Once in Lawrence, we found our way to Exile Records off Massachusetts Street where we raced to the magazine rack with great anticipation. Oscar was the first to spot *Maximum RockNRoll*—the last copy, which he refused to share until he read the review himself.

"Wow, they really think you guys suck!"

"Give me that," Whitaker said, pulling it from his hands. "*This mid-west outfit plays mid-tempo punk with hardcore progressions and chord arrangements. Emotional lyrics with good, catchy phrasings that'll appeal to fans of early Adolescents. The vocals make this tape worth a second listen, not bad for a first effort.*"

"That's it?" Thik asked as he quickly stuffed an Ozzy cassette tape inside his pocket. "That was lame!"

"They liked Frank," Stanley said.

I threw a couple dollars on the counter as the others walked out into the warm summer air.

27

"You guys in there?" the woman behind the cash register asked.

I nodded as she stuffed the bills inside the drawer.

"What band?"

"The Fluorescent Condoms," I claimed with pride.

She delivered a condescending smirk and gave me the receipt. "Never heard of you."

I took the fanzine out the door where the others waited by the curb. The light of day was quickly fading.

Stanley and I paced ourselves a few steps behind the rest as we wandered down the street.

"We should see about getting some shirts made," Stanley said.

"Yeah, good idea."

"What do you suppose is next?" he asked me.

"I think we're pretty far from playing the Outhouse."

"Oh, yeah," he agreed, laughing. "If that'd ever be a possibility anyway."

"I think we should make the next *album*. We obviously aren't going anywhere soon."

"Yeah," he said, pausing as Oscar ran into the street and flashed his pale ass at a Mercedes filled with appalled sorority girls. "I think we've gotten much better. *Lubricated* isn't all that great."

"This review really isn't that bad, though."

"You know, I'm not excited about going back to school," he confessed. "I'm not ready to deal with all the shit again. Education aside—which at that place, it usually is. It's a very humbling experience."

Oscar rushed into a store, dragging Whitaker and Thik with him.

"I suppose we should follow," I said.

"Yeah, I suppose."

I glanced over my shoulder at the narrow street. There was a certain sense of comfort where looking back was not one of defensive measures, but simply the contrast of the steps that delivered the present. It was an odd feeling, just another person on the street.

We walked into the shop where three video games were placed in the far corner. Whitaker stood perfectly still, maneuvering *Pac-Man* through the maze, gobbling all the dots like a true Western consumer. Thik giggled as he jerked the joystick on the *Dig-Dug* game while Oscar jumped, screamed, and kicked at *Frogger*.

We stood a good ten feet away watching as they rotated turns on each game, stuffing quarter after quarter into the big wooden boxes.

"So what are you going to do when we graduate?" I asked Stanley.

"I suppose I'll go to college," he replied. "I want to be a doctor."

"Really? Why?"

"I'd like to help people. I see the body as the ultimate machine. I can fix any damn Harley you bring me. Any American-make automobile—I can fix it. I want to look at the human body the same way. Plus, the money would be good, of course. What about you? What are your plans?"

"I don't plan to go," I told him. "I've had plenty of formal education for one lifetime."

He laughed, but I was serious. All I knew was that I wouldn't be staying in Iola. Where I would go, I had no idea. I was impressed he had a plan—one inspired by an innate passion. I loved only one thing more than myself—music. Little more mattered.

28

"Honestly, most people go to college because it's what their parents expect," I said.

"What do your parents expect?" he asked.

"They expect me to be happy, I guess. Anyway, who cares? I'll have plenty of time to figure all that out. So, what great words of wisdom does a guy like you have for a commoner like me?"

"For a dumbass like yourself?" he clarified. "Well, let me dig deep for that one—"

"Don't dig too deep."

"I would say it's the value of three words. Words most people find impossible to express."

"Are you about to tell me you love me, Stanley?"

"Not those words, jackass. There's nothing difficult about telling someone you love them. In fact, it's all too easy and pointless. Love is probably the most abused word in the English language. No, I'm referring to people's aversion to saying: *I Don't Know*. Sign of weakness to not know everything. Ask anybody."

"I know exactly what you mean."

"Damn!!" Oscar screamed. "Motherfucking frog! I want my damn quarter back. This game ripped me off! I want my motherfucking quarter back!! Fucking frog! If I had this frog in my hands, I'd tear his little legs off. The little fucker..."

"Why are you a vegetarian, Frank?" Stanley asked me, ignoring Oscar as best he could.

"Because I can be."

"Seriously..."

"I'm very serious."

"Do you think it's wrong to eat meat?" he asked.

I shook my head. "It should be required that every child make that kill at least once in their lives. I doubt I'd be in the minority, if that were the case."

"I've made that kill," Stanley told me proudly. "I'll also look forward to the next hamburger."

"I respect that choice. My way is not the right way. It's only right for me."

"You don't drink alcohol ever?"

"Never," I responded quickly.

"Have you ever?" he asked.

"Yes. I'm a control freak. I can't stand to lose it. It's all I have."

"Hey, Frank," Thik shouted. "Why don't we have any songs about rock and roll?"

"Yeah," Oscar said. "What's up with that? You don't even have songs about easy girls."

"What the hell are you talking about?" I asked.

"Every rock band has to have at least one song about rocking out at midnight," Thik explained.

"Why does everything have to happen *tonight* in rock songs?" Whitaker asked. "You never hear: *We'll rock out—today*."

"Frank," Thik announced assuredly, "we need a song about scoring with chicks—tonight!"

I let out an irritated sigh. "You guys are idiots. Maybe we should go to the Outhouse now."

"It's too early," Whitaker said, keeping his eye on the video game.

"Let's find a *Galaga* game," Oscar demanded. "I once had the highest score in San Diego."

29

"Yeah, back when you were a surfer and did karate and had fifteen girlfriends," Stanley said.

"Not fifteen, and I still do karate. In fact, if I kick someone's ass, I can go to jail because my hands are lethal weapons."

"No shit, huh?" Thik exclaimed.

"Yeah, right," Stanley challenged.

"Oscar, I bet there are a lot of girls in the parking lot at the Outhouse, waiting to get drunk," I said.

"Good point." He leaned over to Whitaker's game and pushed the joystick the opposite direction until his *Pac-Man* was tagged by the pastel ghost.

"You asshole! You wasted my game!" Whitaker shouted with an extended, righteous finger. "You're a fucking asshole." He rushed to the door and stomped outside.

"I guess we're leaving now," Oscar said casually. "I don't know what's up his ass..."

The four of us followed Whitaker down the street to the station wagon.

"You're lucky I don't leave you here," Whitaker told Oscar. "I'm serious."

"Come on, man, it was a quarter. Here, have a quarter," he said, reaching into his pocket.

"I don't want your money..."

The four mile trek down 15th Street to the Outhouse had always been one of eager anticipation. I looked out the window, doing my best to ignore their petty dispute as the houses slowly disappeared into the vastness of empty countryside. The sky ahead was dark, lit only by the sunset over Lawrence directly behind us. The crops had a subtle luster from the pink sky, the backdrop being the black of night that swallowed our destination, and soon us.

The car slowed as the light of a flashlight struck our windshield. The Outhouse sat like an island in the sea of corn and wheat. The tops of people's heads could be seen moving beyond the crops like the shells of turtles.

"How many?" the guy asked, shining the flashlight into the car to count.

"Five," Whitaker said.

"Twenty-five bucks."

We exchanged our money for messy inkblots as Thik continued through the gate.

"What are you doing after we graduate, Whitaker?" Oscar asked between gulps of the stolen Black Label beer.

"Going to college."

"Here?" Oscar asked.

"I don't know. Maybe. Then again, maybe somewhere nicer."

"Nicer? Do you mean more expensive?" Oscar questioned.

"I guess so."

"That figures, spoiled bastard," Oscar said. "What about you, Thik?"

"Hell, I don't know. I guess drink a lot of beer."

"That sounds good," Oscar said. "I'll drink to that."

Thik took a sip before continuing the thought. "Maybe I'll pull off a big-time bank heist and get a mansion in South America."

"Yeah, and you can have a dozen Brazilian wives that you bought off the black market," Whitaker said sarcastically.

"You can do that?" Oscar asked. "Maybe I'll be your neighbor and we can swap wives, all thirteen of them."

"And how are you going to have enough money to get a mansion?" Stanley asked.

Oscar seemed offended. "I'm going to win the lottery. I told you that, but you obviously never fucking listen to me. Then I'll drink a lot of beer and have fourteen Brazilian wives. I'll get really fat and have a gnarly beer gut and I'll have my wives massage the rolls on my stomach and then I'll drink more beer."

"How are you going to win the lottery?" Stanley asked.

"How does anyone win the lottery, dumbass?"

"Do you ever play?"

"What does that have to do with it?" Oscar asked.

"Well, do you?" Stanley repeated.

"No."

"Have you ever?"

"No. What's your point?" Oscar challenged defensively. "Are you jealous?"

"Yeah," Stanley said. "I'm jealous. I wish I had your plan."

"What is your plan, then, tough-guy?" Oscar asked.

"I don't know...I kind of want to be a doctor."

"No way!" Oscar said. "Are you going to have Brazilian wives and a mansion, too, Dr. Stockton?"

"I really doubt it."

"A doctor, huh?" Whitaker said with a crooked smile. "Your parents would be really proud of you. And you, Frank?"

"I'd like to keep doing music. Seems to be the only thing I'm inspired to do."

"Would that be much of a career?" Whitaker asked.

"Career? What's that? You asked what I wanted to do, and that's what I want to do."

"So you'll be in a band, play the Outhouse, sell your tapes for three bucks, and then what?"

I felt as if I was suddenly listening to his father. "Then I'll be happy."

"We're almost out of beer," Oscar said. "Let's find some ugly girls who have some decent beer. Cold beer—that'd make *me* happy."

"Okay," Thik said as they walked off into the crowds.

They weren't to be seen the rest of the night.

The bonfire began to blaze, consuming the dark and twisted branches that popped like stiff knuckles. A huge arc of people surrounded the growing flame, seeking comfort in its destructive forces.

"I'm really glad we got this going, Frank," Whitaker told me. "I never would've guessed we'd be in a newsstand magazine with world-wide circulation."

"I think you're overdoing the significance of this review," I reminded.

"The funny thing is, we weren't trying to be something. We were just doing it because it was fun, something we all felt strongly about. Now look at it."

"Whitaker, we've had *one* review," Stanley said. "We're not going down in any books of rock and roll history, we aren't ready to turn the band into a corporation for your parents to invest stock, it's just a little blurb in a fanzine."

"Yeah, but still, it's a great start, and we're just starting our sophomore year in high school. Just think what will be going on next year. We could be on tour, doing interviews—"

"There's a lot of small things to do between now and then," Stanley interjected. "Like you said, the beauty of what we're doing is we simply enjoy it."

"Yeah, I know."

After the last opening band wound up their set, we took our place in the center of the Outhouse and waited impatiently for the Bad Brains. The heat was practically unbearable. Everyone reeked of sweat, faintly stifled by the scent of clove cigarettes. My eyes burned and my feet ached from immobility as we watched the club's back door. Rumors of a cancellation circulated with the excitement. Just as I began to wonder, four black men sluggishly took the stage—their eyes bloodshot, their smiles large and sedate. They appeared as any reggae band with their large dreadlocks, African clothing, and stoned expressions.

"Ah, Jah Children," the vocalist, HR said to the crowd with a pleasant smile. "Rastafari liveth in da underground...yah."

The crowd screamed with fists in the air as the band very slowly acquired their instruments, never ceasing to smile as if a cloud surrounded them. Like a film in slow motion, HR suavely greeted various faces in the crowd. His dreadlocks were long and massively thick. He peered at the rest of the band, stopping at his brother Earl behind the drums. Earl nodded and began with a quiet drum roll that accelerated into *Right Brigade.*

The crowd became a storm as the Bad Brains performed some of this country's best hardcore punk. Dreadlocks thrashed like licorice in the hand of a sassy stepchild.

The music threw me into another dimension, another reality. I was as intoxicated by their music as they were by the Ganja and their belief in their religion—the religion HR claims saved his life.

They immediately burst into their second song without a pause, the title track from their album *Rock For Light.* This was everything I had dreamed—crowds of passionate people defiantly screaming the lyrics to *We Will Not,* enraged and determined to bring about a social revolution.

The future for the Bad Brains would be rocky, as HR and Earl would eventually leave the band. Every couple of years for the next decade they would reform briefly until a fateful performance years later in Lawrence when HR attacked the crowd with the microphone stand. He spent some time in the Douglas county jail, as the band split—so far for good.

On the way home, as Oscar and Thik lie passed out in the back seat—Stanley, Whitaker, and I talked excitedly about the performance. Our ears were near deaf and ringing. We spoke loudly to compensate.

"I would give anything to sing in a band like Bad Brains," I said.

"I'm with you," Whitaker encouraged me. "It's good to get it out of your system."

"Out of my system?"

"You don't think you'll look and dress like this your whole life, do you?"

"Of course not," I told him. "I'm sure I'll change my appearance eventually, and I don't care. Although, I will not sacrifice who I am in the process. I promise you that."

"So, you're going to defy the system to your dying days, sitting in your wheelchair in some nursing home, refusing help from anyone wearing a uniform?"

"I have reasons for my actions," I assured him.

"Of course it seems that way. We're young."

"No, I totally disagree. If that means I'll spend my life making minimum-wage, then that's what I'll do."

"Your parents will love that," he shrugged.

"What would my parents have to say about my life? I've got my life, they have theirs. Should I ever have a child, I'd abide by the same principle."

"If you had a child that turned out to be a conservative, Republican Christian, you'd support them?" he asked.

"Of course, if they really believed in what they were doing, and if their decisions were based on intelligent choices."

"If your child turned out to be a Drag Queen and flaming homosexual?" he asked.

"Sure, why not? I'm not getting my ass kicked by people with half my intelligence just because I feel like being a freak. The words I write to our songs, it's not a phase I'm going through. It has nothing to do with rock music or style—it's what I think and believe. That won't ever change. My looks may, but I never will."

"Well, we'll see at our class reunion," he said. "We'll share information on the Stock Market, impress each other with our brand new cars, and envy each other's jobs. And laugh at this conversation in twelve years."

I closed the conversation with that. The night had been too good to end this way.

Summer vacation had spoiled me. It would take some time to accustom myself to the persistent ridicule and judgment, of which I was equally guilty. Luckily, my second period Psychology class had me seated next to Oscar for the semester. I'd rather have shared the space with Stanley for purposes of cheating on exams, but Oscar's company would do, for company's sake.

"I see we have a new face," Mrs. Webster announced as the bell signaled the beginning of class. "Oscar, tell us a little something about yourself."

He paused briefly to remove his eyes from the window. "My name is Oscar, and I don't want to be here."

Everyone laughed, including Mrs. Webster.

"Where are you from?" she asked.

"San Diego, California. I have the highest *Galaga* score in San Diego. That's all you really need to know about me."

"Really? Well, that's an accomplishment for a man your age. Have you met anyone here yet?"

"Yeah, this joker," he said as he poked my arm. "We've gone to Lawrence to see Black Flag and Bad Brains."

The class giggled.

"What are your hobbies?"

"Karate and girls. Also, I'm going to win the lottery someday."

"Frank, I've been seeing your picture in the newspaper," she said politely. "So, you have a band?"

I cleared my throat quickly. "Yes."

"You've chosen a very interesting name. Very creative, to say the least. I don't think the newspaper should avoid printing the name, as they do," she told me. "As long as the word *condom* is considered profanity, AIDS will spread through that ignorance. It's a good name, Frank. Very timely."

I nodded my head slowly, politely.

"Okay, class. The first assignment this year will be an essay on positive role models in your life..."

We all met at lunch, the five of us sharing our old table in the center of the cafeteria. Lippschitz stood a few feet away, watching us as the Dewie boys took some freshman's lunch money not ten feet away. Jack pulled the boy up by the back of his underwear while Ben declared: "Snuggies! Snuggies! Underwear up your uglies!"

33

"Jesus, look at that girl," Oscar said, pointing at the leader of the pompon squad. "Wouldn't you love to spank her?"

"She wouldn't talk to you," Stanley said.

"My ass, she wouldn't."

"Go talk to her, then."

"You don't just *talk* to them. They'll know you're full of shit, then. You have to ignore them. They'll be moved by your indifference."

Stanley laughed.

"Trust me, they'll be crazy about you—you won't be able to get rid of them."

Suddenly, my eyes locked onto the unexpected vision of a New Wave bombshell. Across the cafeteria, beyond the congregation of drones stood a short girl of poor posture and upstanding taste and style. Her clothes were black, stylish but casual. Her hair was a frightful mess as if she had an allergic reaction to hair brushes. Her expression was one of great curiosity and fear. We watched her, all of us silent as she stared nervously at her shoes. She glanced up to browse the room. When her eyes reached our table, they remained fixed.

"She sees me," Oscar said triumphantly.

"She wants *me*," Stanley corrected.

"Remember Oscar's advice, don't talk to her," I said. "Don't even look at her."

"I wonder who she is," Whitaker pondered. "She's not from Iola."

"Well, no shit," Stanley said.

Upon receiving her food, she immediately walked over to our table, having received the signal of our direct attention.

"Hi," she said with poor English as she sat her tray down and took a seat next to Whitaker. "My name is Pehgan and I'm an exchange student from Denmark. Are you guys the band in the newspaper?"

"They are," Oscar said, "but they suck. I once had the highest score on *Galaga*—"

"Yeah, we're the band," Stanley inserted swiftly with grace and comfort.

"We're the fucking Fluorescent Condoms!" Thik said with uncharacteristic vigor, then laughing at his awkward passion as he sunk back into a tray of mashed potatoes.

"You play music like A Flock of Seagulls?" she asked.

"No, it's punk rock," Whitaker responded matter-of-factly.

"Like the Buzzcocks?" she asked.

"Yeah!" he exclaimed while slapping his knee.

"Do I get to hear it?"

"Yeah, uh...we have an *album*—" he said.

"It's a shitty tape made on a four-track recorder," Stanley corrected.

"I would like to hear it."

"Cool, yeah," Whitaker said. "Yeah!"

"When do I hear it?"

"Today after school?" Whitaker suggested. "We'll have T-shirts soon, and we're also doing another tape—I mean, *album*. We're in magazines also. We've even sold like thirty tapes around the country already. Maybe someday we'll play a show..."

"She doesn't give a shit!" Oscar said. " She's thinking: *Man, this guy's a moron! I wish he'd shut the hell up so I can eat this suck-ass food.*"

"After school?" she asked, staring directly at me.

"Yeah, sure, if you really want to," I said. "I mean...yeah."

"You drive?"

34

I raised my eyebrows—a look that lacked any of this supposed inticing indifference. "Okay!"

"I will meet you after school," she told me.

"By the front doors?"

"Yes. Front doors…"

Whitaker and Oscar exchanged insults against the fear of diminishing an Alpha reign on our pack. The thought of meeting this girl after school was adequate distraction. In fact, it occupied my mind the rest of the day. These were opportune times for me, I figured.

I waited by the front doors as the first grueling day of school came to a close. I had successfully alluded the others and was eager to spend my first moment alone with Pehgan. Thoughts of what could possibly happen raced through my adventurous mind. I stood quietly alone, waiting, fantasizing, smiling. Eventually, she wandered around the side of the school, appearing perfectly and appropriately out of place. It was a quality I immediately liked.

"Front doors," she said as she approached me. "Now we go."

"Do you need to inform your host parents?"

"Of what?"

"Where you'll be."

"Oh, no," she said confidently as we walked together to the parking lot. "They're fine."

"Well, okay. I'm not taking the blame if they freak out."

"They're fine."

"Okay."

We shared an awkward silence, looking at the other students who were busy looking at the other students.

"Which car is yours?" she asked.

"The gray thing over there," I said, pointing to my Ranchero.

"The not pretty one?"

"Yeah, that's it," I confirmed.

"I don't like punk music," she admitted suddenly. "Don't like the Buzzcocks. Hurts my ears, makes my feet sweat."

"Why are you wanting to see us practice?"

"Yeah, I want to see you practice your band."

"Why?" I asked.

"Yeah."

I climbed inside the car. "Okay."

She stood outside a moment, then opened the door and quickly jumped inside.

"Do you have a girlfriend?" she asked as I backed the car out of the lot and advanced down the narrow street.

My heart raced with excitement as I considered her motivation for asking. "No."

"Okay." She placed her delicate white hand on my bony leg and began to softly caress my knee.

I looked down with great concern and confusion. As I pulled up to a stop sign, I fished through that crow's nest of hair to find her eyes. Black rings of eyeliner housed her sexy green eyes. I smiled politely as she flapped her spidery lashes. She yanked my shirt collar—pulling me hard against her, and kissed me. Her firm tongue penetrated my limp mouth.

"Okay, drive," she demanded.

35

Her hand slowly moved away from my knee, northbound to otherwise restricted areas. The pressure of my foot eased from the pedal. She advanced slowly. Slowly. And the Ranchero crawled down the street slowly. Slowly.

She reached her destination before I had reached mine. Her hand stopped at a speed bump hidden inside my pants as the car idled forward. My hormones had reached a meltdown, but time was of the essence. At the present rate of speed, I'd have made the following night's practice—or run out of gas first.

Everything moved in slow motion. Cars lined up behind me, honking as I stared into the rearview mirror with a slagging jaw, unable to figure out what they could possibly want.

"Is the car okay?" she asked, removing her hand. "Is there trouble? It stopped."

"What stopped? Did something happen?" I asked, checking my pants.

"Your car is not moving, and the people behind us seem not happy."

"Oh," I said, stepping on the gas pedal, whipping both of us back into our seats. "Right."

I quickly turned through back streets, disregarding traffic signs until I pulled into my driveway. The rest of the group, along with Oscar waited like protective parents. They stared with suspicious eyes as she stepped out of the Ranchero and took a seat against the wall.

"Hey, Frank, check this letter out, man!" Whitaker said, tearing open all our band's mail that my father had brought home. "Someone wants us to play in Joplin!"

"Where's Joplin?" Oscar asked.

"Southwest Missouri," Thik said as he tuned his drums.

"They're starting to put shows on there. These people...they're from Los Angeles and they used to book for the Circle Jerks and Bad Religion," Whitaker said as he stripped his Oxford shirt off, revealing a worn, holey T-shirt.

"Mild mannered Whitaker MacGregor Junior peels away his stuffy preppy attire to transform into: *Super Punk-Rock-Band-Member Man!*" Oscar exclaimed. "Just don't let daddy know his true identity..."

"Fuck off, Pee Wee," he replied, holding the letter with tense fingers. "They want us to send a tape, and if they dig it, they'll set us up this fall."

"Like, *totally*, dude," Oscar said sarcastically, revealing his supposed disinterest.

"Shall we jam?" Whitaker asked as he fired up his amplifier.

I glanced over at Pehgan who stared deep inside the kick drum. The thought of fondling her small breasts electrified my body. I found myself pulling her into a cozy bed inside my mind where I sat at the foot staring up at her soft, curvaceous body. I studied her feet, feeling the stubble on her legs as I licked from her ankle to her knee. The texture drove me wild. Grabbing her knees, I pushed them further apart as I slid myself face-first up her thighs. I was searching for a scent I knew existed, but had no first-hand experience. Was it as sweet as men so often describe? My curiosity consumed me. I wanted to know. I wanted her to show me. I wanted her...

"Yeah," I said, bringing myself back to reality. "Let's jam."

We sent our tape to Joplin the next day. After two weeks, we had heard nothing. Just as we were giving up on the idea...

"Hello, is this Frank Smith?" a brisk woman's voice inquired over the phone one evening.

"Yeah."

"Hi, this is Karen, you sent me a tape...in Joplin."

"Oh, wow! How are you?!"

36

"Okay! We got the tape and it's pretty cool, pretty cool! We're looking at renting a hall and we've been talking with a band called B.F.E. They're from Arkansas, have you heard of them?"

"No, don't think so."

"Oh, well, they've agreed to headline the show and we're looking for a band to open. Would you guys be up to it?"

"Of course!" I said.

"What do you ask?"

"Huh?"

"Your guarantee?" she explained. "What do you want for compensation?"

"Oh...yeah...I really don't know, I hadn't even thought of that."

"Well, we could give you gas money, and a portion of the door. How about one dollar for every five we make—after we break even on the expenses."

"Yeah, okay. Sure...great!"

"All right, then!" she said. "We're hoping to have the show sometime in early October, on a weekend night."

"Yeah, okay."

"We'll send you details, and some fliers."

"Yeah, okay."

"All right, well, we'll talk to you later."

"Yeah, okay."

"Okay, goodbye," she said.

"Yeah, goodbye—thanks!"

I gently sat the phone down and smiled shamelessly. The Fluorescent Condoms— my very own band—were actually going to play a show!

The next day at school, I gave the unbelievable information to the others. We were well on our way to success, with our *album*, a show and T-shirts on the way...nothing could stop us. *Nothing.*

"Frank," Whitaker said to me after practice one night, "I really need to talk to you. Important stuff...with my parents."

"Yeah, what's up, man?"

"It's the band." His face was scrunchy and constipated. "I mean, it's my parents. It's a fucked-up situation. They aren't finding it funny anymore. They figured I'd have quit the band by now. They're really on my back. They told me if I didn't drop out of the band, they would reconsider paying my college tuition."

"They're trying to scare you. Don't be so easily baited."

He shook his head. "It's a fucked-up deal, man."

His complexion was flushed. I could feel the dread seeping from his pores. It thickened the air between us.

"You have to stick with it, man—for yourself," I told him with a reassuring tone. " If you give in at the slightest pressure, what will that do for you? For your self-esteem—for your pride?"

"I'm not digging it anymore."

"The band?"

He made a throaty noise of awkward discomfort. "There's a lot of shit with being in the band."

"Did you tell your parents how well things were going?"

"The better things go, the more frustrated they seem to get. They don't want me involved."

37

"So, tell me, Whitaker, what do *you* want?"

"I don't know, man. The shit's getting thick—"

"No, man, that's not what I asked."

He paused a moment, and took a deep breath. "I'll play the show, and then I'm out. That's what I have to do."

"We have some new songs, ones that will be on the next album. Like *Persistence, Resistence*—our theme song! We can finish it before the show, easily. Are you cool with that?"

"Yeah."

"I know you want to finish it, right?"

He nodded.

"Are you sure?"

"Yeah, I'm sure. Thanks, Frank."

"For what?"

"I don't know...I wish I had your perseverance. Your parents are so cool about all this."

"We set our own limits, Whitaker. Myself included."

"Well, thanks, man," he said lightly, suddenly casual and loose. "I'm sure we'll laugh at this in ten years."

"Yeah, we'll see."

The sun was slowly sinking beneath the western horizon. The clouds bled a violet hue against a backdrop of fuscia and orange, like rainbow sorbet. The remaining light of day withheld a strong sense of soothing tranquillity. The music we were applying to our environment offered the perfect contrast. Distant neighbors watched from front porches, rocking slowly on old wooden swings.

Orange extension cords enabled us our freedom from the confines of the garage. Thik maintained the center of the driveway behind his small drum set as the rest of us surrounded him. Bright yellow fliers covered everything, advertising the Fluorescent Condoms' show. Our name was dwarfed under three huge letters: B.F.E.

Oscar sat on the hood of my car, staring into the sunset as we cranked out the frenzied chaos, actualizing our reputation like arrogant exhibitionists poignantly aware of our body's youthful defiance of gravity.

"Should we call it a night?" Thik asked as we completed our set-list the second time.

Whitaker clicked off his amplifier. "The jam comes to a close."

"I want our show to be flawless," I commented with a hoarse voice.

"We'll rock," Whitaker said proudly as he lit up a cigarette with a brief, inexperienced drag.

"Bullshit," Oscar corrected nonchalantly. He stepped down from the hood of the car. "You guys still suck."

"Let's get something to drink," Whitaker said. "This is a celebration of sorts!"

"Yeah," Oscar mumbled, "the end of the band..."

"You buying, Whitaker?" Thik asked. "I'm broke."

"Sure. We have a lot to be proud of here. We're going to be playing an actual show..."

Oscar thrust himself upward with coiled fists that jabbed at the sky. "Cool! Whitaker's paying for dinner!"

"No, I'm not," Whitaker corrected as he tugged his bulky amplifier toward the garage. He let go, wiping his brow with the back of his hand. "On second thought, if you take my amplifier inside, I'll buy you something, Oscar."

"Deal."

I walked up to Whitaker and clenched his shoulder. This type of conduct constituted a display of affection between us.

He blew smoke into the stagnant air. "I think we'll put on a great show. It sounded really good."

"My voice kind of suffered, but I'll be able to handle it," I promised as the garage door came down with all our equipment safely inside.

"I want ice cream," Oscar said.

"Well," Whitaker contemplated as he took a quick drag, holding the smoke briefly in his sinus cavity before releasing it. "I really wouldn't mind if we—"

"I want ice cream, dammit!" Oscar demanded.

"All right," Whitaker said as everyone piled into the bed of the Ranchero.

Oscar opened the passenger door and stuck his head inside. "Company?"

"Sure, just don't mess with my driving. Leave your hands off the steering wheel, leave your feet off the gas pedal…"

He glanced out the window at the bruised sky. "Great sunset," he sighed with unnatural reserve. "I'm just kidding about your band, you know. I think your singing is badass, man. When you're screaming, I'm there with you. Stick with it, Frank. You can go somewhere, maybe as far as that sun sets."

"You know our stuff better than anybody—"

"I'll still give you shit," he told me.

"Of course."

"I just wanted you to know."

I smiled proudly. "I'm glad you're here."

"Yeah, right!" he said. "You think I'm an obnoxious idiot!"

"Yeah, so?"

"So?"

"I'm glad you're here, you fucking obnoxious idiot," I told him flatly.

"I'm not going to tell you I'm glad to be here, because I'm not at all. But I have fun with you guys, and I know it could've been worse."

Silence filled the cab as the car halted at a stop sign. I impatiently waved an old woman across the intersection as she stared hesitantly. Laughter from the bed of the Ranchero came in quick spurts, obliviously innocent of the judgmental eyes that glared from decrepit, leaning porches.

"I really didn't have many friends in southern California," Oscar admitted. "There was a group of guys I hung with, they all skateboarded and had those lopsided haircuts. They were pretty cool. They listened to a lot of punk and goth and New Wave. That's where I heard the Stooges. I wasn't that into them, but I knew some of their songs. So, when I say I'm a fan, really…"

"Yeah, that's cool," I told him.

We pulled up behind a large truck at one of Iola's few stoplights. Two scrawny roughnecks sat in the truck's bed, staring at us with dull, haggard eyes. Their cheeks were stuffed with tobacco that seemed to ooze from the corners of their mouths. One reared back and spit an enormous glob of dark juice onto the hood of the Ranchero, staining its dull silver paint.

39

"Fucking boogan," Oscar growled out the window. "It pisses me off to see you take so much shit, Frank. I wouldn't take it."

"It washes away," I said casually.

"Let me tell you something," he began. "Last summer in San Diego, I spent every day at an arcade in a strip mall nearby my house. I really didn't have any friends, and I didn't have anything to do over the summer, so I went there. I spent probably ten dollars a day playing *Galaga*." He paused a moment as he bit his lip, then proceeded. "This was the kind of place that serious nerds would hang out. You know, the type who wear parachute pants and tie bandannas around their calves, trying to breakdance so girls would dig them."

"The kind of guys whose pants don't really fit well?" I asked, looking down at his high-waters.

"I spent nearly every day there. My parents would give me enough cash to get food, but I'd steal a sandwich from the 7-Eleven and blow my money on *Galaga*. By the end of the summer, I had the highest score in the arcade. No one could touch it. Took me the entire summer. You know, San Diego is a large city. I can only imagine the scores at some of the other arcades."

"That's really cool."

"Anybody with that much free time could've done it," he shrugged modestly. "The day I left, I went down to check one last time—an entire year later. Still had the top score, probably to this day."

"That's cool, man," I said as we pulled into the parking lot of the ice cream shop. The others leaped out of the bed like an explosion. "Tell me something...about this karate thing?"

"Yeah," he said, smiling.

"Is that bullshit, or what?"

He laughed as he opened the door. "Who can say?"

I smiled at him as he raced behind the others. I followed quickly after them, the last person in the door, the rotten egg.

"Banana split, Whitaker," Oscar demanded. "That's what I want."

The woman behind the register glared at us, her shiny nametag pinned to her shirt with the engraving: *Anita Mann, Owner.* We stepped up to the counter with hungry smiles.

"Get out," she demanded.

"Excuse me?" Whitaker respectfully requested.

"Do I need to call my husband?" she warned. "Paul! Get up here!"

A large, burly man bounded from the back of the store. I assumed I was meeting for the first time one of Mr. Lippschitz's closest friends. He was what I'd imagine becomes of the star football player after graduation, quite a few beers later.

"We don't want you boys causing trouble around here—*get out.*"

"We just came for some fucking ice cream, what are you talking about trouble?" Oscar inquired.

"Hey, little man, don't you use curse words around here, in front of my wife, in front of my employees. I've got a business to run. If you little shits come in here ever again, I'll call the law on ya'll."

"You want trouble?" Oscar asked. "I'll give you some motherfucking trouble, asshole!"

"Come on, man, let's leave," Whitaker said, trying to calm Oscar. "Sorry, sir, we'll avoid—"

"Bullshit!" Oscar said, backing away from Whitaker. He pointed his bony finger at Paul Mann and shook his head. "Don't worry, I'll never step foot in this fucking shithole again...redneck motherfucker."

"Don't you swear at me, punk!"

"Oh, yeah? *Fuck...You!*" he cried, rushing out the door.

We were right behind him.

"What are you doing?" Whitaker demanded as we followed Oscar to the Ranchero. "We'll never be able to go in there again. Man, when my parents hear—"

"Shut up!" Oscar said, kicking gravel against the side of the building. "Whitaker, if you had a pair between your legs..."

"Fuck this shit!" Whitaker said as he took off toward the street. "I'm walking home."

"Exactly—fuck this shit," Oscar said. "I need a haircut."

The four of us stood in a circle as Whitaker stomped down the street.

"Should we get him?" Thik asked.

"Fuck him," Oscar said. "Let's go before the cops get here."

"Here, have a sip, man," Thik said, pulling a cup from behind his back. His smile loosened the tension. "It's not a banana split, but it's all I could grab. Coke?"

"Coke sucks."

"I'll take it," Stanley replied calmly as he climbed into the bed of the Ranchero.

"I want a mohawk," Oscar announced. "A cool one, like those tall fins you see on postcards. Will you cut my hair, Frank?"

"Your hair is only about three inches long," Stanley said.

"It'll grow."

"Maybe you should relax a bit," I suggested.

"No, either you do it, or I'll do it."

"Okay," I said. "Let's get the clippers."

There were few things I detested more than homework. The essay on positive role models Mrs. Webster assigned my Psychology class was due the next day, and I hadn't even begun. I couldn't allow this annoyance to cut into my personal time. By the end of the day, I resolved, it would be complete—before leaving school.

There were only fifteen minutes left of class, plenty of time to begin and possibly finish. I stared upon a blank sheet of notes as Mrs. Pizzle lectured the finer points of English. I would save the attention for someone who cared to become a writer someday, for which I certainly had no interest.

My essay could be about friends, I initially decided. I knew I didn't want it to be about anyone famous. That would be far too obvious. She'd read plenty of papers about Evel Kneivel and Mr. T.

I thought of the night I had seen Black Flag, but I knew I didn't want it to be about such a successful band. I found more inspiration in the people struggling to get where they were. Something about that struggle that always gets to me in all the right ways...I remembered the Lawrence band, the Jerk Offs whose record I absolutely loved. The passion that exuded from their record had made it one of my all-time favorites. Someday, I decided, I would be in a band like the Jerk Offs. What could be more of an inspiration?

I filled the paper with a train of thought that described every aspect I loved. Someday I would be there, just like them, pushing myself to achieve that greater aspiration that would separate me from the flock. That day would be a happy one. I titled the paper just as the bell rang, taking a moment to scribble at the top of the page: *The Day I Will Know Success.*

I closed my notebook and raced out the door. It was lunchtime, the highlight of my school day.

Whitaker was sitting at our table when I walked into the cafeteria. He smiled as I joined him. It was as if nothing had happened at the ice cream shop the night before.

"How's it going, Frank?" he asked politely. "Have you seen Oscar's hair?"

"I cut it."

"How did you get it to stand up like that?"

"Knox gelatin."

"He looks...radical," he commented as Oscar, Thik, and Stanley joined us. "Where'd you get the combat boots, Oscar?"

"Duh, dumbass," Oscar replied. His head was bald except for a crisp fin of blond hair from the center of his scalp back to his neck, uniformly straight. "My Old Man is a retired military man, where do you think I got them?"

"You look cool," Whitaker confessed.

"You don't."

"Are you still in our band or what?" Stanley asked Whitaker.

"Of course, why wouldn't I be?"

"Well, after last night—"

"Yeah, I'm in the band, until after the show."

Pehgan tossed her tray down at our table and plopped herself next to Oscar.

"Nice hair," she said dully.

"Shut up, bitch," he replied with a full mouth.

"You're an asshole," she said.

"I know you are, what am I?"

"You're such a little kid, Oscar," Whitaker scolded playfully.

"I know you are, what am I?"

"With your new hairdo, you'll fit right in at the Outhouse this weekend," Stanley told Oscar.

"Oh, that show is *this* weekend?" Whitaker asked. "Man, I don't think I'll be able to go this time."

"My Old Man's letting me use the car, so we don't need you to go," Oscar said. "We've got our own ride."

"Fuck you, then, you little prick."

"I know you are—"

"Hey, Frank, we get the shirts this weekend, huh?" Thik asked.

"Do I get to sell them at the show?" Pehgan asked.

"What?!" Oscar protested.

"You aren't in the band, dummy," she said.

"I know you are, but—"

"Yeah, that'd be good, if anyone would want to buy them," Stanley said.

"Yeah, you can sell them," I told her.

"What the hell am *I* going to do?" Oscar complained.

"You can be our roadie," Thik suggested.

"Okay, but I'm not carrying any equipment or setting anything up."

"Man, I'm tired," Stanley said with a yawn. He rubbed his eyes with his knuckles before dropping his hands to the table. "I'm exhausted."

"Why? Jerking off too much?" Whitaker asked.

42

"Probably, but that's not why."

"What's up?" I asked.

"Well, I was problem-solving late last night."

"You're so studious," Whitaker said with respect. "What was the problem?"

"Well, maybe you guys could help me. I know you're a bunch of idiots, but maybe you could pool your limited intelligence together and come up with a reasonable answer. I'll give you the scenario." He paused to drink some chocolate milk.

"Is this going to be some of that gifted class mumbo-jumbo?" Oscar belittled shortly. "People like you make me sick."

"Okay," Stanley began, ignoring Oscar. "Let's say Captain Kirk takes the *Enterprise* into some sort of time warp...and he goes way back in time to a galaxy far, far away."

"And he comes across the *Star Wars* galaxy?" I asked. "That shit keeps me up at night, too."

"Would the Federation stand a chance against the Empire?" Stanley asked.

"There are a lot variables to consider with this," Whitaker said frankly. "Would the Rebel Alliance be involved?"

"No."

"How many Federation ships?" Whitaker asked.

"Just the *Enterprise*."

"No Romulan or Klingon vessels?"

"No, and if you're getting at cloaking devices, I've already considered that."

"So, it'd just be the *Enterprise*?" Whitaker asked.

"Yeah."

"Against what?"

"Say, the second Death Star and a couple Star Destroyers," Stanley said.

"Well, the *Enterprise* would plow through Star Destroyers, it has much stronger fire power," Whitaker insisted.

"Yeah," I added, "but what about a Super-Class Star Destroyer, like the *Executor*?"

"No problem," Stanley said. "The *Enterprise* would smash the *Executor*."

"Yeah, but against the Death Star?" Whitaker asked.

"The Death Star would blow the *Enterprise* away," Oscar said. "It destroys entire planets, I mean, come on!"

"That'd be cool if Kirk tried to meet the Emperor and Vader like he always does," I said. "You know, to talk peace and all that shit."

"And tell the Emperor how cool he is because he's a human, with humanitarian values," Stanley said.

"Vader would kill him," Oscar said. "Grab his throat and strangle him!"

"And he'd say: *I'm a human, like my father before me* and Vader would see the way he's been wrong for neglecting his two kids all these years, and then kill the Emperor," I said.

"Yeah, because the Emperor was the one saying: *Come on, Vader, kids aren't cool, man*," Whitaker said. "One word for you, Darth: Contraception."

"Here's how Kirk would destroy the Empire," Thik began. "After the negotiations were unsuccessful, and after he'd have sex with at least one foxy Imperial Senator, he'd have Scottie teleport a bomb to the center of the Death Star and blow up its core."

43

"I'm giving her all she's got, Captain!" Whitaker said with a poor Scottish accent.

"Yup," Stanley said. "That's what he'd do, all right. The Empire doesn't have that teleportation technology, either."

"Do you think he'd bitch to the Emperor about how Klingons killed his son?" I asked.

"Probably," Whitaker said. "He tells everybody that story. One word for you, Captain Kirk: Psychiatrist."

"That's why Vader would kill the Emperor, because that sappy story of Kirk's would make him aware of his humanity—"

"So, you think the Federation would teach the Empire a lesson?" I asked.

They unanimously agreed.

"I'd root for the Empire anyway," I said, a bit annoyed. "Besides, if it were a ground battle, Vader could kill a thousand Federation—"

"Star Trek," Stanley said.

"Star Wars," Whitaker and Thik said simultaneously.

Pehgan kept eating her peas and carrots, looking at us with oblivious eyes.

"I think you're out-numbered," Oscar said to Stanley. *"Star Wars* it is, so go get your ass over to the *Star Trek* Geeks Club table."

"Is there one?" Stanley asked, looking around. "So long as you won't be there, I'll gladly go, asshole."

"I know you are..."

I lumbered slowly to the turquoise Malibu with a fat box in my hands and a shameless grin on my face. I dropped the box down on the hood as the others crowded around curiously. I stabbed the slick tape with my keys. Shredded paper bled from the incision.

"Don't scratch the paint on the car," Oscar warned. "My Old Man will kick my ass, then yours."

"Here we go," I said, lifting one of the shirts in the faint light of dusk.

The front had a large FC in bright green letters with the word *Fluorescent* over the top and *Condoms* underneath—both words vibrantly orange, wrapped around the large FC. The back shined with an embarrassingly simple drawing of an upright condom glowing of fluorescent green with a bright orange mohawk and grimacing sneer. Our own "mascot."

"Wow," Thik exclaimed with a chuckle. "We have concert T-shirts! I'm wearing one to the show tonight."

"Me, too," Stanley said as he held the new Condoms shirt high with pride. "Whitaker would be doing flips if he were here now."

"He's not here because he's a wimp," Oscar replied.

Stanley brushed at the fabric's crease. "Maybe we should find another guitarist."

"In Iola?" I asked. "I don't think so."

"Can I have one?" Pehgan asked timidly.

"Sure," I said, throwing her one of the smaller sizes.

She peeled off her shirt in the empty parking lot, revealing to us why she needn't wear a bra. We stared until she had covered any differences between us.

"So...what are you guys going to do when you become famous punk rock stars like the Ramones?" Oscar asked.

"Like we ever will," Stanley shrugged.

44

"*What if.*"

"What if?" Thik asked. "First, I'd buy a new drum set. Then I'd open my own microbrewery. Then I'd buy a hot new sports car, like a Camaro or Trans Am, and drink my beer, I suppose."

"I'll help you drink it," Oscar said. "I love alcohol! In San Diego I could drink anyone under the table in my sixth grade class. Would you get a mansion in South America, too, Thik?"

"Oh, yeah, of course! I'd have them everywhere."

"I'd put myself through the best college in the world, and then become a doctor," Stanley said.

"That sucks!" Oscar said. "That's so stupid. That's not even rock and roll. Where's the heroin, and the chicks, and the V.D.? Come on...what about you, Frank?"

"When I become successful," I began, "that is, when I become aware that I am successful, I'll buy a Pepsi—only Pepsi because Coca-Cola sucks. I'll open the Pepsi and dump it on the ground, or throw it away. Something like that. That's what I'll do when I *know* I have achieved something."

"What?!" Oscar shrieked. "What the hell are you talking about?"

"Well," I continued, "if I'm successful, then it wouldn't matter. Either its price would be irrelevant, or I would have no need for possessions. I could dispose of it, and it would make no difference to me."

"Give me a beer, Thik," Oscar said.

"That's pretty cool, Frank," Stanley told me.

"Hey, thanks, man. I kind of pulled that out my ass just now. Shall we move on to the Outhouse?"

"Aren't we going to get the hair dye?" Oscar asked. "Come on, this is Lawrence! We've come all this way and I'm sick of my hair color."

"All right, let's go find some fucking hair dye," Stanley protested as we piled into the car. "I'd hate for Oscar not to get his way for a change..."

Wispy clouds kept the nocturnal view of a starry sky hidden from our ambitious eyes. The darkness of the country cast no reflection, leaving a hollow background as colorful as asphalt. Pehgan and I sat on the hood of the Malibu as the others stood around the blazing bonfire, waiting for the night's entertainment to begin.

"So, did you have a choice in where you were going as an exchange student?" I asked her.

"I wanted Los Angeles, or New York, like everyone."

"Were you upset when you found out where you'd be going?"

"No, I didn't know where it was. Then my host parents sent me pictures of wheat fields."

I took a deep breath of air thick with scents of life and nourishment. It was harvest season, a time of death, and equally a time to reevaluate the life that would continue through it. Autumn always brings out the best in me.

"Why do you come to our practices if you don't care for the style of music?" I asked.

"I don't like punk rock, don't like the Buzzcocks much."

"Right...so why do you bother? Why are you here to see SNFU?"

"What else would I be doing?" she replied.

"If you spend enough time around this music, it'll inevitably grow on you. You'll be tipping cop cars in no time."

45

We sat quietly, both leaning against the windshield, looking up at the gray that hung loosely overhead. The moment was orchestrated by a thousand people holding a thousand conversations over the noise of a dozen car stereos. The enormous fire was surrounded by a circle of onlookers tipping bottles of beer, smoking, and telling larger tales than the next. I could hear conversations I would come to find commonplace amongst punk circles: Who was the best of the four different vocalists that fronted Black Flag? Would punk rock have been a British form of music if it weren't for the Ramones? Could an Anarchistic society work? Did HR of the Bad Brains really record *Sacred Love* in prison?

I listened to the inaudible muck of background noise trying to see how much music I could distinguish. False Prophets, GBH, Butthole Surfers, Big Black, Einstürzende Neubauten, the Exploited, the Specials all echoed through the fields that wrapped around the Outhouse like a quilted blanket. Then there were some recordings I had never heard before, which was the name of the game when it came to collecting underground music. The more obscure, the better the find. If you were the only person with a copy of, say an unknown band from an unknown place like the Fluorescent Condoms from Iola, Kansas, then you were that much cooler than your peers. It was a badge of punk culture to possess what no one else knew, except—of course, yourself. It was easy to tell how long someone had been into *the scene* by how obscure their collection. Those who never listened to the supposed "big bands" were true veterans. As pretentious as the true veterans carried themselves, they never missed a performance of one of the "big bands" even if the decision seemed to be a last minute choice. I could hear several people talk about the plans they grudgingly broke to attend.

"Hey, clowns, don't break the damn windshield! My dad will kick my ass," Oscar said, stumbling toward the car. His brand new Fluorescent Condoms T-shirt was already stained with dirt, spilt beer, and various other substances. A black leather choker was wrapped tightly around his veiny neck.

"Where'd you get the dog collar?" I asked.

"Some girl gave them to me," he said proudly, lifting his fists to reveal two black leather wristbands with rows of shiny silver studs. "Did you see these?"

I nodded my head. "Where are the others?"

"Who gives a shit?" he said as he stumbled away. "The band is about to go on..."

We watched him blend into the crowd as if submerged in murky water.

I climbed down from the large hood. "You coming in, Pehgan?"

"Not quite yet. I'll wait a moment."

"Okay," I replied as I headed for the Outhouse.

The venue quickly began to fill. Without excessive delay, SNFU took the stage with Mr. Chi Pig's wild stage antics and sharp tongue delivering wonderful entertainment for the night.

Leaving the Outhouse was never an easy thing. I did what I could to stall our departure. The only solace I could find was knowing I would return soon, though never soon enough.

"I'm paranoid," I told Pehgan as we drove to my house. "This is our last practice."

"Why are you...paranoid?" she asked.

I rolled up the window and turned the heater low. "Well, we play this weekend, and we haven't even begun recording our second and final *album*."

"You can't finish it after the show?"

"No. Whitaker won't be in the band anymore."

We pulled up to my house and parked behind Thik's station wagon. The remaining Condoms were crammed tightly inside with the windows completely fogged. Like a swarm of bees leaving the hive, the doors burst open with youthful vitality.

"Ready to rock?" Thik screeched into the misty air.

"I think we'll need to practice inside today," Whitaker suggested. "It's wet, and it'll be cold in an hour."

"Wimp," Oscar mumbled under his breath.

I opened the garage as the band quickly took their places behind respective instruments.

"Anything special for the last practice?" I asked as I clutched the microphone.

Everyone looked at Whitaker, making him reasonably uncomfortable.

"Let's just play and have a good time," he said.

The hum of instruments brought the silent garage to life with a sinister hiss. Oscar took a seat on a rusty tool box as the rest of us stood armed and ready for our first and final stand.

"Okay," I began, looking at the set-list as the band circled me, motionless. "This is a song from our upcoming release, *Persistence, Resistance.*"

Whitaker smirked at me as Thik clicked his sticks to usher our anthem. I marched out to the slick, wet driveway. As I sang, I noticed the gray sky overhead being swallowed by black clouds, devouring what little light remained. The wind dragged the thick clouds, chilling my stiff body as I stood motionless, screaming. My wiry, dreadlocked hair flickered like a flame in the open air as I told my stories, giving my life to the unseen listener. They were out there. They listened, but not to my words. The tone of my voice maintained their focus. I was screaming, yet utterly mute to communication. The black storm pressed over me, devouring my attention.

I watched a young girl ride her bike up the street toward us. Her little legs powered the bulky ten-speed as she stared curiously at me on my lone post. She stopped when she reached the end of the driveway. Her brown hair blew wildly by a breath of cold northern air. When the song ended, I turned to her.

"Can I watch?" she asked.

"Seems that's what you're doing," I replied.

"You don't mind?"

"Of course not. Come inside."

She accepted without a moment's hesitation, hauling her bike into the garage between Oscar and Pehgan.

"Who the hell are you?" Oscar asked.

"I'm Kimberly," she returned with polite sincerity. "Kimberly Powers."

"Yeah, so what?" Oscar snarled with snide contempt. "Shouldn't you be in bed now?"

"No."

"Haven't you heard that I eat little girls?" he asked.

"No."

"I bet you have," he challenged for his ego's sake.

"Maybe you should leave me alone, fucker," she snapped fiercely.

Oscar nodded his head slowly. "You're all right."

"Hi, Kimberly," Whitaker offered kindly. "How's your dad?"

"Fine."

47

He turned to the band. "Her dad's the president of the bank down on—"

"Who gives a shit, asshole?" Oscar squealed. "Shut up and play because you annoy the hell out of me."

I stood apart from the others, watching the storm consume our neighborhood. The streetlights came alive with a halo of mist glowing dully. Our set continued as the night converted the hours from dismal gray to black. I concentrated on the numbing of my hands. It helped me avoid the chill of other, more internal senses.

Suddenly it was night.

"Well, that's it," Whitaker said as the band concluded its final song. "We're good to go."

"I've got to get home," Oscar said. "Stanley, will you take me home? My mom's dying my hair fire-engine red."

"Will she dye mine?" I asked.

"Yeah," he said. "I have some other colors."

"Green?"

"You want green? We'll look like a Christmas decoration together."

"Great."

"Oh, wait, did you want to use the green hair dye, Whitaker?" Oscar asked sarcastically. "Oh, I guess that might take some balls. Maybe you should go talk to your parents and get written permission to make such a decision. I'd hate for you to decide something that might affect their social caliber."

Kimberly laughed out loud, innocent and cute.

"Frank, can you take me home?" Pehgan asked.

"Sure."

"How about eight o'clock for the dye, Frank?" Oscar asked. He shot a quick glance at Pehgan. "If you're busy, I understand…"

"I'll be there."

We gave our farewells and went our separate ways.

Pehgan and I took a drive through the countryside, arriving at the remains of the old Kentucky bridge on the outskirts of Iola. Generations of teenagers had spent many intoxicated nights on the decaying and partially collapsed structure. Our footsteps represented a change of atmosphere. Together we sat on the edge, peering into the dark creek with sober eyes. Droplets of rain trickled onto the water, creating a sound like sizzling flesh, smelling of mold.

"I have gone through another change in my life," she told me as she removed her nail polish with a sponge and solution. "My black period is through, and it's time to enter my next one."

"How do you know your black period, as you say, is over?"

"Oh, it is." She pulled a small bottle of dark blue nail polish out of her bag and shook it gently. "Do you think Oscar has blue hair dye?"

"This would be your *blue* period?"

"Yes. It's time I accepted it," she informed me as she slowly applied the polish to her stubby thumbnail.

"So, about how long did the black period last?"

"Seven hundred twelve days. The past seventeen days don't count. They were the blue period. I'm late by seventeen and a half days."

"You must feel dislocated, I guess, having been wearing black during the wrong phase," I joked.

48

"Oh, yes," she returned quite seriously. "I haven't been myself, but soon I'll shed the past. I'll agree with myself, then."

"Yeah, nothing like an argument with yourself. You always end up feeling like a total heel. So, was there a phase before the black one?"

"Green, mainly forest green. Before that was bright orange, when I was young and happy. Before that my mother dressed me in pink. So, I started pink. I'll never be yellow. I'm allergic to yellow. I break out into hives when I wear yellow."

"Now you're blue."

"Now I'm blue. Maybe Oscar's mother will color my hair, too?"

"Yeah, maybe," I said.

"I'm to meet Stanley at eight o'clock. Maybe Stanley will wait for later?"

"Probably so."

"I can't believe this bridge ever connected anything," she said, looking down a deep hole in the center of the ancient roadway. The water flowed below us like motor oil.

"Actually this bridge was built during a time when Iola was a larger community. There was a huge supply of natural gas here and Iola expanded fast. The gas ran out, and so did a large portion of the population. The perimeter of Iola has all kinds of ancient relics such as this bridge. Shows you how fleeting progress can be."

I picked up a rock and threw it into the water where a faint, black ring expanded from the point of impact. I peered down at the flow of water below my dangling feet, feeling nothing but the crumbling concrete frozen against my ass.

Two young boys raced their bikes to the top of the hill on Northwestern Street. Baseball cards clicked rapidly in their spokes as they pressed forward against the threat of defeat.

"I can go faster! I can go faster!" the first exclaimed.

"I can go farther—farther than you!"

They zoomed past a driveway marked *fifteen-zero-nine*. It was noontime on Saturday, the day of the Fluorescent Condoms' show. We eagerly waited by the van my parents had rented for this special occasion. Everyone had spent considerable effort on their image. Even those concentrating on a low profile had succeeded at meticulous casualness.

Oscar's mohawk was tall and stiff and vibrantly red. He looked quintessentially punk rock with his leather collar and studded wristbands, weathered blue jeans and combat boots, worn-out leather motorcycle jacket and stiffly new Black Flag T-shirt.

Pehgan had slipped into her new shade gracefully. Her messy hair shined a blue-black, depending on the light. Her wardrobe now contained only navy blues with tasteful touches of black. A thick, royal blue dress hung loosely to her knees. Blue and white candy-striped leggings sunk into thin-soled black slippers that looked somewhat Japanese in style. Her thin lips were painted blood red, her face naturally flushed white from a lifetime's avoidance of sunlight. Black eyeliner encircled her green eyes.

Stanley was sporting his favorite Dickies' pants. Military green. He could just as easily been ready to harvest the crops, which would've likely been his plans otherwise.

I still had trouble getting used to the bright green coils of hair that hung in my eyes like thick pieces of yarn. My time spent in theater over the past year had taught finer uses of make-up application—such as shading the concave of my eyes to appear gaunt, sunken and hollow like death.

Silence and tension stifled the mood of the trip. Having never had the chance to really take ourselves seriously as entertainers, we were suddenly shocked by the reality of what lie ahead. In a matter of a few hours, the efforts of our passion would unfold to the scrutiny of a trained ear. My heart heaved uncomfortably at the thought. I stared out the window at the brown soil where crops were recently stripped like a whore. Gray skies hung heavily over the level horizon, shining dully on the raped earth like a deep, brown ocean of defecation.

As the van passed through the city limits of Joplin, conversation dropped to nothing. There was an overwhelming sensation of displacement hovering over the van, as if the gray had traveled with us. Our presence seemed intrusive. We belonged in Joplin no more than the streets of Iola we claimed as our own. Like wild game caught in a hunter's ambush, all eyes—it seemed, were on us as they always had been.

We entered into a neighborhood of low-rent houses erected sometime in the 1970's, before the housing boom of the following decade. Faded pastel colors and children's toys sprawled in the front yards was all that separated one from the other, block after block. Slowly, the houses became interspersed with old buildings standing vacant with windows busted from worn, rusted frames. It was the type of neighborhood that couldn't claim any prestigious history. In its finest day, it was probably no less desolate, lacking even the character of being a bad neighborhood.

Everyone came to attention as the van turned down the narrow back street where the hall was located. In the distance, some three blocks ahead, the street was filled with several young kids on skateboards and bikes. There were easily twenty-five—all dressed the same, not one older than fifteen. We studied their actions as if sizing up the other team—their team *Audience*, ours *Band*. We were stoic and immobile, horribly intimidated by the little boys with their baggy shorts and handkerchiefs pulled tightly over their heads like pirates at a junior high school Halloween party.

My parents made the first step into the enemy's land. We sat in the back of the van like troops running our first tour of duty. The side door opened, but no one moved. The kids skated around the van, slamming their boards hard against the curb as we watched, unamused.

Reacting from obligation, I made the first advancement. Oscar was right behind me, ready to back me and cover me like an old buddy. I slowly stepped down onto the damp cement. Oscar followed with the whole troop taking up the rear, and there the six of us stood, lined up against the van like guilt-ridden convicts. The kids stopped dead in their tracks as if someone had whispered: "E. F. Hutton." They picked up their boards and approached with great apprehension. It seemed the appropriate thing would be to smell one another's ass.

"Wow," one of them said, staring at Oscar's stiff, spiky red mohawk. "You guys look like the real thing."

"Yeah, no shit," another said. He looked at my hair and raised a curious brow. "How'd you get your hair to do that?"

"Do what?" I asked defensively.

"Stick together like that. Like Bob Marley."

"Never comb it."

"Wow, that's totally awesome. You guys must be B.F.E."

"No," Whitaker said politely. "We're the Fluorescent Condoms."

"Oh, yeah? Where from?"

"Iola, Kansas."

They all giggled. "Where the hell? Is that by Kansas City?"

"No, not at all. It's west of here," Whitaker informed. "Only seven thousand people live there."

"Where'd you get that 7 Seconds shirt?"

"We saw them about a week ago," Thik boasted.

"You saw 7 Seconds?! Where?"

We were winning this hand, it was clear. Oscar answered proudly to further dispel the differences. "In Lawrence at the Outhouse. With Justice League."

"Wow! Hey, do you guys like D. I.?"

"Sure," I said, cocky in regard to my musical knowledge. "I prefer the Adolescents..."

"Do you guys like N. O. T. A.? They're from Oklahoma, you know."

"Yeah, they're cool," I replied.

"Do you guys play hardcore?"

"Yeah, kind of," Whitaker answered quickly. "Well, we're usually not *really* fast, but some of our songs—"

"You'll dig it, don't worry," Oscar said confidently. "Who's B.F.E.?"

"No idea, but this should be really cool. We've never had any punk bands play here."

"Ah, the Fluorescent Condoms!" an obese woman sang as she stumbled out of the VFW. Her appearance was that of a maid at a turnpike motel. She still had the hairstyle her mother had chosen for her second grade yearbook pictures. "I just talked to one of you fellow's parents and they told me that you just arrived. Great! Who did I talk to on the phone?"

I stepped forward.

"Frank? Hi, I'm Karen. I haven't heard from B.F.E. yet. Would you guys like to set up your equipment?"

With paralyzing apprehension, we assembled our small load of equipment as Pehgan set up a card table for our merchandise. Oscar took a seat next to her and watched as she constructed a cardboard sign using red and black Magic Markers. The hall was bright and spacious. In terms of Bingo parlors, we were on a grand scale.

The skaters gathered at the back of the hall as we checked the levels on the instruments, timidly playing a few notes for the sound-man. We were morbidly aware of their presence, mortified by their trained ears. With their record collections and J.F.A. and Misfits stickers on their skateboards, they'd know.

"Should we do a sound-check?" I mumbled to the band.

"Why?" Stanley challenged, eyeing the young boys.

"Yeah, I'm not sure about doing that," Thik said apprehensively. "Should we ask the sound-man what he thinks?"

"No, don't do that," Stanley said.

"Excuse me," I shouted into the microphone. My voice echoed through the hall with piercing feedback. "Do you want us to go through a song?"

He flicked some dials as the jury of skater boys casually propped up the back wall, watching us like flailing prey.

"If you want," he said.

The band suddenly appeared ill. Their ailment was contagious. It attacked my stomach before charging my heart.

"I think we'll pass," I said, feeling microscopic and pathetic.

I could hear three sighs of relief, along with my sigh of resignation. My body felt tense and weak. I wished to be anywhere else.

51

"I'm so hungry I could eat the ass end of a menstruating mule right now," Stanley said, the tone of defeat somehow buried under the prospect of walking away unscathed.

The rest of the band quickly stampeded for the door like caged animals set free. I stood alone in front of the instruments on the designated floor that would be considered the *stage*. The hall seemed much larger now.

Gently, I set the microphone down and stumbled over to the table Pehgan had set up.

"That's a really nice sign," I told her, trying to overlook the defeat that I was certain would soon determine my existence. "Thanks for helping."

"You guys look like curdled milk," she said, concerned.

"I guess we have the jitters."

Oscar leaned forward and whispered in my ear: "I know you can do it."

"Thanks, man," I said casually. "Would you two care to get some food with me?"

"You bet I would," Oscar said. "Get off your ass, Pehgan, we're going."

When we returned, no one had heard from B.F.E. yet. The place was surprisingly infested with little skaters. Karen had already cleared sixty-seven tickets, with two more hours before we were expected to perform.

I felt my innards churn like a host of parasites were having a banquet. I retreated outside into the street for solitude. I was overcome with anxiety. Who was I kidding? We were just a couple kids from rural Kansas...

Suddenly, the faint sound of music echoed through the street. The headlights moved in on me, slowing as if searching for an address. The smile that lightened my face was the first in hours. It had to be the band. I stepped closer to the street as the loud, indistinguishable guitar-driven music intensified. Just as I recognized the song— the new single from Cinderella, the pick-up truck stopped in front of me. A drunk cowboy hung limp from the passenger window.

"Holy shit, boys!" he slurred loudly over the annoying, anti-punk rock music. "Check out this faggot! Let's kick his ass!"

The passenger door opened as he slid to the ground. Beer cans tumbled around him.

"Faggot! Get your queer ass over here. Why do you look like such a faggot?"

I stared as two cars slowly advanced in the distance.

"I play...quarterback," he informed me desperately. "Everyone loves me. What's your problem, fairy? Why is your hair so...so green?"

"Get in, someone's coming, could be the cops!" the driver demanded as the big truck idled forward.

"See you later, faggot!" he laughed as they sped away.

The two cars pulled up to the hall and unloaded four or five kids each, staring at me in awe.

"Wow," rang several voices as if delayed from the first.

I suddenly realized the air to be bitter and cold. I could see the vapor of my breath leave my chattering mouth. I was horrified by the ramifications of what seemed inevitable. Karen took a step outside the hall with a handful of bills she had just collected.

"I don't think they're going to show," she said. "I've sold one hundred twenty-seven tickets, and as late as it is...I think you guys are the spotlight entertainment. The kids are getting kind of antsy. Are you ready?"

Her voice ricocheted inside my skull: "Are you ready? Are you ready? *Are you ready to show all these kids how pathetic you and your band of dorks are? Are you ready to show everyone—especially yourself—just how unqualified you are to do something like this? Where are you from—Iola, Kansas?!* Are you ready? Are you ready?"

"Yeah," I mumbled, taking one last look down the quiet street before stepping with concrete flexibility to the hall.

"They're going to love you guys," she assured me.

The place was brimming with enthusiasm. The kids generously made way for me as I passed, yet all I saw was the other team. *Them.* The ones who would laugh as soon as I raised the microphone to my mouth.

"I think they want us to go on, man," Stanley said gravely as if informing me of our public execution.

I could only have wished that to be our immediate fate.

Thik and Whitaker sat in the corner with the same expression a baby makes when soiling their diaper. The air hung heavy upon us—the gray had in fact followed.

Oscar sprung up from beside Pehgan and grabbed my shoulders tightly, demanding my attention with a sudden jolt of urgency. "Listen, fucker!" he pleaded, his eyes wide with passion. "Do it, godammit! You can't let me down—not now, not here. Not you."

He rushed to the "stage" and picked up the microphone.

"Testing!" he screamed. It screeched violently from feedback. "Are you motherfuckers ready to rock, or what?"

The crowd stepped forward, forming a huge arc around him.

"Listen up, you fucking pussies, B.F.E. aren't showing—do you give a shit?"

"No."

"Yeah, fuck off. You're about to see the Fluorescent Condoms! They're going to kick your fucking asses."

"Yeah! Hardcore!"

"I like your hair!"

"Eat shit, asshole. I don't like yours. Now, are you ready to rock, or what?!"

"Yeah!!"

"What?! Speak up, you shit-for-brains motherfuckers!"

"YEAH!! Condoms!"

"Frank..." Oscar introduced, dropping the microphone as the kids roared with anticipation.

The audience opened for us, waving exhilarated fists in our faces. Oscar looked upon me with stern, proud eyes. He raised his thumb and smiled.

The band stepped up nervously behind the protection of their instruments. I didn't possess the same barrier. I stood naked—the holder of the bayonet in this Civil War. I picked up the microphone and faced *them.* An ocean of faces vibrated in front of me, stretching to the back of the hall where Karen stood smiling, counting the money. I glanced down at the tiles, trying to find myself between the cracks while the amplifiers hummed. The crowd was stirring with excitement, their voices filling the small venue as the band backed me, quiet and still—lifeless like death. At any moment I felt the audience could penetrate our vulnerability, with the odds against us...as usual.

I turned to Stanley. He nodded without expression, a gesture that would be as close to confidence as I could've gotten from any of them.

"Hello, Joplin," I said firmly into the microphone. I raised my gaze to the faces that surrounded me, that threatened to swallow me. "We're the Fluorescent Condoms from Iola, Kansas. This is a new song...*Persistence, Resistance.*"

53

I could hear the timid clicking of drumsticks, each decaying into the scattered chants from sections of the audience. With the fourth and final click, the slow, throbbing rhythm sucker-punched me against an invisible wall. I scraped myself free, unaware that my feet had left the ground until I landed. My fists rushed to my sides. My body flexed firm as I stepped forward with fierce momentum to claim my area. The stagnation of the wall sought to control me, to chain me. I thrust myself in conjunction with the grinding force of the song's intro, my vision bleeding passion, tainted by a thousand voices including my own who had ever told me I couldn't. My swinging fists impacted the air with cymbal crashes as if igniting explosives.

Time ceased. I glared into the crowd—angered, passionate, and ultimately powerful. Their eyes surrendered to mine as I watched the ocean of faces become engulfed by a hurricane. Their heads chopped like waves. Fists thrust in the air as the storm picked up intensity. The intro reaped eternity as I gripped the microphone with white knuckles. Wandering through the fractional holes of time suspended to the moment, I stumbled onto the song as rehearsed, yet more natural than walking. I raised the microphone to my face—my hand shaking with preternatural confidence as I placed myself within the strength of the music. My body smashed against the crowd, against the band, but never against that wall.

I could see Oscar's bright red mohawk in the wake of motion, moving my direction in a roundabout way. My eyes were glazed, my brow like a lead weight influenced by the gravity of the Earth's fiery core. I screamed my thoughts into the microphone, into everyone within earshot—they were mine. I had them until I would decide otherwise.

Oscar made his way to me, smiling with invigorated eyes. He clenched his fist up proudly before falling back into the stain of bodies that circulated in front of us—the Fluorescent Condoms from Iola, *fucking* Kansas.

Out the corner of my eye, I could see Stanley. He held his bass like a weapon against the turbulence, banging the strings like the fire of a machine gun, knowing nothing except annihilation. It was us against *them*, and they didn't stand a chance.

The song came to a sudden halt and the crowd screamed wildly with praise.

I announced the next song immediately, never allowing my back to be grounded, to return me to human consciousness, human failure. I felt myself towering above the restrictions of my species, so long as the music played, so long as my voice wouldn't give out. I was alive and living, and nothing could stop me. *Nothing*.

Somewhere between instantaneous and eternal, we finished the last song of our abrupt twenty-song set, leaving the audience relentless and hungry.

"We could play a song twice," Whitaker suggested excitedly over the noise as they demanded an encore.

I shook my head firmly. "They can buy a tape if they want more. How about a cover?"

"Sure," Stanley said. "We only know a few."

I turned to the ravenous crowd with a cock-eyed glare. "How about a cover song?"

"Yeah!" one hundred twenty-seven kids screamed with one united voice.

"DC5," I informed the crowd, as well as the band. "*Glad All Over*."

Following our third and final cover, the crowd swarmed Pehgan's card table stand, inhaling every T-shirt and cassette tape with the demand for a great many more.

I stood beside the drums as the band mingled with the audience. I lowered my hands to my knees—eyeing each droplet of sweat falling from my green coils of hair.

54

A pair of combat boots stomped up to my side, grabbing my sweaty neck before patting my flexed back.

"Not bad," Oscar said. "That's what I expect."

I stood erect, towering over him. The young skaters rushed my side, armed with a list of questions.

I welcomed their curiosity.

"All wings report in," Oscar said from the passenger seat of my Ranchero.

I pressed the pedal tightly to the floor as we sped down the gravel road between walls of wheat as if tunneling through a trench. A large Dodge truck pursued tightly.

"Red leader, standing by," Stanley said, who sat between the two of us.

"Gold leader, standing by," Oscar followed.

"Green leader, standing by," I finished up as I held firm to the wheel. I could feel the tires tearing through the gravel with a cloud of dust to trail.

"A small fleet of Rebels have penetrated our defense," Oscar said in an awkwardly deep voice, as if coming from the pursuers. "As ignorant rednecks, it is our purpose in life to destroy them."

"Enemy T.I.E. fighters closing in from the rear," Stanley gave commentary as the truck pursued.

The magnificent walls of wheat outlined the parameters of the narrow road with a golden blur. The truck weaved back and forth as if trying to pass or intimidate me with their ambitious bounty.

"Green leader, this is Base One, do you copy?" Stanley said, as if through some radio.

"Green leader, copy."

"The Empire is within firing range and ready to attack, do we stand a chance?"

"Copy, Base One," Oscar said into his fist. "This vessel has a V-8 under the hood—at least five hundred horse power. Victory by persistence, over."

"Five hundred, huh?" Stanley asked. "I think the radiator brushes for this particular year deflect a lot of the carbon currents leading into the water mount receptacles. Damn near cuts the piston reflex in half. Kills most of your thrust. Do you know what I mean?"

"Pshaw! Of course I do," Oscar said.

"Funny...I don't."

"Fuck off, asshole. There you go, giving me shit again...I'm leaving." He climbed effortlessly out the window into the bed of the Ranchero.

"Do you think they'll shoot him?" I asked as he danced seductively in the bed.

The truck switched its headlights to high beam.

"Shoot him? Don't get me excited," Stanley said.

I kept my eyes on the road, making sure I maintained relative control over the loose gravel. Stanley turned to watch Oscar. The bright lights of the truck illuminated his face through the dust and difference that separated the occupants of each vehicle.

"What's he doing?" I asked. "He's making it hard to steer."

"He's jumping around...now he's taking his shirt off...and waving it over his head. He dropped it in the bed, and now he's taking his pants off."

"You're shitting me."

"He's wearing tighty whiteys...well, he was. He's doing the mashed potato now, or is that the dirty duck? Anyway, he's dancing like he's on *Solid Gold*."

I glanced in the rearview mirror. Sure enough, Oscar's bony, white buttocks gyrated as if skipping through an earthquake. The headlights shined on him, the spotlight attraction, displaying his birthday suit to the dormant countryside and a truckload of appalled cowhands.

"Yeah, he'll be getting shot soon," Stanley confirmed calmly.

My eyes focused on the road with intense concentration as my peripheral vision caught Oscar's ass thrusting at the pursuing truck like a dog humping air. I heard a loud crack against the back windshield. Oscar fell to the bed.

"They threw a massive rock," Stanley said. "They missed, he's up again...and now he's pissing at them...and their wipers are on now so I assume he has a hell of a range. They must not have guns."

"He's got the rock they threw...he's going to heave it back. They're slowing, they don't like this..."

The headlights began to fade in the exuding dustcloud, vanishing in a matter of seconds. Oscar lowered himself into a crouching position as we returned to town.

The trees along the roadside had already begun their transitional coloration. It was as if the road was lined with top-heavy ladies sporting evening dresses from the 1970's—clothes optional, as some were already disrobed for winter. Oscar fit the bill in more than one respect—his mohawk, though less brilliantly red than the leaves, somewhat blended.

"What are you staring at?!" he demanded of parked onlookers at traffic lights.

They stared with wide eyes and lagging jaws. Their curiosity in his animalistic presence kept them enamored. They loved being appalled by him.

"So, what now with the band?" Stanley asked over Oscar's consistent barkings.

"I suppose we're over. Finished. I hate to see it go," I said, turning a quick left to avoid another traffic light in favor of silence from Oscar. "I've been thinking, since we have an album and we've sold it mostly through the mail, I'm going to make a compilation tape. Get a good ninety minutes on tape and sell them through *Maximum RockNRoll*, with ads for it as well as our own Fluorescent Condoms release."

"How would you go about doing this?"

"I'd write letters to the bands, requesting permission for the use of their songs."

"I want to suck you off!" Oscar screamed at a man raking leaves in his front yard.

He stared curiously at the naked guy in the back of my Ranchero, then glanced nervously at Stanley and me.

"So, what about the next album?" Stanley asked. "We have all the songs..."

"I guess we don't do it. Sucks, big-time. So, why did Principal Small talk to you today? Did you get busted for something?"

"There's some state-wide competition going on. He wants me to participate."

"What is it?" I asked.

"A bunch of corporations in Kansas City are funding some competition to reinforce the value of education, or something queer to that effect. They're looking for essays with collegiate level themes from high school students across the state."

"If you won?" I asked.

"The school would get the recognition. Pictures in Sunday editions of newspapers in Kansas City, Topeka, Lawrence, Wichita..."

"What's in it for you?"

"They'd pay the first semester's tuition at any college within the state. I doubt I'll win, there's a lot of really smart people out there. Think of all the schools in Kansas City alone."

"Yeah, but you're a smart guy."

"What's the essay Mrs. Webster had you write?" he asked me, changing the subject abruptly.

"It's about positive role models..."

"What's the theme of yours? I know Oscar's was about Mr. T."

"It's about the Jerk Offs."

"Come get me, big boy!" Oscar screamed to a city worker in a utility truck. "I've got a stiffy here! Climb this pole, honey!!"

Stanley continued. "Don't throw it away. I want it."

"Why?" I asked.

"I like to keep things like that."

"You mean you collect trash?" I clarified.

"Yeah, whatever."

"What's your subject on this state competition going to be?" I asked.

"Well, I've been reading a lot about something called the Chaos Theory."

"Oh, yeah? What is it?"

"Say you want to mathematically figure out the rate of speed of a fifteen pound ball rolling at a thirty degree incline. Mathematics teach you how to go about the answer, but the answer will be essentially incorrect, due to tiny variables in a realistic circumstance, such as the texture of the surface, the wind, any rocks or bumps in the path. All these things will affect the outcome. The proverbial butterfly that flaps its wings in China and results in a hurricane in North America, that's it. This is why we cannot predict weather, because the randomness becomes too overwhelming."

"You can write a whole paper about this?" I asked.

"Sure. See, if you drop grains of sand through a funnel, the contents will form a mound. Although at a certain point, it'll collapse, or the grain will spread. There has to be a constant, predictable factor within the chaos. Possibly an entirely new system of mathematics, which would eliminate the numerical values that we know."

"Like what?"

"They're misleading. There is no such thing as absolute zero. If *zero* is absolutely nothing—an impossible equation, and *one* is whole, or complete, then what's between? How often do we use fractions? Seldom, if ever. Yet, five point three-six-four-nine-eight is as significant a number as five. We only deal in whole numbers, or shades of black and white when real life is nothing but shades of gray."

"Hey, asshole, I'm jerking off while I check out your ass!" Oscar bellowed at a man bent in his decrepit bed of marigolds.

"Humans have a particular weakness for mathematics," Stanley continued. "We struggle with simple multiplication and division, barely comprehending calculus or trigonometry."

"I barely understand algebra," I admitted.

"Can you wear your jeans any tighter, you fucking whore!!" Oscar howled at a woman standing at an intersection.

"So, what are you doing for Halloween?" Stanley asked.

"I don't know. Hadn't thought about it."

"We should do something. Something really fun..."

Across the empty dinner table, out the back window of the dining room, I spied a couple of neighborhood kids engaging in a tense game of Smear the Queer. Rubbing my eyes, I returned to the papers and letters splattered around me as if my notebook had exploded. My fingertips were black from the cheap ink of the *Maximum RockNRoll* issue opened in front of me with smudged and worn pages. On a piece of paper at my side was a list of band names, half of which marked with a check of completion. My hand ached from hours spent writing the stack of letters that corresponded to the check marks.

At the edge of the table were three manila envelopes containing fanzines that had received the Fluorescent Condoms tape and were requesting an interview. I had put them off for a week, and vowed to complete at least one that night. I looked at the return addresses, wondering what their lives were like in Columbus, Ohio or Trenton, New Jersey or Eugene, Oregon. I fantasized what it'd be like to tour, looking at a list of North American cities knowing at the end, you'd have seen and tasted each one—a day in the life, then onto the next. Stress-free living, and living large.

The telephone rang, bringing me back to quiet Kansas.

"Hello."

"Frank, this is Pehgan. Do you want to come over, like at nine o'clock?"

"Sure."

"Okay, at nine o'clock," she said, hanging up quickly.

I held the phone a second while listening to the dial-tone. I stared at the circular dial of numbers on the plastic rotary. Being suddenly struck with a thought, I dialed information on a notion of curiosity.

"What city please?" the operator asked.

"Lawrence, Kansas. KJHK, the college radio station."

"Hold for the number..."

The phone rang at the station for practically two minutes before an irritated voice greeted me coldly.

"Are any shows coming to the Outhouse?" I asked.

With a long-winded sigh, he responded with great effort. "Let me check the concert calendar, hold on."

I waited a couple more minutes to sultry jazz programming.

"Yeah, we have one in November. Cold season, not many shows. The Descendents."

"No shit?! What's the date?"

I quickly scratched the information on the back of the phone bill, thanking him before pressing the chrome receiver down with a wiry, adrenalized finger. I released it quickly and dialed Stanley's number, tapping my finger impatiently as the phone rang once, twice...

"Hello?"

"Ma?" I confirmed casually to Stanley's mother.

"Hello, Frank," she replied. "Stanley's not here. He's working on a paper at Mr. Martin's place."

"Mr. Martin? Who's that?"

"He's the math professor at the JuCo. He's working on the disorder paper. Maybe he's writing about his bedroom. He should be back in a couple hours—"

"Leave him a note that says: Descendents...Outhouse...November. He'll understand."

"Okay, Frank."

"Well...goodbye."

"Bye."

*   *   *

It was exactly nine o'clock—I would be appropriately late to Pehgan's place. I sat up from my relaxed sprawl on the bed warmed by an hour of solitude, darkness, and the comfort of poorly recorded albums. Flipping the switch on my Teddy bear lamp, the color of my room immediately ignited like the blast from a bomb. My eyes squinted—partially shut—as I pulled my worn Chuck Taylor All-Stars on my socked feet. My toes curled into tight fists against the cold temperature of the canvas.

Standing with an immense stretch and light head, I peered with squinty eyes for my jacket. It found me first, its two-dimensional acrylic skull staring from the corner like a rabid dog. I tip-toed through the room, stepping over stacks of letters written and received, piles of dirty clothes, and a scattered mess of fanzines. The jacket felt cold against my skin as I slid into it—the chains rattling like machinery.

I lifted the needle from the Jerk Offs record, leaving it on the player like a throne of monarchy—the quality of its music serving the basis for its rank. Rain tapped gently against the roof. Its peaceful serenity was strickened by the knowledge of the cold that surrounded it—the cold in which I'd soon be immersed.

I left my small quarters, allowing the Teddy bear lamp to illuminate the silence like a proud sentry. Its lampshade bore the crayola design I had constructed during my third or fourth year of life. It was a drawing of my brother and me, seemingly with him knocking me on the head as I cried.

Outside, the cement was lubricated with wet, musty leaves once green with life. They clung to its surface like a wet tarp. The freezing wind forced its way through my clothing, raping my sense of touch, leaving my skin bumpy with erect hair follicles.

By the time I had reached Pehgan's house, the Ranchero's heater had finally summoned the strength to conquer the cold. I felt the urge to savor its comfort, but my hormonal drive over-ruled any such decision. I crept across the spongy lawn, feeling my feet sinking in the ground with each step.

I tapped my clenched fist against the side door and waited a few impatient seconds. She opened it with a wordless greeting. Her thin lips carried the remnants of bright red lipstick. A choker collar of rich blue velvet hugged tightly to her neck, ornamented with a tiny silver bell. A baggy silk gown welcomed me inside.

"How are you, Frank?" she asked.

"Hey, Frank," Oscar said from behind her. His eyes were relaxed. His lips bore the faint smear of red lipstick that matched the stiff mohawk atop his head. "Later," he said to us as he made his way through the lawn.

"What's up with him?" I asked.

She welcomed me inside. "What do you mean?"

"Oh...nothing. So, what's happening?"

"Just listening to music in my room. Come listen."

I followed her through a long, dark hallway. The faint ring of the bell on her choker directed me through the darkness. We entered a small room, lit only by two black candles at opposite corners. The artificially sweet scents of her gender lured my attention. Her room seemed to reflect naturally the fragrance of fresh flowers and all things nice. The bed was a wreck, and comfortably warm as I sat down. The cold rain sizzled against a shuttered window.

"Nice neck thingy," I said. "Where'd you get it?"

"I got it for me."

"Why a bell? Won't that be annoying?"

"What?"

"The bell."

"Why?"

"Because it makes noise whenever you move," I explained.

"No, I need it. So I always know where I'm at."

The tiny bell jingled as she moved closer, smearing the remaining lipstick against my limp lips. I looked down at the sheets piled in a messy lump of fabric as her small hands took full liberty on me without restriction.

My pants became loose before I could remove my jacket. The cold chains and safety pins contrasted the comfort of the bed.

Her gown came off as I pried at my drenched shoes, yanking on the old, bleached-out canvas. My wet socks slid easily from my feet into the accumulating pile of clothes, mine and hers. She sat with Royal blue socks—dry and warm, and baby blue undies with patterns of dancing gray elephants. Her white skin blended with the walls behind her, equally naked with only two posters overhead: Bauhaus' *Bela Lugosi's Dead* and Cocteau Twins' *Love's Easy Tears*.

Her hair seemed to exude a heavenly aura of blue, which was merely the dye acting against the faint candlelight. Her mouth was outlined in a shade of red like a Kool-Aid mustache from the lipstick I now shared. The pulsating sound of Joy Division caressed the bareness of the room with its frigid touch, drowning all colors to a pit of black and white. The water dripped softly down the glass window as if melting the view of the world. We moved apart, void of apparel or feeling, staring with desire.

"It's cold and gray outside," she whispered across from me.

"It's Kansas."

A flicker of light stirred us for a second as one of the candles burned through the wax. An avalanche of black wax poured down the thick shaft, causing the flame to grow higher, brighter. The wax slowly hardened into a smooth puddle, engulfing the base of a small glass container half-filled with clear liquid marked *tears*.

"Should I blow it out?" she asked.

"I think it'll be okay."

"What do you think the first straight line was?" she whispered softly.

"Huh?"

"Every line comes from another, so what was the first?"

"I don't know."

"Come here," she beckoned.

"Why?"

"Come here."

I crawled across the bed and fell into her arms as if her body had been a mold to my own. I felt the urge to explore a tighter union. Her firm nipples rubbed against my chest, her lips clung softly to my neck. My body ached to consume her with a cannibalistic thirst for flesh, ready to devour hers.

I looked into her eyes, into nothing—no past, no life, no love. We were united by our instincts, bound by the hormones that spawned our own existence. The candle burned brightly as the wax dripped to the floor—a vicious cycle that would ultimately bring about it's own self-destruction. I thought how unbearable the clouds in my head that suffocated and killed any ounce of reason. This could be a historical moment, one I'd remember the rest of my life.

I placed my head against her chest, listening to the thumping force of life. I imagined briefly the intimate experience I'd share with someone someday. Someday, but not this day...and not this someone.

*　　　*　　　*

"Homecoming football game tomorrow night," Thik said to me over lunch the next day. By his tone, I knew a secret, covert operation was being drafted in his pale, freckled head. "Tonight. Pre-Halloween bash. We'll pick you up at eight o'clock."

I took a sip of chocolate milk while swirling the fork through my mashed potatoes.

"Okay," I said. "When I hear you knock, say Swordfish—that's the password."

That night I opened the door to two hooligans dressed inconspicuously in black sweat clothes and ski masks. They looked like a pair of Hollywood Ninjas.

"Ready?" Thik asked with a devious grin.

"Where are we going?" I questioned.

"Stealing Jack-O-Lanterns and smashing shit," Oscar screeched triumphantly.

I smiled. "Let me get my coat."

Thik's older brother's truck purred in the driveway where the Fluorescent Condoms once hailed. The headlights sparkled with the downward pull of condensation, thick and cold.

"Get in the back with me," Oscar demanded as Thik climbed inside the cab.

I pulled myself up over the tailgate into a bed filled with pumpkins spread in piles. Several had faces that stared gravely like trash pick-up day during the French revolution.

"Where'd you get all these?" I asked.

"Porches, lawns, fences..."

"There'll be a lot of sad little kids out there," I said as the truck backed into the street.

"Oh well," Oscar shrugged. "Tough shit. That's the way it is..."

We sped off down the street with Oscar and I peering over opposite sides of the cab.

"Watch this." He grabbed a large pumpkin carved up with a maniacal smile.

As Thik rushed through a stop sign, Oscar heaved the Jack-O-Lantern. It impacted the sign with a noisy explosive display of orange vegetative shrapnel. The sign danced back and forth as the pumpkin's remains dripped to the moist ground.

"You know, we could totally demolish this town with these things," he told me. "Think of Lippschitz's car, Small's car, Dewies' bedroom window... Hell, we could totally fuck with the cops with these—"

"Nah, that's okay," I said.

"You take too much shit. It's us against them. We're in this together, and we gotta start biting back."

"You handle things your way, I'll stick with my style."

Adrenaline perched my body temperature to a tolerable level as the freezing rain splattered hard against my face and hands. The truck sped into the town's main public park with the football stadium coming into view like a fortress surrounded by a wire fence.

"We're famous," Oscar told me as the truck rushed over the dike. "Everybody's waiting for something. We're entertainers, let's entertain."

The truck stopped outside the stadium, allowing the rain free-reign upon us. Thik jumped from the cab as Oscar tossed him a pumpkin. With a passive giggle, Thik launched the pumpkin against the wall, leaving a grotesque splatter of orange slime. Pale seeds speckled the wall as the meat of the pumpkin slid to the concrete.

Thik pulled a small can of black spray-paint from his coat pocket and finished Oscar's destruction with huge letters: *Chanute Rules!* He threw another can to Oscar as they walked to the front of the building, painting various Chanute frame-ups.

I climbed the fence into the interior of the stadium, saving myself from the cold rain as my two companions set about desecrating the concrete structure. I walked through the wide corridor up to the benches, covered by a large awning. All sound was flushed out by the sizzle of rain against the aluminum cover overhead. As I advanced up the concrete ramp, the playing field rose over the dark horizon.

Oscar crept down to the grass, beginning at one end of the home team bench: *Millions of Dead Cops.* It was clear they underestimated Principal Small's perceptiveness. We'd pay for this in so many hours.

"Here," Thik said, coming up from behind. "Have at it."

He extended a can of spray-paint. I took hold and popped the red top, shaking it firmly with a rattle that challenged the hum of the pressing rain.

With swift strokes from a steady hand, I laid forth my thoughts on the clean white wall with intense calculation: *I Get Bored In The Flat Fields.*

I rushed along the jagged path through the thick foliage of the dark countryside. Large twisted branches extended from all directions as if the skeletal frames of the live oaks sought to molest me. Overhead, a full moon shined like a lemon, shrouded in a veil of spongy gray clouds.

My lungs burned from the inhalation of frigid cold air. My legs were achy and stiff—my resources feeding from tension and fear. As I passed through an opening in the brush, I glanced over my shoulder to emptiness, darkness. In the distance, a wolf howled longingly at the pale, yellow moon. The wind rustled the drifts of fallen leaves on the eerie path into the dark unknown.

I moved forward as Rod Serling stepped from a twisted tree I had passed—his suit and tie immaculate and dry with tones of black and white.

"Frank Smith decided to take a walk in the quiet countryside of a lake resort known as Camp Crystal Lake," he began as I bounded down the path, frightened and confused. "But Frank found his way down a path off the beaten one—a path...to the *Twilight Zone.*"

I ducked under the low branches that quaked with the force of the howling wind. The path thickened into an open field of tall, unscathed grass. The wind penetrated without resistance, blowing my hair in the cold, night air.

Suddenly, my attention shifted to the rustling trees in the distance like the approach of a nocturnal beast. I could faintly hear the hooting of an owl somewhere lost in the thick forest, within which I was equally without direction. A thick fog rolled over the tops of the tumbling grass like steam over a warm body of water. The commotion across the field intensified as if the beast could move entire trees with the slightest touch, yet making no sound itself.

My eyes widened, when suddenly...Richard Small, the principal entered our well-lit classroom. I looked down at my notes—a clean sheet of paper with a freshly sharpened pencil lying idly across it.

"Mrs. Webster, I would like to speak with Frank and Oscar," Mr. Small announced.

"Okay," she replied.

I glanced over at Oscar who struggled with a Rubik's Cube to no avail. He casually placed it on the desk next to his copy of *Fangoria*. A glare of pride twinkled in his eyes.

Together we followed Mr. Small through the silent corridor of cavernous hallways to the main office. He held the office door wide for us. "Have a seat."

I was surprised it had taken so long in the day for this meeting to occur. This was everything he wanted, a reason to administer our castration.

"I just got off the phone with Chanute high school, after they had questioned a couple of their less honorable students about an incident that occurred last night. Based on certain anti-establishment slogans, I feel confident the problem was designed locally. Are you boys aware of the consequences of these actions, should you be found guilty? We're talking a world of trouble."

We stared at him as the door creaked open. Small's secretary escorted Thik into the tiny office, shutting it quickly as if confining a tribe of lepers.

"As I said, the ramifications of these crimes could hold large penalties—penalties you boys can't afford. Penalties that could affect the rest of your life. Do you realize how much a disgrace you guys are to this school? We have an image to maintain in southeast Kansas—"

"Are you going to tell us what happened?" Oscar asked. "What we're guilty of?"

"The stadium was spray-painted last night, and of course tonight is the homecoming game against our rivals, the Chanute Cocks."

"I plea the fifth," Oscar said. "I mean, I plea insanity. That's it."

"You're out three days, mister! Another word and you'll be skipping a year of school. You don't want to cross me, boys. I'll have you for dinner."

The room was silent as we absorbed the threat.

"Why do you think *we* did this?" I asked politely.

"I know what you guys are about. You're crossing the wrong person. You need to learn to respect authority and power. *My* authority and power. Oscar, maybe you don't understand the way things work in these parts. You aren't in California anymore. We're bound to buck heads, you and I. Let me tell you who is going to win. Me. I carry the big stick, don't you forget it." He shifted his attention to me. "Frank, I keep thinking you'll get better, but you just get worse. I would be in a constant state of humiliation if I were you. How can you live with yourself? Maybe that's the problem with you. Did your parents not teach you any self-respect? Don't you know you won't get anywhere in life without becoming part of the system that clearly works? Can't you see how much easier your life could be if you just gave in? I have no idea what is wrong with you, but I want it clear that I could make it a lot worse for you, trust me."

I nodded my head in a gesture that acknowledged words rather than communication.

"I have nothing more to say, other than I'll be watching all three of you with the eye of an eagle. I won't put up with it. Have I made this clear?"

We gazed blankly across the desk.

He shook his head in disgust and pointed firmly to the door. "Get back to class. Oscar, I better not see your face in three days."

Our exit came without hesitation.

"I'll meet you after school," Oscar told me, gloating over a legitimate excuse to go home.

The door shut firmly behind us as I breathed the air with relief. The three of us stood silent, staring at each other with mi3chievous smiles. The hall was quiet and strangely peaceful. I felt awkwardly free at that moment.

The floor around me was a mess of paper, glue, and scissors. I was trapped within the restrictions of my own disorganization. I made one last adjustment before setting it aside. I rubbed my eyes and stretched my tight back—too tired to be proud of the fact that the cover for my first compilation was finally complete.

The phone rang, announcing the dilemma of my confinement amidst the barrage of shredded paper and supplies. I stood up in the calm center of the circle and leaped to the outer edge of clear carpet.

"Hello."

"Frank?"

"Yes, Stan."

"What's up?" he asked.

"My brain's fried...I just finished the cover to my first compilation tape."

"Hey, way to go! I'm pretty burnt, too, doing this paper. Were you planning to go to the game tonight?"

"No, but my brother is coming up for the weekend, and he'll be there, so I may go down. Let me make it clear that I have no interest in watching the sportos frolic in their provocative uniforms, by the way."

"Yeah, right—I could use a break from this work, myself," he said. "Why don't you get your scrawny ass over to get me? By the way, I have things to tell you."

"What kind of things?"

"Girl stuff."

"Girl stuff? What girl?" I asked.

"I'll tell you in the car, not now."

"Someone around that you can't say—"

"Exactly," he confirmed.

"I'll be over there in like a half hour. Cool?"

"Cool."

I hung up the phone and stepped forward with my eyes focused on nothing. Slowly, the rubber tips of my shoes came into view, then the shaggy terrain of earth-toned carpet that extended like a body of murky water. The pile of papers sat motionless in the center like an uncharted, deserted isle in which I had spent well over a three hour tour. I walked across the water to examine my creation. Refreshed with oxygen, I held up the sheet of paper. Alone I stood, a giant by determination as the paper bent lazily between my fingers.

"Give me the story, man," I demanded of Stanley as he opened the car door, allowing the brisk air to chastise my casual comfort.

"Well, I need to find information about a meteorologist named Edward Lorenz who—"

"Not about the paper, idiot! I'm talking the serious shit—the girl!"

"Oh, yeah! Well, do you know a girl named Jean Martin?"

I shook my head.

"She's a freshman. Her father's the professor who has helped with this paper."

"Is she that little brunette honey with the thick, pop bottle glasses and mole on her nose?" I asked.

"Yeah," he confirmed. "She asked if I'd want to see a movie this weekend or something."

"Like a real date? Did you say yes?"

"Sure. Why not? It's not as if Pehgan and I have something *real* going on."

"Huh?"

"Did you not know?" he asked.

"What do you mean? The question is, did *you* not know?"

"You and Pehgan..."

I laughed. "Oh, yeah. I thought something strange—you know, she spends a lot of time with Oscar, too. And Kimberly Powers. Do you think maybe..."

"Kimberly's pretty young—and impressionable!" he noted. "Pehgan's pretty cool, huh?"

Pleasant thoughts of sapphic lust inspired brief silence. We sped down desolate streets lined with shanty, old houses decorated with cheap cardboard Halloween cut-outs. Soft lights shined from covered windows and porches—its occupants safely within. Two-dimensional witches and ghosts glared from front doors, watching our actions when no one else could. Large bags lined the sides of the street, filled with a collection of fallen leaves rotting the same death as a free-thinking mind in their schools. As we passed, we smiled—oblivious to anything other than the thought of two young girls getting it on together. We'd save the thought for later.

The Ranchero bounced over the tracks, into the park where bundled sports fans swarmed to the artificial light like insects. My headlights brought to life the blue and gold colors of proud Mustang parents reminiscing the glorious day when they were on that field, playing or cheering.

The windshields of dormant cars bore the deprecation of Chanute and praise of Iola in white liquid polish—hatred through grapevines and virgin white shoe polish. Displacement suffocated my comfort once again as I steered the Ranchero through the parking lot. Cops with erect, orange flashlights pointed the way.

We locked the doors and quickly joined the true believers on their hindsight journey to Mecca.

The stadium seemed to glow in the distance under the massive lights. Its surface had a fresh coat of paint that glistened in the air thickened by cold humidity. The marching band could be heard on the playing field, abominating tonality as thoroughly as the Fluorescent Condoms had the previous summer. The windows of the locker rooms glowed on both sides of the stadium containing the heroes of the evening, including the next Homecoming King. I could picture the scene inside—my classmates living a day they'd drink many beers to over the coming decades. I could visualize Ben and Jack Dewie bucking heads and chewing on their cleats as the coach gave a dramatic speech on pride and team spirit. I was glad to be on the outside.

Beyond the gates of the entrance, beyond the blur of blue and gold clothing, a low rumble of voices seeped through the creases of the marching band's rhythm. The sound was a dull monotone based on the conglomeration of people talking about people talking about people.

We flashed our student identification cards to the security guards who stared at each other, then back to us with a slow nod. We proceeded with caution.

With a sudden jolt, one of the guards yanked me aside to a corner away from the crowds. I stared at Stanley with apprehension. I didn't trust the cops, not from previous experiences over the past couple years. He stared with a look of concern—his dark brown suit the color of his skin.

"I won't throw you out," he said to me firmly. "I know your family, they're good people. I see nothing wrong with you kids. Principal Small instructed us to cuff you and escort you away from the premise. I didn't see you, and I have no idea how you guys got in here. Don't make my job hard—stay away from any more games after this. Not everyone here is against you—remember that." He took a second to browse the small entrance. "Now get on with your business."

He quickly turned the other way as we stepped forward through the crowd.

"What was that about?" Stanley asked.

Before I could respond, a group of young girls swarmed us. They snatched at my head with hot-pink claws.

"Are you Oscar or Frank?" one yapped with an annoying voice.

"He's Frank," another snapped. "You don't know *that*?"

"Is your band really called the Fluorescent Condoms? Are you guys gay?"

Their matching baby-blue sweaters gave their Chanute residency away.

"I'm Frank, and if you want to know if I'm gay, meet me outside, you little hussy."

"I bet you guys party a lot," one said, flirting with a hopeful sense of danger.

"I don't drink," I revealed.

"No way!"

"I saw you at a Forensics tournament once...do you guys listen to Heavy Metal music?"

"God no," I insisted strongly. "Metal is for idiots. Dare you insult me like that."

"What do you listen to, then?" she asked.

"It seems I only listen to stupid questions like that one."

"Wow, look at *these* girls!" one exclaimed, pointing to the entrance.

Pehgan and Kimberly approached with lethargic grins beyond a mob of curious onlookers. I found myself as entranced by Kimberly's new look as everyone else. She seemed to have acquired the remnants of Pehgan's black period. Her hair was short and dyed black. The Sisters of Mercy T-shirt she had pulled from Pehgan's wardrobe was ripped strategically to reveal a lacy black bra. For a youngster, she looked good. Too good...

Pehgan was entirely blue—from her hair to her lips, to her fashionable Doc Martens shoes. She carried herself a seasoned New Waver of the goth sect.

"Your school is so cool, why are we stuck in Chanute?" one girl complained.

"We're leaving," I said as we stepped away to join Kimberly and Pehgan.

"Nice hair, Kimberly," Stanley complimented. "You're bound to get a lot of shit for it."

"I know," she boasted with excitement.

"Who were the girls, Frank?" Pehgan asked as we walked up the ramp to the stadium.

"No idea. Curiosity seekers."

The wall of the ramp was taped off with signs warning of fresh paint. How quickly my words wash away...

The lights of the stadium were harsh and blinding—the noise of the crowd equally irritating. We walked up the steps in a single-file line under a shower of wads of papers and derogatory comments.

"Cut your hair, faggots! You're an embarrassment to this town!"

"Your music sucks shit! Faggots!!"

Adolescent boys stepped into the aisle to hinder further advancement.

As the pompon squad took the field, all eyes departed from us as fingers gestured with angry rantings. Oscar and Thik were running wildly across the field with arms flailing in the air. The bright lights illuminated Oscar's red mohawk as he ran as fast as his legs would carry.

"Get that faggot!!"

Security guards rushed from all directions, stopping them at the sidelines. Oscar raised his hands confidently to the stands as the guards dragged them to their knees. Screams of hatred and condemnation shot from the crowd. The adverse opinions brightened Oscar's glowing smile as the cops pulled them away. He threw a proud fist high into the air. The crowd was beside themselves, yet I was shocked to hear a contrasting voice within. A younger voice smaller in size, yet equal in intensity. Their plain clothing blended with the flock of junior high school letter jackets—their cheers to this unlikely hero their only separation.

As I watched them take him away, I realized he was right. Whether they sought a reason to hate him, or stand behind him, he supplied them with news and an easy subject to judge. He was a hero—an anti-hero, of sorts. I was glad he was on my side.

"Hey, Mister," a little kid said to me, tugging at my coat. "I'm you."

I looked down to see a bad hairpiece of orange and green yarn, a poor replication of my dreadlocks. His clothes were torn and cut to represent the ragged quality of punk attire. Two other toddlers—a boy and girl hustled up behind him, attached to the hands of their mother. The other little boy had a stiff arc of red hair going down his head like Oscar's mohawk. His old T-shirt was covered with an enormous FC painted on the front in Magic Marker. The little girl was dressed in black with a frightening black wig frayed into a knotted mess.

"It's what they wanted to be for Halloween. Did I get it right?" the mother asked me.

"Everyday's a bad-hair-day for me. You got that part right," I told her with a smile of flattery.

Tension once again broke the crowd into ruckus as a fight erupted. Opposite a large cowboy hat stood my brother Chet, standing firmly against number and odds. Security guards rushed to stop the progress of the brawl. Brown uniforms peeled the sides away—each backing a cause they knew little about.

"What's going on?" I asked Chet.

"They were talking shit about you guys," he shouted defensively over the frenetic energy the security guards struggled to control. "You may have to leave before all hell breaks loose."

I concentrated for a second on the vicious howlings of the stands, looking up for a moment at the faces. My eyes caught Mrs. Webster, my psychology teacher who sat quietly in the middle of the turmoil smiling proudly, nodding her head in support.

Wadded pieces of paper showered on us as the mighty Mustangs football team burst from the locker room. A line of die-hard fans made a path to the field that ended in a huge ring of paper covered with the words: *Pound Those Cocks!* The team burst through the paper boldly as the crowd went wild with praise.

We took advantage of this timely distraction to make our quiet exit. We quickly rushed down the ramp as the crowd screamed in unison with the cheerleaders: "Beat Those Cocks! Beat Those Cocks! Beat Those Cocks!"

"Hey, dumbass," I said to Oscar who sat quietly at our designated lunchroom table. "You have a sign on your back. It reads: *Kick me! I'm a faggot!*"

67

"Don't take it off!" he exclaimed, knocking my hand away. "I put it there."

I shook my head. "That's clever, Oscar."

"Wait until the first cocksucker tries to kick me," he said, stuffing his face with strips of chicken leg. "Do you want my peas?"

"Sure, do you want my chicken?" I offered.

"I thought you'd never ask."

"Why were you guys running across the football field anyway?"

"Trying to steal the game ball. Thik had a better idea to get it. I should've listened to him."

"You talking about me?" Thik sat his tray next to ours. "If you want a game ball, I'll get you one."

Stanley joined us, scraping his peas onto my plate as customary procedure.

"So, you've been unexpelled?" Stanley asked Oscar.

"Appears that way, doesn't it?"

"How was your vacation?" he asked.

"I played *Asteroids* on my Atari and spent some time developing my *Dungeons & Dragons* character. It was frustrating since I've been playing so many years that I have straight eighteens across the board. I'm an elfin fighter, and a magic user. I think it's time to advance onto Dungeon Master. I've hit that crossroads in my life."

"There's the creep," a girl sobbed over Oscar's shoulder. "You ruined my life!"

She yanked him to his feet, pulling his nose to hers. Her entourage of scantily clad cheerleaders surrounded him. A universal hairstyle united the elite group, a style completely lacking the essence of the very word. Their bangs looked as if a can of mousse had exploded on their forehead with disastrous results. Blue and gold leg-warmers covered their Jordache jeans like knee breeches. Iola existed on the cusp of fashion—the caboose of the motion of time.

"What's your problem?" she asked—her fists firm against her hips as she tapped a quick and irritated elfin boot.

"You're my problem," he replied coldly.

She grabbed his collar with one hand and slapped him with the other. He stepped back as the lunchroom roared with laughter, myself included.

"That routine meant everything to me!" she cried as she sent a fist straight into his stomach.

The firm impact doubled him over with a guttural breath. He crouched at her feet as the troupe of furious cheerleaders went about their way with frizzy curls of damaged hair bouncing with each step. She stared down at him, pausing a moment before joining her comrades.

"You okay, man?" Thik asked as Oscar gasped quickly for breaths, rising slowly to his knees.

"Whoa!" he winced, his eyes bulging. "Do you think she likes me?"

"Yeah," Stanley replied, "but don't act like you're interested, remember your advice."

"That's true," he gasped. "I mean, I like getting smacked in the teeth just as much as the next guy, but not with a stomach full of chicken. Crazy-ass bitch!"

"If I were you," Stanley added, "I would've used some of your karate skills on her."

"Fuck off, shithead."

"Now what were you saying about that sign on your back?" I asked. "What exactly *are* you going to do if someone—"

Stanley cried out with laughter. "I can't believe it, this geek just got pounded by a girl!"

"That routine meant everything," Thik added. "She'll never listen to that Toto song the same again."

"Man, she could've kicked the tar out of you if she wanted," Stanley said. "You're lucky she let you go easy this time."

"Speaking of chicks, I forgot to tell you guys something," Oscar grumbled, ignoring the comment. "I met a girl that just moved to town last night. She was at A&W. She had a gnarly mohawk, big and blond. And I know she likes me."

"Liar," Stanley said.

"No, I'm serious. She was really hot and had buxom breasticles."

"So, what's her name?" Stanley asked. "Or have you made it up yet?"

"Her name's Claire. Claire Clairmont."

"Bullshit!" Stanley said. "Now I *know* you're lying. Claire Clairmont doesn't have a mohawk, and she wouldn't be talking to you."

"Wasn't she the Homecoming Queen a few years ago?" Thik asked.

"Probably," I said, pausing to shovel peas into my mouth. "She's from my brother's graduating class. Everybody wanted her. They called her C. C. Biggs because she had such serious knockers—not to her face, of course."

"I met her last night and she's totally punk now," Oscar contended.

"You're totally full of shit," Stanley said.

"Whatever," he said. "So, what's the big plan for Halloween? Maybe we should get together and destroy some shit."

"That sounds cool," Thik mumbled.

"Maybe we should chill out," Stanley suggested. "Let's meet at the steps of the JuCo tomorrow. Like at nine o'clock."

"Will we go trick-or-treating from there?" Oscar asked sarcastically.

"Yeah, you and your new girlfriend," Stanley added. "You should ask her to go with us."

"Okay, I'll do that," he challenged.

Feeling seasonally festive, I brought a candle into my room and sat quietly on the bed, ignoring the constant ringing of the doorbell by costumed children. The candle flickered under the steady breeze flowing from the house's central heating system. Shadows danced harshly across the walls, cast from objects in the path of the candle's light.

Thumbing through my collection of records, I pulled out the Misfits record *Die, Die, My Darling*. The ghoulish pictures of the band blended well with the season. Their bangs were gelled into a long spike straight down their spooky faces like a tremendous horn. Skulls graced the ends of their guitars and microphone stands, as if the creatures from a campy 1950's horror film came to life and formed a punk rock band.

The telephone rang. I blew out the candle, stopping to inhale the scent of the glowing orange wick before answering the phone.

"Hello."

"So, what do you think?" Stanley asked me. "Do you really think Claire Clairmont—"

"Hard to say with Oscar."

"I'd be surprised—she was pretty popular. She's probably a real bitch. Anyway, who cares...I have some news to tell you."

"Oh, yeah?"

"Yeah, you know that girl Jean Martin? Well, we went to the movie last night. When I took her home, her parents were out to dinner with some friends. So, we went to her bedroom for a while—oh, let me tell you about her room. There's Christ stuff all over the place, Bibles and crucifixes and weird pictures. She's like totally religious, right? Well, we crawled into her bed because we were cold, if you know what I mean. Anyway, things started moving really fast, and we ended up totally in the raw, getting as hot as an armadillo's ass and she told me to give it to her like a bad cold."

"No way!"

"I wouldn't shit you," he assured me. "There we were in her bed wearing nothing but wet socks. I asked if I should get a condom, and she told me to just do it. I'm thinking, all I need is to get her pregnant."

"You had sex?" I asked.

"I did. There's something about Catholic girls, let me tell you. They'll get it on as long as it's not *pre-calculated* sex. If they're caught up in the heat of passion and it happens, they can either deny it, or go to Confessions the next Sunday. Then they're okay since Satan influenced their better judgment. But if they strategize the act, then that's a sin."

"So, you got laid?" I asked.

"I did."

"Congratulations!"

"Thanks. I stopped before the climax, so hopefully there'll be no cigars given out in nine months."

"Was it her first time?" I asked.

"I think so. That, or I'm packed like a Russian race horse."

"Wow," I mumbled. "You've earned your wings..."

"Are you coming to get me or what? It's almost nine."

"Sure, man."

The doorbell rang once again as I hung up the phone. I rushed to the door to see a mob of dwarfed ghouls holding bags over their masked heads.

"Trick or treat!" they screamed at me as I opened the screen door.

"What do you want now?!" I demanded.

"Candy, Mister Rock and Roll!" one said excitedly, clearly under the influence of one too many Snickers bars.

I dipped into the enormous vat of mixed candy. "Here, you trouble-makers, now get the *fuck* out of here..."

Before another troupe solicited the house, I grabbed my coat and rushed out the door to my Ranchero. The windows were marked with fresh soap and wax with various words of slander to sexual orientation and taste. I wiped the egg off the door handle and jumped in the car, quickly bringing to life the gray beast.

The streets were fairly vacant except for those my own age who took to vandalizing the town with soap, wax, eggs, and toilet paper. They hid their numbers in bushes with white T-shirts and flashlights glowing behind sparse shrubbery.

Stanley stood inconspicuously in the shadows of his front porch as I pulled into the driveway. When he saw my car, he rushed to the street, his breath following his path in a dispersing mist. A black sweatshirt hugged tightly to his powerful torso. Old

70

work boots clomped on the frozen ground with each step, echoing through the quiet neighborhood. He looked like a damned redneck, as usual.

"Cold as fuck out there," he said as he climbed inside the Ranchero. "You can actually smell the winter now."

"Maybe you should've waited inside."

"I was hoping to catch some little bastards messing with my house."

"Congratulations, man," I said with a straight face, extending my hand to shake his. "You've been made a man. Do you regret it?"

"No. I feel okay with it."

"Do you expect more to come of it?"

"I don't know if it was that type of thing. It seemed like the thing to do, to get over."

I stared at the envelope of light leading the Ranchero. Objects jumped from invisibility to substance as if oblivion was all within the scope of our vision, and just beyond the cast of headlights lie the unwritten word. It seemed quite plausible that the specimen was I, locked within time and space waiting to act out the final page of this book.

We pulled down a stretch of road to the Junior College—a pseudo-modern structure of poor taste and affordable architecture. The parking lot was vacant, except one Malibu whose hood served as a bench for a couple wrapped in blankets like soylent green burritos. We pulled up next to the car where Oscar struggled on the ground in front of the Malibu, desperately trying to do push-ups for the small audience. The mummified onlookers twisted sideways to reveal two faces—the closer, more prominent baring beautiful, cat-like eyes that watched the two of us with cat-like curiosity. Her face was as fair as a China plate. She smiled politely upon recognition—revealing her perfectly straight, white teeth. My ego sought the imperfections in her entire physical presentation to strengthen my comfort. She was a fine work.

"Oh, God," Stanley sighed with disgust. "That's Claire, isn't it? She looks like a bitch."

I could tell the word he intended was *beautiful*.

She smiled politely at us. The gesture was genuine. I felt the warmth under my collar as I killed the engine.

We opened the doors simultaneously to the grunts of Oscar as he struggled desperately to challenge gravity.

"Th-th-thirt-thirteen!" Thik said. "Come on, you said you could do two hundred in two minutes."

"Hello," Claire said to us quickly. "Please, have a seat."

"No, thanks," Stanley returned. "We'll stand."

"What are you doing, asshole?" I asked Oscar whose arms trembled as he lowered himself to the ground again.

"What are we going to do?" Stanley complained. "It's cold as hell out here."

"We could go to Humboldt Hill and tell ghost stories," Claire suggested quickly, her words so fast they nearly slurred into one.

"Ghost stories?" Stanley asked with more than a hint of sarcasm. "Anything else?"

"We could spray-paint the stadium," Thik suggested.

"We could steal more pumpkins," Oscar offered, sitting up on the concrete with heavy breaths that seemed to freeze in the wind.

"I don't care," Claire said swiftly, sincerely. "By the way, I'm Claire Clairmont."

71

"We know," Stanley said.

"I'm Frank and this is Stanley."

"Yeah, I guess I knew that, too. Just trying to be friendly."

I nodded with a slight smile of generosity, proving my resistance to her historically impressive reputation.

"What's Humboldt Hill?" Oscar asked.

"It's this hill south of town where freaky things happens," she replied. "Supposedly, your car accelerates really fast when you go down it."

"Cars tend to accelerate down hills," Stanley mumbled. "Gravity. Funny thing."

"I think it'd be fun," she said.

"Let's do it," Oscar said. "Who's driving?"

"We haven't even agreed that we *are* going to do this," Stanley protested.

Oscar rushed to his car. "Come on."

"Let's go," I instructed Stanley. "We'll go separately."

The three of them piled into the Malibu as we slowly retreated back to the Ranchero. Oscar laid rubber with a powerful screech of the tires as they sped into the darkness.

"She's a bitch," Stanley said.

"Yeah," I confirmed. "She is a honey, don't you think?"

"I don't know. I guess so—for a bitch."

Keeping up with the Malibu was no easy task, especially through yards and sidewalks.

"What a way to spend Halloween," Stanley grumbled as I desperately tried to pursue Oscar across a ditch. "Out in the cold with Oscar and Claire Clairmont on some ridiculous hill."

"I could think of worse things."

The burning taillights of Oscar's car diminished into the horizon speckled by the lights of distant farmhouses. Iola slowly disintegrated in the rearview mirror with only a faint, pink glow as proof of its existence.

"I wonder what the deal is with Claire," I said. "Why she's all punk now, and—"

"Who cares?" he snapped awkwardly.

The lights on the horizon disappeared as if the night had consumed the little houses, leaving its remnants lost in a void of darkness. The tiny red taillights of Oscar's car rose toward the sky, then vanished. As we followed, the furthest reach of my high beams caught the sudden roll of earth as the road extended upward. A wall of hand-placed rocks lined each side of the narrow road. The Ranchero struggled to climb as the flattened skyline of Iola appeared once again in the rearview. On top, the lights of Humboldt hugged the horizon in the distance. I parked on the opposite side next to Oscar's Malibu as he and Thik jumped on the hood of my Ranchero, mashing their blank faces against my windshield like corpses.

Out in the clear countryside, the wind cut through us like a wall of knives, frozen at the tips.

"This is fucking stupid," Stanley protested again as everyone raced up the hill like a tribe of baboons.

"Are we going to build a fire?" Oscar pleaded.

"I'd probably throw your ass in it," Stanley grumbled from the rear of the caravan. "That wouldn't be good."

"Yeah, let's build a little fire," Claire said with a quick slur of words.

In a matter of minutes, we had gathered a sizable pile of wood. Claire flicked her lighter several times, leaving the diffuse flame etched in our widened pupils like little green balls hovering in space. The final click gave birth to a tiny flame, revealing the dead-earth surroundings of our once invisible environment. The flame connected with the little pile of branches and sticks with only steam rising where fire was intended.

"It's too wet," Stanley scolded as he snatched the lighter from her hands. "Give me that." He flicked it once, bringing it to life again. "We need something dry to start it."

"My bra?" she joked.

"That'd be enough to keep it lit all night," he replied under his breath.

"My underwear?" Oscar asked.

"Please, no," Stanley denied smugly. "Light up those skid marks..."

"How about these?" Thik asked, holding out a handful of crumpled tissue. "I have a cold, but I can use my sleeve. I do, anyway."

With Thik's contribution, the fire easily conquered the small stack of branches.

"What's up with this hill?" Oscar asked nervously.

"It's haunted," Claire answered quickly, assuredly. "Well, they say it's got some really strange magnetic thing."

"The deal with this hill is that the people of Allen county have no idea what to make of a change in the scenery," Stanley explained. "If their car accelerates while going down a rare incline, they assume it has to be haunted because they're too ignorant to understand elementary physics."

"I've heard they've found pails of blood up here with the heads of dolls floating," she said. "This is where all the devil-worshippers do their service."

"Okay," Stanley challenged. "Today is the day our culture celebrates the inexplicable and evil—wouldn't they be up here now? I don't see any black robes, and where are the pails of blood?"

"I don't know," she replied. "It's fun to think, makes the world seem less dull."

"Of course, we're part of the folklore now," he said. "Those stories have gone around for years. A new dimension gets added each generation, and of course, we're probably that new dimension. Cars will pass by ours parked at the bottom of the hill and they'll have their proof."

"That sounds pretty exciting," she said. "Does that mean people are going to call me a devil-worshipper? Cool!"

"Wouldn't that betray your high-profiling reputation?" he questioned.

"What reputation?" she asked.

"Okay," I said, hoping to change the subject. "Have you ever heard the stories of the killings in Iola a couple years ago, Oscar?"

Oscar shook his head with a smile. "You're pulling my chain."

"No," Claire said bluntly. "I remember. I could tell you where I was the day I heard about it."

"Me, too," I recollected.

"You guys are full of shit," Oscar repeated.

"No, seriously," Stanley began. "The guy's name was Yorkie Smith—some social outcast who had taken too much shit. He killed several people in and around Iola, stabbing them multiple times. The first victim was discovered in a field with so many stab wounds, they could barely identify the decomposed body. Then they fished two bodies out of the creek behind the dike in the park."

"I was there the morning they were fishing them out," I revealed. "I was standing in line to go swimming, as I did every day that summer. There were police cars and ambulances and reporters everywhere. Of course, news travels fast in this town, so everyone knew what was up. I'll never forget that."

"One of the guys in the creek survived and had to testify," Claire said.

"Rumor has it that Yorkie wasn't the only person involved," I said gravely.

"You're just trying to scare me," Oscar said.

"No, actually I'm not. Who's to say what's true and what isn't when it comes to rumors in this town? I've heard it's those old bikers that live in Piqua. I've heard they helped. Again, in this town you never know."

"People are always down on bikers," Stanley said. "There's probably nothing wrong with those people."

"How do you know?" Thik asked.

"This girl I used to know in Lawrence had a brother whose friend used to wake up with this horrible pain in his ass," Claire said. "The problem persisted, so he went to a doctor. The doctor told him to have less anal sex. The guy said he had never had anal sex, but the doctor told him that that seemed to be the trouble. He went back to his dorm room and looked through his roommate's stuff and found a bottle of ether. Turns out the roommate was using the ether to knock the guy out, then having sex with him while he was unconscious!"

"I'm glad I'm not going to college," Thik said. "You know, back when my parents were in high school, my dad swears this happened to a friend. This guy dated this girl from Burlington. One weekend he was going to propose to her, but chickened out. On his way home, he saw her hitchhiking by the side of the road, which was impossible because she couldn't have made it that far ahead. Anyway, she got in the car and told him she loved him and asked for the ring from his pocket. He's all confused, of course, not just because she's there, but also because she somehow knew what he intended to do. So, he reached down into his pocket, and when he looked up to give it to her, she was gone! When he got home, there was a message that she had died just after he left—at about the time he picked her up."

"How'd she die?" Stanley asked.

"Uh, I forgot. I'll ask my dad."

"I had this friend who was talking to his girlfriend on the phone once during a storm," Stanley said. "All the sudden, the phone got really static and phased out momentarily. They continued talking for like an hour, except she was talking weird shit. Like specific dates for upcoming wars, who'd be the next President, the specific time and day she'd die—things like that. The next day at school, she asked why he never called back when the phone got disconnected. She said she tried to call for an hour, but the line was busy. She swore that when the phone got all static, it hung up and she didn't talk to him all night. So who or *what* was he talking to?"

"Who'd this happen to?" Thik asked.

"No one, I made it up!" Stanley announced proudly. "These are all urban legends, you idiots! None of these stories are true."

"No," Thik corrected, "my dad swears it's true."

"I have a story that is true, because a friend of mine was there as it happened," Claire said. "I have this friend who works at a place in Lawrence called Headquarters, which is a free counseling center. These people came in with their child who went from being ideal to throwing vicious tantrums and mutilating little animals. It turned out that he would mutilate the animals in a similar pattern. They took him to Headquarters and found he had an imaginary friend. He claimed that the imaginary friend had died in a similar way as his mutilations. When he gave the imaginary friend's name, one of the staff at Headquarters did some research at the library and found that an actual child with the same name had been murdered years before. The child was mutilated as the imaginary friend claimed and the body was placed under the Kaw River Bridge in Lawrence. What's more, the dead child's old house is the house where the troubled child now lives. And the dead child's bedroom is the same room that the troubled child sleeps."

"That's bullshit," Stanley said. "You're just gullible."

"I am, I admit it, but that doesn't change the fact that the story is *true*."

"Why'd you move back here, Claire?" I asked, another blatant attempt to change the subject.

"Money problems," she replied quickly. "I had to get away from the crash-and-burn lifestyle in Lawrence. I can't wait to move back. As soon as I get financially set again. Shouldn't take too long."

"Why the punk music?" Oscar asked.

"You seemed fairly normal in high school," Thik added.

"Normal is what you call people before you get to know them," she replied. "My cousin is the bassist in a band from Topeka called Troubled Youth. He introduced me to people in the Lawrence punk scene."

"We're going to see the Descendents in a couple weeks," Oscar told her. "Want to join us?"

I could sense the dread in Stanley, though not a word escaped.

"Sure, that'd be great! Thanks," she said.

We sat quietly, staring into the fire, watching the flame slowly dissolve into the glowing red coals of burning sticks.

"It's getting cold again," she said. "Does anyone have any more stories?"

"Do they have to be true stories?" Stanley asked sarcastically.

"No, not necessarily," she answered nicely, patiently.

"Do they really say there's another homicidal maniac out here?" Oscar asked.

"Yeah, *right behind you*!!" Stanley screamed, pointing frantically.

Oscar lunged forward to the ground with dust rising around the impact. A second later, he sat up and brushed himself clean. "Don't do that, man..."

"It's Halloween, you're supposed to be scared."

"Let's get out of here. This place gives me the heebie-jeebies," Oscar said. "Maybe we should all piss on the fire."

"It must be that crazy magnetic thing," Stanley said. "These damn hills in southeast Kansas. All three of them, they're all haunted."

"There's this place just outside Lawrence," Claire told us over the dimming light of the fire. "It's actually in the Bible as a gateway to hell. It's between Lawrence and Topeka, called Stull. There's this old church on the hill of this graveyard. It looks really spooky. There's this massive tree next to the church where they used to hang people. They say on Halloween, the Devilman himself is there dancing with people, or something crazy like that. Everyone goes up there on Halloween, so the cops stake it out."

"So, if you go into this gateway, do you end up in Iola?" I asked. "That'd be nice. Save the drive up there."

Oscar quickly unzipped his pants and stood over the fire. "I'm putting this fucker out. Your stories worked up enough piss in me to put out a dozen of these."

Thik joined him as Claire slowly headed to the road with Stanley and me.

"Can we not go back to Iola just yet?" she requested.

"And go where?" Stanley argued.

"To Chanute maybe? I don't know. Anywhere but Iola."

"What will we do in Chanute?" Stanley asked.

"Get some beer maybe? I don't know."

"Sure," I agreed as Thik and Oscar came rushing up from behind.

"We're going to Chanute now," Stanley sighed with exaggerated irritation. "Claire said so."

"We don't have to," she corrected. "Whatever you guys want to do. I'm here for the ride."

"We'll go to Chanute, what else is there to do?" Oscar asked.

"I could think of plenty things," Stanley grumbled as we crept through the stiff grass to the bottom of the hill.

"My damn shoes are going to be ruined in this mud," she griped. "Whose idea was this?"

Stanley let loose a disturbed sigh. "I wonder."

"You know," she began, "you can tell a lot by a person's shoes. If you don't like a person's shoes, you're very likely not going to like them. Style begins at one's feet. Your immediate impression of someone's personality should be derived from their choice in shoes."

"You talk a lot," Stanley said as we reached the cars.

"Yeah, I do. Is there any room in this clunker for me?" she asked, running her gloved hands down the side of the Ranchero.

Stanley glanced at me. I understood his subtle communication and responded accordingly.

"Sure there's room," I confirmed. "You can sit in the middle. Sitting *bitch* as we call it here in *these parts*."

I returned Stanley's scowl with a pleasant smile. I was building his character—he should've been more thankful. Oscar's Malibu tossed chunks of loose gravel as the tires scraped and scratched its way down the desolate road. I quickly caught pursuit of him with Humboldt Hill and Iola gaining distance in the rearview.

"You know," she began, "if these people in this area weren't so ignorant, all the kids in Chanute and Iola would go to Humboldt on weekends. That'd open their options socially. Instead, everyone stays in their own town, mixing with the same dull people, chasing potentially new faces away who venture in from other towns. I never understood why you get chased out of a town for having tags of a different county. It makes me wonder what happens when someone's grandma goes to the other county. Do they also get chased out of town by a truck filled with boogans?"

We both stared forward without a response, gazing at the anti-scenic town of Humboldt.

"I can't wait to move back to Lawrence," she continued. "Look at this town. These people think Iola and Chanute are strong metropolitan areas. It's pathetic."

As quickly as we entered the town, we were exiting it. An enormous rock quarry had to be crossed at the southern edge like a gutted carcass. On the west horizon was a line of monumental houses leaning on the edge of the cavity like an empire in the Old South. Crossing the gorge of gauged rock, we were on our way to Chanute, just a small distance down the road.

76

"Whenever you look at the moon, do you wonder how many other people are looking at it at the same time?" she asked. "Isn't it strange how we only see one side of it? It just kind of rolls around like a ball on a string connected to the center of this planet. Can you imagine how wild it'd be if our planet spun around the sun like that, like a rolling ball? One side of the planet would always be day, the other side always night, and the equator would be like dawn or dusk. The dark side creatures would have big eyes. They'd be really fat because it'd be cold. The creatures on the light side would be skinny and really tanned. And they'd meet at the equator and have massive wars because they'd both want to rule the other side."

"Hmm," I mumbled thoughtfully.

"Isn't that some crazy shit?" she asked. "Sometimes I stay up all night thinking about crap like that."

"In *Star Wars*," I said as the lights of Chanute came into view on the horizon, "something never addressed is that the difference of gravity would play a major role in the outcome of battles. The subtle changes would affect coordination, the oxygen in the air, your energy—it'd be like moving through molasses, or you'd be like Superman. If Endor was a small moon, then those humans should have been near weightless, giving the Ewoks the advantage of locality."

"Yeah," she said, half-interested.

"There's nothing in Chanute we couldn't be doing in Iola," Stanley groaned.

"If you could be any superhero, who would you be?" Claire asked. "Batman?"

"Batman sucks," Stanley snapped. "He's just a rich guy with a lot of gadgets and psychological problems. He's not a *super* hero."

"Spiderman," I said.

"Aquaman is under-rated," Stanley said. "I'd be him."

"How about Space Ghost?" she asked.

"He's not in the legitimate comic books," Stanley corrected. "He doesn't count."

We pulled up behind Oscar at a light where the only reasonable scenery was the closing of the Dairy Queen. We crossed a large overpass with old warehouses and rusty train tracks underneath. It was a very cold atmosphere that apparently seeped into the veins of the locals. We approached Main Street—a continuous strip packed with pick-ups and tiny economical cars.

"Isn't it strange how atoms look like little planets revolving around suns?" she asked. "Don't you wonder if the universe is actually a living organism, with galaxies as molecules, and we're just tiny, tiny forms of life on an electron, moving at a relative speed around a proton—am I getting these terms right? And the atom is part of many atoms that make up our galaxy—"

"Charles Fort came up with that concept long ago," Stanley said. "Frank, do you have any tapes?"

"That'd explain a lot," she continued. "Because that means that in any given atom of our body, there could be entire worlds. And since atomic particles move so fast, a century to us could be the fraction of a multi-milisecond to the organism. So even if the creature only lived to be ten years old, it'd be billions of years to the inner worlds. Infinity would have a new definition—the picture within the picture. That'd also explain the Big Bang Theory and what was there beforehand—a single cell waiting to explode into a life. And if this universe is still expanding, then the creature could still be in the womb, waiting to be brought into its world. If God is everything, the organism in which we live would be our God. What if we live in a slug?"

"Our Lord, the Slug," I said as we turned into the traffic onto Main Street.

A flatbed truck pulled up behind us. A rebel flag covered the grill.

"I bet people in Chanute wear horrible shoes," she said as lines of cars passed, each filled with adolescents too drunk to know their names.

"Okay, now what?" Stanley asked.

"I suppose we cruise like everyone else," she said.

"We could do this in Iola," Stanley complained.

Cars passed slowly, recognizing the Ranchero and its occupants as we crawled down the strip. Taillights ignited in my rearview mirror. Fingers pointed as we passed while hands gestured out the windows to other cars.

"Maybe this wasn't a good idea," I said. "Claire, we kind of have a reputation."

Car doors rushed open as young men with horribly tasteless shoes stumbled out with bent and angry faces.

"Should we leave?" Claire asked as I followed close behind Oscar.

"Maybe," Stanley answered swiftly.

Oscar took a quick turn into the parking lot of a convenient store. He motioned us to follow. I could see a trail of cars in the distance as we pulled into the lot next to him.

"I'm going to get some Cracker Jack," he told me casually through the window of his car.

"We should consider leaving town," I warned him.

"Why?"

"We're not appreciated here," I said. "There's a line of cars coming our way. I hate to be paranoid..."

"We should leave," Stanley agreed. "There's more of them and it's their turf."

"Screw them," he said. "I'm going to get some Cracker Jack."

"Well, we're leaving. You can stay, tough-guy," Stanley said.

Oscar sighed casually. "I'll be back in a second, then we can go."

He strolled inside the well-lit convenient store. The cashier watched him cautiously as his red mohawk moved through the aisles like the fin of a shark.

"Why is he such a pain in the ass?" Stanley groaned.

Bright headlights flooded the parking lot with the sound of roaring engines and screeching tires. A parade of pick-up trucks swarmed us like flies on death. Their headlights burned my eyes through the rearview. In a matter of seconds, a crowd of drunks armed with pocket knives and baseball bats surrounded us.

"Get out of the car, faggot!" one screamed at me as he clumsily reached in his pocket for his switchblade.

"No, man," his friend slurred. "They're not armed."

"I want to carve this faggot up!"

"No, man. Do it fair."

He reluctantly obliged, leaving his pocket to focus his blind hatred on me. I had the foresight to lock the door before he could reach the handle. He grabbed my coat through the window and pulled me hard against the frame, banging my forehead hard on the metal. He tore my shirt with vicious passion as I desperately reached under the seat for my rusted iron pipe for such an occasion. Before I could grab it, he placed a firm blow to my lips. My mouth quickly flooded with the salty taste of blood. I pressed my tongue into my lip, feeling it slip under the skin where the blood was draining. Anger and fear struggled to control me. My hands trembled as I made a hasty attempt to raise the window. I jerked the lever slowly, clumsily as he shoved an elbow into my eye. My neck whipped backward, hard against the seat. I concentrated on the window, forcing it up.

78

Suddenly, the Malibu came to life. Thik pulled out of the parking lot and down the dark street, alone.

Two guys clawed at my locked door, beating aggressively on the window. "Open the door, faggot!!"

Several of them jumped inside the bed, bouncing like wild beasts as they prepared to smash the back window with their bats.

"Get away from that car, you white-trash motherfuckers!" Oscar's voice rang out clearly over the mayhem. He stood alone in the doorway of the convenient store with only a box of Cracker Jack and a determined stance.

"Well, look who's here," one said as the crowd slowly absorbed itself in his direction.

The boldest and angriest of them whose fingerprints were on the interior of my thick and bloody lip lunged toward him with fists hurling wildly. Oscar grabbed his neck, holding him off with one hand as he deflected the flailing fists with the other. The goon towered over him, easily capable of crushing him by the mere difference of weight. Oscar held him off patiently, his eyes calm and calculated. One punch reached his nose, and the blood drained quickly.

"You fucking hit me," Oscar informed him.

Suddenly, Oscar's whole body swiveled with his free arm stretched and rushing through the air in a quick circle that slammed against the guy's jaw. His head whipped aside quickly before he teetered to the ground in a huddled mass. Oscar rushed to a defensive pose like something out of a Chinese action film. As one of the guys reached down to his pocket for his switchblade, Oscar moved in, kicking his feet in some strange way that sent the guy straight to the firm concrete. He plowed through the crowd and dove onto the hood of my car as we stared in awe.

"*Go!*" he screamed through the glass. He climbed the hood to the windshield with blood coloring his teeth a gruesome red. It dripped a path from the hood up the windshield.

I slammed the car into reverse and stomped on the gas pedal, leaving a trail of rubber on the ground in a triumphant screech. Oscar climbed up over the roof into the bed as the Ranchero bounced into the street. He slid into the tailgate with a dull thud as we smashed against the opposite curb. With a firm grip, I pulled the gear down into Drive and sped away. I could see the headlights of cars swarm out of the parking lot as we rushed down the street away from the downtown trap that awaited. My rearview came alive once again with the flashing images of high beams seeking us like rabid animals.

Sirens howled in the distance somewhere, and I knew it was a matter of time before they would catch us, one way or another. A red traffic light glowed in the near distance at the upcoming intersection. My foot hesitated at the brake as traffic crossed slowly through it.

"You've got to go," Stanley said gravely.

I pressed the pedal tightly to the floorboard as we rushed toward the active intersection with impressive acceleration.

A car screeched around the corner in front of us at a high speed. It was Oscar's Malibu. As it passed, it swerved into our lane on a collision course with a row of pick-ups eating our exhaust. His course drowned out the high beams that stalked us. It offered us just enough time to come to a screeching halt as the cars passed quietly through the intersection. The traffic was thick. We wouldn't have made it.

The red glow of amber taillights never signaled the warning of deceleration, proving Thik's determination and insanity all together. The headlights swerved from his path, most of which ended up in yards and through hedges—none colliding with the Malibu as it sailed down the street behind us. As the last car peeled off the road, the Malibu shot down a back street.

"He'll meet us at the JuCo!" Oscar screamed, leaning out the back to the window. "Get the hell out of here!"

"Wow," Claire murmured to herself. "You're not kidding about that reputation…"

The Ranchero raced through the silent and dark countryside with only the light of the moon overhead. Oscar sat calmly in the bed of the Ranchero, wiping his nose and eating the Cracker Jack that he somehow hadn't lost. Tension and relief filled the cab where words awkwardly failed to fit.

As we pulled into the parking lot of the JuCo, Thik sat comfortably on the hood of the Malibu, smiling. In a very odd way, we felt strangely victorious. I swallowed hard the draining blood, feeling my lip bulge a dark shade of purple as I smiled proudly.

I watched with lazy eyes as the small red hand worked its way to the top of the clock. Based on previous studies, my experiment would finalize in thirteen seconds. The thin, red needle passed the third mark between the ten and the eleven. As hypothesized, the bell rang. School was out.

"Did you learn something?" Oscar asked between yawns as he picked up his books.

"Actually, I did. The class ends one minute and twelve seconds before the clock indicates."

"You didn't know *that*?"

His mohawk was firm and erect and luminously red from a fresh dye the previous night. He walked down the hall in front of me, slowly as if half asleep.

"Hurry up, man," I said, passing around him excitedly. "We've got big plans tonight! The proud, the few, the Descendents!"

"I know. I'm just tapped. There's only so much remedial math that one can take. By the way, speaking of math, have you read Stanley's paper?"

"Yes, I read it."

"Where'd he learn those words? Man, I better step up my own vocabulary around him."

"I think he understands you just fine," I assured him.

"Exactly! That's what I *don't* want."

"What's up, sisters?" Stanley asked, perched over the water fountain. He paused briefly to adjust the straps on his overalls. "Your hair looks cool, Frankie. Orange is your color."

"You can thank Oscar's mother," I told him. "She's the artist behind our image."

"She was a hairdresser once," Oscar mumbled as if mere words were laborous.

"What's up with you?" Stanley asked him. "You look dead tired. Are you sick or something?"

"Sick? No. Just feeling…I don't know. Kind of…discombobulated. That's it."

"Discombobulated?" Stanley asked.

"Yeah, discombobulated," Oscar confirmed.

"Sounds pretty serious," Stanley said.

"Do you know what I mean?"

80

"Yes, of course! It happens to the best of us, discombobulation. The discombobulatory state is certainly no laughing matter, pal."

We shoved our books into our lockers, not to be touched for another two days.

"Hey, guys, what's up?" Whitaker greeted us, his hands overflowing with textbooks.

"Going to see the Descendents," Oscar said. "Too bad *you* aren't going."

"Man, I'd love to see them. Maybe next time."

"Maybe," I said.

"Hey, have we sold any more tapes through the mail?" he asked me.

"Yeah, some," I responded. "Not many."

"He's started a record company," Stanley said. "He just did a compilation tape with loads of killer bands."

"Cool!" Whitaker praised. "Can I get one?"

"Of course," I said.

"Hey, have you guys seen Claire Clairmont?" he asked before we got away. "Man, she's hot."

"She's a bitch," Stanley conceded.

"I think she's cool," Oscar said.

"I don't mean to be rude, Whitaker, but we're supposed to meet Thik in the parking lot," Stanley said. "I'd hate for him to freeze his nuts off out there."

"I understand," Whitaker said. "It may snow this weekend, did you hear it on the news? Yeah, it'll probably be really cold out there at the Outhouse." He watched as we happily strolled down the hall together, giggling as we passed through the front doors.

"He's a weenie," Oscar growled as the freezing wind slammed hard against us. "It's an icebox out here! I can feel my nose hairs freezing every time I take a breath. They're cracking when I flex my nose."

"Stop flexing your nose," Stanley said with snide sarcasm.

"Hey faggots!" screeched a female's voice from over our shoulder.

Each one of us stopped dead in his tracks. I could feel my heart come alive as my tongue caressed the hole in my lip that could house a sailor's ransom. We turned to see Claire standing alone with a sheepish grin of chattering teeth. Her hair was teased in a frightful, yet orderly mess—the sides of her head merely dark stubble over cold, tender skin. Rows of small gold hoops hung from her frozen red ears. Her goofy giggle was met with a unanimous sigh of relief.

"What's up?" Oscar asked her.

"I'm supposed to meet you guys here, aren't I?"

"Are you?" Stanley asked.

"I am. I like your flashy new hairdos, by the way."

"My mother does our hair," Oscar said. "She used to be a hairdresser."

"Cool, maybe she could make mine look decent for a change." Her motivated pace surpassed our lethargic gait. "It's damn cold out here, boys. Let's pick up the pace..."

"I think Thik is waiting for us in the parking lot," I said.

"He's likely freezing his balls off," she said. "It happened to me. I can't believe I'm here at this lame high school. I vowed to never step foot on this property once I left."

"There's Thik." Stanley said. "He doesn't appear to be searching for his rocks."

"Are your gonads okay?" Claire screamed across the parking lot.

"What?!" Thik screeched.

"Is your package complete?" Claire clarified.

He looked down to check the buttons on his jeans. "Yes."

"Is Pehgan coming?" I asked quietly.

"No, she's doing something with Kimberly Powers," Stanley answered.

"Bad news," Thik confessed. "My dad isn't going to let me use the station wagon after all. He's on a binge and I really don't want to bother with him. Sorry, guys."

"I can drive," Claire said. "No one asked."

"What do you have?" Stanley asked. "A Gremlin?"

"Volaré," she told him.

"Who cares? It's a ride. Let's do it," Oscar said.

We turned to walk the other way, following Claire's lead. Chunks of salt crunched under our thick-soled shoes, placed an hour earlier by the surly janitor. I looked over my shoulder at the school, happy to see it shrink in the distance. The grounds were a blinding color of white as if the earth had been bleached and drained of all color. In the second-story window of the Drama room, I could make out the indistinguishable outline of Whitaker's head alone, watching.

"I'm glad my parents are supportive and understanding," I said to the others.

"Why do you say?" Stanley asked.

I glanced up at Whitaker's silhouette. "Just kind of hit me."

"I'm glad my parents are always too drunk to give a shit," Thik laughed.

"I'm glad mine just don't give a shit," Oscar added proudly.

"Your dad freaks me out," Thik admitted to Oscar. "He's pretty intense."

"He's a Vietnam vet," Oscar told us. "He's a bit...intense. We don't really get along."

"Nice car," Thik joked, pointing at the faded brown Volaré parked by the curb.

"Yeah, it's a piece-of-shit, isn't it?" she said as we slipped across the stiff vinyl seats. "But it's getting your ass to see the Descendents, so you can shut the hell up right now."

She turned the key a couple times, pumping the gas while Stanley suggested better ways. Finally, it came to life with a monstrous roar. As we pulled into the street, I noticed the gray sky had already darkened several shades toward nightfall.

"Your paper is totally rad, man," Oscar finally admitted to Stanley. "I'll never think of chaos and monkeys the same again."

"I sent it in today," Stanley announced. "We'll see what happens."

"What's it about?" Claire asked.

"Monkeys," Oscar said.

"Where do you think we came from, Claire?" Stanley asked. "Adam and Eve?"

"No. I believe in evolution."

"So, once upon a time there were some fish that had the balls to venture up on land, huh?" Stanley asked. "Probably impressed the female fish, huh?"

She laughed. "A fish strutting around with big balls would impress me."

"Let's say there's this fish who wants to get laid," Stanley began. "How is he going to get the female's attention? What would be impressive? Well, there's always that unknown source of light above. Could be that the fish wasn't trying to get laid. Maybe he was simply curious. Whatever the motivation, it set a standard that was a step in the direction of the evolution of his species. Life and spirit evolve in accordance with chaos. It is my opinion that the only order of biological growth is through disorder. Isn't it odd at the end of the Permian period, as well as the demise of dinosaurs, the evolutionary cycle switched hands? Not all reptilians perished, of course, so what caused the mammals to prevail? Would it be the same reason that the insect would prevail once we fall? We were likely a bunch of rodents to the lizards that survived. Our pesticides strengthen their species by the day. Catastrophic events spawn a birth of evolutionary advancement. By definition, it'd fit under non-linear determinism. Achievement is borne out of chaos."

"Do you feel roaches will someday take our place?" Claire asked.

"Possibly," he told her. "Consider how much our species lacks. We break our nails on plastic typewriter keys. Other animals use theirs to kill. We waste our ability to reason while allowing the television to give us our thoughts. I would say that humans are in a state of regression, at least at this point. We strive to achieve comfort, which is the ultimate goal. Comfort to the point of stagnation and complacency. We spend our lives planning ways to achieve this stagnation. Why have a plan? A plan will have you."

"Where'd you think up all this chaos stuff?" she asked.

"I didn't. Some guy named Kuhn did. And another guy—"

"The animals bit?" she asked.

"That's my slant."

"Wow," Claire praised. "I'm truly impressed."

He paused a moment with a straight face that merged into a stifled smile. "Thanks."

"Do you believe time travel is possible?" she asked him.

"I don't know. I'd say no, but I kind of feel that if we can imagine it, then it must be possible somehow. Time is, of course, a localized concept. It's not as absolute as we think."

"If humans could go back in time, we'd know the answers to *everything*," she said. "There's very little that we would be unable to obtain from the past."

The two of them conversed the entire trip. Eventually, I fell completely from the conversation as I stared anxiously out the window into the darkening world. The vast stretch of drifting snow shimmered under the faint light of the sky. I found myself entranced by the dull view. My eyes began to burn from fatigue. It had been a long day.

As we pulled into Lawrence, my senses came alive once again.

We turned onto 23rd Street where the choices of fast food dining seemed endless. Everyone gave suggestions, yet Claire remained quiet as she steered through traffic. She took the first left before Ousdahl into the parking lot of Yellow Sub. Apparently she had already decided for us.

We walked inside the restaurant where the bright lights forced my bruised eye shut. A young hippie chick stood impatiently behind the counter to take our order. Her bright tie-dye was an irritating eyesore.

"I'll take a four-cheese sandwich," I told her sharply.

She slipped a five of clubs card in my hand and reverted her attention to Thik. I stepped out of their way and found a seat in the corner. Soon the others joined me.

"The Descendents are one of my favorite bands," I told them as we waited for our food. "They've really inspired me in many ways…"

The bathroom door opened and two guys stumbled out, both with poorly fitted sweatpants and tight T-shirts. A patch or pocket protector would've finalized their haphazard, geeky image. They stood at the counter, scratching their shaggy heads and asses.

"Revenge of the nerds," Thik whispered.

"You can see the crack of his ass, check it out," Oscar said, pointing. "Dorks."

"Anyway, they're awesome," I continued as the taller guy with horn-rimmed glasses released a tremendous belch.

"Whew!" his friend said, patting him on the back. "That was pizza! We ate pizza yesterday!"

He laughed, his skinny frame quaking.

I shook my head, trying to maintain my train of thought through the disturbance. "Yeah, so I'm really excited to see them. Milo is my idol as a vocalist. He's actually really educated—"

"Got a fart, check it out!" the shorter one warned, no sooner than the bellowing rumble came.

"*Yes!*" his partner exclaimed proudly. "Good one!"

The two paid no attention to us as they took their food to a corner table.

"Hold on! Hold on!" the tall guy bellowed once again to the otherwise quiet lobby. "It's a good one! Heh-Heh, it's coming!"

"You're going to shit your pants, man!" the other responded.

"Here goes..." he warned, but only silence followed.

"That was lame!"

"Man! I don't know what the deal is..."

"If you were digesting that pizza, maybe. Speaking of stench, what's growing in the van?"

"It looks kind of like this food," the other responded, parting the slices of bread for a more dissected view of its contents. "Maybe it's the procreation of a burrito. Beanage."

"How obnoxious," I sneered, feeling utter annoyance with my inability to express my appreciation over the disturbance. "Let's blow this joint."

"I hope they have that bonfire going," Oscar said as we stood to exit—our food still half eaten in paper wrappers for the road.

"I hope they didn't cancel," I said, mainly to myself. "I've been looking forward to seeing the Descendents for a while."

Claire tuned in KJHK as we rushed off to the Outhouse. To my delight, the programming featured loud, irritating punk rock. I listened intently to the unfamiliar music—the vocals gruff and impressive. It wasn't until the song was over that Claire realized it to be her cousin's band, Troubled Youth.

"To all you listeners out there who aren't frozen," the DeeJay said casually, "and even those who are, we have Billy Christ of Troubled Youth in the studio with us now. Billy, is there any reason the band makes such rare appearances in Lawrence?"

"Actually, there is," Billy said roughly. "Lawrence can't deal with us, we're the real thing, and Lawrence can't handle that."

"What do you mean by *real*?"

"We don't hold back, it's real," Billy revealed. "The blood, the pain—it's all real."

"I see. So, do you have any shows coming up at the Outhouse?"

"No."

"Any records?" the DeeJay asked.

"No, we spend the money we make on beer and drugs."

"No records or shows to plug?"

"No."

"Okay...maybe we should go ahead and play more music. Again, this is Topeka's own Troubled Youth on the Sound Alternative, KJHK. The song that's sure to be a local classic...*All-American Boys*."

Claire's old car descended down 15th Street over the tracks—leaving the city behind. Specks of light from distant farmhouses sparkled clear through the winter air. We followed the entourage of amber taillights, watching them dip at the end of the pavement with a hazy distortion of dust rising from the rear. Just as the Outhouse came into view, we parked by the roadside and walked.

"Frank, hold on," Stanley said, pulling me back as the others scurried with frozen limbs to the Outhouse. "I've got some dirt for you to hear."

"What dirt?"

"Last night, you won't believe it. I don't."

"What?" I asked.

"Well, I was up late, putting last minute touches on the essay at Professor Martin's place—"

"Are you still getting crazy with his daughter?"

"No, I never see her now," he told me. "She used me, but listen...I decided I was going to walk home, which isn't far in Iola. Mrs. Martin offered to drive me home since it was so icy out..."

I laughed quickly. "Liar."

"I wouldn't lie, you know that. So, I agree, and we're waiting inside the car for it to warm up, and God, does it warm up. In many ways! She tells me how lonely a housewife can get. By the time the heater started working, we really didn't need it."

"You nailed the professor's wife?" I asked.

"Well..."

"And their daughter?"

"I'm not lying," he assured me adamantly. "I swear it."

"I believe you. I mean—Jesus! So...which was better?"

"The mother, definitely. I basically just had to lay there and take it."

"She just drove you home, huh? Was it slippery?"

"What, the sex or the road?"

"The road," I clarified.

"Uh, I don't remember."

"Wow," I said as we continued behind the others. "Now what?"

"I doubt I'll ever see them again. Probably for the better. Promise me you won't tell anyone."

"Come on, give me a break! Do I seem like the kind of guy that would tell your secrets? What do you think I'm going to do—write a novel someday and tell the world? Get real."

The cold wind slapped my body like a newborn as I took a step inside Stanley's shoes. I could visualize the dim green lights glowing on the dashboard. Bucket seats spanned a chasm of distance with a cheap bottle of Cherie leaning passively against the firm gear stick. Cherie? Make that a can of Bud. *Rock You Like a Hurricane* played softly as she smiled comfortably. Stanley leaned against the passenger window as she stretched awkwardly across the seats. The stick-shift rubbed against her legs as she bridged the space. Reaching out to his clammy hand, she pulled it toward her, placing it on her breasts. They weren't firm like our classmates that we ogled in school. They were soft and squishy like a rich birthday cake. The urge to gain control over her was unbearable. The attempt would be futile. He'd be no match for her ravenous desire. He found himself at the mercy of her passion, living the dream of every young boy's fantasy—to bed an experienced, older woman.

I idolized this guy.

The silence of the countryside somehow accentuated the low temperature of the air. I could feel my whole body quake as I brushed the thought from my mind. The bonfire never seemed so pleasing.

The sound of the crowd quickly amplified with each step. We handed the gatekeeper our money and proceeded directly to the fire.

"Wouldn't you agree we're in the midst of a massive congregation of rebels?" Stanley asked.

I looked around at the ripped clothing, at the messy, appropriately unattractive hairstyles, at the bad tattoos. "I would say so."

"Do you think a lot of these people are actually rebelling against themselves?" he suggested.

"Themselves?"

"It seems the more someone rebels, the harder they'll go back the other way, unless their nonconformity was backed by reason."

"I don't see myself as radically as I'm perceived," I said defensively.

"You're kind of a let down for a rebel. Hell, you have the celebrative sense of a monk...you're no radical."

"Glad you agree."

We stood by the fire, talking most the evening, checking out the opening bands, then returning to the warmth of the fire. As the final band finished their set, we patiently waited inside.

"Look," Stanley said, pointing to the stage. "That's the guy from Yellow Sub."

Sure enough, one of the two men took a seat on the edge of the drum riser.

"His pants are still drooping," I said, watching as he adjusted his thick glasses.

He picked up the microphone and farted into it, the power thankfully off.

The audience began to thicken behind us as we stood in the center of the pit, waiting for the band to take the stage. The sound-system withered as a large, burly man perched himself behind the drums wearing only a pair of tighty whiteys.

The gangly flatulator stood up from the drum riser and stuck the end of the microphone in his mouth, making obnoxious, guttural noises. "Here's a message from me and Ray," he spoke into the microphone, his thick, horn-rimmed glasses secured around his head with a flexible strap. "We're not going to let the music die...join us if you've got the energy."

Suddenly, and without a cue, the hall filled with frenzied noise of punk rock blazing from the speakers. The crowd thrust me like a silent wave waiting to crash. I found myself blown effortlessly across the hall like a leaf before I could fathom that this was the Descendents! The flatulating man from Yellow Sub...one of rock and roll's greatest bands.

Without delay, the band jumped from the first song to the second, their eyes glazed from passion as they stared into the crowd belligerent with determination, proving when they played, they gave their ALL.

The turbulent energy and passion concealed within the filthy, spray-painted walls justified my faith. So long as I had the music, there was nothing I couldn't accomplish. The music was all I would ever need.

After the third encore, after everyone had left, I stood in front of the stage watching a chubby bald guy sweep its plywood surface clean.

86

"That's it, man," Stanley finally said. "We should motor. It may snow more."

"Yeah," I said, staring at the vacant stage. "I want you to know...someday I'll be up there."

He looked up at the stage, bare and dark. "When you do," he responded. "I'll be right here with you."

I ran my index finger down the rim of my gray felt fedora, feeling its sloping contour. My eyes burned an aching red, concealed under a mean shadow from the overhead lighting.

The bar was sparingly filled—a couple tables occupied with tired couples drinking the worries of the day. Slow blues from the corner piano lightened the still atmosphere. The name of the bar was unknown to me. I didn't care to know, either. Granting it the formality of a name would've deadened the anonymity of it, like the lover on a one-night stand.

I looked down at the dry martini sweating in front of me, saturating the napkin, staining the finish of the wooden table. I fancied the idea of taking a sip, to feel that cold burn scratch my throat, clearing my nose with a deep exhalation. I didn't, and knew I wouldn't. It was there for image. It served its purpose well.

I wanted the night to die at the hands of the sun, scorching the city with life and warmth under the hope of a new day. The creatures of the night surrounded me—undesirables searching that comforting drink, that comforting shoulder. The misery permeated the joint, the bluesy piano the soundtrack to the source. This bar was a retreat for the lost, a place to feel alive within the contrast.

I checked my watch. The night was still young, three hours past midnight.

I felt a sudden chill when the music ceased. The pianist paused for a quick drink. After a few words with the bartender, he returned to the instrument with an impulse of true love, the only love too many musicians will ever know.

"Play it again, pal," I said to him, tipping my hat so the fragmented light could catch my eye.

He nodded politely and began with a toned-down, melancholy rendition of Eubie Blake's *Memories of You*. I edged back in the chair as the music lifted from the soft touch of the pianist's long fingers. I loosened the tie of my zoot suit—just a touch to retain the element of sophisticated style, yet allowing clear passage of air.

The front door squeaked open slowly. The smoke reacted to the visitor, finding its way up and out the door, rising into the bleak night sky. I could feel the draft creeping, cutting in with the intimacy I held with comfort. The sounds of the street followed the new face until deadened by the closing door. Yes, the world was still out there.

I glanced casually over my shoulder, pausing briefly to spy the smoke clinging to the tiles of the ceiling, most of which misplaced or hanging loose.

As I turned to face her, our eyes met, and she came at me, slowly, awkwardly— too in touch with human emotion to carry herself sultry. Her pretty pink dress tumbled from side to side with each step extending my way.

"Of all the bars in all the world, you had to walk into this one, sweetheart," I said, tipping my hat, offering the seat opposite me at the table. "Can I get you a drink?"

"No, thanks."

"Here, have mine."

"No, thanks."

I looked at her soft, red hair—clean and shiny, unlike my own. The fullness of her red lips demanded attention. She brought them to the right place.

87

"What's a sweet dame like you doing in a dive like this?" I asked. "Say, I haven't caught your name yet, doll."

"Molly."

"And your old man would be Mister..."

"Ringwald."

"Say, Miss Ringwald, I have a nice suite at the Marriott. What say you and I—"

"Special announcement," the school secretary said over the shoddy intercom system.

I looked up at the wooden box speaker that people from the 1930's would've referred to as modern technology, and waited for this *Special Announcement*. Could school be letting out for the cold? Unlikely...

"We have just received word from the Superintendent that honor student Stanley Stockton has been awarded first place for an essay on mathematics. There will be a mandatory assembly in the auditorium Monday morning at eight o'clock for the acceptance. Our congratulations for a superb achievement in school spirit."

"Holy shit!" Oscar whispered.

"Yeah," I said slowly, stupefied. "He's a celebrity now."

"I'm stoked! I mean, I'm overwhelmed, subjugated, rectified—"

"Discombobulated?" I asked.

"Exactly!"

"Can this line move any slower?" Oscar grumbled as we stared through the auditorium doors.

The horrendous marching band thumped with several hundred drones clapping to the beat in reverence of their school pride. As we edged closer, the stage came into full view with the pompon squad performing one of their standard routines. The choreography was probably a new idea when my grandmother was equally docile.

"These things make me physically ill!" Oscar screamed over the noise.

Adults with high-tech cameras hovered like birds of prey, some with badges declaring their affiliation with a particular newspaper. Larger cameras worked test runs, focusing on the subjects of newscasters from smaller, nearby towns. All were aimed at the stage like secret assassins, waiting for the subject of the assembly to arrive.

"Stan's become a hero," I said reluctantly as we struggled to find comfort in the old, decrepit wooden seats.

"Should we throw things at him when he comes out?" Oscar replied. "He would for us." He adjusted his jacket, checking all the pins of punk rock bands buttoned on the breast. "Do I look okay for the camera? They may want to interview me. Is my mohawk straight?"

"Straight as it gets," I said.

"I'll scream: *Get off the stage, queer*! He'd probably dig that."

Principal Small entered the stage as the doors sealed us like derelicts. The auditorium silenced as he raised a firm hand.

"Good morning student body, faculty, and members of the press," he said proudly, his hair glistening from a fresh coating of grease. "It brings me great pride to stand up here today, to announce this prestigious honor to a member of our own elite student body. It reminds me of a time when I was a student once, just like a lot of you...the first round of the eighth grade spelling bee..."

Silence hung heavily on the crowd.

He paused briefly to clear his throat. "Stanley Stockton, a native of this town and whose family lineage has served proudly the very district that granted him his education, has excelled with scholastic honors throughout his young life. It gives me a deep feeling of honor and pride in our school to present Stanley with the first place award in a state-wide competition that only a Mustang would have the ambition to achieve. On behalf of the school system, the faculty, and our community as a whole, I would like to present this award to an honored representative of the Iola high school— Stanley Stockton."

The crowd cheered wildly as the photographers embraced the stage, their cameras targeted for the red curtain that withheld the prize.

"Stanley..." Principal Small requested proudly over the applause, extending his stiff hand to the draping red curtain.

With a twitch of the red velvet that sent a rippling wave to the rafters, the curtains spread like painted lips. The flashes triggered to the stuttering clicks of a dozen shutters as Stanley stepped onto the stage. Yet, this wasn't the Stanley I had dinner with the other night. An exact replica stood in his place. His hair was gone—shaved and dyed meticulously rust red with tiny black spots like the fur of a leopard. His eyes were darkened with eyeliner, somewhere between death and pretty. His jeans appeared to have been shredded in a vicious knife fight, splotchy with bleach splatters. A Black Flag T-shirt covered his stocky torso with the Pettibon artwork of a gun being cleaned. The caption read: *I've Been Good Too Long.*

Principal Small's smiling face melted into a scowl of shock and disgrace as Stanley proudly reached out to intercept his hand.

I sat with similar disbelief as Oscar nudged my shoulder. "My mom was up all night doing his hair. Looks killer, huh?"

He accepted the award with a crooked smile. Small's jaw hung low with disgust in this rare moment of state-wide attention. The flashes of cameras hammered at the two of them as they embraced hands, joined together over issues of pride baring no resemblance.

The pictures would make their way to newspapers across the state. When the good people browsed through their Sunday editions and saw the atrocious, Godless attire of the boy with the leopard hair, they'd see the name of his hometown, and the name of the man who claimed responsibility for his education.

"Rewind it again," Oscar said, laughing.

Stanley pressed the button on the VCR once again, sending his image backward across the screen. "We're going to wear the tape out." He stopped it just as his image disappeared behind the curtain.

"...an honored representative of the Iola high school, Stanley Stockton," Small said proudly from the boxy television speaker. "Stanley..."

The living room roared with laughter once again as he walked out like a criminal on parade for the tabloids, the flashes of cameras aiding the mystique.

"There should've been a speech," I said. "You could've talked about the influence Dick's demonstrated throughout your educational career."

"Just like a Daddy," Thik said.

"*Sugar* Daddy," Stanley added. He stopped the tape as the newscaster edged onto the screen talking her biased nonsense. "Okay, boys," he said, scratching the fuzzy spots on his head, "top that."

"I surrender, pal," I demised. "You win."

89

"I'll top it," Thik claimed proudly. "I'll swipe the game ball for the basketball Homecoming."

"You've got stiff competition with this, Thik," I said. "Good luck."

Several weeks later, I caught Whitaker in the hallway—just the guy I was hoping to find.

"Hey, man...check this out," I said. "I figured you'd want to see this."

I handed him the most recent issue of *Maximum RockNRoll*.

"Is your ad in here? Have you sold many?" he asked.

"Quite a few compilation tapes. I don't need a job, I'm getting about twenty bucks a day in the mail."

"Are we on the tape?" he asked me.

"Of course, we're the first band on every tape—do you think I'm an idiot? By the way, it's not the ad I'm showing you. It's the interview. It finally made it to print."

"No shit? Where?" he asked as I flipped through the pages. "Pictures?"

"Yup, every single one."

He looked it over proudly, staring at the historical pictures from just a summer ago. "This is really...*great*."

"I figured you'd want to see it. I've sold some copies of the old tape. Here..." I paused to reach into my pocket. "Seven dollars. It's your portion."

"Aw, no. I couldn't take it."

"What do you mean, Whitaker? It's yours."

"I don't deserve it."

"You deserve it as much as any of us," I told him.

"I'd like to donate it to you. Do another compilation, use this money for postage. Really."

I hesitated.

"Really," he said again, very sure of himself. "I want you to have it."

"Okay," I said.

"Let me get the address. I need a copy of this."

"Sure, write away."

"So, who'll be on your next compilation?" he asked as he searched eagerly through his notebooks for a pencil.

"Haven't written the letters yet. I really can't say."

"Good luck with it," he offered politely.

The ringmaster of the pompon squad strutted her stuff past our cafeteria table, unaware of the temptation that fueled Oscar's desire.

"She's so beautiful," Oscar said. "Wouldn't you just love to tickle her toes and call her Betty Jo?"

"Gag," I said dully. "Her hair looks absolutely ridiculous. Maybe your mother could do something about her split-ends. Shave all that shit off and start over."

"Hmm," he mumbled, paying me no attention as he stripped her down with his seedy little eyes. "Her name's Bernice. Can you believe that? Her parents have a sick sense of humor."

"What's wrong with Bernice as a name?" I asked. "Better than Mable, or Bertha, or Putrid. Maybe you should ask her out."

"No, it'd be better if I pulled her hair, or just kept ignoring her."

Thik sat down, scraping celery and carrots from his tray onto mine. "I don't know how you're going to spend the rest of your life grazing. Are you going to collect berries and nuts when you get old? *Where's the beef?*"

I felt fingers firmly tap my spine with Whitaker's familiar voice whispering softly in my ear: "I need to talk to you."

I turned quickly to face him. "Okay."

"After school. I'll be waiting by your car." He walked away to an empty table where he sat quietly with an open book. He never turned a page or glanced away the entire break.

My curiosity ate at me all day—a good excuse to have no attention in the remaining afternoon classes. As the day came to a close, I stood at the side door, readjusting my collar for a tighter fit as the scent of cold penetrated the space between the glass double-doors. Whirlwinds of snow blew across the sidewalk like tiny albino tornadoes, dying by its own momentum. The sidewalk was slick from a layer of ice on the freshly shoveled walk. Students walked cautiously between the piles of snow.

I pushed the door open as the blast of cold shoved me back a step. My breath burst out my mouth, leaving a temporary haze to dilute my vision of the brilliant white which I was now becoming one.

The path was slick despite the small chunks of sand and salt dispersed by the janitor not ten minutes earlier. I scooted to the parking lot where the shoveled path ended. It was a much safer walk through thick drifts and frozen waves of crystallized ice.

Whitaker stood by my Ranchero, bundled tightly and jumping in place on a mound of dirty snow.

"Take your time," he said irritably.

"You didn't scrape the ice off my car," I joked, noticing the snow was deadening all sound. My voice seemed muffled at close range for a more personable effect. "What good are you?"

"It's too cold to bullshit, so you can go ahead and fuck yourself right now and we can skip to the chase."

"Chase away," I said.

"You must think I'm a total puttz."

"Is that a Yiddish word?" I asked.

"I want to finish what I started. The tape, the songs."

I was shocked. "To reinstate the Order of Condom?"

"To participate once again in the state of Condomonium," he clarified. "So, what do you think?"

My pride demanded me to decline, yet my overwhelming desire to continue with music was too strong to resist. "I don't know. Of course, I'd love to, but the others?"

"I've already talked to Thik about it. He's totally up for it."

"What about your parents?" I asked. "The grapevine is pretty thin, and the driveway is mighty chilly this time of year."

"Thik's dad owns a warehouse on the west side of town by the old train station. It's large, there's no one around, no one can hear. I'll bum a ride with you or Thik and before the word would ever get out, we'd have finished the tape."

Despite my excitement, I wasn't so sure this plan would work. "You'd be in a world of trouble if news got out. I don't know what I think about that."

"With all due respect, I really don't give a shit what you think. It's my choice. The consequences would certainly suck, but it's a page unturned. I'll open myself to the possibility of the walls caving in. In such a case, that'd be *my* problem."

"You don't have to do it," I told him. "There's no hard feelings."

"Exactly. I don't have to do it. I *want* to do it. What else do you need to hear, asshole? So, what is it? Are you with me, or against me?"

Thik kicked the old wooden door with a shower of loose snow tumbling from the awning overhead. "It always does this."

"Hurry up, jackass, it's cold," Stanley scolded lightly. His leopard spots were already fading with the growth of new hair.

"Got it," Thik said, shaking the key in the lock. With a firm push, the door creaked open to reveal a hollow shell of an enormous wooden box. "This is it."

The interior of the warehouse was dark with harsh shadows cast from windows high on the walls. Most had been broken out years ago. Years of neglect had colored the concrete floor a sickening shade of brown. In the far corner sat Thik's drum set with a row of space heaters surrounding it. It stood like a mystical shrine. Once again, we had reason to believe.

"Help me load some of this stuff," Whitaker said as he carried the head of his amplifier into the old warehouse.

I picked up the guitar case and walked inside. The inner air was as stale and cold as the exterior.

"Well, at least there's no wind," I said.

"The space heaters work great," Thik boasted as he relocked the door. "I got a really good deal on them, too, if you know what I mean."

We pulled the equipment across the old concrete floor, scratching it clean with shiny gray streaks following like the trail of snails.

We erected our new fort within the orange glow of space heaters, connecting black cords to power outlets and extensions across the floor.

"We can make some serious noise out here. Nothing but abandoned buildings," Thik said. "And the cemetery."

"The residents there have more to worry about than our music," Whitaker joked casually as he opened his polished guitar case.

The heaters generated a comfortable dry warmth—so much that it was almost tolerable without a coat. Almost.

Whitaker took the end of the cord and shoved the hard shaft inside the guitar's plug. It made a crackling sound as the cord penetrated, bringing the strings to life with the slightest touch. The distortion of the instrument hummed as he stood holding the neck of the guitar, waiting for Stanley.

I picked up the microphone as the bass rumbled through the warehouse, shaking the rafters with tremendous force. Thik pounded on the snare while making small adjustments with the specific placement of each drum. I stood quietly, waiting. All eyes met with mine suddenly, silencing the warehouse to the dead sound of winter.

"Ready?" I asked softly, quietly embracing the anticipation. I looked at each person with a cocky smile as I raised the microphone to my mouth. Bitter determination met me from all angles. One more chance to breathe the life. "We're the Fluorescent Condoms," I said to an audience of mice and termites. "This is a song from our next release, if we remember how to play it. *Persistence, Resistance.*"

With the words falling from my mouth, Thik began with four clicks, sending the force of the song through the warehouse, off the bare walls, and through the rafters with the delayed effect of a concert hall. The tempo was quicker than before. We played to destroy—starting with the decrepit ruin that now housed the resurrection of our dream.

I screamed the fast-paced lyrics, feeling the intensity more than I had ever before. By the fifth song, my voice was gone, but we continued through the old set until the only light available was the orange glow of the space heaters. Nightfall summoned our demise. This time I knew it was only temporary.

As we walked outside into the cold night air, three large men stood on the loading dock with Harley-Davidson motorcycles perched side by side under the streetlight. Their demeanor was rugged with leather jackets and long beards and mustaches drenched with snot. Their jeans were tucked into leather motorcycle boots, ornamented with shiny silver studs. We recognized these people from stories of legend. I had heard enough about the old bikers from Piqua to know there was plenty to fear.

"What the hell was that noise all about?" one asked with a wandering eye of glass.

"So, you little kids are the Fluorescent Condoms," another laughed. "All this talk about a bunch of little fucking kids."

They surrounded us, circled us, examined our hair, our clothes. At this point, I realized the beardless one was actually female.

"That's some wicked hair," the man with one eye said, clenching his red, chapped fists in the cold.

We stood nervous and speechless, waiting for them to do what they had come to do.

"I don't know what to think of that music," One-eye said. "I've been hearing about the stunts you guys have been pulling around these parts for quite a while now. Quite a while..."

The other guy kicked the ground firmly, releasing chunks of ice from his pant leg.

"Figured you'd have dropped it by now. You don't seem too frightening to me," One-eye said, basking in the absurdity. "You kids seem to have this town on its toes, whatever this shit is about."

"I don't like the music," the other guy said flatly.

"Whatever this shit is, you're really true to it. In this town, I know how hard it can be to stick to your guns," One-eye said, sticking his hand out to Whitaker. "Put it there."

Whitaker grabbed his hand, shaking it humbly, awkwardly.

"So, this hair," the other guy said. "I can do that with some Elmer's glue," he told Oscar, "but what the hell is with this leopard skin? And how the fuck did you get your hair to stick together like that?"

I smiled, pointing at my throat.

"He's the singer," Stanley said. "His voice is shot. They're dreadlocks, like in Jamaica."

They laughed, making casual motions to highway 54. The dry stretch of road had been cleared of snow days ago.

"So, really," the other guy said, scratching his scraggly beard as we walked to the street, two separate generations of rock and roll hellions. "What is with that music? You need to slow down, let it groove. Learn some Zeppelin, then we may come and check it out. But this hyperactive shit...I guess I'm too old."

They climbed on the massive frames of their motorcycles, bringing them to life—except One-eye's. It sputtered and backfired, sending booming cracks of thunder throughout the quiet landscape.

"Dammit!" he exclaimed angrily.

"I was sure your carburetor was shot," the other guy said loudly over the quaking engine.

One-eye pulled a screwdriver out of his inner coat pocket. "It *was* shot. I figured I'd solved this fucking problem."

Stanley stepped forward and stared at the engine. "My second cousin had a 1972 FLH Electra Glide. I worked on it some before he sold it."

"It's the timing," their female cohort offered as the heavy machine vibrated between her legs like a mechanical horse.

One-eye stepped down off the Harley as it rocked uncontrollably, spitting backfire through the exhaust pipe.

"I'll need to get it back to my barn where I can take a look at it," he said.

"You can ride with me," his buddy offered.

"You can't just leave your ride here," the female warned.

"Can I borrow your screwdriver a second?" Stanley asked with coy reserve.

"You'll need more than a screwdriver," he said, extending it to Stanley's grasp.

Stanley placed the tip of the screwdriver against the engine—his ear against the handle. He listened like a stethoscope a few seconds. "It's not your timing. Your timing's fine." He handed the screwdriver back to him and looked to my Ranchero. "I'd say your intake gaskets are worn and leaking air. As it heats up, it should get worse. We can get some grease from the front wheel baring of the Ranchero and smear it on the intake gaskets to seal off the inflowing air. That should smooth out the idle enough to get it home. Since there aren't any stores open at this hour, you can cut a section from an old radiator hose if you need a temporary fix for tomorrow." He walked over to my car and looked down at the front wheel. "Frankie," he said, bending down to the tire. "Mind if I take this center cap off to get some grease? It won't affect anything."

I nodded affirmatively as he and One-eye pried the cap off and scraped away some sticky grease with their fingers. We stood back, watching a quick maintenance of the hefty ride. As the grease was administered, the engine regulated to a consistent, steady vibration.

"Well, I'll be a monkey's ass. Thanks a bunch, partner," One-eye said to Stan, slapping him consistently on the shoulder. "Take it easy, and keep your hearts pure, boys."

We waved as they sped down the highway, their engines rapping with each elevated shift of gears, echoing throughout the countryside as their amber taillights disappeared over the horizon.

"Don't think the wrong thing," Oscar said to me a few weeks later as we sat in my car, waiting for the others to arrive at the warehouse. "I'm cutting my hair."

His words caught me off-guard. I tried to conceal my thoughts behind a poker face. "Why?"

"Well...I'll just go with a shaved head for a while."

"Is something up?" I asked.

"No, not really."

"Not really?" I asked, trying to summon a better reply.

"Well, my parents are getting weird with each other, and with me."

"Over your hair?"

"My dad doesn't dig it. He's a military man, he doesn't get it."

"Your mother is the one who does our hair," I reminded him.

"I know."

I could sense his discomfort. I didn't want to add more. "You'd look cool with a shaved head."

"Yeah," he agreed calmly, "I think it'd look decent. Probably look pretty damn tough."

"When's it going to happen?"

"Tonight."

"Hmm," I said, looking at his tall, liberty-spiked mohawk. I was sad to see it go, though I could sense his uneasiness. I opted a subject change on his behalf. "Have you noticed Claire has been taking Whitaker to all our practices?"

He nodded casually.

"What's with that? Is Whitaker getting up with Claire?"

"No," he said flatly.

"I wonder what the deal is?"

"Have you noticed who she talks to? Who she watches? Check it out."

"You think she's got the hots for one of us?" I asked.

"Uh-huh. Any shows coming to the Outhouse?"

"I don't think so, it's too cold."

"That sucks," he complained. "This town gets really boring."

Stanley and Thik pulled up alongside us, staring through fogged windows.

"Time to brave the cold," I said as I opened the car door to join them.

"I hate this weather," Oscar grumbled to himself.

Thik jabbed the key into the lock, shaking it roughly until it turned. With a forceful shove, it creaked open. The hinges squeaked of gritty rust. We strutted confidently to the opposite corner where our equipment awaited in cold silence.

The four-track sat on a couple milk crates with cords rushing in and out, feeding into the little mixer board with microphones covering various drums. The last rehearsal had completed the recording of the drums, mixed tediously down to the first of the four tracks available. Stanley unhooked the cords and neatly placed them in a large cardboard box.

The front door opened and in walked Whitaker, followed by Claire who banged her pink mittens together to release the snow.

"It's cold out there!" she exclaimed through chattering teeth. Her button nose was bright red. She batted her long lashes thick with mascara as her smile lit the room.

"It's cold in *here*," Thik added.

"Are you ready to lay down your basslines?" Whitaker asked Stanley.

"In a minute," he complained as he struggled with the tangled mess of cords. "Did the Dead Kennedys ever have to deal with this crap?"

"I bet they still do," I replied, staring straight into the heater.

"Stanley, my car's messed up," Claire said. "Do you think you can take a look at it later?"

"What's wrong with it?" he asked.

"It's not working."

"How is it not working?"

"Oh, you know, it's just not...working, or something," she told him. "Probably the radiator."

"Do you have any anti-freeze in it?"

"My brother puts all those things in it," she said.

"Can't your brother fix it?" he asked.

"He's probably busy."

"Sure," Stanley agreed, closing the top of the cardboard box. The leopard dye had almost completely faded from his hair. "I'll check it out later."

"Oh, man, I had the wildest dream last night," Claire said quickly. "See, I was reading this book about that UFO that crashed in the desert in 1947, you know?"

"No," Thik replied.

"Anyway, this UFO crashed, right? And the government has this ship and these alien bodies at the Wright Field—"

"Is this a movie?" Whitaker asked.

"They say it's real...anyway, I dreamt these aliens landed in my backyard, but then it became my room somehow, and then it became a swimming pool...and these aliens looked at me with these crazy eyes—"

"Was it like that dream I always have," Oscar said, "where you're at school, and suddenly you realize you're naked—luckily no one has noticed, and you try to sneak away to get clothes and the teacher makes you sit down, and then you get nervous because if you make a scene, everyone will notice you're naked..."

"I always dream I'm in front of the class giving a speech and my teeth keep falling out," Whitaker said as he repatched the cords on the four-track to record the bass.

"I never remember my dreams," Stanley said. "I know they're black and white, though."

"Anyway," Claire said loudly. "I hate to be so rude as to talk while you guys are interrupting me, but these aliens—what was I saying?"

"Something about how the aliens told you that you talk too much," Stanley said.

"Anyway, when I woke up, I thought—*Damn! That was really weird!* So, I started thinking, what if that really did happen, and the government is keeping it a secret? Wouldn't that be wild if the secret is they found a crashed saucer, but they found it in the 1940's, as opposed to it crashing then? And they discovered that it had crashed a long time ago, like a *long* time ago. They found that it had maps of this solar system and pictures of their home planet, which would be Mars from like a long time ago. Mars was inhabited—this is back when Mars had water, right? As its atmosphere depleted, they tried to colonize this planet, but were unsuccessful—except one ship crash landed here. The occupants were forced to regress back to a barbaric culture because the flimsy, sophisticated culture they had known was gone and they were on this planet like *Lost in Space.* Anyway, these creatures were humans, originally from Mars, and we are their descendants. *We're all Martians!*"

"Wouldn't there be remains of cities on Mars?" Whitaker asked as he picked up the headphones.

"No, because their atmosphere changed and thinned out. So the planet became a desert—susceptible to meteors and space debris. It wouldn't take long to destroy what was there. Think about our own culture," she said as Whitaker put the headphones over his ears. "Most everything we make in this society is built to degrade within a few decades. I mean, if things last over two hundred years, we stick them in museums. If our species died off today, how long do you think it would take for nature to totally consume this planet? In a couple centuries, what would remain?"

"Interesting point," I said quietly as I sat immersed in the warm glow of the heater.

"Thanks."

"Give me a level," Whitaker said confidently as he fondled the tiny knobs on the four-track.

Stanley played his bass as the sound echoed through the warehouse. Whitaker turned buttons, flipped switches, and adjusted knobs until he finally found the right tone.

"This is it," he said, removing the headphones and handing them to Stanley. "I'm going to play through the first song on the four-track to check the levels." He pressed the *Play* button on the cassette deck as red lights lit up the four-track.

Stanley played along with the tape we couldn't hear, nodding to the rhythm. "Sounds good," he said as he completed the song. "Make sure it's loud."

"Okay," Whitaker announced quite seriously. "Are you ready?"

Stanley nodded confidently.

"Everyone quiet," Whitaker instructed.

He looked at Stanley for approval as he placed his finger on the *Record* button. With a nod, he pressed down—causing the four-track's dials to perk slightly. Stanley stood quietly with a firm grip on the pick while staring down at the soiled concrete. It was quiet enough to hear the faint clicking of the drum sticks on the tape. After the fourth, the bass boomed through the warehouse to the rhythm of the drums—silent to all but Stanley.

After almost an hour, the bass track was completed on tape.

"These wide open acoustics are going to make this thing have a lot of natural reverb," Whitaker said.

"Is that bad?" I asked.

"I don't know. Maybe...maybe not."

"Time for the guitar?" Stanley asked.

"Yeah," Whitaker responded quickly as he rushed to his instrument.

"I'm going to walk down the street to get some grub," Stanley said. "Do you need me for anything, Whitaker?"

"No."

"You're walking all that way in the cold?" I asked.

"It's just four blocks. Do you want to come?"

"Hell no."

"I'll go," Claire offered.

"Oscar?" Stanley asked.

He shook his head.

"Okay," Stanley said as he buttoned his coat. "Are you ready, Claire?"

"Yes."

"Whitaker," I said as he powered up his amplifier. "I don't want to do the vocals tonight, even if we have the time. I'd rather wait until tomorrow."

"Why?"

"The anticipation is good for me. Also, I'll fast tomorrow, so when I do the vocals, I'll have that extra edge, extra passion."

"Whatever you want," he said.

"That's what I want."

*   *   *

"Take my peas," Oscar pleaded over the table at lunch the following day. His velvety shaved head shined under the fluorescent lights of the cafeteria.

"I don't want your peas," I told him.

"Why aren't you eating? That's so stupid."

"Because, it'll give me that extra edge," I said.

"You'll have an edge by not eating my peas? Yeah, right."

"Eat your own damn peas for a change," I told him. "They're good for you."

"Oscar," a soft voice whispered over our shoulders. "You look better now that you cut that ugly thing off your head."

I turned to see his heartthrob, Bernice—the honcho of the pompon squad.

"Yeah, thanks," he mumbled, merely glancing at her, then back to his food.

She walked on with an edgy grumble.

"What a bitch," I said.

"Whew," he sighed. "I want her *so* bad."

"You should've talked to her."

"Can't do that. If I do that, I won't stand a chance in hell."

"Yeah," I mumbled.

"She's got the kind of beauty that stops hearts, that starts wars. It tortures us men," he explained. "It's like a virus in your brain, it eats at you. It lingers like a bad odor, hours after you see her. Now that I've seen her, I'm sure the next six hours will be spent trying to get it out of my head."

"Trying to fumigate her scent out of your head? To each his own, I suppose."

"Just think what one could accomplish without being chained to hormones," he said. "Sucks being a guy. I don't want to have to look at every girl that walks by, I don't want to be the slave that I am. Life could be so much better if I were free from it."

"I'm not sure we wouldn't be in the caves still if it weren't for that hormonal drive, though. Why would we care to invent the wheel, invent the computer, send machines to space? It's all exposure."

"Do you think?" he asked.

"Take, for instance, a scientist struggling to create an antidote for allergic reactions and rashes. His motivations are probably fairly standard—a nice house, a nice car, a hot woman at his side. Analyze those choices. What's the house for—just him? Why the classy ride? It all goes back to one thing: door number three."

"Is that *your* motivation?" he asked me. "Is that why you're the band's frontman?"

"My motivation is different due to the circumstances. At this point, I feel I have something to prove, if only to myself."

"Being in a band has nothing to do with meeting members of the opposite sex?"

"No, it's not my motivation," I replied. "I'll leave that attitude up to the Metal bands. When I sit down to write the lyrics to the songs, I have my agenda, things I want spoken. I can honestly say it's one of the rare times that I'm *not* thinking about girls. When I pick up the microphone, it's a release of hostility. I don't think punk rock is attractive. I don't feel like a heartthrob rocker when I'm frothing into the microphone. It's the expression that motivates me, the release of tension."

"Doesn't that prove your statement wrong, if you aren't an example yourself?"

"A vast majority would easily fit this picture. I do believe that some people out there simply love to create, and it's a very pure and wonderful thing. They're rare, though. When they create, it's a very intense, genuine work. They set the standard for

98

everyone to copy. It's the copiers who see the impact this person's honest creation has made, and they mimic it for similar results, feeling nothing of the original's authenticity. It's those people who leach from the vision of others that represent not only my example, but the largest part of society."

"And you place yourself above this part of society?" he asked.

"I don't mean to sound as arrogant as I am, but yes, I do."

Pehgan sat her tray next to Oscar's.

"So, Pehgan, would you say that everything you do is simply to get laid?" Oscar asked.

"No."

"See, Frank, you're wrong."

"I'm not feeling very well today," she said. "It's the tenth today. The tenth day...I'm allergic to this day."

"Allergic?" I asked.

"This is the day I will someday die. Not necessarily this month, but the tenth day for sure."

"Are you talking suicide?" Oscar asked. "If I were to off myself, I think I'd eat six bags of strawberry pop rocks, then drink a can of Coke. That's how Mikey from the commercials died, you know."

"The tenth is a very cold day. It's icy bluish-white," she said. "A very cold number."

"Numbers have colors?" Oscar asked.

"And letters have colors," she told him. "When I learned the alphabet and numbers, the teacher had put cardboard letters on the wall that were different colors. So when I learned the number or letter, I always memorized the color along with it. Now every name and number has a unique blur of colors. When I memorize a number, I memorize the color combination, too. That's how I remember phone numbers, by the color."

"What color is my name?" Oscar asked.

"Red with a bit of white, burnt orange, and brownish-black. Frank, your name is very dark. A shade of burnt brown and black—like chocolate fudge."

Stanley sat his tray next to mine and plopped himself abruptly in the plastic seat. "Are you still not eating?" he asked me.

"No."

"Not even peas?"

"No."

"The recording sounds good," he said. "It's going to sound much better than the old one."

"I got this letter yesterday from some guy who works at the college radio station in Manhattan, Kansas," I told them. "He's trying to put on shows at this old theater. He saw our interview in *Maximum RockNRoll* and wants to know if we'd like to play there. He says there isn't a big scene, but it's growing."

"Did you write back?"

"No, not yet."

"Maybe we should talk to Whitaker."

"About what?" Whitaker asked as he joined us.

"A show in Manhattan," Stanley said. "What do you think?"

"I really don't know. I'd like to," he said, sighing. "What night? A weekend?"

"Probably," I told him. "I could make sure of it."

"I suppose I could tell my parents I'm staying the night with Thik or something."

"It's up to you," I said. "Don't even look at me."

Whitaker withheld his silence a moment. "If it's on a weekend, and it's soon, I'll do it."

Thik sat down at the table, and looked at us. "What's up?" he asked. "Everyone looks all serious, what's going on? Frank, take my peas."

"We're going to play a show in Manhattan," Whitaker said.

"Really? How?"

"I got a letter yesterday," I told him.

"Here's the deal..." Whitaker said, pausing to make sure his words were being digested properly. "I'm finishing the tape. We're almost done. After we play this show, I've *got* to call it quits. I know it sounds totally lame, but it was a stretch for me to go this far. All this has been behind my parents' backs, lying each day about studying and doing extra-curricular work for school. Does everybody understand this?"

"We're cool with that," Stanley agreed easily. "By the way, about the show, I was only asking. If you don't want to do it, let's not do it."

"No, I want to do it. I *will* do it. Set it up, Frank."

"Check," I said into the microphone as everyone sat in front of me, watching.

"Keep talking into it," Whitaker instructed with the headphones wrapped snug over his head.

"Check mate, check your pockets, check in the mail..."

Whitaker twisted a couple knobs like a veteran engineer. "I'm going to play a bit to get a level. Sing the volume you'll be singing. I think I got a good tone on your voice. Here, take the headphones."

I placed them over my cold ears. The foam padding was warm and comfortable. Whitaker pushed the *Play* button, and within a few seconds the music was roaring in my ears, loud and clearly. I sang my words as the band played, pieced together over a couple nights, now ready for the final touch—me.

He stopped the tape and I could hear my voice echoing briefly throughout the warehouse. Everyone stared at me, startled by my sudden calm demeanor.

"Okay," Whitaker said. His finger tapped softly against the *Record* button. "You ready for the real thing?"

"Lay it down, Sally."

He pressed the button and my legs began to shake. I shut my eyes and listened as the intro to *Persistence, Resistance* raged in the headphones. Without my vision, I found myself encompassed within a safety bubble of conviction. I couldn't be touched. My voice and opinion were all I had and all I needed to survive.

As the song kicked into high speed, I was riding over the top, standing high on the song, owning it. The ferocity of the rough recording stood firmly behind me as I screeched into the mic. My empty stomach enraged me. It supplied that little straw needed to veer from complacency. I felt enslaved by the microphone. I wanted to throw it across the warehouse, to watch it break into a thousand pieces. I wanted to feel the restraint of nothing. Yet, at the same time, it was the only weapon I possessed. I used it with accuracy, staring into the eyes of oppression that stared back from all corners. The mirror came before me, and I stood before it Superhuman as the song raged. Somewhat animal, completely articulate, overwhelmingly alive. Hungry in all respects. I could feel my anger swell as the song came to the finish. I threw my head up in the air with open eyes, staring straight into the rafters as the music ceased. I was back in the warehouse, cold and musty.

"Wow," Whitaker said as he stopped the tape. "That's a keeper."

"Go to the next," I said shortly. "What is it?"

"*Person On The Street.* Here goes..."

The tape rolled again, bringing forth the fuel of my existence. I screamed into the microphone as if biting at it—fire from the Dragon's mouth.

I completed the whole thing in one clean sweep like a live performance, which it was to me. The recording was complete.

"You must be hungry," Stanley said as Whitaker packed up the four-track in the cardboard box. "Let's get some food, Frankie. That was awesome."

"It's been a long time since I rock and rolled." I stepped up to Whitaker and patted him on the back as he packed away cords and colored wires. "Whitaker," I mumbled. "Thanks."

He looked up at me and smiled proudly, returning quickly to his work.

The green and white lights showered upon me. I could barely see the small audience that stood before us, beyond the stage monitors. Scarlet fliers littered the floor of the club, torn by the weight of military boots and a pleased crowd. Their hungry eyes silently urged us to continue with the music's momentum.

Only one song remained. This was it. The end of the set, and the end of the band.

"Don't miss Curious George and Nine Lives, up next," I told the crowd. I felt a strange rumbling in my stomach. I wasn't hungry, but my body ached as if it was. "We have a new cassette. *Time Spent Beating Around the Bush.* Please buy it. This is our last song, ever. *Rest.*"

The echo of my voice fell to the crashing impact of the music's intensity. I could feel my voice crackling with passion, crackling like fire. The words meant everything to me. The words were my life. Within them, I lived.

In a flash, it suddenly was all over.

The loose and skimpy mosh-pit slowed to a clumsy halt. Applause followed naturally.

I lowered the microphone and caught the firm glare of Whitaker. He appeared different all the sudden. Almost gallant, completely confident. We were heroes, if only to ourselves. Stanley stared directly into the audience with a thoughtful and almost nostalgic expression. Sweat dripped from the tip of his nose.

A line quickly formed in front of Pehgan, exchanging money for the product of our passion.

Oscar greeted us with a nonchalant swagger as we dragged our gear off the stage.

He had cashed in his father's old combat boots for a new pair of Adidas jogging shoes. His hair was growing out its natural color of dark blond into a disorderly crew-cut. He sometimes mashed a handful of mousse in it to make it somewhat spiky, but still modestly tame by comparison of the old style.

He helped Stanley lift his ragged Peavey bass speaker. The black surface had a tear that hung loose like the skin of an eggplant.

"Leaving?" Walter, the promoter asked us as we gathered our equipment at the rear door. His eyes conveyed deep concern and guilt. The lines on his face responded accordingly with stress. He had worn the expression often in his life.

I nodded politely. "The weather is really bad, and we have a good distance to travel. Two of our guys aren't supposed to even be here. We're supposedly having a slumber party."

He laughed. "Well, here," he said, reaching into his pocket. He handed me a wad of bills. "It's not much, I know. Bad turn-out. I didn't think the weather would be this nasty...to make it up to you guys, I do have your new tape, and I'll be playing it a lot on my shift at KSDB."

"Wow, on the radio," Whitaker said proudly. "That's really cool."

"Oh...one more thing I almost forgot," he said quickly as he shuffled away to the sound-man. He returned with a cassette tape. "From the board."

It was a live recording of our entire show, and became the third and final release of the band: *The Fluorescent Condoms Live!*

"Well, take it easy, Walter," I told him. "And thanks again for the show."

"You bet. Any time you need a gig, give me a call."

We opened the rear door to a turbulent blast of freezing wind. We kicked through thick drifts of snow that buried the knee, hauling our equipment clumsily to Thik's station wagon. It was submerged under a mound of snow that slagged over the roof like frosting.

The street appeared as an endless flow of creamy white pudding. The bowl from which it was poured would take a lifetime to lick.

"So, that's it," Whitaker said to me as we stood in the freezing wind, pushing the snow off the station wagon.

"That's it," I replied. "You know what would've been easier than all this?"

"What's that?"

"If you had just kept your mouth shut during those bus trips."

He laughed. "It was just too funny an idea to not pursue. Besides, had we not become Condoms, I'd still be playing in the garage for no one. Don't get me wrong, Frank. This hasn't been a joyride by any stretch of the imagination." He flashed me a toothy grin as the wind whipped his flat and conservative hairstyle.

"Look at you, you preppie piece-of-shit! You're the ideal kid! Fucking Thik...he's probably stealing the soap out of the bathroom as I speak. Me and Oscar, what do I need to say..."

"I always imagined high school to be something memorable," he mused. "Nothing quite like this."

Pehgan stumbled out to join us while concentrating on a piece of fuzz that she held between her fingertips. "What do you suppose this thing is thinking?" she asked. She stretched one stiff arm in the air, while scratching her ass with the other. "Do you think in twenty years lobotomies will be cool?"

"Are we ready to go?" I asked Stanley, who struggled with the final piece of equipment.

He nodded shortly as he slammed the rear door shut. "Let's go."

We climbed inside the station wagon, fitting ourselves within the small amount of room that remained.

Thik slowly brought the station wagon through the drifts as if steering through a Root Beer float. The wind howled desperately as the tires cut through the snow that seemed to shift the road.

Otherwise, there was only silence solid as ice.

An hour later, Whitaker spoke. "Are you feeling tired, Thik?"

"No," Thik responded lazily.

102

The level plains were invisible through the swirling flurries, just a vibrating wall of crystallized precipitation. The station wagon plowed through the thick snow like a chocolate bar through whipped cream. The sound of the snow scrunching under the tires sent an unnerving chill up the spine like nails on a chalkboard.

I stared uneasily out the window. I didn't move for several minutes as the snow slurred my perception.

Suddenly, the road became painfully bumpy. Pehgan started screaming as the station wagon angled toward the ditch, plowing through the snow. Thik turned to her with dazed eyes.

Whitaker—who occupied the passenger seat, pushed at the steering wheel, forcing it the opposite direction. The station wagon jumped back up on the road and quickly veered off into the other ditch. We impacted a snow bank that brought the station wagon to an immediate halt.

Everyone was shaken and very much awake at that point. We quickly jumped out of the station wagon into the harsh winter flurries. We made a mad rush through the virgin snow, kicking it high in the air so it showered back on us, tingling our faces with pinpricks of cold.

The station wagon purred with its headlights illuminating the falling flakes. The tires were hidden under the sweep of a thick snowdrift, as if submerged in clam chowder. The snow hammered softly against the windshield, creating an immediate mound.

Thik shook his head. "My God...I fell asleep. I dreamt I was flying a plane."

Pehgan, the little girl blue counted her fingers repeatedly.

"We had just passed a gas station," Whitaker said, pointing to the dark road behind us. "It was closed, but we can call someone to get help."

"There's got to be other options," Oscar insisted. "We're not supposed to be here, you and I."

"My parents are out of town at Pitt State, visiting my brother," I told them.

"My parents are likely drunk at the bar right now," Thik said.

Stanley cleared his throat uneasily. "My mother's car wouldn't make it in this weather."

Oscar plunged his fists in the snow that surrounded the station wagon, digging like a dog with short-term memory loss. He fell quickly to his knees, holding his frozen fists over the snow bank.

"We'll need a shovel," Stanley told him. "For starters."

He bowed his head in defeat. "My Old Man has one. He will kick my ass for being here. I mean, he will *really* kick my ass."

"Come on, man," Thik said to him. "I'll go with you to use the pay-phone."

Oscar slowly brought himself to his feet as he wrapped his arms around himself. Together they stumbled down the highway, into the darkness.

"Your parents will find out, huh?" I asked Whitaker.

"Maybe...maybe not. Doesn't matter now, does it? I did what I set out to do."

"Now you pay the consequences," Stanley resolved with a deep sigh.

"I'll be a better man for it."

"I hope it was worth it," I said.

"I wouldn't change a thing," Whitaker decided with ease. "In ten years, we can look back on this. I know I will."

*   *   *

I saw Whitaker very little after that night. He went on to get his bachelor's degree in Drama at the University of Kansas, later to teach in some remote town in southeast Kansas with his wife, a native of Iola.

Oscar went his own way shortly after that night, spending less and less time with us as his style became everything he was once so adamantly against. Bernice and he enjoyed a short fling of a romance the following year before he joined the Navy.

Several years later, I met Oscar again in Iola for a brief and awkward visit. We fancied the fact that our ban had expired as we enjoyed some ice cream in the park in front of the stadium we had once graffittied. A vicious tornado had struck Iola in the years between, tearing away the aluminum awning of the stadium, leaving only a concrete frame.

"It's not that bad," Oscar said calmly of the military. "I live off the coast of Florida, no bad winters away from this place. I have to get up early, but all I do is fly to Caribbean islands to photograph sunsets. Not bad for the money. So how is living in Lawrence? You've been there since graduation, haven't you?"

"Been living in Lawrence for about five or six years now," I said. "Actually, I'll be moving away this summer to Austin. My girlfriend Jill is going to graduate school at the University of Texas."

"Weren't there a lot of old punk bands from Austin?" he asked.

"The Dicks, the Big Boys, Butthole Surfers..."

"So, you have a steady hitch?" he asked.

"Girlfriend? Yeah, we've lived together a few years now. Things are going well."

"*Really* well? Are you getting married?"

I laughed. "I don't know. Things aren't too bad."

"How'd you meet her?" he asked.

"Kind of a funny story, really. I owe it all to this one fateful day when I made some pizzas for this ballerina...you know, it's a long story. Some other time maybe."

We finished our ice cream, watching a carload of rebellious youths storm through the park in an old, beat-up jalopy.

"I guess Small is still dealing with radicals," Oscar said.

"When we graduated, Kimberly Powers and her buddies carried the torch. Hell, I don't even know these younger people, and they likely know nothing of us. Funny how things pass."

"I doubt we were forgotten that easily," he decided quickly. "If I could change things, I would've stuck with it. We could've *really* fucked things up. But the family—"

"I know. No skin off my back."

"Your parents were always really cool."

"Yeah, still are," I said.

"Sorry about my parents coming into your parents' office after that Manhattan show, screaming at them like they did in front of customers. They needed someone to blame."

I laughed, still feeling the wake of those events. "Ironic that your mother was the one cutting our hair, and somehow it was my parents who were responsible."

"Yeah, that was fucked up, I know. There was so much shit going on back then, so much adversity."

"Good word," I complimented.

"Thanks. The whole town was at one end or the other, teachers leaving and all that. It was a crazy time."

"Really crazy," I said.

"I tried to meet Mrs. Webster because she was really cool to us, but she wasn't there."

"She left after we did. Dalton did, too."

"I hear the Dewie boys work for the City of Iola now?" he asked.

"So I've heard. Did you also hear they had some problems a few years ago keeping their jobs after they set fire to a black guy they had beaten senseless?"

"I believe it. I believe they still get respect in this town despite that."

"Shit," I groaned. "Acts like that *earn* the respect."

"So you actually lived off those tapes throughout high school?" he asked.

"Three compilations, three Fluorescent Condoms tapes. Not too bad."

"Are Stanley and Claire still married?"

"Yeah. Very happily," I added.

"Man, they've been together for years now. What about Pehgan? Do you ever hear from her?"

"No. She sent that one picture at graduation, the one where she's all dressed in red, head to toe."

He smiled.

A family pulled up next to the stadium, unloading a group of youngsters for football practice.

"I wonder if Thik still has that game ball from our Senior year," he pondered.

"Probably. I guess he still lives here. I hear he hosts parties every weekend at this old farmhouse north of town. High school girls go there and strip for the drunk guys, and of course the guys give all their money."

"Sucks being a guy. A guy and his money are soon parted when hormones are involved." He nervously twisted the wedding band around his finger.

"Man, it's really quiet out here," I said, watching the autumn leaves blow in circles around my car. "I'm not used to it."

"It sucks here. You know, I wish it had turned out differently."

"It was fun while it lasted," I said.

"Yeah, it was. Put many miles on your Ranchero being chased around. They fucking hated us here."

"Sure is quiet now, though," I said. "They finally got what they wanted. Seems impressively dull. What a pain in the ass we must have been."

"Man, we turned this town upside down," he said proudly.

I laughed, feeling a lump in my throat as I remembered the look on his face years ago, so proud, so defiant. There he sat next to me quiet and harmless, the two of us immobile and completely unnoticed in a park crawling with life.

I envisioned the Ranchero cutting through a country road, splitting the fields of wheat with dust as a massive truck pressed against the rear, fueled by aggression. Oscar's starchy, bright red mohawk resisting the wind as he stood naked in the bed of the Ranchero...

He leaned down with a steady hand to his shoe, wiping a blemish of dust from the black shiny polish. "Well," he said, straightening his collar, "I should be getting back to my parents' house now. My wife will be wondering where I'm at."

"Okay," I said, standing firm on the asphalt.

"Good seeing you, Frank." He extended a hand to receive my diplomatic embrace.

"Nice to see you again, Oscar. Take care of yourself, and enjoy life. That is the point, you know."

"I'll see you at the class reunion." He stepped away, turning his back to me once again.

I watched him climb inside his rental car, cautiously putting the seat belt over his shoulder as he waved one last time. I returned the gesture as the car pulled away, disappearing into the history of my life.

I stood quietly alone, treasuring the silence. I listened to the brilliance of nothing—all the little things we filter to better attune to daily worries. The crickets chirped loudly, and somewhere, far from where I stood, someone pushed a lawnmower, sending a scent through the air more appetizing than candy.

I recalled the vision through the Ranchero's windshield as I left town immediately following the high school graduation ceremony. My eyes were fixated on the yellow lines splitting the road, paying no attention to the scenery I had become too much a part. As the car bounded over the tracks—rocking from the dire need of new front shocks—I smiled at the moment of my life's biggest triumph. The countryside stretched as far as the eye could see, an ocean of golden wheat swaying with the pressing wind. The Bad Brains orchestrated my departure as I watched Allen county regress into a memory behind me.

Tried to see if I'd give up, but there wasn't any luck...now I'm movin' on.

I kept my eye on the advancing mile, each a step forward to life. My northerly destination was just beyond the limits of a vast horizon. The landscape stretched in calm waves like the rolling contours of a desert terrain—treeless and empty.

The Ranchero burst through the fields, freedom abound with the invigorating charge of life in motion and fraction of time realized to the second. I was on my way home, just in time for dinner. In Lawrence I would sleep the first night of my awakened life.

"Flight 432," the woman says over the airport's speaker system. "Now boarding for Kansas City. Flight 432..."

I pick up my bags and take one last sip of water from the melted ice. Spare change jingles in my pocket as I stroll out of *Betty's World Famous Apple Pie*, free at last to travel north, to return to Lawrence.

I bound down the narrow gate into the plane. The vinyl carry-on bag pulls tightly against my shoulder as I forfeit my boarding pass.

"Have a nice flight."

Life In A Northern Town

"So, Frank," the petite brunette whispered in my ear.

I opened the passenger door of my Jaguar for her to slip into. She stared at me with sleek brown eyes. Her soft burgundy lips seemed wet enough to stir. The scent of Nag Champa oil on her pale skin delivered a thirst that begged to be quenched. I beckoned a sip. Ravel's *Bolero* hummed from my car's massive Martin-Logan speakers.

"What would you like to do now?" she asked. Her cotton dress glided with the gentle breeze like waves rippling under soft moonlight. Her long, claw-like nails were painted like wine, matching her dress. Dark emerald earrings sparkled amidst her soft, straight hair. Her perfectly shaped legs sunk into thick-soled Doc Martens.

I wanted her now more than anything on earth.

"Well, Miss Hunter," I replied nervously.

"Please, Frank, call me Paisley."

"Okay, Miss Hunter, I mean Paisley...I guess we could go back to my suite at the Four Seasons Hotel and..."

"Hey, Mister!" the young boy exclaims, forcing my elbow from the small armrest that separates us. He points to the window over my right shoulder where runways scatter the flat landscape. "I want that seat."

I glare at him, studying his bulbous strawberry-blond head and freckled face. His rosy cheeks are prickly from pre-pubescent razor stubble. "Too bad, asshole."

"Come on! I'll let you read my magazine," he offers, flashing his *Spin* magazine in my face. "There's a story about the Media Whores."

"That's nice..."

"You don't even know who they are, do you?" he challenges. "You're too old."

I laugh in response.

"Who are they, then?"

"You're annoying."

Holding up the glossy magazine, he shakes it noisily. The Media Whores stare at me from the cover.

"Not a chance," I tell him.

"You suck, dude. See if I talk to you..."

He quickly flips through the pages, admiring the glamorous photographs of the Media Whores. Their matching black outfits smother them with an air of mystique and self-righteousness.

His attention wanders to the advertisements of pretentious rockers striking pseudo-intellectual poses to sell their record company's product. If the product doesn't sell, then it's back to delivering pizzas and summer college courses. They could someday tell their grandchildren they once almost made it to the Big Time. The cheap, glossy pages of the magazine would be proof.

I look out the window at the various landing strips. The warm sun is reflecting against their smooth surfaces, casting a radiant sparkle. The grass permeates a natural shade of green, its life slowly returning after a long and hot summer. Now, late in the autumn season, the landscape lives once again—the climate finally tolerable for all living things.

After a few short minutes, the plane shoots upward into the puffy white clouds.

"You're from Austin?" the boy asks me.

"I am."

"Do you have a job, or are you a tax burden?"

"I have a job," I tell him. "I manage a bagel bakery on the Drag."

"They call Austin the *Live Music Capital of the World,* you know. Do you see a lot of bands?"

"Not if I can help it. Some of the worst music I've ever heard has been in bars. Maybe I've just spent too much time in them when I was younger."

"Were you in a band?" he asks.

I nod. "I was the vocalist."

"Why'd you quit?"

"I'm too emotionally secure to do something like that again. You seem to like music a lot. Do you like good music, or that shit on the radio?"

"I like good music," he tells me as he browses through the magazine. "I like the Media Whores. I want to learn guitar, but my dad doesn't think I'm serious about it."

"Are you?" I ask.

He nods affirmatively.

"You should consider bass or drums. Guitarists and singers are dime a dozen."

"But I want to play guitar. The guitar carries the mood of the music, especially for a punk band like the Media Whores. So, what's wrong with the music on the radio?"

"They play the same five songs over and over! Trust me, more people are writing songs than those five or six. Creativity has no test market, can't calibrate the sales, so why bother with expanding horizons? There'll always be another Media Whores out there to satiate the flock."

"You don't like the Media Whores?" he asks.

"Few people are as proud of those guys as I am."

He closes his magazine and leans forward to challenge me. "If what you're saying about radio is true, then why do people listen to it?"

"Mediocrity is a natural by-product of democracy. It's just one of those things. Our media controls the public mind with an underlying bias. Corporations own the media, and they decide the trends. Take rock and roll, for instance. As long as the kids *think* they're on the edge, then everything is fine within the machine. If kids dress punk and listen to a sugar-coated replica of the real thing with the same name, then it discredits the whole underground genre from the beginning. A lie is most effective in a field of truths. If something like punk threatens the machine, the system will strangle it by popularizing a cartoon version. And that is what we have seen of 1990's music."

"So *why* are you going to Kansas City?" he asks.

"My best friend died recently."

"Oh...was this person a musician, too?"

"Yes. Inspired my life, as a matter-of-fact."

Out the window, floating clumps of misty clouds cast large shadows on the ground below. The sun angles overhead, preparing its dissent toward the horizon amidst the thicker clouds.

The young kid had finally fallen silent.

I reach into my bag, pulling out a decorative wedding invitation with a postmark of the previous year. It was an event I had intended for years to share the starring role. Myself and the bride, Jill Johnson. The worn envelope represents something of closure for me. Our idealism sent us down separate paths. I'm happy the decision has worked out for her.

I lean back in the chair and close my eyes to avoid further conversation.

A while later, I deliver my attention to the ground below. I spy a small town hidden under the mask of gray clouds. I study the streets, finding it strikingly similar to the layout of Chanute, Kansas. A road stretches north out of town, leading into another smaller village. An enormous cavity rests on the south side as I had guessed—the little town of Humboldt. I keep my eye on the road, one I had traveled many times before. A tiny hill spans from east to west, Humboldt Hill. The road ends at Iola. I can scarcely see motion on the streets below, unchanged for a quarter century. One blink and it's all just a bad memory.

We continue north over highway 59. In the far distance, I can see the flatlands churn with wooded hills. Small patches of snow spot the landscape, filling ditches by roadsides stretched miles through linear rows of brown, skeletal trees. Tiny towns pass below the plane, just another speed trap for the unsuspecting motorists.

The ground's contour begins to ripple as the landscape seems to have been graced by a coat of white paint. Suddenly, the horizon fills with the lights and activity of a large metropolitan area spread throughout the land like a mystical city.

"We're starting our descent into KCI airport," the Captain comments lazily through the speaker. "For you basketball fans, below us out the right side of the plane is Lawrence, Kansas—home of the Kansas Jayhawks."

The football stadium on the north edge of campus is lit like a green soup bowl. Up the hill, a small hockey game is in progress on Lake Potter. The entire north side of Mount Oread is housing the perfect slope for a troupe of sleds under the Campanile Tower.

Massachusetts Street is alive with traffic, all crammed down the narrow avenue of shops. The courthouse rests like an enormous stone block at the south end.

I follow 15th Street into the country in search of the dormant Outhouse. Small shacks are stretched far apart through the bare, harvested fields. The venue had been closed years ago, following a brief stint as a strip bar. It is nowhere to be found, only its legend standing erect in a field, just a footnote in the town's musical history.

The plane veers east to Kansas City. I look back at the glowing skyline of Lawrence, almost clear from view as the plane sinks into the gray sky of a harsh midwestern winter.

It was a hot summer day. The leaves had faded to a dull green—their nutrients exhausted from the bright sun overhead.

Clutching the Ranchero's proof of insurance with sweaty hands, I returned to the courthouse once again. Its grayish stone was dry from a long summer. My footsteps reverberated through the small building with a ghostly presence as I returned to the end of the line.

The dreadlocks of my mohawk hung to my chest, brought back to their natural color of sandy-brown. My empty stomach ached from the stress of moving a few weeks earlier. The job hunt had turned up nothing, and the small amount of money saved from the previous two years of mailorder was dwindling fast. I desperately needed work.

"Pizza?"

I turned to a short, stocky Native American carrying two flat pizza boxes. Long, black hair streamed down his shoulders. An archer's arrow was tattooed on his darkly tanned forearm with the words *Red Power* over it.

One of the clerks waved a rotund arm, signaling him excitedly. He couldn't have missed her. He placed the pizza box in her healthy hands and snatched the money that lie on the counter.

As he turned to leave, I suddenly realized I recognized him from the Outhouse, years prior. This stranger's voice had inspired me at a vital time in my life.

"Norm?" I muttered as he passed. He stopped dead in his tracks to face me, a perfect stranger. "You sang for the Jerk Offs?"

He nodded.

"I have your record. I saw you guys open Black Flag. You were one of my all-time favorites."

His eyes widened with a sincere and humble smile. "Gosh...thanks!"

"Did you break up?"

"No...not that I've heard of, at least. They never tell me anything...we're playing in a couple weeks, I think."

"I still listen to that record. I wore it out when I bought it."

"I'm flattered. We talk about doing another one. We have...organizational problems." His voice carried with it the innocent laughter of a child. His calm presence was contagious. My own posture loosened comfortably in accordance. "Thanks for the compliment. It really means a lot...you know, coming from a stranger in the courthouse."

"Just moved to town," I told him. "You wouldn't happen to know where I could get a job, would you?"

"You could try Pizza Shuttle. They hire everyone. If you're in a band, it's the place to work." He shot a quick glance at the clock. "Go down there—23rd and Ousdahl Street. They'll hire you as long as you don't use my name as a reference." He gave a brief and sincere smile before turning to leave. He took the time to tickle the bells hanging from the door's tacky decorations. It reverberated through the hall in an annoying clamor like the bells of Notre Dame.

"Next," the large woman behind the counter groaned.

I approached with sleek apprehension, happy to not be helped by the other cranky woman who sent me out to my car the first time. I placed my information on the counter. She snatched up the papers with thick and pale fingers ornamented with cheap rings of gold. Long, red nails the color of Coca-Cola Classic cans clicked on the wooden tabletop as she scanned my information. I waited for her to send me for some bureaucratic proof of something or other. Instead, she casually requested the fee as she lifted a tiny sticker from the desk. I handed her the money and swiped the sticker from her slow hands.

"Next," she grumbled as I hustled out into the blinding light of mid-day.

Crouching behind the Ranchero, I wiped the dust off the license plate, rubbing firmly against the sticker in the upper left corner. The golden AL shined brightly against the navy blue background that represented the county of Allen, the county to which the vehicle was registered.

I meticulously placed the new sticker over it to conceal the evidence of history. The shiny new DG shimmered of gold in the summer sun, officially declaring me a native of Lawrence, Kansas. Just like an eraser on a chalk board, my past was all just a memory, and my future, well...

"Can I get an application?" I asked the girl behind the counter at the pizza joint.

She stared at me with blood-shot eyes as she sloppily chewed her gum. Slowly, she reached below the counter, stirring a mess of papers before slapping an application in front of me. Yellow hair streamed from underneath her cap. "Here."

"Thanks," I replied, taking a seat at one of two dining tables inside the doorway.

I took a moment to scan the environment for which I was requesting to be a part. The walls were a blinding shade of yellow. The phone rang furiously in the background. It had an atmosphere of some demented waiting room, equally clean. There was virtually nothing relaxing about the place. I figured I would fit well.

I slowly filled out the application. Upon signing the bottom, I brought it to a thin yet muscular man holding firmly to an enormous pizza peel. A pack of Camels was rolled up in the sleeve of his Def Leppard concert shirt. Acid-washed jeans pegged at the ankle fit quite snugly against his slim legs. His body was compact and muscular. He looked like a gladiator of the working class, a hands-on kind of guy.

"Tom," he announced himself as he clutched the peel gallantly. "What do you got here?"

I placed the application in his callused hands.

He looked it over from top to bottom, too quickly to actually be reading it. "We're pretty well off now," he said shortly. "If you want to come back next weekend, we may have something."

"What day?" I asked.

"Oh...I guess Sunday."

"What time?"

"Uh...like five o'clock."

Finally! A positive response! It was the first *maybe* I had received. Things were looking up.

When I stood at the counter the next Sunday at five o'clock sharp, he told me: "Come by next Tuesday. I'm too busy to talk now."

"What time?"

"I don't care. Say...six."

When I stood at the counter the following Tuesday at six o'clock: "Come by this weekend, maybe we'll have something then."

The next weekend he shook his head and greeted me once again.

"Well, let me be honest," he said with a condescending smirk. I could see in his fiery eyes that he had no qualms about telling it as straight as he saw it. "I think your hair is a disgusting mess. No offense, but do you ever wash it? This is a food establishment with an image to maintain." He shook his head. "Can you pull that shit back if you wear a hat?"

"Of course."

"Do you have a car that runs decent?"

"Yeah, it's a Ranchero. It runs like a champion."

"Do you know the town very well?"

"Uh...yeah."

He scratched his chin, glanced at the clock, then back at me. Taking a split second to make sure no pizzas had come through the conveyor oven, he smiled. "All right. Come in Wednesday at four-thirty and I'll start you as a night-shift delivery driver. My name's Tom, ask for me when you get here—you better show up."

"Thanks, Tom. You made a wise choice."

"Yeah, whatever...I'll see you on Wednesday. I'm busy now, so..."

My bedroom was bare with an annoying glare from the afternoon sun. The window was painted shut, yet a draft had somehow mysteriously penetrated. My few possessions were still packed away in brown cardboard boxes. It was a temporary sublease. I planned to live there no longer than I had to.

"Frank!" one of the hippies screamed up the stairs at me. "Some guy named Stanley is here."

I leaped up from my lazy slumber and rushed down the stairs. When our eyes met, we embraced one another with smiles, and it seemed only like yesterday that I had left.

"Where's the ball and chain?" I asked him.

"She's coming. Making her drag the bags in, you know...put the Ol' Lady to work."

"My ass," Claire said as she rushed through the door with a small duffle bag over her shoulder. "How's it hanging, Frank?"

"Pretty low. Having you guys here should change that."

"You know just what to say, don't you?" she replied happily as she fixed her lovely eyes on me.

"Around you? Yes. Are you folks hungry?"

They both nodded. We wasted no time finding the door.

The crisp air smelt of rich color, the sound of my partner's voice warm to the ear. There was a weightless feeling in its warmth. It was good not to spend the evening alone for a change.

The meandering stream of time eventually delivered us into the student ghettos where a house-party was rumored to be. We parked off Tennessee, about a block from a massive social event that bled into the street, saturating the shanty neighborhood with conversation of the menial sort. Loud, aggressive music generated from the historically ancient house.

We merged in the factions clumped like rice. The space between each clique was a maze to the house. The music lured us like cheese to the laboratory rat, a quest to be amongst the living. We climbed the steps of the porch, each lined with rugged adolescents—students by day, pan-handlers by night—attending the University by their parents' funding.

"Two bucks," the roguish tough patrolling the door demanded.

"Why?" I asked. "That's three dollars too much."

"To pay for the beer. It's my place that's being wrecked. Two bucks."

"I don't even drink, what the hell? Are the Pain Killers playing? That's what I heard."

"Their last show," he said. "Bass player quit. He's moving to Rhode Island to join Verbal Assault. See them now or never again."

"Surely you jest," I challenged.

"Curtains for the Pain Killers. Two bucks, or get the hell off my porch."

We reluctantly handed over our cash and waded through the dense sludge of hipsters to the dining room where the Pain Killers were in the middle of their set. We watched attentively, drinking the history of each song's final performance.

Merle's hair had grown out a natural shade of brown since last I had seen him. It was cut into a tight, starchy flat-top. He looked good.

112

They broke into their final number with great intensity, ending abruptly with applause. The room was alive with smiles and handshakes. I wandered up to them, taking my place in line to speak with Merle. With the demise of the band, he was now no more than another face in the crowd, yet somehow it didn't quite fit him.

"Frank," he said to me. "I never forget a face, especially one attached to those dreadlocks. I saw you in *Maximum RockNRoll*. You're quite the mover and shaker in those parts, huh?"

"You saw that? I'm flattered."

"Why? Everyone reads that rag. How's the band?"

"No band. I live up here now," I told him.

"Really? We do, too. Moved over the summer."

"I hear your bassist is joining Verbal Assault," I pried.

"Yeah, I hope it works out. So, what did you play in your band? Bass?"

"No, I was the singer."

"We should talk. Do you know James Macey? He was in Cock Ring from Topeka. Not familiar? They played the Outhouse a few times. Anyway, he's a drummer. I play guitar. I'm not really interested in singing these days. Care to jam sometime? We could do some crappy renditions of Weirdos songs or something. Just for kicks."

"When?" I asked.

"I'll call you. I'd like to hear your old band. You made a tape, didn't you?"

I grabbed a pen from Claire's purse and scratched my number on the edge of a deposit slip. "I'll bring one."

"Cool," he said, taking the number and sticking it in his ear. "I'll call you. Probably tomorrow."

"Sounds good."

"Later, gator." His eyes caught the gaze of an on-looking girl that yanked at him like a magnet.

"Sounds like a band opportunity," Stanley told me over the loud ruckus of the party.

"Charming guy," Claire said. "Two points off for being so aware of it, though."

"He could probably sell ice in Greenland," Stanley said. "Watch guys like that. Sometimes as crooked as a dog's dick."

"I think he's on the level," I said. "He's just...what would I say? Zealous?"

"Yeah, good word," Claire mumbled. "Zealous..."

"Sounds promising," Stanley decided. "Spirits high? Good...I have some news that you probably won't like. We inherited my house. It was my mother's wedding present to us. She's moving back to Yates Center. We pick up the payments next month."

"What about college?" I asked. "I thought you were moving up here with me!"

"I could go to the JuCo. Then KU eventually."

"While owning the house?" I questioned, clearly unable to cover my annoyance. "Weren't you raised in that house? There's so much in the world to experience, I'd hate for you never to leave home—literally."

"I won't stay forever," he challenged defensively. "It's a good deal, and I could probably get a decent job through my family to save some money. All the while we can fix up the house and sell it, take the money and be that far ahead."

"Don't let so much potential waste away in that town."

"That won't happen," he insisted.

"I hope not."

"Don't get all heavy," Claire warned both of us. "Do you see any of your coworkers at this party, Frank?"

"No, I don't know anybody in this town."

"Let's move around, do some crowd-watching," she suggested. "Nothing makes me feel better about myself than watching others."

We ended up on the porch where the gibberish ramblings absorbed into the comfortable night air.

"Can you imagine what the world would be like if humans had tails?" Claire asked. "I think you'd have a nice tail, Stanley. Do you think it'd be a body part we'd cover?"

"I'm sure Christians would have found something evil about it," Stanley sighed.

"I wonder what our tails would be like, dogs or cats," Claire pondered. "Cats are really sleek, with slow, liquid motions. Dogs are clumsy and wag theirs when they get excited."

"If we used it like dogs, it'd add a new element to bluffing during card games," Stanley said. "I could see a bunch of guys watching a stag film as some girl wags her tail. *Call me.*"

"Speaking of dogs," Claire began, "do you think time is different to them? That their whole body is on a faster level, and that's why they die sooner than we do? I wonder if when we walk, they see us as if we're in slow motion, and when we talk, they hear...us...like...this."

"I bet gravity plays a role with smaller creatures," Stanley said. "Like flies. I'm sure we move in slow, slow motion to them."

"Do you think there are variations of gravity on this planet where time would pass slower or faster to us?" Claire asked. "If gravity weren't as strong, it would lessen time, wouldn't it?"

"I think so," Stanley replied, unsure.

"Couldn't there be inconsistencies where time just gets kind of screwy? That could cause some major distortions to the brain," she said. "You know how some places just feel kind of funky? I wonder if the gravity is simply abnormal to our bodies."

"Who knows," Stanley said. "Have you noticed when a day seems to drag that other people tend to comment on it, too? I don't think we truly understand time. It's not as linear as we believe."

"I was thinking the other day just how Freud was really onto something," Claire said. "Everything—every logo, every piece of equipment is based around phallic representation or the inversion. What would a world be like where an asexual being was the dominant species?"

"Their culture would advance a lot faster without that ignorant chase constantly ruling the mind," Stanley said. "Probably no wars."

"Their daily living?" she asked. "What would their society be like?"

"Entirely different," Stanley said. "Hmm...makes me want to polish my shotgun just thinking about it. That's a strange reaction, isn't it?"

"You guys ever been to Village Inn?" she asked.

"Do they have shotguns there?"

"Let's go get some coffee," she said. "The night is young...and so are we."

The grill of my Ranchero blurred in the reflection of the Toyota truck's shiny black paint. I looked up the steep hill of Mount Oread to the house numbered 1011.

The porch overlooked the traffic of Tennessee. Cars raced down the street, the southbound vein of the student ghettos. I climbed the concrete steps to my destination thus far in life. The old wooden porch was sturdy and well managed. A thin layer of green turf covered the surface. There was a faint scent of flowers, but none were to be seen.

I pushed both doorbells—one for the second floor apartment, the other for the first. With the crescendo of approaching footsteps, the door creaked open. A tall, gangly guy, roughly my own age stared curiously through the screen.

"You Frank?" he questioned, his wiry glasses low on his nose. He pushed them up nervously with a wrinkled brow and studied me, expressionless.

"You James?" I asked.

"Yeah, come on in," he offered loosely.

I followed him into the first floor living room. The blue sofa matched the stiff fabric of the curtains. A copy of Munch's *The Scream* was mounted and tacked to the white wall. The fragrance of vanilla sifted up into the air from a Waxman candle. A corkboard coaster rested under a sweaty glass of grape juice on the oak coffee table. The place was immaculately clean.

"Don't mind the mess," he told me.

"James!" Merle screamed from the kitchen. "Was it Frank?"

"Yeah," he responded loudly. He glanced at me quickly with nervous tension as he ran his long fingers through his thick, short hair. "Did you bring your tape?" he asked the floor.

"Sure did, here it is." I held it out across the coffee table, releasing it into his hand.

"*Time spent beating around the bush*," he read aloud with a rigid chuckle. "What will you kids think of next..."

"Hey, Frank," Merle greeted with a tall glass of whole milk. A dark blue bowler's shirt hung loosely over his shoulders, unbuttoned. It revealed his smooth chest, firm with muscle. The nametag embroidered on the breast was *Skip*. Plaid Ocean Pacific jams hung over his knees, covering his hairy legs. A long dog chain hung around his neck with a silver padlock fastened over his hairless chest.

"Has your bassist left yet?" I asked as James put the Fluorescent Condoms cassette in the tape deck.

"Left over the weekend," he told me.

"What about the rest of the Pain Killers?"

"They're taking off for Seattle," he said, taking a sip with a residual white mustache. "Everyone's moving there. They think it's this country's secret haven. No one would guess without being on the Sub-Pop seven-inch mailing list. The music scene is said to be thriving, on the verge of an explosion. Who knows..."

"Are you ready to hear this?" James asked as he pressed *Play* on the cassette deck.

With a brief silence of leader tape, the music burst through the room. Its poor quality seemed strangely improper to the nicely kept quarters.

"Great energy," Merle commented casually between soft sips of milk.

"Who's the drummer?" James asked.

"A friend, no one you'd know. His name's Thik."

"You sound pretty angst-ridden," Merle mused. "Right on. What's this one called?"

"*Persistence, Resistance*."

115

"Great song," he mumbled when it ended. "That's enough, stop the tape, James. I like it."

"Yeah," James agreed as he ended the quick presentation.

A thick feeling of awkward curiosity had suddenly left the room, and it wasn't until it was removed that I realized its presence.

We went down into the basement through a long stone corridor. Pipes from various plumbing fixtures lined the ceiling like an old speakeasy. At the far end, the small practice room awaited with enticingly soft light. The stone walls were impressively decorated with a montage of colored fliers. After a few casual comments amongst themselves, they squeezed behind their instruments. I walked up to the dead microphone and edged my lips romantically close.

"Well," Merle said, gripping the neck of his black guitar. "We know a lot of Black Flag's *Damaged*, a couple tracks from Circle Jerks' *Group Sex*—"

"How about a Pain Killers song?" I requested.

Merle's expression turned to a pompous smile. "Flattery will get you everywhere with me, Frank."

I named the song and we broke into it fast and heavy. The room was suffocating with tension and discomfort from lack of familiarity. We managed about an hour of old punk rock songs before our repertoire of known covers concluded.

"Sounded good," James surmised, standing firmly over the drum set. "Can you tell I've only been playing about three months now, Frank?"

"I thought you were in a different band before this?" I asked.

"I played bass. I sucked at bass, so I'm switching to drums. I make a better drummer."

"Sounded really good, really strong," Merle said to James. "So what about a bass player? Do you know someone, Frank?"

"No—well, I have a friend who plays bass, but I don't think he'll be moving here after all."

"I think the Philistines would be a cool band name," James suggested.

"Yeah, if you sound like the Cure or the Smiths," Merle said. "What do you think, Frank? Do you feel up to pursuing this?"

"Absolutely."

"The covers were pretty elusive so far as what I plan to write," Merle said. "Punk is dead. I'm tired of doing punk. Tired of punk rockers. We're talking about a slower, more powerful approach." He placed his guitar on the shiny metal stand. "I'll call you when things solidify more, Frank. I think we can work with this. Would you be against two guitars? My coworker at the record store is a great lead."

"That's fine, whatever," I said enthusiastically. "Let's do it."

Looking at the ceiling of my bedroom, I had never noticed that the cracks seemed to form a face, with two watermarks for eyes. I'd never be able to look at the wall again without the gaze being reflected. This was my perception. Our eyes retrieve information, our minds do the sorting, constructing the reality in which we choose to exist. In my lonely room, another face smiled gravely upon me, and I appreciated the company.

I felt myself wandering in the cold, dark stretch between hope and reality, dream and accomplishment. It seemed as if I were rushing to an invisible light, and all I knew was the start and finish. The roadmap between the two points remained elusive. I ached with a hunger to explore.

116

The phone rang. I stood firmly on the hardwood floor and stretched to reach it.

"Frank?" a familiar voice asked. "This is Merle. I got a bass player! We jammed the other night and it worked out really well. In fact, we have three songs prepared. Want to come over tomorrow night?"

I felt a sigh of relief overwhelm me. "Definitely."

"How about seven at my place again?" he asked.

"Sounds great."

"By the way, my coworker and I got together and things seemed cool. So that second guitar may be worked in as well."

"Whatever, I just want to play," I told him. "I've been sitting here too long."

"You'll like our songs. They sound just like what's happening in the music scene these days. I think there's a lot of potential for success. Are you ready to be adored by the masses? You've got the right image. Your dreads are killer!"

"Thanks. So the songs—are they intense?"

"Yeah, they're cool," he assured me casually. "They aren't very fast, but neither is the music we're trying to play. They'd make a good demo tape. We could send them out to all the labels and see what happens. Maybe we could get signed and hit the road in style."

"It must sound really good by the way you're talking. Tomorrow at seven? I'll be there."

"It's about that time," I told Stanley over the phone the following evening. "I should be going."

"Don't forget me when you're the man," he told me. "By the way, don't throw out that can of pop when you're a success. I'll drink it. Give it to us lowly working-class types."

I laughed, recalling the soda pop analogy that would equate to my success. "Good memory. Today's the day, I can tell."

"Good luck. Talk at you soon."

"Later on..."

I rushed out into the tranquil serenity of summer's end.

I stepped up to the Ranchero, fumbling with the keys. The old car sparkled a dull gray in the fading light of the descending sun. Pink and orange clouds splattered the western sky. I stopped a moment to examine the beauty of it as the excitement of a full band rehearsal danced wildly around the fires of my faith. This was it. This was the beginning for me. My dream realized. I pictured the square frame of a soda machine standing before me with a glowing slot beckoning quarters. I would reach into my pocket, relieving myself of a weighty load of silver to purchase one canned beverage I didn't care to possess. The can would slam to the bottom, its cold exterior collecting condensation as I would walk away—a prize for the next wandering soul.

I turned the ignition of the Ranchero and proceeded to Merle's place. A smile of wild excitement engulfed my face as I rang the doorbell.

"Frank!" Merle exclaimed happily. "Come on in. Everyone's here."

I followed him into the living room where a congregation of stylish rockers were gathered.

"Everyone, this is Frank," Merle said. "Frank, this is everyone. You've already met James. This is my coworker Raymond, he plays a mean guitar and can solo like Vai—I jest, of course. He was in a band from Kansas City called Staple Diet. Never heard of them? A lot of people really dug them and that'll help us when we play. By

117

the way, you'll need to get out there and socialize so people are familiar with you. Nothing wrong with a little ass-smooching. This handsome lad is Jeremy, the bassist. Did you ever see a band called the Monotonous Thugs? No? Well, they were from Lincoln—I mean, Omaha. He was the rhythm guitarist. They had a record out on this independent label from Pennsylvania, and maybe we could use that connection as leverage. Frank here knows how to push a band. He's been in *Maximum RockNRoll* several times."

"Let's do it," James announced excitedly as he led us into the musty basement.

"Anybody thought of a name?" Jeremy asked with an annoying voice that cracked like an adolescent. "Nothing too offensive, don't want to turn off the wrong people."

"I like the Philistines," James said as we entered the small practice room. "Or the Samaritans."

"I've been thinking about it," Jeremy began, "and I think we should be called the Twirps."

"Sounds too punk," James resolved quickly.

Everyone took their places behind the instruments. The room was snug tight with just enough space to stand perfectly motionless. My ears buzzed with the activation of amplifiers geared for high volume.

"You'll be surprised how much we got it together," Merle told me with a devious grin. "Should we go through the chunky one first, or the slow one?"

"The slow one," James said.

Jeremy tapped on the thickest string with his fat pick. He gripped the tuning peg with his left hand and slowly tuned the bass from E down to D for a more guttural crunch. "Ready."

James clicked the sticks together four times, releasing the blast of music like the turblence of a Kansas tornado. It was as thick as snot, and as slow as one would imagine moving through a room of it. The dual guitars chopped in unison for space, each playing the same chords for optimum power. The drums smashed slowly, firmly with force. It was through and through the grungy sound of Seattle as heard on KJHK. More than that, it was Metal by another name. Metal in a very pure sense—a strange concoction of one part Black Sabbath and one part latter Black Flag. The Black Flag portion lacked the raw uncontrollable anger, leaving an empty, eroded shell of what once was defiance turned fashionably friendly. Its aggression was a mockery for all that it stood. There was no danger in it. It had been done for decades. As fads go, a new label was slapped on it, aided with better technology for instant regurgitation of trend resurrection.

I liked what I heard. In fact, I could appreciate every effort created. Yet that was the obvious conclusion. Everything I deemed sacred in music was betrayed by its accessibility. It could easily have been theme music to those who sought to destroy me in years past. I felt a resistance to it.

As the music ended, all eyes looked upon me—the sole critic, the first of many for them—and possibly the harshest.

"Well," Merle said. "Do you see some potential?"

"I do," I told him objectively. "I could totally hear that on college radio, selling hundreds of albums."

"Cool!" he replied. "Want to hear the next? We only have two more...so far."

"Chunky," James announced as he introduced the song with four clicks.

The wall bombarded me again. The force and volume sent a chill down my spine. It had power, I stood firmly behind that. Yet, power comes and goes with those

118

conning the masses. Integrity maintains beyond death in the creation that the creator bled. Nothing oozed from these melodies. There were no wounds from which they poured. A different motivation had spawned these songs. A motivation generated not by passion, but by a need for recognition from a faceless public.

"What do you think?" James asked me at the demise of the second song.

"What did you call it? Chunky?"

"We titled them as we thought they felt," Merle explained.

"Chunky for sure. Good choice," I said. "That chorus has a hook from hell, you could catch Jaws with that. What's the third one?"

They continued with their blistering onslaught of controlled noise, sluggishly churning the momentum with fueled adrenaline. Their hands bounced firmly against their instruments to the beat. It was infectious. I, too, felt the urge to unify with the drone, my head bobbing like a headbanger at a Mötley Crüe concert.

"Excellent demonstration, guys," I said as they completed the third and final song. "You've written some tight songs with seriously strong catches. I think you'll see some great feedback when you play this stuff live."

"The kids love it," Merle joked. "So?"

I stood silently a moment, wondering what to say and how to say it. "Merle, let's chat, shall we?"

His smile quickly washed away. "Sure."

We walked uncomfortably into the tiny backyard by the alley.

"What's up, sailor?" he asked.

"You guys are onto something," I told him in a no-bullshit tongue. "I'm searching to be onto something else."

"What's the problem?"

"I guess I have a jaded opinion, and maybe I'm too motivated by revenge and hatred, but it's not as pissed off as I'd like it to be."

"It's not heavy enough?" he asked.

"Plenty heavy. It's not that. I believe I need the aggression of straight-forward hardcore."

"Punk is passé," he insisted. "Time to move on."

"Time isn't a concern to me. It's what I feel, and how I'd like my emotions expressed. If there isn't an audience, that's okay. It's the strength of communication, and punk is the vehicle for me. It's what I need to do."

"Is what we're doing that far from punk?" he asked.

"Yes, and no. No to the consumer, yes to me."

"We could do some faster songs."

"Your songs are great. It's how I interpret them. I never was into the Metal thing. Never liked Judas Priest or Iron Maiden."

I could feel his defensiveness in his tightened posture. "We aren't doing Metal."

"I really don't know what to say," I told him grudgingly. "I'd hate to leave you guys in the cold, but I just don't know if I could give all that I'd want to give. I wouldn't want to let you down."

"Well, if that's what you want..."

"I wouldn't be satisfied with my contributions," I said. "In turn, you wouldn't, either."

He smiled. "We'll be in touch. I have your number."

"Use it," I implored him. "I'm a stranger in town."

"I will, Frank."

                              *   *   *

A brisk summer wind worked its way through the back lot of Pizza Shuttle. Norm stood in front of me, absorbing the details of my recent musical exploits. I could sense the compassion in his concentrated stare as I presented the details of the experience. He agreed with my decision.

"You should go to Hashinger Hall some night," he told me. "All the art students live there. Surely some are musicians. You'll find something. Life runs its course, and your plans are irrelevant to its current."

I nodded.

"Go to Hash Hall. Even if you don't meet music people, you'll meet people regardless."

"I will, and thanks. I'll keep my hopes high."

He gave a friendly smile. I hadn't noticed before that he had a missing front tooth. The braids hanging over his ears twisted like cobras as his head turned from side to side. "Watch out for hope. The mind can concoct some absurd illusions. Imagination can taint your vision, a blanket over your limits of control. Relax, my friend. Smell the air. Can you smell that?"

I inhaled deeply. "French fries?"

"Smells great, huh? Coming all the way from Arby's or Perkin's, but who cares? It's a moment in our lives. The sun is about to set, see that? Beautiful, isn't it?"

I looked to the horizon over the tops of the run-down buildings to a clear blue sky, slightly dulled by a thick and sticky atmosphere. "Beautiful? Sure."

"Ah, but think, once that sun goes down, this day will never be lived again," he said. "Only in memory. We live now. We grow old tomorrow. It's in your heart, my friend. Nowhere else. Certainly not your pocket. Look at that sunset. There's more to appreciation than the aesthetic. *It's your life.* Beautiful, isn't it?"

The following afternoon, I found a vacant parking space somewhere by Ellsworth Hall and walked the short distance to Hashinger. The setting sun reflected a tasty shade of orange on the windows. The weathered bricks were a soothing backdrop, shifting the dominance of stature to beauty, then back.

I walked up the short steps and past the hippies with their acoustic guitars and greasy hair. The building's old interior accurately represented the dated exterior.

"Can I help you?" the girl behind the wooden counter asked me.

"Maybe," I said. "Do you know a lot of the people who stay here?"

"Some. Why?"

"I'm hoping to get a band together—"

"Isn't everybody in this town?" she resolved. "Let me guess—do you sing or play guitar?"

"I sing."

"Figures. What kind of music?" she asked.

"Hardcore."

"Figures. No, I really don't—wait. There's this girl—"

"Let me guess, she plays bass."

"Yeah, how'd you know?"

"Figures," I said. "Go ahead."

"Her name is Lilith. I could ask her—"

"I play guitar," a voice interjected. A young man stood alone, eavesdropping on our conversation as he browsed articles of junk mail. "What do you have going on?"

120

"At this point?" I asked, looking at his properly trimmed goatee and thick sideburns extending from a shaved head. He wore a knitted cap despite the warmth of summer's final stand. "I don't have anything other than a great desire."

"Let's go out and talk," he said quite seriously, leading me to the front steps where all the hippy children sat. "So, what do you do? Sing?"

I nodded.

"Ever sang in a band?" he asked.

"I was in a band called the Fluorescent Condoms."

"Never heard of them. I was in a band from Kansas City. Dead Youth. Heard of us?"

I shook my head.

"A lot of people have," he returned defensively. "We never performed, but we knew a lot of people."

"Have you played a long time?"

"About four months or so. I'm good enough," he assured me as a couple girls walked up the steps with shifty hips. "Hey, Jennifer, how are you?"

She rolled her eyes and passed without hesitation.

"I need to be in a band," he said. "Girls really dig guys in bands."

"So I've heard."

"What kind of hardcore?" he asked. "Not that New York Metal shit that's posing as punk rock, I hope. Metal will kill punk, yet."

Music to my ears, I thought. "No. Straight-forward hardcore."

"77 or Oi?"

"Neither. Something like the Jerk Offs. Like False Prophets' faster songs, or D.I.—"

"Dag Nasty?" he asked.

"Sure."

"Social Distortion?"

"They suck," I confided to the response of a sagging jaw. "Mike Ness is weak-minded idiot. Mommy's little poser...no offense, just an opinion."

"That's fine, I have a lot of strong opinions myself."

"I wouldn't want to get all thick with the politics," I warned hesitantly. "A lot of punk bands wear their inane political perspectives like a badge. Political ideals come and go. I'd rather construct something a little more timeless."

"See, I have a need to speak to the people," he informed me. "I have some really important issues to get across. Most people don't know what's going on in the world, but I do."

"You do?" I asked.

"Uh-huh. I read a lot. I have fanzines coming in from everywhere. I probably have the largest collection of fanzines you'll ever see. I know what's going on in towns most people don't know exist."

"Wow, that's pretty impressive," I replied dully.

"There is no government," he revealed. "They find these people when they're children and groom them throughout their lives. Reagan knows, he is one of them."

"How do *you* know this?" I asked him. "Were you groomed? You going to be the President?"

"Hell, no! I'm an anarchist, and when I'm running things, anarchy will be the system."

"So, who is running everything now?" I questioned.

121

"The Illuminati. They've been running things since the beginning of time. Kennedy knew. Hitler knew. Napoleon, Caesar, Queen Elizabeth—they all knew."

"It's all a big conspiracy?"

"Oh, yeah. I can't tell you everything. I sometimes wish I didn't know all that I do."

"How do you know?" I asked again.

"Research. Some other sources...but mainly research. All those suicide cases at Jonestown, they were murders. The CIA. The public never saw the close-up pictures, the gunshot wounds in the heads of all those people. It was a concentration camp, an experiment by the government. One of these days, the shit's coming down. I'll be ready. That whole grape thing with Cezar Chavez? That was another experiment. They were spraying the workers with a chemical that turned them into mindless drones, killing machines for the New World Order. Cezar Chavez knew, he knew too much."

"Did the Illuminati kill Kennedy?" I asked.

"Ssshhhh! Not so loud! Yes. He was going to tell the people in Dallas, and they popped him."

"So, you've researched this?"

"Yeah. I'm also a member of the Church of the Sub-Genius. Bob knew everything, and they killed him, too."

"Bob?" I asked.

"Bob Dobbs. They say he's still alive, but I know better."

"Sounds like you're a marked man. Why would I want to be in a band with a guy who knew too much?"

He laughed proudly.

"I think you're taking the political articles in *Maximum RockNRoll* a bit too seriously," I told him. "They'll probably get you before we'd even play our first show."

"There's a lot of truth in those articles."

"Those articles are written by a bunch of kids," I said. "Let me guess, we never went to the moon?"

"We've had spacecraft since the turn of the century. You've heard of the massive waves of sightings of airships in the 1890's, and the foo-fighters in World War One, haven't you? Yeah, we had been to the moon several times. It's all conditioning. The public wouldn't be able to handle the truth, so it's slowly revealed. In the next ten years you'll be seeing a conditioning of the Zeta Reticuli beings."

"Huh?"

"The little space aliens with the gray skin, huge heads, big black eyes?"

"Yeah, like in Close Encounters," I said.

"Well, in ten years time, everybody will know that image. It'll become as commonly known as Mickey Mouse. T-shirts, bumper stickers—"

"Which one of you wants to be in the band?" a girl snarled over our stiff shoulders.

She looked down upon us with vague hostility. Her foot tapped impatiently, firmly. Her short, dyed fuscia hair was pulled back with a child's plastic bobby pins. Her forehead was marked with ridges from a permanent expression of disgust. Her pale white skin was flawlessly smooth, free of cosmetics.

"Both of us," I said.

"I play bass. I'm Lilith," she sneered.

"I'm Frank."

"Call me Bob. I like your hair."

122

"There's more to me than just a body, pal," she said with a firm, straight face. "The patriarchy of this country has you brain-washed! I expect a lot more from a couple guys with punk rock values and ideals."

"I was just referring to the dye in your hair. Sorry..."

She shot him a harsh glance, ignoring his retraction as she scratched the hair of her armpit. She put forth a great deal of effort to look unattractive, and seemed irritated by her failure at pulling it off.

"Hardcore, eh?" she asked firmly. "What do you play?"

"I play guitar and I'd sing a few songs."

"I sing," I replied modestly.

"That wouldn't make you the leader of the band," she warned me. "A band can only work if all the members have equal say."

"I agree," I replied.

"Do you guys eat meat?" she asked.

"No," Bob answered proudly.

"Why do you ask?" I questioned.

"I'm not going to be in a band with people who are doing nothing to save our environment. The goal of our band would be to save the planet before humans destroy it. Are you anarchists?"

"Yes, I am," Bob boasted. "I attend all the meetings of the Anarchist's Society. In fact, I've been elected to be on the council."

"I was late for a meeting once and they kicked me out," she said proudly, flaunting her wildly erratic behavior. Her eyes shifted to me. "So what about you?"

"No, I'm a realist," I replied. "Have you played long?"

"What, just because I'm a female you think I can't play? The last thing I need is to be in a band with a sexist."

"I'd write the songs," Bob said quickly. "I have a couple ideas. We'd need a good drummer, though."

"I've got some songs," Lilith said. "I'd need to sing some of the songs, too. I have something to say to this oppressive white male society. Paying women less than men, sexually harassing women in the workplace—males should be castrated and enslaved. I'm a stout Earth Firster, too."

"Yeah, I've researched some of their beliefs," Bob said, matter-of-factly. "They have a noble cause."

"So Earth First is all about stopping the destruction of this planet at all cost, even by ending lives?" I asked.

"Yeah, sure as hell! Humans are destroying the planet," she snarled.

"Environmental issues are issues of the preservation of life on this planet," I told her. "I fail to see the reasoning behind destroying life for the sake of environmentalism. It's a contradiction of terms. Your points and interests are counterproductive."

"You're a Nazi!" she shrieked. "And a sexist! I'm not going to talk to you. You clearly have no idea what is going on. Find some *man* to be in your fucking band."

We watched her stomp back inside. Her stride was awkwardly geared for a larger stature.

"Wow," Bob said. "What a great ass. Wonder what her deal was?"

"She's having trouble coping with the reality that she'll be voting Republican in five years," I said sarcastically.

"When we get our band going, we'll have babes like that at our disposal after each show. How about the name Rump Rangers?"

"It's getting late," I said as I stood to stretch my stiff limbs. "I'll see you around."

"What about our band?"

"Our *band*? Watch out for those Devildogs of the Illuminati. Later."

Dust spilled onto the Ranchero's hood like smoke from a brush fire. I could smell it seeping through the vents, reminding me of an old cellar. Suddenly, a light burst through the haze, catching my windshield. I pulled over and lowered the window as the cloud finally caught me. It paralyzed my vision as the light slowly approached, extended from a tiny flashlight.

A skinhead with a firm build bounded to my car. He shined the light through the window, into my eyes. "Three dollars." His dark hair was smoothly shaved into a crewcut. His sideburns reached down his forceful jawbone. He was quite attractive.

I slipped the money into his hands. "You're in the Jerk Offs, huh?"

His firm brow wrinkled from contemplation as he unsuccessfully tried to place me in his memory. He nodded.

"I'm just a fan," I told him. "No one you know."

"Specky," he said, reaching his hand into my car to shake mine.

His grip was firm and strong, much like his guitar technique. His arm was tattooed and powerful with rippling muscles. The sleeves of his T-shirt were rolled into orderly little folds. The basic black print across his chest bore the drawing of a mallet crashing down upon the words: *Smash Racism.*

"My name is Frank Smith."

"Actually," he began slowly, "you look familiar. Where have I seen you? Are you in a band?"

"I was." I stared deep into his stern, brown eyes. "The Fluorescent Condoms."

"Ah!" he said with a smile, signifying a recollection that caught me off guard. "From southeast Kansas."

I nodded slowly. "How the hell..."

"*Maximum RockNRoll*," he answered. "I remember your picture. How's the band?"

"Defunct. I moved here to find one."

"Good luck."

"Thanks. So, why the nickname, Specky?"

He stared down the dark stretch of road with a thoughtful, resilient expression. "I don't know. I don't remember, actually. One drunken night years ago that has stuck with me."

I smiled. "Hey, it was nice chatting."

"I'm sure we'll talk again," he said as I advanced through the gates.

I found a parking space near the entrance by the old, mangled tree. Its massive limbs sheltered the bonfire like a protective parent. The fire was small, proportionate to the crowd that had gathered to see a local show: The Jerk Offs and Troubled Youth.

"Hey, hey, Frankie!" a voice bellowed happily from the edge of the fields.

I turned to see Merle with his back turned to me, urinating.

"There are bathroom inside, you know," I told him as I stepped out of the Ranchero.

"That bathroom is a pit," he replied. "Hold on, let me shake it. Not too many times—may lead to other things." He zipped his black vinyl pants and stepped into the light next to me. His sunken eyes glared at me as if peering through a skull painted with sour cream. A horseshoe scar split his left eyebrow, giving the effect of a total of three.

"How's the band?" I asked.

"Not bad. I've been singing again."

"Got a band name yet?" I asked as we stumbled closer to the Outhouse. We lingered by the dumpster, just a few steps from the door.

"No, we talk about it all the time. Mostly, it leads to arguments, then we drop it. Nothing can destroy a fledgling band like choosing a name."

"Hey!" cried a friendly voice from the group that crowded the door. Norm stepped forward, separating himself from the rest. "Frank, Merle—what's the word?"

"Not much, buddy," Merle said cordially. "Are you guys going to let my band open the Jerk Offs when we get our shit together?"

"If *we* get our shit together enough to schedule another show," Norm joked, revealing that gap of a missing tooth in his unreserved smile. "How goes it, Frank?"

"Fine."

"Did you go to Hashinger Hall?" he asked me.

"I did."

"Hey fellas," Merle interrupted as his short attention found a new focus. "There's my future ex-girlfriend. Maybe I should go introduce myself. Talk at you later." He followed a buxom peroxide blond inside the Outhouse.

"How did it go?" Norm asked me.

"It was annoying and disheartening," I said.

He nodded casually as if he had anticipated my words. "You don't drink, do you?"

I shook my head.

"Did you ever?" he asked me.

"I have before, when I was like fifteen. Didn't do much except hinder my thoughts. I can't find anything less enjoyable than being unable to rationalize."

"I used to drink," he confessed. "Fought all the time, sought out trouble. I knew where to find it, too. The stereotypical Indian with a drinking problem, that was me. Couldn't say no, and if I had one, I had a six-pack. Hard times. That's probably when you had seen us. I was at my worst then."

"You don't drink now?" I asked.

"No. I don't need it. That's the problem with these people out here, they need some form of stimulus to activate their minds. They look to some substance to generate the creativity they lack, or the ambition. Just add beer. Couldn't do it on their own, had to have a crutch. Weak minds are accepting minds—minds that question nothing. It's the American way. Sieg Heil Old Glory—red, white, and blue—emphasis on white."

"What brought you to Lawrence, Norm?"

"Haskell Indian Junior College. I've since dropped out."

"How do you feel about being in a band with a skinhead?" I asked. "Aren't they notoriously racist?"

"Truth is…people are notoriously racist. Specky and his friends here in Lawrence are very much into unity and racial integration. There will always be those confused people out there, and those are the ones who get the exposure. It's ironic because skinheads have represented black and white unity for decades. The only thing that has changed is the focus of the attention from the press. Personally, it's not my thing. Too rigid. I prefer my individuality."

Another sporty car entered the mud lot. I could sense his attention meandering as the car emptied.

"There are more Kansas City people here than I would've guessed," he said.

"Do you know *all* these people?"

"Not all. I can generally tell where any of these people are from by how they wear themselves," he said. "Kansas City people always look good. They tend to have style and generally wear more black than, say, that group of Topekans over there. The dirty, rugged ones are almost always from Topeka. The plain T-shirt and faded jeans are Lawrence. Not always, but almost." The sound of a guitar aroused our attention. "Troubled Youth are about to start. Care to check them out?"

"Sure," I said as we stepped inside the venue.

The stage was kept by a group of haggardly men. Based on Norm's style association with local geography, these folks were from Topeka.

The bassist lingered back with the drums, standing close to a bottle of brandy that teetered on the edge of his Peavey amplifier. His face was hidden behind a veil of dirty blond bangs.

The guitarist took center-stage as the band broke into a sludgy introduction of tonal muck. His expressions were stiff, his posture poor and relaxed. His body was thin and pasty, smothered by a black leather biker jacket lined with spiked silver studs. His age was lost within the range of a couple decades from a premature graying. A comb hadn't touched his messy hair in years, it seemed.

"We're the Jerk Offs," the guitarist said into the microphone as the band released their rage through the gritty music. "I mean, we're Troubled—or the Jerk Youths...Youths...oh, hell—who gives a shit anyway?" He smiled bitterly at the crowd, revealing a silver cap amongst a row of crooked teeth. Razor stubble splotched his buttermilk skin. His green eyes peered through a small pair of wire-rimmed glasses with round lenses. "My name is Harold Saucerocket," he told the apathetic crowd. "This song is called *Rich White Kids From Kansas City Going to Outhouse Shows and Pretending They've Had It Rough.* The next song—should any of you pretentious low-lifes care—is called *Rich White Kids From Kansas City Who Went to Outhouse Shows Last Year And Now Belong to Fraternities.* You're all the same, you fucks."

The band's notorious vocalist, Billy Christ slithered pathetically to the stage with a bottle of Jack Daniel's swinging freely in his limp hand. He climbed the microphone stand, using it as support for his swaggering body. He appeared as the walking dead, straight from a George Romero flick. His presence was strangely captivating. He was born to be a superstar. Fate apparently had other plans.

He yanked a black pistol out of his pants and turned to the crowd. I could feel the discomfort infect the audience as he shoved the end of the barrel into his mouth and pulled the trigger. The dull click was drown by the vicious music. He smiled to himself with bent satisfaction as his teeth clamped the barrel of the gun. He dropped it at the edge of the stage and grabbed the microphone with a jittery hand. Black nail polish, partially chipped, covered his long nails.

As the music began, he smashed the microphone into his face to release the blood as he screeched the lyrics of bitter contempt. His jet-black, enormously spiky hair remained perfectly in place like the hide of a porcupine. He writhed slowly on the filthy stage, fueled by pure self-hatred. Blood dripped from his mouth, coloring his lips like a vampire fresh from a kiss. Between songs, he violently ridiculed the audience, provoking people to stand against him. No one seemed to care enough to oblige.

126

After a few songs, he stumbled off-stage, burying himself below a bottle. The band ended its set shortly after.

I waited with eager anticipation as the Jerk Offs systematically assembled their gear. Through persistence and time they had honored an allegiance of a small, yet devoted following—a following that resembled a kinship rather than teen idolization. They were the epitome of my wildest dream, adorned by their own stamina and will, purveyors of conviction and integrity. To some people present, it was just another local band playing a social event. To me, the Jerk Offs were one of the country's best.

As Norm took to the microphone, the crowd came alive with praise.

"Thank you," he said, unwinding the cord from the shaft of the microphone stand. "We're the Jerk Offs."

Fists shot into the air as the tension circulated throughout the vibrantly energized crowd. Norm paused casually to smile upon every member of the band. His expression was warm and strong. Collecting their attention, he raised the microphone to his thick lips. "This is a night of your life. Live it accordingly."

The band came to life with the throttling ferocity I had vividly remembered. The audience had become a torrent storm, a filter of the band's energetic pulse reamplified through the faith of some two hundred true believers. I was one of them.

Their music intoxicated me. I knew no bounds, no restrictions under the influence. Problems of the day deceased to triviality, paled by the illumination of a unified vision of hope and passion. They jumped from song to song, allowing no chance to rest. The set was long and vigorous, ending too short for me when nothing could have been too long.

"Thank you for your time," Norm said as the band walked off the stage after the final song of the last encore. "Keep the faith." He faced the audience, his braided hair swinging from side to side as he stepped down into the pit to greet the people who honored his respect.

I stood at a distance smiling, proud to be there.

"Excellent show," I told Norm the following day at work.

"Thanks." His attention remained fixed on the circular flats of dough that would soon be formed into pizza crusts. His hands were covered with flour. "It's very inspiring to be up there like that."

"You guys define the form. You deserve the respect."

"I'm glad you feel that way, but I can't continue."

I swallowed uncomfortably, suddenly overwhelmed and distraught. "Huh?"

"I've exhausted my fuel with the band. My path leads me another direction. My heart has a lot to learn. So, I'm leaving."

"Leaving? How? You can't do that. The band..."

"The band is great," he told me. "I love it, of course. But, it's time for me to move on."

"Norm!" Tom exclaimed from the other side of the oven. "Are you rolling dough, or gabbing?"

"That would be gabbing, sir," Norm answered as he wiped the white flour from his dark skin. "Look what this place is doing to me—I'm becoming white!"

"Where are you going?" I asked seriously.

"The Dakotas. In time for winter. I have some conditioning to withstand, to better myself, purify myself. I've got to build a sweat lodge to release the toxins and negative spirits. I can't begin my journey otherwise. I'll begin fasting on Sunday and stop a week later."

"When would you leave?"

"Sunday."

"Norm!" Tom scolded again. "Can't you work any faster?"

"Hey, man...it takes a long time to go this slow," he replied casually as he continued to roll out the balls of dough.

"What about the Jerk Offs?" I asked.

"For a whitey, your eyes are wide open," he said with a friendly smile. "Keep alive your perception. There's much to taste out there, you'll see. Mankind has left behind the creation of thousands of years. We don't have enough hours in our lifetimes to consume it all. Your faith is pure, your heart is strong. Live every day. Appreciate all that life gives. I believe you will, Frank."

"What does the band think of this?" I asked.

"They don't know yet. I'll tell them tonight."

"So, the Jerk Offs are defunct?"

"As it stands."

I had become entranced by the face on the wall. I felt a need to take a felt marker to the watermarks to better bring out the eyes. I needed another face inside my room, inside my life. The world outside was quiet. My room was quieter. The wind stirred the leaves on the trees, causing the harsh shadows to dance about the neighborhood. I shut my eyes, wishing it was late enough to become a new day.

The phone rang, and my eyes sprung open. I crept through the empty, quiet house to answer it.

"Hello."

"Frank?" asked a strong voice over the phone. "This is Specky. You've talked to Norm?"

"I have."

"So you know he's taking off on his spiritual adventure, so-to-speak?"

I laughed at Specky's lack of belief. "Yeah."

"He'll be sticking hot spikes through his chest, hanging from a tree for a couple days without eating. Sounds hardcore, doesn't it?"

"More hardcore than me," I admitted.

"Yeah, me, too. Want to stop in to catch a practice? We're getting together at around three o'clock."

"Where?"

"13th and Ohio. If you have a pen..."

I walked up the steps to the sidewalk, steeply towering over Ohio Street. I compared the house number to my notes. It fit the description: dark brown Victorian with white trim. I stepped up to the door and gently knocked.

Specky opened it quickly. "What goes, Frank? Come on in."

The remaining members of the Jerk Offs sat on a single couch. Musical equipment filled the rest of the sparse room, lit only by candles. The fragrance of peppermint struggled against a powerful musty odor. The peppermint was losing.

"Where's Norm?" I asked the three of them. The question was met with silence.

"Frank," Specky said, "do you know George, our bassist?"

"Nice to meet you, George."

128

He smiled briefly.

"This is Hazel," Specky said, introducing the short little girl drummer. "Witch Hazel, Hazel Nut—whatever you want."

"Hello," I offered politely.

She declined words with a simple nod.

"So, Frank," Specky said quickly, "you have the Jerk Offs' seven-inch, don't you?"

"Yes."

"Listen to it much?" George asked me.

"I lived by that record in high school."

George chuckled slightly. His piercing eyes revealed the rippling of deeper thoughts. His intelligence kept them well concealed.

Specky took a seat on the couch, facing me. "We talked last night, Norm included. We haven't heard your tape, but we'd like to jam. Nothing heavy. If things work out—"

"It's hard to say," George butted in bluntly. "A lot of people came to our shows to see Norm."

I struggled in disbelief over what I assumed to be hearing. "He had quite a presence, that's for sure."

"Give it a whirl?" Specky asked.

"Sure. I mean, absolutely."

They quickly took their places behind their respective instruments.

"Now?" I asked nervously.

Specky flipped the power switch on his amplifier. "Sure."

I felt hesitation restrict my movements, paralyzed by doubt and the fear of failure. Within two minutes of walking into the room, they were asking me to rehearse with them, and I had no idea what all of this was about. I could only hope that my intuition was correct.

"Any song off the first seven-inch?" Specky asked me.

"I know them all."

"The microphone is over here," Specky said wryly.

They watched every calculated step. I felt cowardly small, a dwarf amongst giants of accomplishment. I reached out to the microphone and tapped on it. The sound reverberated through the small room.

"It gets really loud in here," Specky warned. "I'm moving soon, though."

I stared into the black tip of the microphone, losing myself in the grooves of the wire mesh. I found great comfort within.

"Ready?" Specky asked the band. "Frank?"

"Maestro?" I whispered into the microphone.

"How about *Crack in the Wall*, Frank?"

I nodded slowly.

With closed eyes, the force of the bass guitar shot through the room. When the band kicked in, fronted by the ferocity of Specky's ravenous guitar, my muscles loosened immediately as the intensity flooded my fires of self doubt. I opened my eyes and stared straight into nothing, far beyond the restrictions of vision and perception.

I reared back and growled angrily into the microphone: "There's this huge white wall right here in front of me. It's a boundary, I know. Life is what I want it to be. It's filled with scuff marks, but I still can't be seen because I haven't done a thing. I still only dream..." The band roared tensely, properly below the weight of my delivery like

129

the soundtrack of my own passion. I was amazed how well my voice mixed with the mad fury of Specky's instrument. The thought of such a union pushed me harder. "I am just a spot, possibly only one inch tall, but someday I'll make my own crack in the wall!" I wailed furiously into the microphone, steering the song to a crashing halt.

"Jesus!" Specky exclaimed. "Yes...*Yes!*"

"*In Your Place*," George announced quickly.

With eight clicks, the song impacted me only to be consumed and conquered to the end. We ran through every track I knew, then rushed through the five songs again for posterity.

"Give us a minute," George said shortly as he removed the bass guitar and led the others into the kitchen.

I sat on the edge of the couch, feeling torn and ragged from the surging death of adrenaline. I felt cleansed and aligned, happy to have joined one of the nation's best for a good half hour.

"Frank," Specky said as the three of them returned to the living room. "Got a question, do you have an answer?"

"Want to join the band?" George asked squarely.

"To sing?" I asked in disbelief. I responded with the first thought that came to mind: "Man, the first crowd would kick my ass for even thinking I belonged—"

"Didn't ask what people will think," George said flatly.

Hazel stood quietly, watching.

"Of course I'd want to join," I decided quickly, pondering the ramifications. "*Yes.*"

"You're in," George declared poignantly. "Before Norm leaves, we can get the lyrics to the rest of the songs, the newer ones. We have some jambox recordings that would give you an idea of the phrasings."

"I'll see Norm tomorrow at work," I told them.

"I'll call him tonight and make sure he brings it," Specky said.

"We practice on Mondays, Wednesdays, and Thursdays," George continued. "Seven o'clock. We practice as late as midnight. If Norm brings the tape to you tomorrow, you'd have plenty of time to have *all* the songs figured out by Monday's practice. Also, bring a tape of your old band. Take all those days off from now on. No excuses."

"Congratulations, Frank," Specky said, shaking my hand. "You're one of us."

I shrugged my shoulders in disbelief. "Do I get a shirt?"

"The hell!" Stanley said over the phone, exasperated. "You're in the Jerk Offs? Listen, when you buy that can of pop, don't throw it away. I want it. I'll keep it the rest of my life. I'm serious."

I laughed. "Sure, man."

"I hate to rain on your parade, but the old ball and chain is heckling me to watch this movie."

"Sure, I understand," I said. "Tell her I said to fuck off, and I love her."

"I will. Take it easy, partner. I'll talk down to you later."

I gently sat the phone down. Within a few seconds, it rang again.

"Frank! This is Merle, I just talked to Specky and heard the news. Congratulations!"

"Thanks, man. How's your band doing?"

130

"Very well," he replied. "I guess you're who I'd talk to about getting a decent opening gig..."

I laughed. "Don't know anything about that yet."

"Man, someday I could tell my kids I was almost in a band with Frank Smith. By the way, we finally decided on a band name."

"Oh, yeah? What's that?"

"The Media Whores," he revealed.

"Has a certain ring to it. I like it."

"Can you see it in lights?" he asked.

"It's a keeper. Stick with that," I told him.

"Well, had to contact you before you became a rock star," he said. "Good luck, Frank. I'm happy for you."

"Thanks, Merle. Good luck with the Media Whores."

"Here's the tape of the band," Norm said as I met him at the back door of Pizza Shuttle for the last time. "Sounds horrible, but you'll get the idea. Here are the lyrics."

I removed the items from his dark hands. "Your last day?"

"Was. I'm out of here now."

"Bags packed?"

"Don't own anything," he said proudly.

"Good luck."

"The same to you. Take care of the band. And...just one thing—if ever you stop feeling the passion of the music—quit. That's all I ask. Don't tarnish the name of the band with insincerity. As for yourself, keep believing, and keep living. Our paths will cross from time to time. I'll be back through."

"Good luck, " I repeated.

"Take care, whitey."

"Oh, you know I will, red man. That's all us white people know."

He went on his way, walking with the sun to his back—the glare shining brightly against his red flannel shirt. As he walked, I breathed deeply, absorbing the scent of fried fast food. He turned the corner and out of my life, leaving me with a rich inheritance.

I looked down at the tape in my hands with a long list of song titles scratched on the J-card. I put the cassette to my nose and inhaled deeply. It smelled of plastic with a faint aroma of patchouli oil from Norm's touch. I still remember.

My work was cut out for me, work inspired by a lifetime's dream. I walked inside the bright eyesore of a restaurant to grab my first delivery of the night. I had waited years to hear more music by the Jerk Offs. Now it was me.

Alone in the solitude of the Ranchero, I spent the entire night studying my future, making the songs my own.

The wait was over.

Taking a deep breath, I knocked on the door. Footsteps across hardwood floors accelerated to a sudden halt. I listened to the slow turn of the door lock, clicking as the door swung open. Hazel stood before me with a straight face. Her hair was dyed fuscia, pulled back with plastic ducky hairpins. It was a common style in town. She crossed her arms and glared at me with hazel eyes.

"Come in," she said dryly. "Any trouble with the tape?"

"Not really. I may forget some lines here and there. The songs are great."

131

"The new ones are better," she told me.

The rest of the band waited on the couch.

"How's it going, Frank?" Specky asked, scratching his elaborately tattooed shoulder. Skin tone was invisible under the multi-colored tattoos of pride and strength, all skinhead in nature. "Ready?"

"Definitely."

"Well, I just got a call from a friend who promotes shows at the Outhouse," Specky said. "I guess everyone is talking. He's curious about the change, so he has a show for us in a couple weeks, if we want."

I stood quietly, waiting for him to continue.

"There's this new band from southern California he's booked. He says they're really good, but virtually unknown. He wants to know if we could headline to draw a crowd, and they could open. With a new singer, it'd probably bring out a lot of curiosity-seekers."

"Who's the band from California?" I asked.

"Some band called the Offspring. I'll be getting a tape of them tomorrow. What do you think? We'd have a little bit less than a month to prepare."

"Did you bring the tape of your old band?" George interrupted.

I pulled it from my pocket. "Here it is."

He reached out and grabbed it, examining the simple packaging.

"Would you be ready?" Specky asked me.

"I believe so."

"Okay, I'll set it up."

"Let's practice," Hazel said irritably.

The first rehearsal flew past as if time had folded, passing two hours like tunneling through a wormhole. By the end, my voice was rough and my throat sore. I looked over to George who had smiled for the first time that evening.

"Sounds really good," he confessed.

"Could you tell I forgot half the words?"

"Thank God our speakers suck. Can't hear shit," he said.

Specky crouched by his custom-built cabinet with EV speakers sliced down the cone. He picked up a couple of broken picks and placed them on his shanty, solid-state amplifier. "Yeah, that was good. Really good. How about some food?"

"I've got a test tomorrow," George said. "I need to study for a change, before they kick me out of KU."

Specky looked at Hazel who looked down at her well-kept hiking boots. "Frank?" he asked. "We could go to Taco Johns, see who can eat more tacos."

"Sure."

"See you guys next practice," Specky said. "George, make sure the place is locked up."

"I think I can handle it…" he grumbled as the door shut behind us.

"Hope Norm is doing okay," I said to Specky as we descended down the sloping hillside of Mount Oread.

"I'm sure he is. It's where he wants to be."

"Which Taco Johns?" I asked as we climbed into the Ranchero. "South? North?"

"Downtown."

I pulled away from the curb into traffic. The dying glow of a faded sunset had fallen beyond the hillside spotted with old Victorian houses. It resembled the play-set of Mr. Rogers' neighborhood. The narrow street was lined with rows of compact cars, most from other counties in the state. Several blocks down the street, some college students played with a hackey sack, obscuring traffic in the heart of the student ghettos.

Massachusetts Street was calm and slow, retiring with the day's demise. A small line of people stood outside the Granada and Varsity theaters waiting to purchase tickets for the motion picture features.

"We're moving out in about a month," Specky told me. "Found a huge house at the corner of 15th and Rhode Island. Has a lot of rooms, some still vacant. Need a place to live?"

"Yes, I do," I assured him. "Count me in. I'm living with a bunch of hippies right now."

"That's pretty funny...fucking hippies, treehuggers..."

We approached the counter where two young schoolgirls waited with tacky hunter green uniforms.

"Four tacos," Specky said to them. "And a Mr. Pibb."

"Five tacos," I said. "No meat, beans instead—you don't put lard in your beans, do you?"

"No, sir."

"Beans instead, and super hot sauce. Mr. Pibb."

"Can you add one more taco to my order?" Specky requested.

She gave us the order number and price. The food followed quickly, delivered on cheap plastic trays. We retreated to the far corner alone.

"So, how'd you get into this music, Specky?"

"A lot of my friends such as Harry from Troubled Youth were into it," he began between bites. "There wasn't much to do in Topeka, so we collected records. I was a serious homebody before I started hanging out with those guys. I was into goth before punk. I like it all, it's all the same to me. If it's underground, I collect it. You should see my collection."

"How many records do you have?" I asked.

He smiled proudly. "Hundreds."

"How do you feel about your own recording?"

"Well," he said, taking another bite before answering. "I prefer the live show, by far. The energy, the intensity, the aggression. Recordings are only effective if they can capture that element. I generally avoid the quality recordings. It's the friction in one's life that fuels passion and creativity, in my opinion. Once you take away the conflict, you take away the artist. If someone has done well enough to have made a spiffy recording, then they have lost touch with what they had to say—desensitized by success. Once you've made it, you're finished. You've blown your wad, it's all over. Time to pick up gardening."

"You do want this band to succeed, don't you?" I asked.

"Of course I do. I'm human. I care about the band's success a great deal, but I'd still do it even if no one came to our shows. Overall, though, it's the music, the energy. It's the highest human achievement. You'll never get the same satisfaction from a person. Too many variables, too many emotions at stake. Music is pure. That's all there is in life. All my life I have listened to great music, wondering how a stranger could make me feel so much. That, to me, is love. I wanted that power, that power of expression. It's our only chance to grip immortality."

"Do you think punk is about to burn out? Do you think it's dying?" I asked.

"It's very much alive. That's the beauty of punk—it doesn't rely on large-scale exposure to thrive. Its history is similar to jazz. Punk will be remembered as a staple

133

aspect of music from this era. I think punk will rise out of the underground within a decade. It will eventually become mainstream. Maybe in fifty years we'll be collecting Legends of Rock postage stamps, the Punk Rock years. Agnostic Front, the Germs, Ramones, X, Fear, the Freeze. American music at its finest."

"Another taco?" I asked.

"Sure," he said, reaching into his pocket. He patted his firm belly. "I'm pretty full."

"Two more?"

"Ah, man...okay."

We walked to the counter, placed our order, and waited quietly by the soda machine as the staff created our meals, sloppily without regard. I laughed at the thought of where evolution had delivered our species, to a point where the basis of our survival is merely a hassle in our pointlessly busy lives. We took the tray back to our table where our drinks collected moisture, half full.

"I'd like to do another recording," he told me between bites.

"I would, too."

"We need to schedule it. Everyone would have to pay their share."

"No problem with me," I told him firmly. "I could schedule it. That's something I do quite well."

"That's it for me," he decided as he leaned back. "If I eat anything more, I'll be wearing it later."

Just as we stood to exit, some dully dressed girls entered the restaurant. We walked past, barely aware of their presence.

"Excuse me," one mumbled apprehensively, tapping my shoulder. "Is your name Frank?"

"Do I know you?"

"You don't, but I know you. Everyone knew you. I went to Marmaton Valley, near Iola. Every guy in my school wanted to kill you. They went to Iola on weekends to find you, but never could. They said you hid in caves outside of town."

"Hate to give away my secrets..."

"I always thought you and your friends were pretty cool for being the way you were. I respected you."

"Thank you," I told her as we continued out the door.

"What was that all about?" Specky asked.

"I'm from Lawrence. Iola? Never heard of it."

"Okay, don't talk any louder than the check we did," the DeeJay said as the commercial came to an end. "Three...two...one...you're listening to KJHK, your sound alternative. In the studio, we have with us the Jerk Offs. Tonight they will be playing at the Outhouse, their first show with the new vocalist, Frank Smith. So, how did you come about joining the band, Frank?"

"Timing. I don't really know. Norm, the old vocalist and I worked together."

"Norm suggested it," George revealed.

"Any plans of a new Jerk Offs recording?"

"We've been talking about another seven-inch by the year's end," Hazel said.

"Make sure we get a copy down here," the DeeJay told us. "For your listening pleasure, this is a track off a new seven-inch that arrived at the studio last week. *Junkies Running Dry* by Operation Ivy—a new band out of the Bay Area."

134

The record played softly over the speakers, giving him time to take some calls. He put them on hold to cue another record. He leaned over to the microphone and prepared to speak as the song ended. "We're here in the studio with the Jerk Offs. We've opened the phone lines for questions. Caller, you're on the air."

"Hello?" a gruff voice said over the speakers. "Yeah, the Jerk Offs are—I mean, *were* my favorite band, man. How could they go on without Norm? Who are they trying to fool?"

"Can I answer?" Specky asked. "Caller, this is Specky."

"Hey, Specky, what's up?"

"You, pal. Come down with the rest of us. Lighten up. Get over it. Next caller..."

"Next caller," the DeeJay said, cueing another.

"Yeah, hello? Hello?"

"You're on the air."

"Okay...hello?"

"You're on the air, caller."

"Okay, I'm not going to another one of your shows. You guys suck. What, do you play Metal now, too?"

"Yes, we do," Specky declared. "See you at the show tonight. Next caller?"

"Hey, kids! This is Merle. More power to you. Frank rules, you will all bow at the stage. Oh, by the way: *Rock on, Lawrence!*"

"Thanks, Merle," I said.

"One more call before a word or two from sponsors," the DeeJay said.

"Hello? My name is Stanley. I'm right outside of town. I've come all the way from southeast Kansas to see this show. I just walked out of my job for this. I wouldn't miss it for the world. You're the man, Frank."

"Don't miss the Jerk Offs tonight at the Outhouse with special guests, the Offspring, from California. And now a word from our sponsors..."

"What do you mean you walked out?" I asked Stanley in the parking lot of the Outhouse as we sat on the hood of the Ranchero. It felt like old times again.

"They wouldn't let me off. No big deal, just a shoddy garage. I could get another job just like it tomorrow."

"I'm flattered."

"Don't be," he said, staring up into the night sky. "I promised years ago. This is your dream, glad I could witness it."

"I hope I don't let you down."

"You won't," he said. "You never have."

Silence suddenly consumed the environment as the California band completed its final song. The door burst open and a line of people exited into the mud lot.

"Better help your band load equipment," he said to me. "Do or die."

"We'll see what determines that." I stood to face him, concentrating on the warm smile that softened the rigid angles of his firm jaw. I felt immense comfort in his expression, and dreaded the first step away into my new life. "Thanks for being here."

He put a firm arm around my shoulder and patted me on the chest with a thick and powerful hand. "Wouldn't miss it. I keep to my word."

I smiled and nodded as he walked away, alone into the muddy lot of the Outhouse.

Hesitantly, I proceeded the opposite direction to the core circle of my awaiting new band, the Jerk Offs.

"This place attracts the biggest idiots," George scoffed irritably as I joined them. "They take this so seriously, like all they have to live for is this band."

"Maybe that's the case," I said.

"Maybe they need to get a life. Start their own band."

We stepped aside to allow the Offspring to clear the stage for us.

"That's the last of it," Hazel said impatiently as she peeked through the door beyond a clear stage. "Let's go."

I reached in the van and grabbed the stack of cymbals in one massive vinyl bag. The cool breeze lapped at me as I walked through the rear entrance into the stuffy dive. The bitter eyes of a skeptical audience smothered me with attention. I couldn't have felt more out of place. I did all I could to avoid contact, yet nothing held my attention more.

"Bring those over here," Hazel instructed me.

I followed her to the drum riser as the rumble of voices tapped at my back. I was temporarily protected under the guise of a poor fool loading equipment—just another name on the guest-list.

I stood by the edge of the rear door viewing not faces, but an alliance of people numbering upward of two hundred. I felt all the imperfections of my body cry out as if instructing them of all my weaknesses. My back slumped forward, my limbs skinny and bony. I felt grossly naked against the backdrop of my wildest dream.

My heart began to race as the amplifiers came to life. The music blaring throughout the club died down to reveal the naked badgering of the crowd which stood before me. I took one step forward from the drum riser, struggling desperately to keep my posture firmly upright. I stepped between Specky and George to the microphone, clenching my fists in an effort to release the pressure.

This was Norm's place, not mine.

I edged back, allowing my vision to concentrate on the faces that would scrutinize my every move. Shaved heads and irritated eyes were all I could see as the crowd bled into the back wall of the Outhouse, far stretched through the darkness. I stood immobile for what felt like an eternity. I was in a daze, as if I were drooling with a slagging, insolent expression.

Then my eyes found Stanley.

He looked at me with a straight face, perfectly at ease. I held his gaze, feeding off his lack of expression. This was just another show at the Outhouse to him.

I reached up and grabbed the microphone. Staring straight into Stanley's firm eyes, I asked calmly: "Are you ready?"

He nodded, and I could feel my hand grip tightly the cold microphone with stiff, white knuckles. Four clicks delivered the music like an anvil to my skull. I pulled the microphone stand against me as my body was ripped away from its dormant pose. Muscles tightened. I could feel the electricity of the music surge through me, igniting the hairs on my body. Specky's guitar grinded into my right ear, so nasty and full of contempt that I involuntarily spit at the first row now churning like my stomach.

From the mass of human limbs, people jumped up at the rafters, pulling themselves over the pit, swinging like apes. Bodies flipped upward from the swarm, tumbling on stage with smiles, then back into the heaping mess. I stood over it tall and strong. A shower of beer exploded from the mouth of a pleased listener, glazing my face. Projectiles of spit shot from the chaos, landing on my forehead in a warm mass that dripped down over my lips. Faces blended together in the pit with eyes and fists bringing me to attention. I was suddenly united with the passion that drove my deepest ambitions—the passion that delivered me to this incredible destination.

Bodies flew over my head. Hands yanked me into the crowd and ripped at my shirt. I sang the words with closed eyes, remembering the years I had spent locked up inside my bedroom, listening to the same song on my old Jerk Offs record. There was a deep affection for this song, and this moment on stage with them was nothing by comparison. Their music would live on—it would out-live me. I was only there for the ride, there to entertain my dearest friend.

A lanky skinhead jumped up to me as the lyrics poured like a fountain of hostility. He stopped at the foot of the stage, watching, singing every word. I pulled him forward by his shirt collar. Together we screamed, united with one goal, one vision.

Somewhere out there stood Stanley, as promised. That was all that really mattered to me.

The three-story house lumbered like a fortress on the corner of 15th and Rhode Island. There was no missing it. It was a pale color, the shade of a rotten lime. A tall wooden fence contained a tiny backyard and a foul heap of compost. The concrete steps to the front porch leaned lazily from an unstable foundation.

The place itself was lifeless.

I stepped out of the Ranchero and walked cautiously across the poorly kept lawn. I glanced back at the Ranchero once before stepping onto the porch. The bed was overflowing with material objects—the lifetime accumulation of working class hand-me-downs. It was all I owned.

I knocked gently on the door of my new residency and waited. I was met only with brief silence.

"Come on up," someone's ominous, edgy voice invited me from above.

I pushed the door open slowly. Inside, it was bare and unfurnished. Several windows allowed a flood of light to lift the atmosphere of the old, stale environment. To my right was the path to the living room and kitchen. To my left was the staircase. I could faintly hear the sound of footsteps coming from one of the floors above me.

The hardwood floors creaked with each step that delivered me to the wooden staircase. The floor—as well as the steps themselves were worn from excessive use. They could use a serious waxing. I felt certain that the maintenance wouldn't take place over the next year of our lease...

At the top of the steps, I found a hallway with rows of doors—each marked with the name of a future tenant. Mine was directly to my right.

I pushed the wood door, finding a long room with two windows. Out the front window, I could see the roof of the porch, as well as the legs of a person lying deathly still. The Ranchero was in plain view on the street below. It appeared that looters hadn't yet stripped its contents away.

I walked up to the window and forced it open. The person lying on the roof was Harry Saucerocket, the guitarist from Troubled Youth. His black leather biker jacket shrouded his frail shoulders. Shiny silver studs encircled the cuffs, reflecting the blinding glare of the sun. Its heat must've been merciless underneath, I assumed.

"What's up?" I asked him politely as I leaned my head out into the warm air.

He turned toward me, staring at me through circular, wire-rimmed glasses. "This is my space."

"Oh, is it? I thought it was mine. This is my room, after all."

He pointed to the other window. "That one is mine, mister Johnny-come-skately."

137

"My name is Frank."

"I don't care."

I laughed. He didn't.

"Where's everyone else?" I asked.

"Who is everyone else?"

"Specky. Is he here?"

"Third floor. He's got his little goons helping him fix up his room." He stood quickly, towering over the neighborhood behind him. He rearranged the package of his tight jeans. "First door on your left."

"Thanks," I said, just as the sound of heavy footsteps ricocheted throughout the hallway.

Specky leaned his head in my bedroom door and smiled. A stocky skinhead stood next to him. "Hey, Frank, I want you to meet my best friend, Clifford Skitovich. You can call him what everyone else does: Skeet."

I stepped forward to greet him.

Skeet extended a hand that grasped mine firmly with charge. He was a large man of proportionate confidence. His face read mischief, but the chubby cheeks and freckles were simply too cute for harsh prejudgment. His second chin was twice as pronounced as his first. He would likely spend his life playing Santa Claus for the in-laws. "I really enjoyed the show the other night."

"I did, too," I told him.

He brushed his forehead with the back of his hand in an effort to clear the sweat of hard labor. He panted uncontrollably like an old dog. His skin was splotchy and red from exertion. Droplets of perspiration speckled his rosy cheeks. "Need some help with your things?"

"Maybe you should take a breather first," I suggested.

"I have beer waiting in the fridge. First thing we moved in—and the most important."

"I'll see you guys later," Specky said as he continued downstairs.

Skeet motioned for me to follow him downstairs. "Come on, let's do it."

A troupe of young skinheads passed us on the way out the front door. The contents of the Ranchero were still intact.

"This house is immense," Skeet sighed as he yanked on the bed frame, forcing it from the confines of the Ranchero. "Got the Outhouse four miles down the street. William Burroughs lives only a couple blocks away. You never see him around, though. He's getting old."

I nodded politely as I helped him lower the frame to the ground.

"Have you met Spike?" Skeet asked as he paused momentarily to gaze down 15th Street. He pointed to an approaching black hearse.

I shook my head.

"He's rather...eccentric. His parents died in the infamous Hyatt Regency catastrophe when that catwalk bridge collapsed and crushed all those people on New Year's Eve. He's up to his ears in cash now."

The hearse pulled up behind the Ranchero in a shroud of mystery. There was brief silence as the driver glared through the tinted window at us. Eventually, he opened the door and stepped morbidly slow in the mid-day sun. He was a very sturdy man, firm in build and slovenly in appearance. His hair was dyed black—a frightful, fashionable mess. Thick layers of black eyeliner circled his bloodshot eyes. His lips were painted bright red, and if it weren't for his awkward masculinity, one would be apt to consider him dainty by apparel alone.

"Hello," he mumbled softly to us as he stepped away from the hearse. A small white French poodle was tucked carefully under his arm. "Say hello to Bootsy, boys."

"Hello, Bootsy," I said to the dog.

"Bootsy doesn't understand," Spike corrected bitterly. "Le Bootsy du France."

"Bootsy is French," Skeet whispered to me. "Oui, Bootsy," he mumbled politely to the dog.

"Oui, Bootsy," I said. "Viva la France."

"Spike, this is your new roommate. Frank."

Spike leaned toward Skeet, whispering in his ear: "He's in the Jerk Offs?"

Skeet nodded.

"So many bands..." He sauntered off, pausing to place the poodle in the grass. *"Vas te faire la merde sur la pelouse jaune, Boots."*

He turned once more before climbing the steps, looking me up and down, then back again.

"Nice wing tips," Skeet mumbled to himself. He turned to me and smiled. "So, you've met Harold?"

"I don't think he cares much for me," I confessed. "It appears he's not into new faces."

"Those Topeka guys see your pretty-boy face, and they don't like that," Skeet said as he raised the end of the bed frame.

I laughed. "They roughed it out in Topeka? Going to Topeka for the weekend was a vacation for me. What about open-mindedness and acceptance and tolerance? Isn't that what punk is all about?"

"You know," he began as we squeezed the metal frame through the front door and up the stairs. "I used to live by the old records, still love them. Where do you want this thing to go?"

"By the window."

"Contradictions...have you ever met a relaxed hippy? The most uptight people I've ever encountered in my life were hippies. People seek their niche based on their weakness. If you're an uptight person, wouldn't you be attracted to the hippies and their lifestyle? Now, think of all the classifications for underground music—punk, ska, industrial, goth—you choose punk? Well, there's peace punk, oi, Straight Edge, 77, crossover, garage punk, dirge, skate punk, hardcore—I chose oi. Oi, of course, represents the skinhead sect. The skinheads in Lawrence call themselves L. A. S. H., who are affiliated with the A. R. A., or the Anti-Racist Action. For a genre of music derived by misfits and outcasts, it sure has a lot of order. Anarchy? Yeah, right! You'll never meet a laid-back hippy, and you'll never find a punk scene that wasn't anything other than a humorously complex social club of who-knows-who. You have an interesting position being in the Jerk Offs. You're bound to get a lot of respect without judgment. Lucky break, I guess."

"That's too bad," I said as we stumbled down the steps and outside once again. "I'd prefer the judgment."

"No one cares, to be honest. If they decide you're a spoiled brat who discovered this music last week, then that's what you'll be through their eyes. You're in the scene now. You're just another candidate running for office and caliber. Now, what about this mattress? Is it heavy?"

"It's not bad. Just grab the little rope handles."

"Here, you get that end," he said as we lifted it up out of the bed of the Ranchero. "I look forward to seeing you guys play the house-warming party tonight."

"I'm looking forward to playing," I told him as we struggled with it across the yard. "You love the music, don't you?"

"I do," he admitted passionately. "More than anything. I live by it. That's why Specky and I are such good friends."

"I'm honored to be in this band."

"You should be," he said. "Before the Jerk Offs came onto the scene, no one cared about the local bands. Of course, there were the Micronotz a few years back. After the Micronotz, everyone was apathetic about the scene. The Jerk Offs changed all that. There definitely exists the potential for a larger audience. That is, if someone has the fuel to motivate the band again. Norm's departure practically killed the band."

We sat the mattress down on the frame and paused for a breather.

"The Jerk Offs were my favorite band for quite some time when I was in high school," I told him. "Listened to that record until I knew every word, every mistake on it." I paused to straighten the bed. "The mattress looks good against this wall. I only have a couple small boxes. I can get those. Thanks for helping."

"No problem. You have very few possessions," he said as he stumbled through the boxes. "My girlfriend makes moving hell. She could fill three cargo trucks and still need more space. She collects all kinds of junk."

There came a knocking at my door. I turned to see a bald head glaring inside with a stoic expression.

"Vernon!" Skeet exclaimed excitedly. "Come on in, meet Frank."

The scowl on Vernon's face seemed permanent. It was as if his skin was chiseled from stone, hard and cold. Anger seemed to have dissolved his soul. His name was embroidered on his flight jacket in white cursive letters.

"Frank just moved to town," Skeet said to the fierce man who stared at me momentarily before nodding. "Vernon's one of my roommates." Skeet stood quickly, turning to me before leaving. "It was nice to finally meet you, Frank."

"Thanks for the help, Skeet," I told him.

He smiled. "The pleasure was mine. We'll talk again sometime."

My room quickly cleared, giving me time to finally suck in the environment so rich in freedom. The gentle breeze of summer whipped through the open window. I climbed outside onto the roof of the porch. The rooftop was black from an ancient tarring, its surface hot to the touch. I leaned against the wall, slumping casually to sit in the sun.

Below, a group of skinheads under the supervision of Specky combined their strength to lift a dresser from a truck's bed. Their communal effort warmed me with a feeling of relief, as if I had withheld a breath for years. This was where I belonged.

An obnoxious thumping pulled me from an extended nap later that evening. The house was already churning with belligerent voices and high-spirited music. I rubbed my eyes and stretched with clenched toes and trembling muscles.

"Knock, knock," someone spoke outside my door. It was the gruff and boisterous voice of a female. I perked up at once. "Where's the new guy?"

I rushed to the door, tripping twice over boxes placed blindly on the floor like booby traps. I opened the door while shielding my eyes from the light of the bathroom down the hall.

"Did I wake you up?" she asked. "Aw, poor baby! Wake up, it's time to socialize, there's a party downstairs."

I lowered my hands from squinty eyes. Before me stood a stout woman with a lovely smile. She appeared to be years older than me, possibly in her mid-twenties. Her eyes were bright and suggestive, her hair brown and cut in a fringe, or Chelsea— shaved to the scalp except for fluffy bleached bangs. A green plaid mini-skirt hugged tightly to her pronounced hips. Black fishnet stockings ran down her muscular legs. Small tears in the fabric revealed her smooth, delicate skin. A pair of black steel-toed boots covered her feet, untied. The leather had been worn off the left toe, revealing a shiny metal plate under the tear. Her robust chest stretched the material of a thin white tank-top. Her black lacy bra was clearly visible beneath it.

She smiled at me comfortably, revealing a shiny barbell that pierced the center of her tongue. The skin on her face was extraordinarily smooth. "My name's Xanthe and you're being rude."

"I'm Frank."

"I know," she said quickly. Her long lashes fluttered like the wings of a bat. She leaned forward and pinched my cheeks. "Look at you, aren't you a cutie? Now get your ass downstairs and talk to me."

"It's too early...are you always this...lively?" I asked as I followed her to the first floor.

"Depends on how much coke I've done."

We walked to the dingy couch that seated at least four scrawny skinheads in matching uniform, all of them with their mouths open to the ceiling like a nest of baby robins. Skeet stood over them with a tiny bottle, placing droplets of a blue solution on their tongues.

"Do you trip, Frank?" Skeet asked, holding the bottle out at me.

I shook my head.

Skeet tucked the bottle in the pocket of his flight jacket. "Saving the rest for you, Specky. After you guys play, we can drop together." He tucked a sheet of paper in his old leather briefcase. Rows of tiny planet earths covered the page.

"I don't know what people are into where you're from, but acid is the choice drug of this scene," Xanthe told me as the others talked amongst themselves. "Acid and Shrooms. There's always coke and speed, but these jokers can't afford it on a busser's wage. Everyone smokes pot, that's a given."

"Hey, Specky, look at my new tattoo," one of the young skinheads requested as he removed his flight jacket and rolled up his sleeve. In large Olde English letters, the initials L. A. S. H. were tattooed with stark black ink. "Do you like it?"

"Yeah, that's cool, Lank."

"Good, thanks," he replied happily, relieved.

Vernon stood firmly at Skeet's side like a stoic sentry. The words *Untied Skins* were tattooed across his forearm. I assumed the intention was *United Skins*.

"Check this out," Skeet said to the others. He pulled his bottom lip down to reveal the word *Skinhead* tattooed on the inside of his chubby lip.

The praise was unanimous.

There came a knock at the door. Specky sprang to answer it. A gaggle of young punks strutted through the door, striking up loose conversation like a family reunion. I stood awkwardly silent as the room came alive with smiling faces and empty words.

"Where you from, Frank?" Xanthe asked.

"Iola, Kansas."

141

"What brings you here?"

I glanced at the occupants of the room. "Music. Are you from Lawrence?"

"Graduate of Lawrence high school, thank you very much," she responded proudly. "That was a number of years ago, I must admit. I'm moving to Boulder, Colorado in the spring. I'll begin my first semester of college at CU next year."

The door opened again, allowing a new stream of young punks into the quickly shrinking room.

"So, where do you work?" she asked me.

"Pizza Shuttle."

"The old standard, huh? That makes sense. You're a band guy, you should work there."

"And you?" I asked.

"Pink Flamingo. The Ol' Dirty Bird."

"Waitress?"

"Dancer. I show my tits to hard-up guys for lots of money, basically. Is that a problem?"

"If guys would pay to see my chest, I'd do it," I told her.

"Glad to hear it. I feel self-conscious about it sometimes, mainly because a lot of girls look down on me for doing it. I don't think it represents sexism so much as sexuality. I'm in control, I know what I'm doing. It's my choice to be there, so how can that be sexism? If men are willing to offer money simply to see my body, then what's wrong with that? No one's getting hurt."

"If the naked body wasn't viewed so criminally in this country, we'd have fewer problems with sex offenders."

"Well," she said, reaching out her hand. "To sexual oppression."

I gently shook her hand. Her grip was tight and strong. Our hands fit comfortably.

Two young girls wandered by, trying to lick the numbers off a five-dollar bill while they ranted on about how the color red tastes. Everyone in the room appeared to have recently visited Arkham Asylum.

"So, Straight Edge is passé?" I asked.

"Don't know how hip it was in the first place. People need their vices," she said, reaching into her purse to retrieve a clove cigarette. "Most of the people in this room were probably Straight Edge at one time. Just another trend for this crowd to follow."

A young girl stumbled up to me with wide, frightened eyes. She stared, horrified.

"Come here, Susan." Skeet comforted her as she trembled like a child. "You're having a bad trip, let's get some milk." He pulled her away to the kitchen as she clawed at various people, ineffectively shielding her eyes from the illusions around her.

"Looks like fun," I said sarcastically.

"Nothing like watching someone's face melt off. Begin to have a bad trip, and you've got a good twelve hours to deal with the horror of it. Most of these people are too young to cope. The thing about a bad trip is you'll never forget it. Any time you drop, you come off it a different person, good or bad. Some people can be enhanced or enlightened, while others...have considerably less fun."

"Interesting choice," I said.

"Each person has a drug that will suit their personality. I can tell already that you're a ludes kind of guy. Speed is my thing, any upper. Give me an eight ball and I'll be happy."

George walked into the room with alert eyes that rolled once he scanned the occupants of the party. He stepped forward to greet me as he fastened the top button on his collar. "This is a fucking freak show." His sober articulation contrasted the surrounding conversations. "Ready to play?"

"Always."

"Where's Hazel?" he asked.

"Haven't seen her."

"George, do you remember meeting me?" Xanthe asked.

"I remember, but your name..."

"Xanthe."

"Oh, yes, that's right," he said shortly. "I'm sorry."

"That's okay. I forget it sometimes myself."

"Hello, boys," Spike sang as he approached with a flowing black sequin gown. His neck was weighted by rosaries and gaudy pennants of crosses and crucifixes. Bootsy sat comfortably under his arm—the fur dyed a vibrant shade of pink. He lifted his limp hand to George with his knuckles arched upward, loosely. "So many people, so few friends."

"Indeed," George replied.

"Alas," Spike breathed heavily as Hazel walked through the front door. "Another member of the Family. Getting rather straight and narrow in here."

"Ready to play?" George asked her.

"Now? I just got here," she moaned.

"What difference does that make?"

"There are people who will want to talk to me," she said quite seriously.

He sighed as she absorbed into the party atmosphere with a tacked-on smile.

"Let's go," George insisted as he directed me to our equipment. "I don't want to be here all night."

We grabbed Specky by the arm as we passed.

"Are we playing?" he asked.

"Yes," George said flatly. He powered up the small P. A. system and raised the microphone to his thin lips. "Hazel, let's do it," he demanded before placing it in my hands.

The crowd quickly caved inward, surrounding the small playing area, breaking down the barrier of band and audience.

"Hi," I said timidly into the microphone as Hazel unwillingly broke away from a conversation. "We're the Jerk Offs."

With a few eager seconds falling to silence, Hazel quickly broke into the first song, bringing the band to life and the audience alike. The house suddenly unified into a congruent allegiance. Hollow eyes covered me with full attention, flooding my vision with direct responsiveness. Heads and bodies moved quickly with the rhythm, aligning me with the single presence of one direction, one goal, one motive.

Applause showered upon us, piercing our ears with shrill cries of praise. Each song was a burst of energy—short, intense, and directly to the point.

The burnt and confused eyes removed themselves from me, from the music. Those individuals were gone. They would return with the sun, sharing surreal tales of our world through impaired vision. My vision remained unaffected, strong and alive.

As our last song came to a halt, I dropped the microphone casually and left the house.

143

"Where you going?" Xanthe asked as she pursued me out the front door. "That was a fantastic performance."

"Thanks. I agree," I admitted quickly.

"Don't get all snobbish, pal—I'm no fucking groupie," she growled. "Musicians are so arrogant."

"Arrogance is pretense, confidence is knowing. *I know*. If the listener feels a fraction of what I feel, then I've succeeded. Besides, I know the music is good. I've been listening to the Jerk Offs for years."

We sat on the porch away from a group of young girls chain-smoking cheap cigarettes.

"Been in this scene quite a while?" I asked her.

"Only a few years," she replied with a more calm tone. "Honestly, you may laugh."

"At what?"

"Well, part of my past is kind of embarrassing."

"Oh, yeah?" I beckoned.

"I'd hate for you to think I'm frumpy."

"Because of your past? I couldn't care less. It's not what someone has been, it's what they could be. Go ahead, speak."

"Well, my parents were hippies, thus my name," she said as she reached into her bag to pull out a cigarette. "To rebel against hippy parents, one tends to lean conservative. I was a cheerleader. I had that hairdo that looks like a rabbit's ass. My parents were mortified."

"What changed?"

"I wasn't happy. I would carve things into my stomach with a razor blade, like *slut* and *whore*. I was in a bad state for certain reasons. I'd go into my closet each night after school and cry for like an hour. I wouldn't eat, wore a lot of make-up, cared only about what others thought."

"Look at you now."

"Yeah, look at me now," she boasted as she held her arms out proudly. "I finally got my shit together. I was pretty lonely, though."

"What will be your major at CU?" I asked.

"English."

"You write, huh?" I asked.

"Uh-huh."

"I can't imagine writing," I decided quickly. "It's a very slow process, and besides, I haven't got enough of an education. I don't know the difference between a noun and a pronoun."

She laughed.

"Honestly. I don't."

A short chubby girl waddled up to me, diverting our attention to her imposing presence. Her expression was somewhere between excitement and discomfort. "Good show, man. Welcome to town."

"Thank you," I replied as she quickly scurried away.

Specky threw the front door open, scanned the porch for a head count, and placed himself between the two of us. "Hey, is the party out here now?"

"Just waiting for the pigs to show," Xanthe responded casually.

"This party isn't going to get busted," he said as he stuck his tongue out to reveal a tiny square paper. "Fucking cops. It takes a certain kind of person to desire a job like that."

"Someone's line of work tells a lot about the person," she added.

"Yeah, you for instance," he said.

"That's right," she returned swiftly. "You're one to talk, Specky. You have no morals whatsoever."

"I love women, what can I say? I have a fruitful sex life."

"Proves your masculinity, huh?" she challenged.

"Sure does," he said. "And stripping proves your femininity?"

"Sure does, but do I get diseases from dancing? No. By the way, speaking of contracting diseases...who was that nappy skinhead girl clinging to your arm last weekend at the Lynch house?"

"Some girl from Arizona passing through town with a caravan of punks. I forgot her name, if I ever knew it. She was a freak."

"How's that?" I asked.

"She had a few mental tics. I'd hate to know how they originated. She was kind of...what would I say? Masochistic? To say the least—the *very* least. We were engaging in coital activity, nothing out of the ordinary, right? Then she asked me to slap her. I playfully accommodated her request. Then she says: *Hard!* So, I obliged. She wants it harder, like violently rough, bruises and all that. I thought—*man, this needs to stop!*"

"So, did it?" Xanthe asked.

"Of course not."

"You just kept serving the blows?"

He laughed. "Someday I'll be a dirty old man. But for now...I'm just cool."

"When are you going to return my Fluorescent Condoms tape, Specky?" I asked.

"Actually, that's why I came out here. Not to return it, but to ask a question. That song *Persistence, Resistance*—it's a great song. Any chance we could revive it as a Jerk Offs song? I'd love to play that one."

"I know the words," I told him. "Of course. I'd love to."

"Hey, check this out," he said as three young punk ladies walked up to the front of the house. "Debutantes."

"Specky, those girls are probably in middle school," Xanthe said.

"So, they're a bit old."

"They aren't even attractive," I added.

"Exactly. Attraction is dangerous. You should only be so attracted to your bedmates. The best sex I've ever had has always been with fat women."

"Is this the party?" one of the young girls asked.

"No," Xanthe responded loudly. "There's just a hundred punk rockers hanging out on these people's porch. What do you think?"

"Yeah, let me show you in," Specky said, jumping quickly to escort them inside.

"Specky has a one-track mind," Xanthe told me as the silence briefly returned.

A large, black car pulled up to the curb, dropping Billy Christ onto the yellow lawn. He stumbled to the porch with a bottle of beer in his hand. Within a few seconds of entering the house, glass shattered.

Xanthe sighed. "I've been searching for Howard Roarke my whole life...I've only met Holden Caulfield, many times over, come to think of it. Never fails."

"I don't think I know either of them," I told her flatly. "Sorry."

145

"So, when are the Jerk Offs playing again?" she asked me.

"I don't have any idea."

"You should get some shows for the band," she suggested. "Someone needs to. Their disorganization has always kept them from a much larger audience. The potential is clearly there. So far they've only amounted to Lawrence's best-kept secret. They're old hat, they need someone to motivate them."

"George seems motivated," I told her.

She shook her head. "George quit recently, at least that's what I heard. I can't really see him sticking with it for very long. It isn't his thing. Skeet was there the night Norm broke the news. Apparently, the band was ready to call it quits. When your name came up as a replacement, the tone slowly changed. Your involvement is kind of make or break for them. If you want this band to succeed, you need to take control. They're counting on it."

Later that night as I lie in bed trying to sleep over the noise of the disintegrating party, a fight outside caught my attention. I jumped to the window and thrust it open, allowing the cool air to blow through the dark room.

Specky stood in the street below with one of the legendary town locals, Nick the Barbarian. Nick was an old biker that refused to give in to the establishment. He spent his life collecting government checks, drinking beer, and hanging out with the younger generations. His sense of style hadn't changed in fifteen years. He looked like the cast of *Easy Rider*, a human relic of a forgotten decade.

Specky knocked Nick to the ground, circling around him wildly.

"I'm not going to be like you," Specky cried as he kicked at Nick's swaggering head.

Nick stared up at him, frightened and disoriented from the alcohol—Specky looked down upon him, frightened and disoriented from the LSD.

Nick climbed to his feet just to be knocked to the pavement again.

"I'm not going to end up like you," Specky declared as he dragged Nick to the curb by his hair.

"Let him go, man," Lank requested cautiously, squeamishly.

"I can't fucking stand him," Specky exclaimed as he punched Nick in the face.

Nick's jaw gaped, rendering him incapable of words.

"He's drunk, man," Lank pleaded. "He doesn't know what's going on. Come on, let him go. You're just tripping, man. It's the acid, man. It's the acid."

Footsteps came noisily up the stairs as I watched the scene below. Breaking the clear silence of my blind surroundings, someone banged forcefully at my door.

"Where's that guy?" a voice slurred beyond the closed door. "What was it—Johnny-come-skately? Yeah. Open up, you fucking pussy. I've got a beer for you."

I stepped down onto the floor, making my way through the unpacked boxes. When I opened it, Billy Christ leaned against the frame, smiling belligerently.

"There you are," he mumbled angrily as he barged into my room. "Step aside, asshole."

"What's going on?" I asked.

"Fuck you," he growled as he turned on the light and propped himself against the wall. "Who the fuck are you?"

"Frank."

"I didn't ask your name—I don't give a shit about that. Who the fuck do you think you are?"

"Someone trying to sleep? You tell me."

"Where did you come from, and why do you think you can just walk right into this scene and..." He slurred a moment, losing his train of thought. "When I came around here, you got your ass kicked first. My buddy Spit, when he went to his first punk show, they kicked his ass and made him leave. The next time he came with a gun, and they said: *You're all right, man.* Then they allowed him to come around. So, who...who do you fucking think you are?"

"It's late, you're drunk, and I'm tired. I don't know you—"

"That's my fucking point, you asshole! No one knows you," he said with an extended pause as he tossed his bottle at my wall, merely ricocheting onto the bed where the remaining contents spilled out onto the sheets. "Hit me."

"What?"

"Hit me. Come on."

"It's late," I shrugged.

"Hit me, asshole! If I had asked Norm, he'd have pounded me. He and I used to be drinking buddies, I've had my ass kicked more than once by him. So, come on..."

"I'm not Norm."

"Fucking pussy. We don't need any more fucking vegetarian hippies in this scene. There's enough hippies in Lawrence...you fucking Straight Edge motherfuckers..."

"Do you need help leaving?" I suggested.

"You could try to make me...or I could just keep you up all night. Depends on what you want." He slouched lower against the wall as he stared at me with hostile eyes. "I don't like you."

"Sorry to hear that," I said in a deadpan voice.

"You know...you straight....you straight.....you straight...edge..." He slid down the wall to the floor, ending up in a motionless mess in front of my door.

I dragged him into the hallway at the top of the steps and returned to bed.

The sun returned a few hours later. Voices whispered outside my window. The house was otherwise quiet and motionless except those preparing for sleep after a rough night. I leaned forward, careful not to sit in the spilt beer on my sheets.

Young boys bickered in the schoolyard across the street, arguing about the events of a football game in progress. Spike and Harold sat on the roof, leaning against the house with their attention focused on the young athletes. Bootsy sat at the edge of the roof, staring at the ground below. The poodle's freshly dyed fur seemed to glow like cotton candy in the bright sunlight.

"Look at the one with the red shorts," Harold mumbled between drags on a cigarette.

"Like a miniature Greek statue," Spike whispered succulently. "Still, the one with the half-shirt—Lord, have mercy on this Queen."

I rolled out of bed, stretching my limbs as I slowly pulled myself forward.

"I always wanted to be a quarterback," Spike confided to Harold. "To feel the sweaty crotch of the other boys when they hand me the ball between their legs. I still have fantasies about football teams..."

I walked down the hallway to the bathroom, cautiously stepping over Billy's twisted body sprawled on the beer-stained hardwood. The floor creaked with each slight step, sticky from years of neglect. The bathroom had a perpetual stench of rot from the poor utility and maintenance over several decades. The wooden floor had deteriorated to a disgusting shade of dark brown, bowed under the weight of the ancient tub, ready to collapse at any moment.

I turned the water on, allowing the steam to rise up over the water-stained, plastic shower curtain nailed to the tile ceiling. I stepped inside. The warm water flowed down my stiff coils of hair. My feet were firmly stationary under the resistance of grime and hard-water build-up.

The door slowly opened, followed by the sound of agitated footsteps.

"What's going on, Frank?" Specky grumbled as he began brushing his teeth.

"Up rather early, aren't you?"

"No, up rather *late*. Came down a few hours ago, so we walked home from downtown."

I reached out of the shower to the tabletop where all the tenants' supplies were sectioned. I grabbed a small container blindly, one the same size of my shampoo. I brought it inside the shower, only to realize it wasn't my shampoo, but a similar container with a piece of tape marking it liquid LSD. I replaced it and searched again. "What were you doing downtown?"

"Downtown...who knows?" he replied with a mouthful of toothpaste. He spit the contents into the sink. "Why is Billy on the floor?"

"That's where he ended up for the night, I suppose," I said casually.

"Good place for him."

"Hey, Specky, do you mind if I try to set up some shows for us?"

"Do I mind? Yeah, I do," he said sarcastically as he opened the door. "While you're at it, avoid setting up some studio time to do another recording. We don't need that either." He quickly left me alone in silence.

As I shut the water off, I could hear the tiny clicks of Bootsy walking down the hallway. I peeked around the corner to glimpse the fluffy, pink creature sniffing a puddle of Billy's drool.

I returned to my room, stepping over Billy at the top of the stairs. Boxes covered the floor. I felt a strong desire to claim the space as my own. I tore open the box at my feet and sorted through a stack of old keepsakes. At the top of the pile was the scarlet flier for the Fluorescent Condoms' final show at Bombers in Manhattan, Kansas. I separated it from the others, admiring the small print of my former band's name at the bottom of the paper, just above the promoter's address and telephone number. I reached around the corner for the telephone. Bootsy stared up at me with wide eyes and a friendly tilt of the head as I dialed the number.

"Hello?"

"Hello, is Walter there?" I asked.

"This is Walter."

"Hi, this is Frank Smith. I sang for a band called the Fluorescent Condoms...we played there—"

"How's it going, Frank? It's been a few years."

"Doing fine. Got a new band—actually, I joined an existing band."

"Oh, yeah? What band?"

"The Jerk Offs."

"Really? I saw the Jerk Offs at a party last year in Lawrence. Good band."

"You wouldn't happen to be promoting shows at Bombers these days, would you?" I asked.

"Yeah, same old thing. You guys looking to play out?"

"Do you have anything?"

"Yeah, I do. The scene has grown here. You'll be pleasantly surprised. Hold on a minute." He sat the phone down momentarily. I could faintly hear the shuffling of papers. "Okay, let me see...I've got a couple shows coming up late this month. Got one on a Wednesday. Have you heard of a new band called Operation Ivy?"

"Heard a little bit...I like it, but no one knows them."

"Or, on a Saturday night we have Dead Silence and Dissent."

"Both bands on a weekend? That'd probably be a great turn-out."

"I'm hoping," he said with a laugh.

"Well, given the choice...our drummer and bassist are students, and I doubt many people know Operation Ivy, so I'd prefer to open the bill for Dissent and Dead Silence."

"That's great. Do you remember how to get here?"

The warm air of the day's end filled the narrow street with a smooth tranquillity that could levitate the most solemn spirit. People wearing shades of purple walked aimlessly through the thoroughfare of shops in Aggieville, the heart of Kansas State University.

Walter stood outside the back door of the club, smoking a cigarette as we parked our van alongside two others.

"I recognize those dreadlocks," Walter announced as I stepped out of the van. "How's it going, Frank?"

"Not bad. How was the Operation Ivy show?"

"Great show. Had maybe three people come out, but the band was great fun. How are things for the Jerk Offs?"

"We're going to record a seven-inch next week, actually," I informed him.

"You'll have to send me a copy. I can work it into KSDB's rotation."

"That'd be great," I told him as the rest of the band started unloading our equipment. "You wouldn't happen to know of some type of magazine that carries a listing of college radio stations around the country, would you?"

"Try either the Gavin Report or College Music Journal. In fact, if you're interested, I've got several old issues in my car. I just cleaned out my office the other day. I'm parked out front, if you'd like..."

"You don't mind?"

He laughed. "It'll save a trip to the dumpster." He stepped back inside the club, disappearing into the dim visibility of the musty venue.

I followed blindly, allowing the neon beer signs in the distance to guide me. A game of pool was in progress. I assumed the players were members of the other two bands. Hazel bumped into me, wandering in the dim light.

"This place is nice," she said.

"It really is," I responded. "You know, we have a couple hours before we play...would you want to get a bite to eat—"

"I've got to study," she told me. "Test on Monday..."

She quickly walked away.

As I stepped into the center of the building, I felt I had slid into the past, as if the Fluorescent Condoms were about to take the stage. Years had filled the gap of that cold, winter night, stretching the timeline without notice. The place hadn't changed since, and I suddenly felt an urgency to hear Stanley's voice—the voice of a past that had washed away all but memories.

"How was the show your old band played here?" a voice asked over my shoulder.

149

I turned to George, who stood calmly at my side.

"Crazy night, bad weather," I replied casually. "It was our last show."

"Big fight?" he asked.

"No, we got along fine considering the circumstances. Being in the band meant a lot to us in one way or another. I suppose the circumstances could've been the sole bonding factor, something to rally around."

"Let me guess—you couldn't wait to get away from all the ridiculous games. Kind of a rude awakening when you met all the Bozos in Lawrence, huh?"

"Why do you say?" I asked.

"Maybe you just haven't met many people or gotten to know them yet. They're far from troopers, far from it. No one gives a shit in the bigger scenes, they have no reason to. They're surrounded by so many hands patting them on the back that they wouldn't know which way to turn without someone to lead."

"You really aren't into this style of music, are you?" I asked.

"It bores me. Same old shit, same old attitude."

"What do you listen to?"

"Schöenberg, Bartók, Schnittké, Messiaen, Hindemith... Rock music is restricted to so many rules. Even the instrumentation, it's always the same. Never varying, always the same combinations of chords."

"Are you guys going to help haul the equipment or what?" Specky grumbled as he carried the snare drum to the stage.

"Let's go," George told me. "We'll talk later."

We followed Specky out the door to the van.

"So, who formed this band?" I asked him.

"That was before I came around," George said as he lifted the head of his bass amplifier. "I was the last to join. Specky and Hazel started it. I didn't even know them. Skeet introduced me. He and I worked the graveyard shift at Packer Plastics, so we'd hang out and drink together when the sun came up. That's how I met Specky. One drunken night he asked if I'd like to jam with Hazel and him, and I agreed to check it out. My band experience to that point was Metal cover bands. I liked it, so I joined. I couldn't give a shit what kind of music it was, or what it was called."

"Where are you from?" I asked as we raised the bulky bass speaker out of the van.

"Everywhere."

"Military family?"

"No. Broken family. Can you lift your end higher?" he asked as we slowly brought it through the door. "Connecticut, Illinois, most recently Kansas City...to name a few. Grew up in Connecticut, moved to Illinois when I entered middle school, then Kansas City for high school."

"Parents still married?" I asked.

"No, not my natural parents. My biological father was not all that positive a role model, to say the least. I will probably never see him again—which is the plan, at least. We never had any money. We were totally lower class. My mother remarried when I was becoming a teenager."

We sat on the edge of the stage as Specky carried the drumsticks through the back door.

"Had a lot of trouble with the family when my mother remarried, though," he told me. "In fact, every person in my family has at one time had a bloody lip or black eye from another member of the family. My parents included."

"How are things now?" I asked.

150

"We got through all that. Those were rough times, you've got to understand the circumstances. I wasn't raised with comfort surrounding me." He stood and began to walk to the loading door. I followed. "I had a lot of trouble with acceptance growing up. I did have some friends, but I was always on the outside of everything."

"Wouldn't you say that all those things made you stronger?" I asked.

"Never really thought about it. Would I say that the hatred caused me to want to succeed? Yes."

Walter greeted us at the back door. He extended a stack of publications with a generous smile. "You have about four months here. Kind of dusty."

I quickly flipped through the pages. "Man, this is great. Thank you."

"If ever you need more, call KJHK," he told me. "They'd probably have old copies they'd unload onto you."

"What is all that?" George asked.

I handed him a couple. "Radio journals. They have the recent playlists of North American radio stations."

"Yeah, so? Why do you want to know what these stations are playing?"

"I don't," I said, pausing to point at one of the playlists. "Look...the station, the location of the station, and the station's telephone number."

"Are you thinking about sending our next seven-inch out to these places?"

"Not just that. This is the key to getting shows anywhere. For instance, this one in Burlington, Vermont. Let's say we want to play there. All we do is call them up, find out the name of clubs and promoters in Burlington that are doing our kind of shows, and there we have the contact. We send the station a copy of the record coinciding with the upcoming date in town, and viola—Band promotion 101. We can get shows most anywhere," I explained. "We could even set up a tour."

He stood silently for a moment while studying the pages of listings. "Let's do it. Next summer. I'm serious. I'm *very* serious."

"Knock, knock!" Xanthe screamed from the other side of my closed bedroom door. "You're supposed to be ready! I'm coming in."

"Come on in," I mumbled after she opened the door. Stacks of papers surrounded me on my bed, each one a hand-written letter to radio stations throughout the midwest. "Don't mind my privacy."

"Fuck you and your privacy, bastard—you were supposed to be downstairs waiting for me. What the hell are you doing? Is this for the band? You don't even have the records back from the plant yet!"

"I want to send them out the day they arrive, which will be later this week. I'm busy, and I'm resourceful."

"These are to fanzines?" she asked, picking one up.

"Some. Most are to college radio stations."

"Radio! Wow, I'm impressed! Will you talk to me when everyone in this country is singing your songs?"

"I doubt it. Let's go," I said, stepping up from the bed. I took a second to admire her impressive fashion sense. So alluring was her impeccable sense of style, I really had no choice. Her black leather mini-skirt devoured my attention. Red leggings covered the length of her powerful legs. The shiny left steel-toe of her boot peeked up at me through a ripped leather trestle. An oversized long underwear top covered her impressively large chest. The sleeves were rolled up over her elbows like a construction worker on break. She looked good to me. "Where are we going? What are we doing? Have you decided my night's plan for me yet?"

"Yeah, actually I have," she said. "You're going with me to a get-together at the Lynch house. Ready?"

"Your car or mine?"

"Neither," she said as we hustled down the wooden steps. "We're walking."

"I see."

"Everything is only a few blocks away in this town," she rationalized as we stumbled out into the brisk, autumn night.

We walked silently down Rhode Island Street, absorbing the change of season. We walked a full block without speaking. It was a comfortable silence—a comfort which I felt we both shared.

"Have you heard our recording session yet?" I finally asked.

"Of course I've heard it."

"Well, what do you think?"

"Honestly?" she asked.

"I wouldn't expect anything else."

"It's really good. You sound very...into it. I like that—turns me on. Were you nervous?"

"Not really," I told her. "It was odd to be in an actual studio environment, though."

"The recording quality is very punk."

"It's all we could afford. George hates it," I said as we arrived at the intersection of Mass. Street. Our destination, the Lynch house sat ominously across the busy street. We waited for traffic to clear. "So, this place is haunted?"

We made a quick break across the street before she could answer.

"They say. Some hippy claiming to be a professional psychic told us some girl got killed there over a hundred years ago. Her spirit just floats around from time to time."

I followed her up the stairs, one step behind her assuredness as we entered without knocking and proceeded to the haunted den.

The living room was moderately crowded with a specially selected elite crowd, each carrying on with their personal motif. The Cramps first album played loudly from a jambox like a soundtrack for the pretentious scenester's aloof disposition.

We took a seat on the old, dusty couch.

"How are things, Frank?" Skeet asked me politely, beer in hand, smile on face.

"Not bad. And you?"

"Doing okay. Day to day."

"How's work? Where *do* you work?" I asked, expecting proud tales of the working class.

"I don't have an actual job. I make ends meet by whatever means necessary."

"Skeet's a dumpster diver," Xanthe explained.

"Trying to get a job?" I asked. "Pizza Shuttle is probably hiring, if you want I could—"

"No, I'm doing fine," he replied confidently.

"Seriously," Xanthe said to me. "He makes a living in dumpsters."

"How? Do you find old TV's and fix them to sell or something?"

"Not objects, paper," he told me. "One good find and I'm set for a while."

"Receipts," she specified.

"Do you know the Eldridge Hotel down on Mass. and 7th?" he asked.

I nodded.

"When they throw out their trash, they toss all the credit card receipts. If a husband sees the transactions are for shoes, he will pay the bill and think nothing of it. I use a pay phone so it can't be traced. I place orders for products to be delivered, usually from England, like Doc Martens. When they get here, I sell them at a lower cost than any store. Anything you want, Frank, I can get it cheaper than anywhere else."

"You have to sign for the shipment when it arrives, don't you?" I asked.

"No, it comes through the mail. Anything that arrives in your mailbox is your possession. Everything is addressed to Lorenz Hart, which is one of the names on our mailbox."

The bedroom door opened and Specky came stumbling out, squinting in the harsh light. Vernon retreated inside the room after him.

"Frankie, what's happening?" Specky said as he sat next to me on the couch. "Tell me about that call. Sorry I didn't have time to hear about it this morning. I was going to be late for work as it was."

"Some guy named Bloody Mess from Peoria, Illinois called about the Fluorescent Condoms. He wants to start putting on shows. He liked the band's name and thought we were some kind of radicals doing shock-rock."

"Sounds like he wants Troubled Youth," Skeet said.

"I told him we weren't anything like that. He was obviously looking for a band with an outrageous, yet printable name for the Peoria newspaper. Trying to create news to sell his own records. I told him I was in a new band called the Jerk Offs. He said he'd give us one hundred fifty dollars guaranteed if we played in Peoria."

"Did you accept?" Specky asked.

"Yes. The show is the weekend after Thanksgiving. We'll have our records then."

"Cool," he said excitedly. "Our first out-of-state show!"

"Can I be the roadie?" Skeet asked.

"Sure," Specky said. "You can drive." He turned to face me again. "George told me you would be able to set up a summer tour."

"It would be possible," I told him. "Would you want to tour?"

"Hell, yes! I'll take that summer vacation road trip!"

The bedroom door opened and Vernon rolled out, rubbing his eyes. His Fred Perry was unbuttoned and partially tucked. An American flag was tattooed on his firm chest.

"That was fast," Skeet mumbled as he stood and walked into the bedroom.

"What's going on in there, Specky?" Xanthe sighed with disgust. "Never mind, I don't want to know."

The front door creaked open and a short skinhead crawled pathetically up the steps. His nose was leaking blood.

"What happened, Lank?" Specky asked, rising to his feet.

"Frat boys in South Park." Lank propped himself dramatically against the wall. "Down Mass."

Specky jumped forward with clenched fists as the rest of the skinheads scrambled courageously to their feet. He rushed out the door. Vernon joined him, his actions slow and calculated, his gait as solid as the expression on his face. The clan of young skinheads all stomped down the staircase in an angry mob.

153

"That's one way to clear a room," Xanthe said. "Instant skinhead repellent, mutter the word *fight* and there they go like a bunch of idiots. Lank probably just tripped on the steps."

We stood up as the bedroom door flung open and Skeet stood with his pants undone.

"Fight?" He walked calmly to shut off the jambox. "Where?"

"South Park," Xanthe responded with a smile. "Better hurry."

He rushed out the door and down the steps, leaving us alone in the house.

"Never a dull moment with this crowd," Xanthe said in the contrasting quiet. "Shall we go?"

Suddenly the silhouette of a woman glided through the darkness. It was the ghost! My heart raced as it came toward us, entering the light with her blond locks flowing, the look of death written on her gaunt and pale face.

"Anybody got a cigarette?" the ghost asked with a husky, southern accent.

"Yeah," Xanthe said casually. "I do."

"Where did everyone go?" the young girl slurred as she adjusted her jeans.

"There's a big brawl going on," Xanthe said as she handed her the cigarette. "Who are you?"

"I'm Sylvia," the girl said as she placed the cigarette between her limp lips. The remains of cherry lipstick was smeared up the side of her face. She looked exhausted. "Traveling around the country. I'm from Alabama."

"How old?" Xanthe asked.

"Old enough."

"Old enough to have a train pulled on you by a bunch of skinheads?" Xanthe asked.

"I need a light," the girl said, ignoring the question.

"From Alabama, huh?" Xanthe asked her as she struck a match and lifted the flame to the girl's haggard face. Xanthe's actions were firm and deliberate. There was nothing weak about her, yet she was absolutely feminine. "Running from what?"

"I don't need—"

"You're welcome for the cigarette," Xanthe growled as she pulled me to the steps by the collar of my shirt. "Make yourself at home. Seems you already have."

I followed her down the stairs as if on the end of her leash.

"That girl could clean out their house," I told her.

"That's the price to pay for degradation," she replied with cold hostility. "They stole all that shit in there anyway. It's their Karma. They revolt me."

"Suppose they were paying her?"

"With what? They don't have money. That's the problem with me—I hate men, but more significantly, I hate the fact that I am so attracted to men."

We walked briskly down Mass. Street, not a word mentioned from either of us as we came upon South Park. The courthouse sat in the distance on the other side of the park where the downtown lure of shops begin.

"Over there," Xanthe said, pointing across the street.

The unsuspecting frat boys were clearly out-numbered by the attacking mob of skinheads. A red BMW was parked by the street. Its windshield was cracked like the web of a spider. It was something I had never seen—the odds in favor of what I had always known as the minority.

We stood in the dark shadow of a towering oak tree.

"I've been on the other side, and I really don't see the difference," I mumbled.

154

I watched the blood pour. I remembered.

The morning before Thanksgiving, I was awakened by a tapping on the window. I sat up to see Norm smiling in at me from the roof over the porch.

I opened the window, allowing him to bring a cold draft into my room. "Where have you been?"

"Everywhere and nowhere, at the same time." He climbed inside and sat at the end of the bed. I could smell the scent of winter on his clothes. "In town for only a short time. I've got to be in Iowa tomorrow. Just wanted to see the old town, see what's going on with my band."

"Your band is doing fine," I replied with a groggy voice and a smile. "We have a new record. Over there in those boxes, take one."

"I've got one, thanks. I heard it last night. Great work."

I rubbed my eyes, still having trouble focusing.

"Sent copies out everywhere yet?" he asked.

I nodded. "We plan to tour next summer, so we've all agreed to pitch in on a third page ad every month in *Maximum RockNRoll* until we leave, just to promote the name."

"I knew you'd take the reigns. It's nice to be right."

"How was South Dakota, or was it North Dakota?"

"An experience," he said, lifting his shirt to reveal two massive scars on his upper chest.

"Did you learn anything from it?" I asked.

"So much that I couldn't even begin."

"So, you're going to spend Thanksgiving with the family?"

"I am," he replied.

"You celebrate Thanksgiving?"

"I take advantage of the time to see my family," he told me. "I don't celebrate it, no. It doesn't mix well with my ancestry. What are your plans?"

"No plans. I'm not into the holiday, really. It's a very shallow and selfish tradition."

"It's the American way—gluttony," he said. "Bathroom down the hall?"

I nodded.

He excused himself, shutting the door behind him. I rubbed my eyes and waited for his return. My body felt warm and comfortable. The sheets conducted my body-heat like a tropical plant in a greenhouse. I felt as if I had melted comfortably to the bed. I stretched my limbs and yawned, waiting for the door to open again. It never did.

Norm's words stuck to me like velcro. That was the first year I fasted on Thanksgiving.

Peoria, Illinois was cold and hard, an industrial town by appearance with grave, washed-out faces occupying the lifeless streets. It had a restricting atmosphere. Having been raised in Iola had caused me to develop a severe reaction to geography and community. Very few towns gave me comfort. This one was no exception.

I could hear the opening band struggling through their set as I waited patiently outside in the van. Their vocalist, Bloody Mess pranced about the stage in striped leotards and hot pink undies. Strangely, he believed that his presence was somehow threatening and dangerous. He looked more like a middle-aged woman with a bad perm and horrible sense of fashion than a rock and roll deviant. His stage-name was humorously non-representative of his juvenile and harmless character. Between songs, he chattered his accomplishments to the unspirited audience. By now, it was more than clear that the serial killer John Wayne Gacy would be doing the artwork for his upcoming record. If their record's quality would equal their performance, it would be plagued with errors and incompetence.

On the dashboard of the van lie a torn and wrinkled clipping from the Peoria newspaper. In the article, our name was mentioned once as the opening act traveling from Kansas. Skeet ensured that the billing would remain as quoted. After a brief and private conversation with Bloody Mess, Skeet returned with not only a promise of the billing, but with the entire guarantee paid up-front.

Hazel sat quietly in the back of the van, catching up on some homework. I felt a curious desire to strike up conversation with her, but I knew she hadn't the time. She was the mysterious figure in the band, the one I knew least. I could tell this wouldn't be the night to break the ice.

As Bloody Mess announced their final number, Hazel immediately dropped her homework to step inside the venue. George and I sat alone in silence.

"Tell me a story about your life," I requested.

"What story?"

"*Any* story. Your choice will say a lot about your personality."

He laughed.

"Seriously! I don't know anybody in this band. Give me some slack, pal! I'm the new guy! Here, I'll give you a nudge—have you ever been in a fight?"

"Of course I have," he told me.

"Besides with your family, I mean."

He chuckled. "Yeah."

"What was the grounds of your first fight? What case were you defending?"

"Wow...so long ago. Let me see...I guess that'd have been second grade. On the kickball field. Some guy named Perry was laughing at me because I went to kick the ball and missed it. Almost fell on my ass, and of course everyone roared with laughter. This guy Perry, he had the nerve to call me a pro. Not a *pro*, but a P. R. O."

"Ah, the old Pregnant Retarded Ostrich insult. Those are fighting words for sure."

"How about you?" he asked. "Whose ass did you kick?"

"Fought with my brother, but that's what brothers are for. No, I was the fightee, not the fighter. Never been a participating member of a fight."

"Okay, I have a fight story for you," he said. "One of revenge."

"My favorite topic."

"It was my Junior year of high school—"

"This is Kansas City?" I asked.

"Yeah, Blue Valley. Anyway, there was this cretin named Billy Bob Duft. He was the kind of guy that wore the tight, dark blue Wrangler jeans, cowboy boots—"

"Yeah, I think he went to my high school, too. He and about three hundred of his close relatives. Go on..."

"He liked to fight, can you believe that? He'd fight old drunks just to provoke a lawsuit since he was underage. Anyway, there was one New Waver in our high school. A guy named Cash. He was small, not too masculine. He had the hairdo—not quite A Flock of Seagulls, but nonetheless he looked the part. Cash and I were really good friends at the time. I wasn't a New Waver, I listened to the music somewhat, but never really got into it like he did. Anyway, Billy Bob thought Cash was gay—"

"Of course."

156

"One day in the lunchroom he and his friends started some shit with Cash. I knew there was no chance in hell he'd be able to stand his ground against those guys. Keep in mind, this Billy Bob was like a bear. So, I stepped in and told them to back off. Of course, this makes them think I'm Cash's gay lover—"

"Of course."

"So, there goes my reputation—one night I had my parent's car. It wasn't the classiest ride, but nevertheless, it's my parent's car. I was returning home from a weekend night out. I stopped in to get some gas, when a massive truck pulls up next to me."

"And there's Billy Bob," I said.

"Actually, no. There's his little sidekicks, four of them. They surrounded me, pushed me, attempted to provoke a fight they'd easily win. I finished pumping the gas, went inside to pay, and there they waited for me outside. They were all drunk and falling over themselves—"

"Of course."

"I wasted no time getting in the car and getting the hell out of there—*quick*. As I'm driving off, they threw rocks at my parent's car! Dented the sides, cracked the windows...I was totally pissed. I mean, this was my parent's car!"

"Right."

"So, I hauled ass down a country road. They were right behind me, headlights up my ass. I finally ditched them, right? I told my parents, and they weren't happy. Well, I was a lot less happy. The following week at school, I sought out each one of those guys. I found one the first day and kicked the shit out of him. I got suspended two days for it. My first day back from suspension, I found another and kicked the hell out of him. Suspended two more days. First day back from that suspension, I found the third and made him kiss the floor. Another suspension. When I came round for the fourth, Billy Bob was keen to my plan and stepped in. I told him this was my deal, to stay out. My problems were with his trolls, not him. I then admitted to him that he could easily kick my ass. It all ended there. I guess all he wanted was for me to admit that."

"All because they called your friend a homosexual?"

"Kind of. I mean, it escalated from that point. To a certain extent, yes."

"That's very noble of you."

"Do you have a good fish story to match?" he asked. "Keep in mind, the next time I tell that one, there'll be five guys, not four. That's northeast Kansas, tell me about southeast Kansas."

"Man, do I have a decent story? That was a good one." I thought a moment.

"Aw, shit...here comes Specky," George said. "And he's with some nasty-looking girl."

"Guess he's going to want us to give up the love wagon for him." I rolled down the window, allowing the cold breeze to seep inside. "Yes?"

"You guys should check out the band," Specky suggested with a mischievous smile. A rather unattractive, stumpy little girl clung excitedly to his arm.

George laughed. "The band sucks."

"Let me rephrase that," Specky said. "I'm giving tours of the van and you guys are in my way."

I opened the door and slid out. George followed me, sacrificing the keys to Specky.

The street was already littered with beer cans and plastic wrappers of junk food. An adolescent couple sat on the sidewalk, putting forth a great deal of effort to look pathetic. We walked inside the noisy hall that reeked of cigarette smoke.

"This place is going to burn my tender eyes," I complained.

"I hate cigarette smoke. Did you ever smoke?" George asked.

"No, I never needed to. No one I cared to impress. I suppose I've always been too secure and confident. Call me an arrogant bastard…"

"You're an arrogant bastard," George declared positively.

"So, how am I doing?" I asked as silence finally prevailed with the diminish of the opening band.

"With what?"

"The band, what else?"

"No one's kicked you out. I guess that says something," he said. "No, actually you've really impressed me. When Norm quit, I was ready to go, too. In fact, I had decided to do so the night before you came to practice with us."

"Were you and Norm close?"

"I respected Norm quite a bit, actually. I wouldn't do what he does, but I respect the lengths he'll push himself. He's made an impression on me. I hope he's doing well."

"So, why would you want to quit?" I asked.

"Can't stand all this." He gestured toward the crowd of scenesters huddling in elite circles. "All the stupid games. You never escape them. You can only isolate yourself. Motivation based from your inadequate social standing is a pretty hollow goal. Norm never bought into that. Neither did I. I'd rather be respected for my accomplishments."

"I'm sure these people respect the music you create," I said.

"Exactly my point. Music for the Special Ed. I'm capable of creating much more."

"More complex music, you mean?"

He nodded assuredly.

"Our music hits a nerve somewhere deep," I told him. "That comes from a fan, not a member. There's something to be said about that, something that goes beyond these social circles."

"To answer your question, yes, you're doing a great job," he confided. "I can feel these songs again through your own belief in them. You deliver an intensity that is very pure. When we're on stage, I know I want to be up there. It's one of the few times I'm totally sure about that."

"I'm glad you're satisfied," I told him.

An hour later, we began an invigorating set to a very receptive audience. A few songs into the performance, the guitar suddenly fell silent. An old drunk with a greasy, rockabilly haircut had yanked Specky's cord from his guitar. The old guy twirled the cord victoriously in the air over his head, swinging it inches from Specky's face.

The music quickly ceased and the venue fell strangely silent.

"That sounds better…" the middle-aged drunk said as he stumbled backward. "You guys suck."

Several inhibited and anonymous groans responded throughout the crowd. It was clear that this man had a reputation in town.

"Get lost, Stork," someone spoke squeamishly, safely hidden in the audience. "Get a life."

"Who the *fuck* are you?" Stork asked as he gripped tightly to the cord.

158

Out the corner of my eye, I could see Skeet stepping forward from the wings. Specky took off his guitar and leaned it against his amplifier.

"Who the *fuck* are you?" Stork repeated to the stiff crowd. "You people are pretty damned uptight." He ran his thin fingers through his thinning hair. The grease kept it in place momentarily. "You people think you're so damned liberal and on the fucking edge. You go so far left, you end up right. That's what you mama's boys are all about."

Skeet meandered through the crowd until he found himself face to face with Stork.

"Leave now, before I kick your fucking teeth out," Skeet warned calmly. He seemed perfectly at ease.

Stork stood in front of him, watching and laughing. He lost his balance momentarily. He grabbed a nervous and horrified young girl whose presence seemed based on a dare.

Specky stepped to the edge of the stage, towering over the two of them. "What do you think, Skeet?"

Skeet smiled, lighting his rosy cheeks. The dimples of his smile seemed innocently cute. "Drop him," he mumbled as if words were too much effort.

Specky casually leaned forward, grabbed Stork's greasy hair, and yanked him to the stage.

"Drop him," Skeet sang.

With one hand mashing Stork's head against the platform stage, Specky kicked him repeatedly in the face with his steel-toed boot. The Oxblood coloration of his boot seemed to melt with the dripping of blood down the heel. Specky gave in to Stork's resistance, dropping him to the floor in his own fluids.

"Leave," Specky demanded calmly. "Don't ever come back here."

Stork lie motionless.

"Get up, motherfucker, or we'll set fire to your greasy, hippy ass," Skeet said with a strangely sweet tone.

Skeet leaned down and clutched a handful of Stork's hair. He dragged him through the venue and out the front door. Stork gave a futile struggle with flailing limbs. He covered his swollen and bloody face while he desperately tried to release himself from Skeet's powerful grip.

The venue was stunned and silent. All eyes were upon Specky.

"Let's go home," Specky said dully, quietly. "Show's over."

The wind pelted the fine crystals of icy condensation against the windshield of my car, lifting the shelf of solidified snow from the hood in massive clumps. I pulled into a parking space along Mass. Street, just in front of the Taco Johns. A young, minimum-wage earner scraped the Christmas decorations off the window. The holiday season had come and gone. Another year of hope lie ahead.

A small stack of red fliers sat at my side. I had spent half the day posting them around town, publicizing an upcoming show. I wouldn't be able to sleep until I knew our name was posted on every corner, every bulletin, every post. It was an arduous task that demanded hours of my time weekly.

I shut the engine off, waiting in the warm comfort of the car's fading heat as I watched the snow swirl about the street like white sand.

The power of the cold penetrated my car as the door thrust open, killing the warmth instantly. Swift steps as rigid as the cold air brought me to the door of the restaurant, its occupancy low and quiet.

Specky waited at the booth nearest the door. He was bundled from head to toe, each garment branded with a tag of quality. "Kind of late, aren't you?"

"Had to post fliers," I told him. "Spent six hours and a tank of gas wandering through the snow. Eaten yet?"

"Hell," he protested as he stood to join me at the counter. "Waiting on you. Five tacos, please."

The cashier scribbled his order on a note pad. She looked up at me with untainted, youthful eyes.

"Six tacos, please. No meat, refried beans instead, and give me tomatoes."

"Can you throw another taco on my order?" he requested.

We paid and waited patiently for the plastic trays to be slid across the counter.

"So," Specky said as we found a booth in the farthest corner. "Are you ready to play?"

"That's still going on?"

"Of course. Why wouldn't it?"

"Isn't it to be outdoors?" I asked.

"It's supposed to stop snowing."

"It'll be twenty degrees, at best."

"What's it to you? You aren't the one banging your hands against metal strings. Can't take it?"

"An outdoor show in January?" I asked. "Come on! There's three feet of snow."

"Well, if you really *cared* about the music... It's a conquest, man," he said enthusiastically. "Are we not men? Are we not men?"

"Conquest for what? The highest level of stupidity? We'll achieve that."

"Women. Think about all the women. What else is there?"

"Music," I reminded him. "You have something about women, what is it?"

"I'm a male, what do you expect?"

"So am I, but I'm not quite so...preoccupied as you."

"I love women, what can I say? How do I love women?" He took a healthy bite of the taco before continuing. "Let me count the ways..."

"How many women have you had sex with in your lifetime?"

"Seventy-four."

I shook my head in disbelief.

"Seventy-four," he confided proudly. "I was a virgin a few months ago. See, I had this party where seventy women showed up, and I got a few beers in me...of course, I'm kidding. It took a long time to acquire such an impressive collection."

"I don't know seventy-four girls—I don't even know twenty girls. You could catch something deadly, you know."

"And die a hero."

"Is it a power thing?" I asked.

"I just enjoy it."

"Enjoy what? The conquest, or the experience? You can't tell me all those experiences were good ones."

"No." He slowly took another bite. "Why?"

"Just curious. I've never known someone as sexually active as you."

He laughed proudly.

"What's the worst experience you've ever had with a woman?" I asked.

"During sex?"

"Not necessarily."

"The worst experience involving a female in general? That must have been the time when my mother burned me with a cigarette." He raised his shirt. Four small, cylindrical scars circled his bellybutton. "Haven't seen her since. I grew up with my father."

"Oh..." I mumbled. "I'm sorry..."

"So, what's the deal with you and Xanthe?" he asked.

"No deal."

"Come on, don't shit a shitter. I know better."

"Haven't laid a hand on her," I assured him.

"It'll happen."

I unwrapped another taco. "I don't think so."

"You don't find her attractive?"

"No, I do. We're just different people."

"Would it be that she's a stripper?" he suggested.

"Well, that would be an issue if I were to get serious, I suppose. We have a different perspective on entertainment."

"You mean the drugs?" he asked as he tore into another taco. "I respect your choices, but this is the real world. People drink, they experiment with drugs, they have casual sex. Don't let your idealism limit your options. Life's too short. You've got to live it while you can."

I sat quietly eating, watching him as I listened.

"If the shoe fits, slip it in," he advised. "You'll be happy you did." He took another quick bite. "I always thought Xanthe was gay."

"Because she wouldn't have sex with you?"

"Who said she wouldn't have sex with me?" he asked defensively.

"She did."

He smiled. "Yeah, maybe."

"Any woman who wouldn't have sex with you would have to be gay, huh?" I asked.

"Of course. You know, I could eat another two more."

"Well, you win, then. I'm had."

The stinging sensation in my fingers had resided long ago. I found myself repetitively examining my hands, making sure they still gripped the microphone. Rows of headlights illuminated us from the steep incline of cars parked in the alley up the hill. An impressive number of people lined the side of Mount Oread in the tiny backyard, watching us play our short set in the deathly cold night air.

My chattering teeth chopped at the microphone between songs, echoing through the cold silence of the student ghettos.

"Last song?" Hazel asked the band.

"Two more songs," Specky insisted.

"My heads are going to crack," she groaned. She succumbed with a reluctant nod.

"Okay," I said into the microphone, my voice suddenly small and inaudible over the rustling wind.

George rushed to check the board. "We've lost our power."

"Get off the stage, queer," Billy Christ screamed to me. He propped himself against the wall and smiled.

"The thing must be blown," Specky said as he and George flipped the switches. "Maybe it's the cold."

"Equipment shouldn't die in the cold," George said as he fumbled with the power button. "Maybe the fuse blew."

"I could break this bottle upside your fucking head," Billy said to me as he stumbled up on the back porch where the band was set up. "Are you too chickenshit to make me leave, pretty-boy?"

"Show's over, people!" Specky screamed at the audience. "Get out of here...go to the heat."

The crowd grumbled unpleasant remarks as they returned to the warmth of the house. Billy followed.

"Jesus!" George said as he lifted the board in his hands. "Look at this!" The cord dangled in his fingers. "Someone unplugged it."

Specky stopped to notice. "It was plugged over there—"

"By Billy," I said. "That's just great."

"It was too cold anyway," Hazel resolved. "Come on, let's load our stuff."

We toted our equipment up the icy incline to the alley. The backyard grew vacant and quiet.

"Done already?" Xanthe asked from the porch down the hill.

"Yeah," I said. "Where the hell were you?"

"You're assuming I'm going to stand out here in the cold to watch you play? Give me a break, pal. I guess I just *look* stupid."

"While you're standing there, you could grab that guitar case and bring it up here," I suggested.

"Sure, dear," she complained as she picked it up with gloved hands. A thick, black sweatshirt and black leggings kept her weather-resistant. "Do you want to eat, or do I need to take you to Lawrence Memorial to get your frostbitten hands removed?"

"I've already eaten," I said, blowing warm air into my cupped hands. "Thanks for the offer."

She climbed the snow-covered steps to the alley. "All right. We'll go to your place, then."

George took the guitar case and gently placed it on top of the heaping stack of amplifiers and drums. The rear doors enclosed the material of a mutual dream, together in the silence of a faceless alley.

Xanthe shuffled through the snow to my car.

"You're driving," I told her as I scooted across the icy path, following her lead. "I can't use my hands."

"Give me the keys."

"In my front coat pocket. Get them."

"What would you do without me?" she asked.

"Where to begin...make my own plans for a change?"

"Get in the car, bastard."

"Yes, dear," I joked.

The tires crunched through the snow, slipping along the gravel glossed with an even layer of ice.

"Billy sabotaged the end of the set," I said as we shivered in the silence of the Ranchero.

"He'll keep pushing you until you stand up against him," she told me sharply.

"I don't want to fight him. I have no reason."

"He'll find a reason. He'll study you until he finds what will push you to that edge."

162

"I'll make sure I don't give him the pleasure."

"I can respect that," she said as we rushed south down Mass. Street. "There does come a time when you should just put your foot down. In any case...people will naturally strive to go that mile, and they'll provoke the inch to go on."

"So, how was Christmas for you?" she asked me as we pulled up to my house.

"Same. Another Christmas spent alone."

We hustled to the front door.

"Best way, in my opinion," she began as I fumbled with the keys to unlock the front door. "People are just trouble. Being single is the only way. Monogamy is not a natural state, and it's been a highly unsuccessful experiment."

I threw the door open as a blast of heat escaped from within. Removing all my winter clothes, I rushed upstairs to the bathroom with Xanthe right behind me. The house was unnaturally still with all the tenants throughout the town seeking some substance for thrill. I turned on the faucet until the water flowed luke warm—no hotter—then stuck my frozen hands under the stream.

"Nice," Xanthe said, standing behind me, pointing at the toilet bowl.

In the scum built up under the surface of the toilet water, someone had scraped the word *love* away, leaving the clean porcelain as letters.

"I can feel my hands," I declared as I gradually increased the temperature of the water. "I get to keep them." I turned off the water and wiped my hands on my shirt. They were red and stinging.

"This place is a pit," she said as we left the bathroom. "I don't respect the artist, so-to-speak, who carved that in the toilet bowl. That's really revolting."

"What's that—the word, or the effort?"

"I guess both...fucking hippies. Love is for the idealist—I'm a realist. Love is an addiction, not a good thing. My independence is all I have." She led me to the bed. "And another thing...this whole making love crap. We're animals, for God's sake! There is no love-making, there's only sex...the grind...the horizontal dance...bumping uglies. I believe it just so happens that humans are capable of expressing adoration. So, we try to put the two things together—sex and emotion, and they can fit together, but they don't necessarily belong together. It's all about procreation. Where does this love garbage come into play? I'll tell you where, it's through the society that we have created, the reality that we have warped to fit our morals."

"Our culture is pretty uptight about sex—"

"Damn straight it is!" she declared. "I make a decent living off the side-effect. It's sad and pathetic—not on the part of the men, but on the society for forcing these morals that are so incongruent with the fact that we are simply another species on this planet. No better than roaches, no better than dogs."

"You sound pretty self-righteous."

"As righteous as you'd expect from someone who's been independent so long as I have been."

"I do believe in love," I said, lying back against the pillow. "I believe that people overuse the word and desensitize it. I'd rather express my feelings through actions. The word gets thrown around like loose change. It's heavily overused."

"And over-rated. Like sex. People think too highly of it. You know what would be ideal?"

"What's that?" I asked.

"This wouldn't go over very well in proper American society, but it'd make life much easier. In our society, it's all or nothing. Either you're single, or you aren't. Of

163

course, there's the whole dating thing, whoever does that. Anyway, take two people. Both are too busy to play with people's emotions—too goal-oriented to deal with someone's insecurities. So, they decide to form a commitment. Companionship when time allows. No bullshit, no games. Sex, going out to eat—that kind of thing. The commitment would be that they communicate honestly. Sex only with each other, but not restricted to each other. If that exclusive engagement should ever change, the other person would be informed for whatever difference that would make. Emotions don't come into play, and if they do, then it's over. It'd be a pact to offer pleasure to the other person, and exclusive only to that extent."

"Interesting, but is it too idealistic?"

"I also think people would benefit by being more open about sex," she said. "I feel that if you see an attractive person walking down the street, it'd be a compliment to ask them if they'd like to have sex. Of course, you could simply decline, but that'd be pretty complimentary."

"Every guy would be asking every girl that passed by..."

"Yeah," she said, resigning to laughter. "Probably so. But there's nothing wrong with asking."

"Do you want to have sex, then?"

"Sure."

"Hello."

"Yeah...like...I'm looking to find the Jerk Offs?"

"You're talking to one," I said into the phone. "Who's this?"

"Marty Straw. Salisbury, Maryland. I've seen your ad in *Maximum RockNRoll*. Hittin' the road—yah?"

"Yes."

"Killer name, by the way, bro."

"Well, thank you, sir..."

"No problemo," he said. "Got any dates on this cross-country extravaganza?"

"I'm collecting numbers right now."

"If you're rockin' DC, you should motor my way, dude. I'll be chillin' in Ocean City, Maryland like I do every summer. I'm a lifeguard."

"Think we could get a show there?" I asked.

"Dude, why would I call? Surf, sun, sex, and drugs. This is the place to be."

"Great."

"Cool, you'll dig it. Bitchin' beach, dude. Bodacious waves. Got the innie connections, you guys will be stylin'. Just let Marty play papa, bro. By the way, I'm a vinyl collector—"

"I'll send some copies," I assured him.

"Cool," he said. "Got a pen?"

"Got one." I wrote down the address and significant information. "I'll call you when I get a better idea."

"Cool thing, bro."

"Talk to you later, Marty."

"Kirk out," he said as he hung up.

I sat down the phone and gazed at the calendar. Taking all the information acquired over the past month from the radio stations, I penciled in a rough idea of a tour route. Each date on the calendar marked with a city contained the name of the club and the phone number.

"Are you still on the phone?" Specky asked as he climbed the stairs with a plate of food. "Let me see." He tilted the calendar for a better view. "Two months?"

"And four days."

"Never been to any of these places. Pennsylvania, Maryland, Georgia...wow."

"These shows aren't coming easy. We can forget about getting the guarantee. We'll be playing for the door, whatever that'll be."

"I'm glad *you're* doing it," he said.

"A lot of programmers at these radio stations have been seeing that ad every month. A lot of people are calling to set up a show or just offering us their place to stay, simply because they've seen our name so much."

"If we're lucky, our interview for *Maximum RockNRoll* will run while we're on tour."

"Or before," I said as the phone rang.

"Here, let me get it." He reached down for the phone, balancing the plate with the other hand. "Hello? Yeah, I'm with the band...hold on, here's the guy you need to talk to."

I reached out and grabbed it from him as he proceeded up to his room on the third floor. "This is Frank."

"My name is Jules. I'm the program director at WFMU in East Orange, New Jersey. I got a promo copy of your record in the mail. I really like it."

"Thanks."

"How are things going? Sold many copies?"

"We have very few left. We only pressed three hundred, and we got distribution immediately which practically cleaned out our stock. The rest have gone to shows."

"Who's distributing it?" he asked.

"Rough Trade, Dutch East India, and Blacklist. Konkurrent is handling it overseas. Locally, we can't keep up with it. It's been on four *Maximum RockNRoll* Top Ten lists, which hopefully will generate sales outside our regional following. We're going to press another three hundred copies just for the tour. I'm expecting we'll have to double the entire production when we return from tour if the distributors run out. I believe they will."

"Glad things are going well. It'll enter our rotation soon," he told me. "I'll be playing it quite a bit, actually. We broadcast over the tri-state area, covering a good portion of New York City. There's this club nearby in Newark called the Pipeline. We have a deal. See, every Thursday evening we have a band play live on the radio, then they play the Pipeline later that night. Great exposure. I'm calling to extend an invitation for you guys to play on the air this summer."

"Live over New York City? How many people would be listening?"

"Your guess would be as good as mine," he told me. "It's a large city."

"Yes, we'll do it," I decided quickly.

"Do you know when you'd be available?"

"I have my schedule here," I said, looking at the empty calendar covered with penciled dates. "How about the last Thursday of June?"

"Okay," he said slowly. "That looks good. The week before is booked, so that works out well. I'll contact the club. Let me give you directions to the radio station. Where will you be coming from?"

I looked at the empty calendar. DC was penciled a couple days earlier.

"Ocean City, Maryland."

"Okay, first..." he began as he slowly gave the directions into New Jersey.

"What's the deal with the club?" I asked. "How much would we be making?"

"What are you expecting?"

"We have a guarantee of one hundred dollars a show, but, you know..."

"If people come, you'll make your money."

"So, the radio thing is just promotional?"

"Yes."

"Fair enough."

"Well, then...I guess we'll be seeing you this summer."

"Great," I told him. "I look forward to it."

"Have a good night."

"You, too. Goodbye." I slowly put the phone down. "Specky! We got our first confirmed show! A cool one, too."

"So, what's the story," Xanthe asked as she stumbled with heavy strides through the front door. The changing spring air followed her. Summer edged close behind. "Did they like you guys?"

"Yeah, both were very good shows. Sold a lot of records, made enough money to make at least one hundred T-shirts for the tour," I said as we walked to the kitchen. Spike's door opened and Bootsy—now with dyed blue fur rushed out.

"Time to defecate," Harold said as he walked out behind Bootsy. His black leather jacket covered his skeletal frame. "Hey, Frank, I need to talk to you."

"About what?"

"About the tour," he said. "I want to go."

"Skeet has already agreed to be the roadie," I told him.

"Last I heard, he decided to stay. I can do sound, drive the van, whatever. What do you say?"

"Skeet's really not going?" I asked.

"That's what I heard."

"No one told me," I mumbled. "If that's the case, then sure."

"Cool. I'm going on tour! Harold and some other jerks—I mean Jerk Offs!"

Bootsy came running back to the room, pushing the door open with her nose. The music of Specimen seeped through the dark, cavernous room. I peeked inside, having never seen the interior of Spike's domain. The walls were covered with black trash bags, consuming any light that should dare enter. The decor was universal: religious objects stolen from various Catholic churches around Kansas. A large red velvet robe hung over a statue of Jesus that overlooked his massive bed.

"Spike and Priests have a rough history," Spike said as he wandered from the kitchen. His long, black gown followed him like a train. He looked like a bride fallen from grace. "Please excuse me."

Harold turned and walked upstairs.

"Your house stinks," Xanthe told me as we continued to the kitchen.

"Smells like Bootsy's ass," I added. "The dog doesn't make it to the door." I pointed to a small room by the kitchen where a washer and dryer once stood. In its place was an old mattress covered with months of fecal accumulation.

"That's revolting."

"That's the cesspool, as George calls it. And yes, it is pretty disgusting," I said, laughing.

"Glad you have a sense of humor," she scorned lightly.

"It's my only option living here."

166

"I'm not hungry after all," she said. "Let's go to your room. Then you can tell me about the trip."

We walked through the messy house once again to the stairs. "I think our place is being watched."

"By who?"

"The cops."

"Why do you say?" she asked.

"There's an unmarked car that sits out by the house when all the parents are picking their kids up from the school. When all the cars leave, it does, too."

"Never picks anyone up?"

"No. Just blends in with the others. I've been pulled over three times in two weeks while delivering pizzas."

"They think you're the runner," she said as we slowly walked up the steps. She groaned as we reached the top. "What's all this?"

"Marijuana plants drying—"

"I know what it is."

"They're not mine." I glanced down the hall at all the plants hanging upside down from the ceiling.

"Doesn't matter. You live here."

"Well, we could sleep in the van tonight. That's where I've been crashing lately, now that it's getting warmer."

"I'm not sleeping in here, that's for damn sure," she insisted. "Not if your place is about to get busted. Come on, let's get what we need. Can't believe I'm going to be sleeping in the street."

"You won't be sleeping in the street, you'll be in the van...in the street."

"Jesus, you guys are a mess," she complained as we rushed back down the stairs. "I'm surprised the place is still standing."

I opened the front door for her. "Ready for my story?"

"Sure."

"Okay, so we arrived in Fayetteville, Arkansas on Friday and played with a band called Big Drill Car. There was a good turn-out, so we got paid. Pretty uneventful, as shows go. The next day, we played in Oklahoma City. We headlined at some Knights of Columbus type place." I reached into my pocket and fished out the key to the van. "Anyway, after the Oklahoma City show, this old man pulled up by the van. He opened his car door—keep in mind there are like one hundred punk kids standing around the street, talking. He opened the car door and he's got a shotgun in his lap! He just sat there, looking at no one, aiming the gun at the crowd!"

She ducked under the blankets. "What'd you do?"

"We just hid on the other side of the van. Someone called the cops. Took them twenty minutes to show up."

"Was it a bad side of town?"

"Didn't seem all that good, but what do I know? Anyway, we waited for the cops while this old man sought to clean up the neighborhood."

"That's probably how he saw it. So what happened?"

"Not much. The cops came with their sirens blaring, so the guy just took off. I guess he didn't like the band all that much."

"He didn't buy a record?" she asked.

"Not that I was aware of..."

167

We sat quietly as cars passed down 15th Street. I reached up and placed my hand gently on her freshly shaven head that shined in the glare of the streetlights.

"I was amazed at how many people were at your last show," she whispered. "I've never seen a local punk band pack the Outhouse like that. There must have been over four hundred people there."

"Something like four hundred thirty, if I remember right. Yeah, we're doing okay these days."

"A lot changed after you guys opened the Dirty Rotten Imbeciles. All your efforts to promote the band has really paid off. You guys have the buzz."

I smiled proudly. "I'm going to miss you when you leave."

"Don't get all sappy on me..."

"I'm not saying I couldn't live without you. You aren't *that* good at sex."

"Not that bad, either."

"Okay, and my point—which has nothing to do with—"

"Not that bad, either. Wouldn't you say?"

"Yeah," I replied. "Not *that* bad."

"Now, what were you saying?" she whispered softly, sweetly.

"What I meant is I enjoy your company. I look forward to telling you all the stupid things that no one else cares to hear. Those trivial conversations are priceless. Thank you for listening to every one of them."

"Sure thing," she said.

I rubbed her bald head endearingly with the tips of my fingers.

"I have some advice for you, and I hope you take it," she said.

"Okay."

"The band won't last forever, and I don't know what you plan on doing when it ends. You'll know the next step to take when you need to. But one thing: you need to be the one to abolish the band. Have that control, have that respect. Otherwise, it'll control you. Your ambition leaves you wide open for obsession. When the time comes, be aware of it."

"Sure," I responded slowly.

"Always know where the exit is located. Not necessarily using it, but knowing that you can, and not being afraid. For instance, at my work, that's what keeps me from leaving some nights. Just knowing I can walk out at any moment makes me hang in there. Once you realize the freedom you have over a situation, you master it. I don't want the band to ever outweigh your own sense of pride. There's more to life than recognition...recognition from total strangers."

"Like what?"

"Like good sex."

"Yeah, I should find me some of that." I wondered if having sex in a parked van on a busy street would constitute a decent locker room story. I smiled at the thought and turned to her as another car passed.

"I've been raped before," she said softly.

My eyes widened. I spoke the first thought that came to mind. "High school?"

"Actually, once in high school, and once last year." She paused momentarily to collect her thoughts. "In high school, there was this guy whom I barely knew. He hung out with me and my friends occasionally. Never cared to really know him. Anyway, one night my parents went away for the weekend. He was hanging out with us, it was a Friday night. I guess it had been a topic of conversation that I would be at home alone.

168

Anyway, later that night I awoke to him standing over my bed. He had a knife in his hand. I didn't know what to do. So, I didn't do anything."

"Did you beat the dogshit out of him later?"

"I wasn't the boisterous bitch I am these days. So, no, I acted as if nothing had happened. In fact, I was probably nicer to him based out of the fear and humiliation that I was trying to conceal."

"That must've eaten you alive."

"Everything was gnawing on me back then. It was an awful time."

"You should find that guy," I said.

"He lives here in town, has a family. Not worth my effort. It's behind me now—right where I want it."

"It happened again?" I asked.

"Different situation. I was dancing one weekend night, and this older guy, probably in his forties or fifties was tipping me really well all night, asking me questions about my life, if I were in college, all that shit. As a stripper, you make up some sob bullshit so they'll fork over their cash. Later that night as another girl and I were leaving, he met me by my car. He seemed to have something in his pocket, but I don't know. I didn't want to risk it. He demanded that we give him oral sex. I've never told this story to anyone. That's as far as it went. Makes me never want to touch a man again."

"You've touched me."

"You're no man," she said with a smile.

"Well, thank you."

"I trust that you will respect me enough to keep it here."

"You can count on me," I told her.

"I really appreciate all that you've done. You've been very cool, and it's helped me a lot."

"Well, it's been no party for me, that's for damn sure."

"You're an asshole," she said lightly, comfortably.

"Yeah, well, the best of us are."

"Ever had sex on 15th Street?" she asked me.

"Let me see...now that you mention it—no, I don't think so...but..."

"Me, neither. Want to fuck me?"

"Well, uh...sure."

My throat felt as if it had been slashed with razor blades. It was a good performance. I opened the door to my bedroom, happy to have made it home before the other tenants arrived. Out the window, I could see a trail of lights coming down 15th Street—the remaining crowd from the night's show at the Outhouse. I studied the headlights of each car, wondering what was being said about our performance, about me.

I climbed into bed before the house filled again, quick to turn off the light to elude others to my presence elsewhere. I didn't want to be bothered. The night was going too well to be brought down by my housemates.

Car doors opened, filling the street with the busy chatter of familiar voices—voices that would likely keep me up all night.

I smiled as I looked up at the rough contour of the ceiling over me. The attendance had overwhelmed my assumption. Five hundred fifty people.

Someone came stumbling up the steps, tripping backward down a few, then continuing to the top. A forceful knock came at my door.

"Open up, asshole."

I sat quietly, wary of even breathing.

"I know you're in there, open up."

"Leave me alone, Billy. I'm tired and I need sleep. Some of us have jobs."

"Fuck you, pussy," he said as he stumbled in and turned on the light. "I'm going to stand here all night until you make me leave." He walked further into my room, looking at the pictures pinned to the wall. He focused on one of Stanley and me performing with the Fluorescent Condoms in Joplin, Missouri. "Is this your boyfriend?"

"Sure."

"Well, here's the deal," he said. "I'm going to rip it up unless you stop me."

"Just get the hell out of here."

"Make me leave. That's all I ask. Beat the shit out of me, pretty-boy."

I sat silently.

"Okay," he said as he ripped it from the wall. "I'm tearing it up. Going to stop me?"

"I have the negative," I shrugged casually. "I'll make another."

"Fine," he said as he ripped the picture down the middle.

I bowed my head, finding myself somewhere wedged between self-pity and hatred. There was no negative, and no other print. I didn't know how to handle this situation. All my life I had been so diplomatic toward conflict. This person shared my passion—our interests were perfectly aligned. Where did all this go so wrong?

"Going to make me leave?"

I stood up from the bed, dressed only in a pair of cut-off sweats. "I'll escort you to the door." I pulled on his leather coat. He wouldn't budge.

"Not that easy," he mused at my ego's expense. "Come on, hit me. Hard as you can. I'm opening myself up to you. Defenseless. Lay into me."

I pulled his coat harder, yanking him uneasily to the door. He knocked my arm away, pushing me back against the bed.

"What is your problem?" he shrieked. "You are such a fucking pussy! I don't know anyone who would take this kind of shit and sit back like such a fucking loser!"

He stumbled out the door and down the hallway, mumbling some snide remarks as he slammed into the bathroom.

I stood up—humiliated and small—and turned off the light to immerse myself in the darkness.

"Why do you put up with that shit?" Stanley asked me as we sat on the roof outside my bedroom window. "If it was me, I'd tear him up, like he wants. Hell, I'll do it for you."

"Nah," I sighed. "It's really no big deal."

"Bullshit! It is to me. I respect your ways, but I wish you'd sacrifice your ideals long enough just to level him out. Stand up for yourself."

"I see it more as resistance," I said.

"Resistance from what? Your pride? Pacifism is a nice thought. In an ideal world, I'd say you're doing the right thing. But in *this* world," he said as he pointed out to the surrounding neighborhood, "you'll be walked all over. You need to toughen up, loosen up your ideals before they have you for dinner."

170

"I'm becoming very disillusioned by this whole thing."

"Your views of this sacred integrity that you read into this music, I must confess—you can stand to salvage some of that. Just don't tell me that your determination with the band is waning. That'd make me feel lower than a turtle's ass. Your inspiration carries me. Always has."

"No, the music is all that really keeps me going. I still believe in the music, and I always will. I once thought this supposed movement was alive and strong, ready to take a stand and make a change. Rising where the hippies fell..."

"Not so?" he asked.

"Well, consider my comrades here. Bunch of drunks hustling for a piece of ass. The music means nothing to them. The attitude and ideals mean nothing to them. The ones who do stand for something stand blindly, tacking a label on themselves and adopting all the views of that particular mold. They accept the whole package deal, and itemize nothing. Hardcore leftist liberals wear the badge they're supposed to wear, preaching their beliefs only to the converted, never troubling themselves with challenging any opposition. Easier to talk your shit within your circle so no one can disagree. Safer that way. You never fail when you don't assert yourself. I used to think there was something special about this whole thing, that those who chose this path had something they believed in and stood behind. These people are special, all right."

"Maybe it's just this town," he suggested.

"Maybe, and I'll soon find out on the road."

"Could it be that you're looking too much at the broad picture and not focusing on the specifics? Maybe if you stopped looking at people as punks, or hippies, or metalheads, and just referred to each individual...I think you've done quite well for yourself in just one year. Consider where you were last year."

"Last year? I was looking forward to graduating," I said.

"See? Now look at you. You joined one of your favorite bands, and that last gig at the Outhouse...you guys stole the show from the headlining group. Everyone left when they came on. You're doing something right. Your records are everywhere, your music is on the radio all over the country—what more?"

"When I look into the crowd, I may as well see masks. Maybe I was meant to only be an observer, not a participant."

"You want to know what I think?" he asked.

"Sure."

"No, do you *really* want to know what I think?"

"Go ahead, man. Shoot me down."

"No, it's not that. Open your eyes, yes. Shoot you down—well, that's up to you. What was the draw at your last show?"

"The last one we headlined?" I asked.

"Yes."

"Five hundred something."

"A year ago you'd have considered this heaven. Now you bitch about it. You expect too much of people. You can't depend on them to come through. They just won't."

"I know..."

"Your own walls are closing in on you," he told me. "You've become so obsessed with accomplishment and determination that it's poisoned you. You only see the flaws and failed ways. What about the things these people have done? What's their story? Is it any less valid? Why do they do what they do? Let me tell you one thing: one year

171

ago today, you wouldn't have been bitching about this. You'd be so wrapped up in all of what you have done that nothing else would've mattered."

"And a year from now?" I pondered.

"Time will tell. A lot can change in that time. Actually, very little will remain the same. You're here now, and what you came to Lawrence to do you're allowing to suffocate you. You need to chill out. The water is as deep as you want it to be. So, tell me about this chick you've been scoring with..."

"She's a stripper. Big, busty girl who does a lot of coke and speed."

"Does she eat meat?" he asked.

"Yeah."

"Good for her. What else? Getting serious?"

"She's moving away in about two weeks," I told him. "Right before we tour."

"So, you'll be leaving this town with no strings attached. Not bad. Hope you don't end up staying some place out there."

"We'll see how well the van does. If it breaks down, we may be stuck working in the salt mines in upstate New York, or something."

He laughed. "Look at your life! You're on a fucking roll! Now, about that celebrational can of pop—"

"I should never had said anything."

"You know the problem with you? You'll never accept what you've done. You could own the world and still be pissed at yourself for not taking the moon. You'll never honor yourself or your accomplishments with that soda because you'll never be able to appreciate the small steps, the intimate details of life."

"Maybe you're right," I shrugged.

"Hell, yes, I'm right. I know everything, did you forget that? How many shows do you have left before tour?"

"We have one more. It's in Kansas City at some new club called the Oasis. They're having us play the grand opening to establish a clientele. They're hoping to pick up on the old Pogo's crowd."

"You guys headlining?" he asked.

I nodded.

"I'll be there."

The disco ball shot luminous bubbles throughout the club, lighting the faces that filled the space before me. Out the pane glass windows, a faceless neighborhood stretched beyond the strip mall. It was a bland neighborhood which I wouldn't have cared to ever return to.

The owner of the club came to the stage, beckoning me to announce upcoming shows and events at his new investment. As he turned to walk away, he leaned to me. "There are almost eight hundred people here."

I turned to the crowd that seemed to fade into the darkness of eternity. Each person carried with them the story of a life, rich with triumphs and failures. Maybe their motive was to simply get drunk, but that was irrelevant. This was everything I wanted.

I glanced over my shoulder to Stanley who had perched himself high up on the bass amplifier. I smiled at him, never allowing my eyes to fully leave the crowd that spread itself around me like a comforting blanket. I knew he understood.

"I'd like to thank all of you for coming," I announced to the wildly excited audience that tossed plastic cups at me. "We're the Jerk Offs—" The crowd's cheering forced me to pause a moment. "This is a song off our record. *Persistence, Resistance.*"

As Hazel struck four much-anticipated clicks, the music consumed the audience, animating them in a turbulent frenzy of mayhem. I looked to the back of the venue, trying desperately to see where the crowd ended. As far as I could see, and for all I knew, it didn't.

"So, this is it," I said to Xanthe as I loaded the last bulky box into her compact car. "I thought you had more than this."

"I did. Had to sell it to pawn shops so I could afford the trip. Wouldn't fit anyway."

We stood in front of each other as the car's engine rumbled quietly. Her torn fishnet stockings clung to her pale, stout legs. I could see her bra through her thin white tank-top. That particular bra had been on my bedroom floor countless times.

"Are you going to visit me?" she asked.

"Maybe we'll play a show out there sometime. I kind of wish the band wasn't leaving so soon. I'd like to be able to play for one thousand, and so far, we've only made it just under eight hundred. Another couple months—"

"I'll see if I can find out where all the good bands are playing in Boulder."

"You have my address?" I asked.

"You'll be moving in how many weeks? Make sure you get a forwarding address so my letters get to you."

"I will," I promised.

We paused silently as the awkwardness of the situation loomed heavily. I could feel the sweat collecting on my brow. Luckily, the heat provided an adequate diversion.

"Well, it's been fun," she said.

"Yeah, sometimes."

"You'll miss me. Admit it."

"No problem. I'll miss you."

"Thought so," she said victoriously.

"You have inspired me, and that'll stick for quite a while."

"Like a scar?"

"More like cancer," I said. "But close."

"I'll miss you, too," she said softly, seriously.

"You've really helped," I confessed as I hugged her tightly. "You'll never know."

"I do know. Thank you." She backed uneasily to the car. "Come on, don't get all sappy on me, you softy. What's with men these days?"

"Get the fuck out of here."

"I'll write."

"So what?" I smiled and waved slowly. My face fell straight and serious. I watched the car pull down the street, waving until it was clearly out of sight. A warm breeze was blowing against my face, I hadn't realized. It was the soothing warm breath of summer—the summer that was about to change my life forever.

I never heard from Xanthe again. Either no letters were written, or they never found their way to me. Several years later I was informed she had intravenously contracted HIV.

*   *   *

173

The shrieking scream of my alarm clock punctured my peaceful somber. I reached up and clicked it off, rubbing my eyes as the sound of chirping birds came through the open window. The sun was high overhead, cloudless and dry. I crawled out onto the roof and sat quietly with my back against the wall. It was the last time I'd ever be able to do it, and I had to take advantage, if for no other reason.

"You going to help me carry this?" I heard Harold ask someone on the porch below.

"Hell, no," the person responded with hefty machismo. I vaguely recognized the voice, though I couldn't immediately place it. "I'd be likely to drop something, throw it down, whatever."

"Yeah," Harold said as he dragged Specky's speaker out to the van. He loaded it effortlessly, despite his docile physique. He paused to spy a group of kids preparing a soccer game in the schoolyard across the street, not noticing me sitting up on the roof when he returned. "You want anything on the east coast?"

"Yeah, actually. Sabotage this tour, make them look like idiots."

"They already look like idiots," Harold joked.

"Yeah, fuck up just one show...for me. Will you do it?"

Harold laughed.

"Will you do it?" the person repeated.

"Isn't that too obvious?" Harold asked. "And too easy?"

"Okay, then have a bunch of skinheads kick the shit out of Johnny-come-skately."

"I've got to get this equipment loaded," Harold said, laughing. "I'll see what I can do."

"I know what you can do, you're the roadie. See if you have the balls to do it. Well, I'm taking off before these clowns show up. What time are they meeting here?"

"About now," Harold said. "The van is running really badly. Missing out, backfiring—makes me paranoid. I may need you to send me a bus ticket."

"Yeah, good luck," the voice sneered. "I'm leaving. Have a good time. Don't hold your breath on the ticket home, traitor."

"See you later, man," Harold said just as Hazel pulled up behind the van.

Harold and Billy Christ walked from the porch to the street. Billy continued through the quiet neighborhood, never looking back as he disappeared down Rhode Island Street.

I climbed back inside and prepared to take the last shower at the house, and unbeknownst to me, my last shower for quite a while.

"Are you ready?" Specky asked me as I walked out of the bathroom, ducking below the hanging leaves of marijuana.

"I feel we'll return entirely different people," I told him excitedly.

Smiling, he turned to me with a heavy duffle bag over his shoulder. "There isn't going to be much room for anything. I tried to pack light, but how do you pack for the next two months? There's so much shit we could use—or is it that there's so much shit we won't use? I guess we should just bring the essentials, like underwear, and socks—that sort of thing."

I walked into my empty room to make one last check. "I have all that. I've got about a week's worth of clothes packed. Hopefully that'll last two months."

"Well, let's do it. The band is waiting."

"Can't let the band wait," I said anxiously. "Guess that's it. Who knows, maybe we'll be walking back into town in two weeks with our tails between our legs."

"Yeah," he said as we stumbled down the stairs for the last time. At the bottom of the steps, he looked up at me and smiled. "You never know."

The Highway Through Hell

"Green."

"Wrong," he announced as the sound of a car raced down the street. "Red."

I looked up, glancing in the rearview mirror at a red Datsun. It braked at a stop sign before proceeding through the quiet streets of Normal, Illinois.

He adjusted the collar on his scarlet Fred Perry shirt while rubbing a flat palm across his freshly shaved scalp. "Here comes another one. Cover your eyes...it's a truck."

I listened to the roaring of the engine, visualizing it mentally. "Gray."

"Nope. Silver."

"What's the difference? There isn't any," I insisted. "I get that one. See, I *am* a psychic."

"There's a big difference between gray and silver."

"Maybe we should fight over it," I suggested. "You love to fight."

"I don't either."

"The hell you don't! I've seen you beat the hell out of how many people?"

"Defending my honor," he boasted. "I have a lot of pride. What can I say?"

"You and your buddies sure aren't afraid of the odds being in your favor."

"It's been the other way more times than not, trust me. I've stood alone against many men, sometimes in droves."

I glanced down the quiet street, inhaling the atmosphere of an unknown landscape which I would soon have a one-night musical affair. There was something very pleasing in the thought. "Like how many?"

"There was a time when I was in Kansas City...a couple of skinheads were giving me some trouble—"

"Skinheads were?" I asked.

"Yeah, well, when these baby-skins pop up with Docs and a shaved head, they better have made their presence known to us first. We usually kick the shit out of the ones who don't, and take their Docs from them. We aren't going to allow just anybody to be a skinhead without our consent. A couple of these guys had formed their own little clique, and Vernon and Hefty had buckled some heads because of it. One day I was in Kansas City and they spotted me. They caught up with me in an alley near Westport."

"Took your Docs?" I asked.

"Yeah, right. They could've shredded me like a mill. Funny how when you stop with the bullshit talk, few people are ready to just throw down. They just stared at me. I walked right passed them. Often times it comes down to the loudest roar. Mine can be pretty loud."

"Did you ever run across them again?"

He took a second to light a cigarette with his shiny silver Zippo lighter—or maybe it was gray. "No, in fact there are a lot of them now. They're into Skrewdriver and other racist skinhead bands. The skins in Lawrence and the skins in Kansas City aren't mixing like the old days. I know you don't agree with my way, but let me tell you, there's a lot to be said about someone who will stand up against the odds, ready to fall for one's pride."

"Have you ever really had the snot beaten out of you?" I asked.

"Comes with the territory. Can't win them all."

"Doesn't make you the slightest bit apprehensive about leaving the house, knowing that someone for some reason stemming from a drunken night may seek revenge?"

"No, not at all. Makes life exciting."

"So what do you fear?" I asked.

He took a long drag from his cigarette. "To be like my father."

"That's a stock answer. Be a little creative."

"No, I don't mean wearing the suit, dressing the part, having a real job. I'm talking the choices he made, the hollow sacrifices."

"Like what?" I asked.

"He's only loved one woman. My mother. His vow was sincere, he will always love her—the pathetic fool. She's a loon. She's as neurotic as a woman can be. She's very materialistic, very vain. She looks plastic, like an old Barbie sat too close to the fireplace, melting. My father sure dug on her. She put him through hell. Constantly cheated on him. Playing the fool, he'd run right back to prove his love. It was a vicious circle. It went on for years."

"Did she not care for him?" I asked.

"No, she did. She was just too insecure to be satisfied with one lover. What he loved about her was the concept of her. She looked good on his arm, a trophy for a night out. She wasn't someone he could talk with, she was someone that would satiate his own flailing ego. She justified his existence somehow. Nice looking, very sweet, yet hollow like those chocolate Easter bunnies. Now he drinks himself to sleep, watches television all night, talks like he knows everything when he doesn't know shit."

George walked out of the venue on the quiet corner, holding a lime green flier. He strolled away from the crumbling old building that peeled brick like the shedding of a leper. He passed the flier through the passenger window into Specky's hands. "Lots of hot girls in there."

"Oh, really?" Specky examined the flier and passed it to me. "Are they really young, like fifteen?"

"Yeah, in fact, some are even *younger*," George replied as he balanced himself on the edge of the curb.

I paused to study the flier. "We aren't even headlining. Who the hell are NOFX anyway?" I stepped out of the van, paying special attention to locking the doors. The street had a very used smell to it, like dust and old wood. I didn't trust it.

George sighed as he kicked a rock against the side of the old brick building. "Seen one hardcore band, you've seen them all."

"They're from California," Specky replied as we walked into the dim cavern of a venue.

"We're a legit touring band!" George suddenly exclaimed over the loud clamor of recorded music. "Maybe I should get a stage name. Something clever like Billy Christ."

"George Esposito doesn't cut it," Specky said. "How about George Thunder? Or George Dagger?"

"We'll be made when we get to stay in motels," I said. "You aren't a truly made rock star unless you throw the television out the window—no less than fifth story."

"Man, that is one of those strange truths," George pondered. "Wonder why they do that?"

"Some covert, secret organization, or something," Specky suggested. "Maybe that's how you know you're a rock star, when you find out *why* you're expected to destroy the hotel's television set."

"There's also the chewing off of the live bat's head," I said.

"That has to be bullshit," George protested. "Who was there to tell? What, a bunch of stoners in the front row? Give me a break. I bet they also believe Iron Maiden's *Eddie* is a real guy. Idiots. It's all part of the show. That's like that whole Rod Stewart and the thirty gallons of sperm in his stomach story."

"Rod Stewart?" Specky asked. "I thought that was Freddie Mercury? I heard it was only four quarts."

"Four quarts, thirty gallons—what's the difference?"

"No," I corrected. "It was Rod Stewart. Hell, I'm sure it's happened to everyone who's famous. Another one of those things that goes with fame. You get your name tagged onto that story and you're there. No bones about it."

"The trick is," Specky added, "to achieve immortal fame in the music industry, one of your band members has to overdose on heroin, or anything, really. Heroin, of course, is the rock star drug of choice."

"I think it's less restricted than that," George challenged. "We're talking about a seriously ignorant institution, rock and roll. As long as you die an embarrassingly stupid death, you'll be remembered as a hero. For instance, choking on one's vomit. You could also simply choke on your tongue as long as you're drunk. If you die while totally wasted, you'll become a legend—even if your music blows like a two dollar whore."

"Good point," I said. "But who in our band, Specky, would die such a ridiculous death?"

"Yeah, Specky?" George asked. "Which one of us would be stupid enough to choke on their own puke?"

"Or tongue?" I added.

"We're going to need you to make that sacrifice, Specky," George prodded. "We're counting on you."

"Yeah, you've got some time to consider," I said, looking about the stale atmosphere of the lifeless venue. "Right now we're about to play a small show opening some virtually unknown California hardcore band," I said lightly with charismatic enthusiasm. "And we'll be sleeping on the cement for the next two months."

"Yeah, plenty of time," Specky said.

It was early in the afternoon when we pulled out of Cincinnati, birthplace of *Hustler* magazine. It was the third date of the tour, and fourth day on the road. Our show in Cincinnati was at the Top Hat on a weekday—filler for a night at the local bar.

People often say that the audience response is irrelevant to a quality performance. In theory, it sounds very noble. In practice, it's a pure test of will and ego to stand on a stage playing for a crowd of ten that are trying desperately to talk over your life's creative efforts. Anybody who claims they're unaffected by a bad show is someone whose honesty is not to be trusted.

*　　*　　*

178

The drive from Cincinnati to Columbus was quiet yet thoroughly exciting. Each mile was a step further into the realm of an optimistic future, the place where dreams are made real with careful, meticulous planning. The horizon was our domain and destination. The only limit was the ticking of the clock. Patience was my virtue—one of many, and I was prepared to wait for what green pastures lie beyond like virgin snow.

The air that clung to the sprawling country breathed green life. Each inhalation was like the intimacy of sweet-nothings spoken at point blank by a well versed lover. It was a magical, beautiful day.

A pleasant breeze drifted through the open windows. It made no difference that the van was not equipped with an air-conditioner. We would definitely see worse weather on the tour.

As the skyline of Columbus came into view, the engine suddenly engaged in a loud, thunderous eruption. The euphoric expressions worn by my bandmates melted as a thick cloud of smoke rolled up over the hood. The van noisily quaked to the shoulder of the road as the speedometer fell lifeless and the traffic of the world passed us by.

Everyone evacuated the van as Harold cautiously raised the hood, sending to the heavens one visionary smoke signal. It matched the color of Harold's leather biker jacket, absorbing the heat of the sun. The underside of the hood dripped of fresh oil like inkblots conveying our sudden dismal fate. I felt if I looked hard enough, I would find my life's dream dripping into a steaming puddle onto the pavement.

"What's the deal?" I asked nervously.

Harold bent over the engine, looking bravely through the smoke as the cars passed in a blur. "I don't know," he grumbled, "but it's not good."

"Can it run?" Specky asked.

"Well, it *is* running," Harold replied. "We'll need to keep putting more oil into it because it's burning right off. Which is not a very good sign."

"What happened?" George asked.

"I don't know," Harold answered swiftly. "I was driving it, then *bang*. I think I've seen this before. Ever heard of a head gasket?"

"No," I responded.

"Good, you don't want to." He lowered the hood. "Let's get it as close as we can. Hurry up, back in the van."

Once inside Columbus, we very slowly found our way to the club. It was a large venue deep in the suburbs. A massive green canopy over the front read Flamingo Isle in yellow and red letters. It was the type of place one wouldn't expect a punk rock band to play. The promoter had seen our ad in fanzines and was excited to have us close the final night of the club's existence. We were hosting a going away party. It seemed only fitting under the circumstances.

"Well," Harold said as he shut down the engine and leaned back in the captain's seat. "This turned into a big piece of shit really quick."

I opened a bag of crackers that my mother had the foresight to pack for us. Unfortunately, it wouldn't last long.

"Does anybody have a felt marker, or did we sell that already?" Harold asked.

I reached into the box of T-shirts where we kept the essentials: duct tape, three-prong adapters, and felt pens. "No, we still have it." I tossed it up front.

He popped the lid off and focused his attention to the white interior of the van. Above the driver's seat, he wrote in enormous letters: *This Turned Into a Big Piece of*

Shit Really Quick. Below that he scrawled *Days of Hell* and underlined it. He put four marks underneath, a tally we would keep to the end.

Specky sighed, putting his bald head down in his hands. "I guess we could live in Columbus for a while."

"That's an option," Harold agreed.

"This pretty much means our engine is gone?" George asked.

Harold nodded. "Pretty much. I could be wrong, but that's the gist of my automotive knowledge."

"Okay, let's deal with that," George said.

"I called the promoter and he's coming down," I told them. "He sounds really young, His dad owns this place. He's expecting a good show. We could really use it."

"I. D. Under?" Specky asked as he looked at the fliers taped to the inside of the front door's glass.

"They're the headliners," I said. "From Chicago. They're supposed to have a following here."

"I'm going for a walk," Harold said quickly. "Anybody want to go with me to get some smokes?"

"Yeah, I need a pack," Specky said as the two of them sprang from the van.

George impatiently shook his head, slapping his hands on his knees to hoist himself vertically. "I can't sit around here. I'll be back." He left quickly, going the opposite direction as the others.

"Well, Hazel," I said as the two of us sat alone. "Here we are."

"Yeah."

"You know, I hardly know you," I admitted.

"I know."

"Is there anything to know?" I asked.

"Other than the fact that I'm a drummer and a lesbian? No."

"Did you go to school with Specky and Harold?" I asked.

"Specky and I were classmates. We used to be in a cheesy goth band called Graveyard. The Jerk Offs formed from the ashes of that, actually."

I watched her toy with her bangs, teasing her wavy brown hair into swirling curls.

"I'm going to cut all my hair off," she said. "It'd look cooler, don't you think?"

"I guess."

"I'd probably end up looking like a boy. Instead of everyone asking about the girl drummer, they'll ask about the little boy behind the drums. I'll have to flash my tits just to let them know."

I laughed.

"Do you miss Xanthe?" she asked.

I chuckled, somewhat surprised. "We really weren't an item. Just close friends."

"Sometimes closer than others." She teased her hair, gazing into the reflection of the van's rearview. She looked at me coldly, unintentionally and then smiled. "The band is good for meeting people. A lot of lesbians come to our shows."

"I never noticed."

"Never noticed the audience?" she asked me.

"Yes and no. I see only eyes. I judge the level of intensity through them. I feed off that."

"Yeah, and those eyes jump on stage and pull equipment down..."

"Yeah...bastards."

180

"By the way, you've done a good job at pushing the band the past year," she complimented rigidly. "We've increased our audience a lot in that time. Now when I go places, like to the store, people recognize me. It's pretty weird, but it doesn't affect me. You're really ambitious about promotion. I would say it's been your assertiveness more than your singing that did it."

"Yeah, for a shitty singer, I can really promote a band."

"Yeah, you can," she said with a smirk.

"Should I thank you for that?"

"I didn't say you were a bad singer," she corrected. "You did."

"No, I didn't. Anyway, thank you. I'm glad everything worked out."

"Worked out?" she questioned suspiciously. "Look where we are."

I gazed out into the parking lot, hard and noisy. It was covered with cracks like black veins through a layer of gray flesh. I feared this would be somewhat a home for a while. I dreaded how long.

My attention was diverted to a timid tapping on the window. I glanced over to see two very young girls peering curiously inside. Both shared the same sense or lack of fashion. Red handkerchiefs covered their bleached hair, tied in the back like pirates. The taller, chubbier of the two was wearing a Sonic drive-in smock. The smaller one was covered with a worn, over-sized Crimpshrine T-shirt that fit like a dress.

I leaned forward and rolled down the window.

"Are you the Jerk Offs?" the pudgy one asked me.

I looked down at the pad of paper that she clutched with thick fingers. "Are you the paparazzi?"

She smiled. "I have a zine called *Ample Time*. Any chance I could get an interview?"

I was moved by the determination that challenged her soft demeanor. "Sure." I stepped outside into the warm summer sun. Hazel was right behind me, adjusting her hair.

"My name is Heather," the portly one told us. "This is my friend Cathy."

"Hello, I'm Frank. I sing. This is our drummer Hazel."

"I had read somewhere that you guys had a girl drummer," Heather said excitedly. "I'm actually working on an issue dedicated to women in punk. Do you mind if I have this interview exclusively with Hazel?"

"No," I replied indifferently, stepping back against the van. "It's your thing."

The three of them took a seat against the wall of the club as they pounced Hazel with undivided attention. It was the happiest I had seen her in days.

"That was great!" the little Asian boy promoting the show told us as we departed form the stage. The audience cheered enthusiastically for more. He held out a wad of bills to me. "Two hundred dollars, that's your part."

"Wow!" I exclaimed over the ruckus of the crowd. "That's great."

"You guys were awesome, you deserve it!" he said happily. "Get back up there and give them another shot."

I turned to the band, revealing the lump of money with a quirky grin. This tour would be a very profitable venture at this rate, but there existed the van problem...

I stepped up to the stage once again and lifted the microphone to my mouth. The audience hushed immediately. "Thank you very much," I told them. "You may be seeing more of us for a while. We're experiencing some vehicular trouble that we need to resolve. If anyone has a couch or a floor to offer, we'd gladly accept."

181

We played a brief couple of numbers before turning the stage over to I. D. Under. I could see a line of people waiting to purchase our merchandise. Harold had his hands full, collecting the money while sorting through shirt sizes.

"That was fantastic!" Heather told me as I weaved proudly through the crowd. "About that interview, you know, earlier when I skipped you so I could have a femme issue...well, I *need* to interview you now. After the show you just gave, I'm your biggest fan!"

"Thanks."

"I'll talk to my mother about letting you crash at our place," she offered.

I figured her age to be no more than thirteen. I smiled politely. "Don't worry about us. We'll figure something out."

"Let me talk to her first," Heather insisted.

"Excuse me," an older gentleman interrupted as he prevented further movement with his restricting posture. He held up an emaciated hand to capture my attention. His body was feeble and long. His face appeared as a skull wrapped in caramel. "How many days are you going to be in town?"

"A few," I told him.

"I do the booking at a venue called Apollo's, across from Ohio State University. We have an opening on Wednesday night. It's a slow night, but it'd be something to do. If you want—"

"We'll take it," I said flatly.

"Here's my card," he told me as he extended it forward. "Call me tomorrow."

"I will."

He slipped back into the crowd like a giant mantis.

"I'll talk to my mother later," Heather repeated to me. "She'll be here to get me at midnight."

"Okay," I said, humoring her.

"Almost one hundred dollars in merchandise sales," Harold told us later that night as I. D. Under completed the final song of their encore. We had gathered in the van to establish a plan before our options diminished to a vacant hall. "That puts us at three hundred dollars for this show."

"Not bad," Specky said.

"I suppose we could live in this parking lot a while," I suggested. "That's if we don't get towed away."

"Well, when we get the van in a shop, we'll have to stay in a public park a few nights," Specky reminded.

There came a loud thud on the side of the van. We opened the door to a middle-aged couple. The woman was tall and busty with frizzy blond hair. Her man was stocky and firm with at least two days growth of stubble on his face. I could smell the alcohol on his breath from where I sat. It appeared they had just finished square dancing. I could easily sense the influence of *Hee-Haw* on their lives.

"I kind of thought I should meet you people before I offer my home," the woman said. "My name is Theresa. I'm Heather's mother."

"Oh," I said, somewhat surprised. "I'm Frank. I didn't know I should take her seriously."

"Well," she chuckled, "I've learned at this point to take her interests as seriously as she does."

"I'm Specky," he said before introducing the others.

"Why do you need a place to stay?" she asked. "And for how long?"

"Until we get the van fixed," I told her. "And that answers both questions."

She took the time to study each of us by our outward appearance. I'm one to find such an impression very accurate.

"Know any mechanics?" Harold asked.

Theresa smiled. "Maybe. Have I introduced my boyfriend? This is Joey."

Joey nodded slowly with unbridled reserve. The act of speaking seemed a wildly erratic behavior to this stoic man.

"He has a shop," Theresa said. "It's out by our house in Marysville. I don't know how booked up he is…"

"I can fit it in," Joey said coldly. "No discounts."

"No problem," George said swiftly. "We just want it done right without trouble."

"How many days are you thinking it would take, Joey?" Theresa asked.

He scratched his rough chin as his dour expression maintained during deeper thought. "Oh…it depends on the problem."

"Head gasket, I would say," Harold told him.

Joey's face soured briefly. "Depends on what we have available as far as engines. I would guess a good four to five days."

"I could handle that," Theresa confessed. "Before I turn my house over to you, there is one condition outside general courtesy."

"What's that?" I asked.

"Heather's birthday is Thursday. It sounds like you would be around still, and we have a big birthday party planned for her. I want you guys to play for free."

"We could do that," Specky agreed.

"Well, follow us," Theresa said casually. "Our country home is yours. We'll get this van to the shop first thing in the morning."

Joey nodded with half-baked eyes.

Their home rested on the edge of a small town beyond the outskirts of Columbus. It was a small, cozy house where the only character was the years of neglect that made it their own. The chipped paint had faded to a dusty white long ago. Shiny red shutters adorned each window to create the illusion of charm, resulting in an eyesore. Each side of the front porch had a stack of railroad ties that enclosed small flowerbeds. A porch swing hung limp on rusty chains to the sound of tiny windchimes. A fake deer guarded the front yard.

I slept that first night alone on the hardwood floor in the sewing room. I used a pile of pastel afghans for a mattress. I rose with the sun, just the perfect timing to help Harold transport the equipment to the garage before taking the van to the shop.

A thick fog clung to the quiet countryside. I watched the tired van disappear in the haze with the rupture of an enormous cloud of dust to follow. Our fate was out of our hands once again.

Theresa stuck her head out the front door. "I've got some toast and juice."

I found myself standing alone, stuck in a daze. "Okay."

I followed her through the house, stepping over the bodies that covered the living room floor. She owned the most impressive collection of wooden and ceramic ducks I had ever witnessed. An entire bookshelf was dedicated to the presentation of these items. Not a speck of dust existed anywhere.

The kitchen was equally clean with little ceramic duckies for salt and pepper shakers and a giant cookie jar that required the removal of the duck's head to find the goodies.

"I've got to go to work now," she whispered. A white plate heaping of buttered toast sat on the gingham tablecloth before an empty chair designated as my own. She poured me a glass of grapefruit juice as I sat down in the uncomfortable wooden chair.

"Sorry about the intrusion into your life," I told her.

"No bother," she said as she tied a stiff pink scarf around her neck. She looked better without it. "Feel at home here."

"Thanks," I said as she walked out the door.

"We're going out behind the garage to get a tan," Specky told me as he, Harold, and Hazel walked outside the old farmhouse one lazy afternoon. "Come with."

I followed for lack of a better option. They placed their towels on the stubby lawn and passed a bottle of baby oil between them. This would be the first time I would ever see Harold without his leather jacket. I wasn't entirely sure that it could be removed. My answer came moments later.

"I'm getting an all-over tan," Hazel said as she peeled her shirt off.

She removed her bra effortlessly, revealing more than her comfort with us. She scratched underneath her breasts casually, oblivious as the rest of us completely disrobed. She tossed her panties at my feet. I looked up at her hairy legs—hair that thickened naturally at the crossroads, concealing the details of everyman's fancy.

"We can now see why Specky gets all the dates," I announced as we baked under the sun.

Harold made a point to examine Specky's parts, shaking his head in protest. "We can?"

"Dates?" Hazel asked. "I wouldn't say he ever went on a date in his life."

"C'mon, now," Specky shrugged, adjusting the angle of his Ray-Ban impostor sunglasses.

Harold chuckled to himself. "Specky's idea of asking a girl out is, would you like to get some cheap beer and fuck, or do you not drink?"

"Gotten laid on this tour yet, Specky?" Hazel asked.

"Not yet."

"Where's George?" I asked.

"Doesn't want to ruin his complexion, or something queer like that," Hazel said.

Looking out into the vast stretch of farmhouses and fields of crops, I could easily believe that we had never left Kansas. The mid-west had practically the same look, all the way through to Ohio. I wondered at what point I'd be perfectly aware that I had actually traveled somewhere.

"Did you cancel this week's tour dates?" she asked me.

"Yes, did it yesterday morning," I told them. "Cleveland and Ann Arbor, down the tubes. I held off canceling further shows east. I think we can make it to our next one in Harrisburg."

"We'll see how long it's going to take to get that motor installed," Harold said.

"I'm hot," I complained as I covered my eyes. "That would freak me out to get a sunburn on my ass. I'm getting my pants back on."

"Chicken shit," Harold challenged.

"Oh, I forgot," I said as I stood. "I have to prove myself."

"That's right."

"Join the Topeka punk fraternity because I'd want respect from a drunk like Billy."

"He is a friend of mine," Harold warned me.

"Yeah, just the company I'd want to have. I'm going inside."

"Good idea."

I picked up my shirt and walked back to the house, dressing myself as I strode through the green lawn. I rushed back inside, blasted by the cool wall of artificially chilled air. George was in the living room watching some history show about World War Two. I sat on the couch next to the display of porcelain ducks. The cushions were soft and comfortable, its surface pleasantly cool to the touch.

"What's up?" I asked George.

"I hate being inactive like this."

"We had a show tonight in Ann Arbor," I reminded him.

"Now we have a show in Columbus *again*."

"Maybe I should take another nap," I said. "Just sleep through this whole week."

"You know, if this is comfort, then I never want it. I can't imagine a worse fate than living for nightly sitcoms. The moment you stop being productive you should just off yourself. There's a choice to be made the rest of our lives. It's either comfort or productivity, one or the other. I can't live like this," he said as the sound of bombs rained down on England.

Looking at the van, I could see nothing different with it, though I didn't recall that it was polka-dotted and pulled by a caravan of elephants. The thirty-foot tall clown was desperately trying to motivate the beasts to move it, to no avail.

"Frank, dammit!" Tom screamed at me over my shoulder.

I turned to him, feeling the grief and frustration of knowing that my pizzas would be about seventy-two days later than the time we quoted.

"Sorry, Tom," I said slowly. "But the elephants—"

"The elephants?" he interrupted. "To hell with the elephants! We have blimps, we have submarines! Who needs these damn elephants? These pizzas are probably getting cold by now."

He tapped the pizza peel on the grass where the large conveyor oven sat on Theresa's lawn. Empty containers of body lotion and beach towels lay scattered across the yard in front of the oven where pizzas seemed to pour like molten lava. Each time he lowered the peel to the ground, the grass would ripple briefly from a deep green to a burnt orange, then back.

A row of benches had been placed in front of the old garage, and everyone I loathed from Iola was seated. They watched me, and they laughed.

"So the birds won't fly?" Tom asked as the German Luftwaffe approached on the horizon.

"Birds? Not birds, elephants."

I turned to the van. To my surprise, a circle of ostriches sat huddled in front of the van, smoking cigars, playing blackjack.

"Well, the Germans should be attacking us soon, so we'll need you to get those pizzas out of here. How long are you going to be sitting around this place doing nothing?" he asked.

"Who knows."

"This is the rest of your life, Frank," he told me. "Don't fool yourself. *The rest of your life...*"

Suddenly a voice descended from the heavens like the roaring engines of fighter airplanes. "Frank." The voice echoed like thunder as the clouds seemed to spread. It was so powerful... "It's time to eat."

185

I opened my eyes, unaware they were closed. The couch had branded its pattern on the side of my face. Hazel hovered over me. "It's time to eat," she repeated. A large beach towel was wrapped around her thin waist like a dress. Her bony, hairy legs looked like two microphone stands, buckled at the knee.

"You must have been having a stressful dream," she said.

"Yeah."

"Missing your lady friend? Here..." She reached up inside the towel. Scratching her crotch under the privacy of the linen, she lowered her fingers to my nose. "Bring back memories?" She laughed and turned away. "George made pasta for everyone. Get up."

I stood slowly, stretching my tense body. Various joints cracked with each step as I found my way to the kitchen. George stood over a pot of spaghetti sauce, his face peering through the steaming concoction as he stirred and examined.

I yawned slowly, stepping up to gaze over his shoulder. "What's this?"

"What the hell does it look like?" Specky said as he scooped himself a portion.

"This is my own recipe," George answered.

"He puts cocoa in it," Specky revealed. "That's the secret ingredient. Can't taste it, though."

"Esposito family recipe?" I asked.

"No, it's mine," George said as he stirred the mixture with a wooden spatula.

"Was I asleep long?"

"No, not too long," George answered. "We have a show to play at Apollo's. We need to get down there sometime soon."

"Man, I hope there are some easy women there tonight," Specky said. "I think I've cranked it more this week than any other week in my life."

"Yeah, me, too," George admitted. "Idle time and a free hand."

"What do we know about the van?" I asked.

"I guess it's on schedule," George replied. "Harold is down there now. Hopefully we won't have to cancel anymore shows."

The show at Apollo's was quiet and utterly pointless. The effort to get there was far more demanding than the pay-off. Theresa was kind enough to load our equipment in the back of her pick-up. She and I rode in the cab as the rest of the band watched the equipment in the bed as we returned to Marysville.

"Doesn't this get annoying?" I asked. "Having to run all over the place for your child's whims?"

"That's why I had a child," she told me. "I wanted this. Didn't your parents do the same?"

"Yeah," I commented in a happy reflection. "They did."

"When you have kids, you'll understand," she said. "When you love them, they become your hobby. Their interests become yours."

"So, you're getting into this music, too?"

She smiled without a response.

"What do you think of her musical and social interests?" I asked seriously.

"I've grown an appreciation for it. It's made a big difference on Heather, which makes a difference with me. Two years ago she was not doing well. I know she took a lot of heat at school for her weight. She got that from her father...anyway, I prayed to Jesus that she would find the courage to overcome it. When she found this music, she discovered a lot of pride with it. I think it gave her an identity beyond the snide comments, snickering, and heckling. I guess my prayers were answered in a mighty strange way. I can't complain. I'll support it and anything else she believes in. She's become a strong woman in the past year. That's everything I ever hoped."

The following afternoon, I was sitting on the old porch enjoying the quiet serenity before the birthday party. The aroma of the flowers filled the air as the chimes rang softly over my shoulder. The flowers looked like an explosion of colorful fireworks ceased in the fabric of time, twisting in the gentle breeze. The ass of the fake deer on the lawn caught my attention. The paint was chipped with half the white tail revealing a ceramic base. They weren't going to fool many people or deer with a chipped ass...

I was distracted by an eruption of dust spilling into the air through distant crops. It approached with a low rumble that slowly intensified. I stood, feeling a strange sense of curiosity. Even the traffic had become interesting in such a lackluster environment... To my pleasant surprise, it was our van! Joey had finished early.

He pulled into the driveway and revved the engine twice before killing it. He stepped down, still looking rough as sandpaper. He already had a beer in hand.

"It's done," he said as he joined me on the quiet porch. "Here's the keys."

I reached up and snatched them. "Did my parent's check arrive?"

"Yup. Good people for covering the bill."

"Yeah, they are," I told him. "That was quick...and cheap for an entire engine. I thought there were no deals."

He took a hearty gulp from the beer before wiping the foam off his stiff lip. "Maybe I'm just fair."

"I thought there were no fair mechanics."

He laughed for the first time. His teeth were crooked and stained. He looked better when he didn't. "I do what I can for Heather."

"How did you meet them?"

"I went to high school with Theresa. Never dated, just friends. I always had a crush on her, I was just too darned shy to tell her. She married a guy that was no good for her. I told her so, but she wouldn't have any of it. Didn't last long, but long enough to have Heather. I do what I can for them. I'm no rock and roll fan. Never was. I do it for Heather."

"You'd find we're no different than you."

"I've already found that," he said shortly as he finished the beer with one furious gulp. "Can I offer you a brewsky?"

"No thanks," I said.

"I reckon I may get me another."

"Thanks for everything, Joey," I told him.

"No problem. You guys are doing a good thing. People like Heather are really excited about your songs."

"It's people like Heather who keep me doing what I'm doing," I told him.

He nodded quietly. "Too hot out here. I'm going for another beer."

I watched him hobble away as I fumbled the keys between my fingers.

We were back.

"This last song is for Joey," I told the occupants of the garage as my voice echoed with feedback over the excited jabbering. "For fixing our van."

The kids had absorbed all my space. I had no place to move. Specky and George were already crowded against their amplifiers that were propped up on lawn mowers and tool chests. The sound within the room was awful, yet our spirits were high. We broke into the final song with intense vitality. Morale amongst the audience was the highest we had experienced on tour. Even the parents were impressed with our performance as they watched their kids wreck the garage with enthusiasm and style. It was one of the more successful performances on the tour so far.

When we arrived in Harrisburg, night had already fallen and the show at the Fire House was well under way. We pulled into the parking lot alongside no more than twenty other cars.

A band called Sticks & Stones was playing to an enthusiastic crowd in a corner of the small building. Pulling a flier from the wall, I saw that we finally were billed the headliners. I smiled to myself, a personal satisfaction to making the show by the skin of our teeth.

Sticks & Stones ended the song with a roar of applause from the frenetic little crowd. "This is our last song. I've been told the Jerk Offs canceled. So this is it."

My jaw lagged as the band ripped into their final song. I stepped forward to notify the singer of the contrary, but the song was painfully short. By the time I had arrived at the stage, it was too late. The crowd had already found the door.

Our set was short and uneventful. The few people who remained were adequately pleased. They sang their words of praise as I stumbled off the stage, disappointed.

"I liked your band," an attractive female said as I walked out the back door. Thick, black lashes flapped in a rousing effort to gain my attention. The perfect cut of her bob hairdo shined an unnatural black—jet-black, thick like her eyebrows. I was taken in by her mouth, the way her glossy red lips appeared swollen. A white base of make-up worked to conceal a cute array of freckles on her cheeks.

I shook my head and forced an artificial smile. "Thanks for sticking around," I told her. "We woke up in Ohio this morning and barely made it here."

"Well, I came solely to see you guys. I enjoyed it."

"Thanks," I said.

"Where next?" she asked.

"DC, New York, Syracuse, Pittsburgh, the south..."

"You guys are scheduled to play on WFMU, aren't you? I work in New York City."

She walked over to a pink Karmann Ghia with New York license plates. A vinyl sticker of Faith No More clung to the bumper speckled with rust.

"Well, thank you for coming out," I repeated. "Seriously, it means a lot."

"My pleasure." She slipped into her car and closed the door. The tinted window slowly lowered as she started the engine. "My name is Rebecca, by the way. I'd give you a card, but that'd be tacky. So I won't. And you are?"

"Frank. Frank Smith."

"Good to meet you, Frank. Take it easy. We'll probably meet again," she said as the car quickly backed out of the parking lot and down the dark street.

Harold stood shaking his head as he put the equipment back inside the van. "I don't know what the deal was with the show. I told the guy on the phone..."

"It cost us," George said. "We have about fifty dollars to get us to Washington DC. We'll be broke by the time we arrive."

He was right. When we arrived at the BBQ Iguana late in the afternoon, the venue was empty, as were our pockets. Several people wearing staff shirts were loading amplifiers out the front door. The bar had a worn-out feeling about it. By the looks of it, a show had just ended.

188

We pulled up alongside the club where an employee swept the entrance.

"What's with the show?" I asked.

"The show's over."

"What? We're one of the bands—"

"Ah, you must be the Jerk Offs. What was the deal?"

"We're to go on at twelve—"

"Did you think midnight? No, it was a matinee show. That was twelve noon. You guys were to be the first band."

"We have no money," I mumbled dully to myself. "What about a show tonight?"

"No, can't do it. Got Soulside in here tonight. Too big a draw, and we already had a tough enough time deciding on an opening act. Sorry. Beat it."

The band sat quietly without expression or words. Their attention strayed somewhere over my shoulder, out the passenger window. I turned to regard their interest only to be faced with a trio of young thugs dressed in spiffy though cheap, black suits. Their white shirts were properly ironed with thin, black ties covering the buttons. Cheap sunglasses concealed their eyes. Sweat clung to their brow, dampening their short haircuts under black porkpie hats. The frontmost one had a Selector button pinned to his jacket. Another read *Rude Boy* in hot pink against a black and white checkered background. He tossed a piece of dice in the air with his left hand, catching it swiftly with his right.

"How's it going?" he asked me.

"Missed our show here," I revealed to them.

"Which band?"

"The Jerk Offs."

"That sucks," he said casually. "It was a good show. What kind of music? Ska?"

I looked down at his black and white wingtip shoes. "Hardcore."

Specky leaned forward, revealing his shaved head and loose association.

The leader of the group reached out his hand to Specky. "I'm Willy. This is Trent and Hal."

We introduced ourselves in return.

"Where you from?" Hal asked with an irritatingly nasal voice. The sun shined brightly against his clean-shaven, unblemished face. They were all quite handsome.

"Kansas," Specky told them.

They laughed. "Where you going from here?"

"Ocean City, Maryland," I said. "Tomorrow."

They paused to stare at each other, sharing unspoken communication.

"Need a place to crash tonight?" Trent offered.

"Sure."

"Can't say we have big plans for the night," Willy said. "Spent all our money at the show."

"That's fine with us," Harold said.

"Follow us…"

They strutted down the broken sidewalk like cut-out hooligans. We idled closely behind as if we were special agents working a Mafia bust. They stepped up to a white 1979 Ford Mustang and waited as Hal unlocked the doors. Each of them checked their reflection before stepping inside.

They delivered us to a placid, suburban neighborhood in Arlington, Virginia, high above their standard-of-living.

189

"I take care of my grandmother," Trent told us, addressing our apparent curiosity. "This is her house. Both my parents have passed away."

He unlocked the front door, inviting us into a cozy room decorated with elaborate, priceless antiques. Each appeared as a family heirloom, purchased new at one time by past generations. Stepping quickly through the room, he opened a scratched wooden door, revealing a sunken fortress immersed in darkness. We stumbled down the steps into the musty corridor as Trent yanked a string that brought light into the dungeon dwelling. It had a strong musty scent of mold and mothballs.

"My place," Trent told us proudly.

The plain white walls were decorated with fliers from DC shows as well as posters of the Jam, the Who, the Specials, and Madness. The furnishings were sparse. One couch with a card table, a black and white television set, and a stereo system. Nothing more.

"Plenty of floor space," Trent told us as he loosened his tie. "There's probably some spaghetti sauce and pasta upstairs."

Willy and Hal placed their hats on the card table as Trent trampled up the wooden stairs in search of a meal. Willy reached inside his pocket as we all took seats on the black tiled floor. He pulled out a deck of cards and slapped them on the table.

"Gin rummy?" he asked us as Hal discovered a bag of pot between the cushions. He sniffed the contents of the bag for freshness.

Specky and Harold stepped up to the card table. "Sure."

After a couple hours of small-talk, George and I left the smoky cave and returned to the van.

"Seem like nice guys," he said as he snuggled under a torn, ratty blanket.

"I'm sorry about the matinee confusion. It was my fault for not paying closer attention."

"There is no fault, only consequence. We deal with it—no guilt, no blame. We're fine tonight. That's all that matters right now."

"Goodnight," I said.

"See you in the morning."

It was well past midnight by the time we arrived in Ocean City. It was a Sunday, and the weekend getaway at the beach had come to a close for those with real jobs. The resort was being cleared for our arrival, or so it appeared.

"Should we call this Marty guy?" Harold asked as we crept through town.

"Maybe we should just sleep in the van tonight," I said. "It's nice out."

Harold didn't agree. His irritated, uneasy throat-clearing revealed this. "I'd like to get some decent sleep for a change."

"I say we crash on the beach," George said to me. "Everyone else can have the van."

"Sounds interesting," I agreed.

Hazel sent a vicious eye to the two of us. Her preference was clearly to call Marty. She didn't speak a word, she just stared. And stared.

Harold made a wide turn, bringing us to an amusement park with a Ferris wheel and water slides. He brought the van to the far end of the vacant parking lot at the water's edge. Hazel was already preparing her sleeping quarters when we took off to the beach in a mad dash.

The breeze coming in from the ocean was cold, as was the thick sand through which we stumbled barefoot. We strolled past the lifeguard stands, placing our towels on the opposite side. The waves kicked up at the shore, leaving a glistening sheen on the sand before it receded back. I glanced back at our tracks where the waves had already crept up and erased every step to the present.

"This is it," George boasted as we stared into the vast horizon. The separation of water and space was blanketed in the pale glow of moonlight. "I never would've guessed that this band would make it to the Atlantic Ocean. You know what's on the other side of that water? Europe!"

I reached down and picked up some sand, letting it fall through the cracks between my fingers in an unsteady stream to the ground. It was finally clear that we had, in fact left Kansas. "I've always dreamt of this."

"Me, too," he said. "To be somebody...to make a difference."

I found my thoughts drifting with the waves that lapped against the shore. I gazed down the stretch of shops along the Boardwalk to the kites that hovered perpetually over the beach. It was very tranquil, and very much away from home.

"I want my music to out-live me," George continued. "All of it—rock and symphonic, whatever I create. I want my name spoken in universities two hundred years after my death. I want to someday redefine symphonic music."

"I want to know I made a difference on someone's life," I said. "Like others have for me."

"We're barely pulling this tour off," George mused confidently. "Knock on wood."

"Knock on sand," I corrected, digging my fist into the cool, wet earth. "I wonder if the tide will sweep us away if we sleep out here."

"I doubt it. The lifeguard chairs are too close to the water to worry about that. I lived in Connecticut when I was younger. I've been to this ocean countless times, swimming in there with the horseshoe crabs—disgusting creatures."

I stretched the musty blanket out underneath me, separating half my body from the sand. With my duffle bag as a pillow, I was ready for sleep. "It's good to be here." My words tapered with a lazy yawn.

"See you in the morning," George said, sitting, staring into the deep water. "I have a lot of good memories with this ocean. I'll be up a while, don't mind me."

"Goodnight."

"Hippies on the beach! Hippy alert!" exclaimed Specky.

Children screamed as they raced around the sandy beach, drowned under the thunder of crashing waves. Daylight of an exhaustive temperature summoned my return from a deep slumber. I raised my head, squinting under the blazing heat of the morning sun. The sun burnt my eyes. My skin was sweaty and hot.

"You look red," Specky informed me. "I'd get up if I were you."

I slowly pulled myself forward, wiping the sweat off my brow as I tapped George's shoulder. "Get up, man. You'll look like a lobster."

"Oh...fuck," George groaned as he curled into a tight ball. "Bound to get cancer...whose idea was this?"

I stood and brushed the sand from my sweaty body. I could feel the sting from the redness that covered my skin like the surface of Mars.

"Let's get out of here," George said. "Did anybody call our guy Marty?"

"Not yet," Specky responded lightly. "Waiting for Frank. He's the numbers man."

The three of us walked back to the van where Harold lay on the roof continuing his tan. His leather jacket lay safely at his side. The amusement park was a madhouse with hordes of people screaming in mayhem and bliss. The resort atmosphere plagued the occupants of our van—we had no choice but to assume this *was* our summer vacation. There existed a new sense of comfort that eased the pressure of any recent bickering.

"Is there a phone around?" I asked, feeling edgy from the heat. My body conducted it like the surface of Venus.

Specky pointed to the far end of the parking lot, opposite the amusement park. "I called Skeet just a bit ago. I went to that restaurant over there."

Brushing the sand off my sweat-stained T-shirt, I strolled across the parking lot with the sun fertilizing the burn on my neck. I could feel the tiny grains of sand sticking to my scalp, glued by the dirt and sweat of over a week without bathing. My stomach ached, and my only hope to appease the hunger was that this guy Marty would have the foresight to offer us a meal. Otherwise, we'd have to scrounge the streets for change. Nonetheless, I knew I'd come up with a meal sometime that day. At least I hoped I would.

Inside the restaurant, the air was cool and comfortable. It was my first chance to view the oceanside for what it was. The deep blue waves developed their strength into a tumbling mass of white that crashed against the bright, reflective shore. People ran gaily on the beach, retreating to dry land with each passing wave. Far on the horizon, a massive battleship perched itself like an immobile island, its belly filled with young American sailors—at least I hoped they were American. That would be the luck of the tour. I could see the news:

...and in the remains of what was once Ocean City, Maryland, a piece of scrap metal was discovered amongst the ruins. It read: *This Turned Into A Big Piece of Shit Real Quick!* It was the last known relic, believed to be part of a Dodge van. It will begin an everlasting tour of museums as a reminder of the unforgettable late 1980's surprise attack on Ocean City...

Two bikini-clad girls passed by the window, giggling, kicking sand in the air as they chewed on caramel apples. The caramel dripped slowly down their chins from the moist fruit—half-consumed, sticky and sweet.

A young trio of kids with hooded Champion sweatshirts stood at the phone as one of them chattered pointlessly to a friend about the size of the waves. I waited patiently, absorbing the type of comfort I took for granted as a child on family trips.

The skinny, young kid quickly hung up the phone, staring at me as they passed. I fished the phone number out of my pocket and slid a coin down the slot. The three kids stood close behind me as I dialed the number.

"What-up?" the voice asked on the other end of the phone.

"Is Marty there?" I asked.

"He be me. Whooby-you-be?"

"Frank Smith. I'm the singer for the Jerk Offs."

"Word, Chief! Dude, you made it—that's raucous! Where ya? I'll motor down."

"I'm at some restaurant facing the ocean. There's an amusement park with a haunted house right by the van, it's dark blue. 5th and Washington, I think."

"Right on—half hour—see ya."

"Yeah," I replied before hanging up.

My skin felt as if it would spontaneously combust. I resisted digging my nails into my tender skin. As I turned—not watching where I was going—one of the hooded young boys stepped in front of me. His weathered Vans were nearly on my toes. I looked up from my red complexion, straight into his alert and perceptive eyes.

192

"Did I just hear you tell that person you are in a band called the Jerk Offs?"

I nodded.

"You guys are in *Maximum RockNRoll* scene reports all the time, aren't you?" he asked.

"Indeed so."

"You're playing at my friend's pad. Don't you have a song about being Straight Edge? It was on some compilation, a song called...*Persistence, Resistance*."

"The lyrics are a lot more vague than that, but I could see how you'd interpret it that way."

He stuck his hand out firmly to grip mine. A black X of fresh ink was painted on the back of his hand. "I'm Smiley. This is Chip and Posse. They're my boys."

I shook their hands generously, careful not to allow the X's to stain my hand.

"How long have you guys been out?" Posse asked. He stared with firm, attentive eyes. He toted a skateboard under his arm. I could tell he rode often by the scratches and bruises. His ballcap had the words Hard Stance written with blue ink on the upturned bill.

"About three and a half weeks."

"Has it gone well?" he asked me.

"It's gone as these things do. Not making much money, equipment problems, van problems. All the things you've heard before."

"Can I offer lunch?" Smiley asked generously.

"Oh, no thanks, I really—well, actually..."

"It'd be no problem at all, man," he assured me. "My mom set me up with twenty bucks for the day."

"Honestly, I'd love to turn you down out of kindness, but I'm fucking starving. I'll give you a record in trade."

"Sure thing, man. Let's have a seat."

I followed them to a table where we sat uncomfortably together—me the outsider—immersed in awkward silence. We placed our orders and looked at one another as if searching for a topic of conversation. Each one of them had the same look. Each represented the clean-cut boy next door, the one you envied for getting all the breaks, the star quarterback with the starched shirts and unbroken families. The kid who lived in the picket fenced house that never had trouble, and never would have trouble. The ideal American boy, the kid who always did the right thing. The kid who didn't even drink alcohol.

"I'm kind of a mess," I said uncomfortably. "Haven't had access to a shower in a while."

"It's the life, man," Smiley said. "I can imagine how it is. I really respect it, putting yourself out there like that for what you believe in. We have to stand together, help each other. Make a difference, you know?"

I smiled, surprised. "I agree."

"So you're Straight Edge, huh?" Posse asked me.

"My personal philosophy resembles the trend, yes."

"We're Straight Edge. Clear thoughts to make a difference," Smiley said to me calmly. "I saw Bold a couple weeks ago at City Gardens in Trenton. It was amazing. I still feel the fires of the inspiration. I'm going to become vegan. It's time for me to take that step, to move beyond vegetarianism. Are you vegan?"

"No," I answered. "You guys are from New Jersey?"

193

Smiley answered for all of them. "No, we're from DC, but I used to live in Salisbury. DC is where it all started, you know?"

"What's that, hardcore?" I asked, preparing to disagree.

"Straight Edge hardcore," he clarified correctly.

We paused our unsteady conversation as the food arrived.

"We've got a band going," Posse informed me. "We're called Stomp. Anybody who brings beer to our shows, we're going to stomp on them."

"Sounds like Slapshot," I said. "Would that be plagiarism to beat drinkers with hockey sticks?"

They all laughed.

"Kind of seems ridiculous to me, no offense. Inflicting violence on those who have different views, those who made different choices in their lives."

"The choice?" Smiley asked me. "This is a movement we're backing—a cause. Are we just going to fall like the hippies? Lose our identities to drugs so we have no idea whether we've won or lost?"

"Won or lost? What, is this some basketball game?" I asked, suddenly feeling guilty for arguing with this person who supplied me with a much needed meal. "I don't need to make a deal of it myself, this is the way I am. Cool or not. No offense, but I'd rather listen to *More Beer* by Fear any day before Bold, Judge, or, Uniform Choice...sorry if that offends you."

There was silence for a long and uncomfortable spell as we ate our food. Smiley was the first to break the fasting of speech. "That's your opinion, I'll respect it."

"Take away all the lines, all the difference between hardcore, punk, Oi, ska...we do need to stand together, I agree," I said. "We're outcasts, it's all we have—each other. Thanks for the meal."

"No problem."

Not another word surfaced throughout the meal, which ended rather quickly. As we stood, I shook their apprehensive hands once again.

"I'll get that record, our van is just over—"

"Don't bother," Smiley said coldly. "I don't want it."

They turned and walked away.

I got my meal for the day. I was content.

"S'up, homey?" a young stoner asked me as I returned to the van.

His hair was long and clean with curly locks blowing in the soft ocean breeze. Small braids hung from his bangs over groggy eyes. His cut-off jeans were old and ragged. An old navy blue football jersey with a faded white number 58 hung loosely on his limp body. Dried mustard stains offered a nice splash of color for contrast. Cheap, lime green foam sandals protected his tanned feet.

"Marty?" I asked. "I'm Frank."

"Dig. Your fellas told me, said you never arrived from making the call."

"Some young hardcore kids bought me some food—"

"Score!" Marty exclaimed with fists punching the air obnoxiously. "I had some spaghetti in the works, though."

"There's room for more if you're offering," I assured him.

His warm smile revealed every white tooth in his thick head. "You're under my wing, call me Dad. Nothing but chillin' on the beach."

"About that food..." Harold said.

"Ah-ha-ha! Someone's hankerin'! Grub, everyone?"

194

The response was quick and affirmative.

"Off to the party pad," he said as he retreated to his crashed-up jalopy. He paused a moment before stumbling back to the van. "Do you guys trip?" He cautiously pulled a clear bag out of his pocket, its contents two psychedelic mushrooms.

"Nice of you to offer," George said. "But no, thanks."

"No problemo. On the rebound...this-a way—follow the finger."

I twisted the weaves of pasta in small circles around the teeth of the fork, listening to Marty tell brave and exciting stories of lifeguarding. He wasn't afraid to talk, that much was clear.

"We could cruise the Boardwalk tonight," Marty offered as his audience finished their meals. "Lots of folk just checkin' shop, cruisin' and hangin'. Game?"

Specky, the only one of us without a mouth filled with pasta, responded. "That sounds great. We could use a break."

"Yeah, close quarters, tight spots," Marty said. "I did the tour thing with my old band, the Sickos. Changed my life. The tour killed the band. All the better, anyway. I've got some advice: you need Bill. He saved our tour, and I know he can help you guys out."

"Huh?" I asked. "We have a full load—"

"There's room, you *need* him. Last I heard, he was somewhere in Bermuda, or it could have been Tulsa. Anyway, he's flighty, but he's responsible for *everything*. Catch my drift?"

"No."

"He's the quintessential scapegoat. He scheduled the tour, he forgot to change the oil, he's the idiot who didn't put the fliers up the week before the show. It's his fault. If he wasn't off in Japan, you'd have his ass. You can bitch all you want, he deserves it...the fuck-up."

"Interesting," I said as I sat the clean plate on the coffee table amongst the tiny marijuana seeds.

"Don't let the road get to you," Marty began—rather continued. "You can enjoy the ride or let it ride you. Life is to be enjoyed."

The phone rang, causing him to spring from his seat to catch the second ring.

We were suddenly left with silence.

"Skeet and Lank took off to Los Angeles," Specky told us.

"Why?" George asked.

"Bored. Didn't want to hang out in Lawrence another summer. One night they just left."

Marty slammed the phone down and returned to the small living room. "That was my bud Carl on the phone. He works the door at the water park—you know, where you guys were parked? He'll let you slip in there tomorrow. I used to date the manager of the haunted house..."

"That's great," Harold said. "Thanks a lot for the food."

"Thanks for everything," George added.

He dropped himself on a lime green beanbag. "No problemo."

The tentacles of the serpent ripped the waves, digging through the sand with monstrous force. I stood behind the rows of military units armed and poised for battle. They crouched in the sand, steady as a bowl of gelatin as the searchlights struck the beast. It reared its head from the depths of the unknown, a ghastly abomination that belonged in the dark watery realm of the deep Atlantic.

"On the count of three," the decorated General announced to the troops. The serpent swept a forceful tentacle across the shore, leveling the tallest waterslide as if it was constructed by a protractor set. "One...two...three!"

The sound of the gunfire was deafening. It rained upon the creature like Independence Day. The monster raised its menacing head and roared viciously into the night sky before sinking its powerful jaws into the roof of the haunted house. It chewed it mercilessly like a Tangy Taffy. The bullets had no effect.

It slithered from its nautical environment up the shore, edging closer to the civilized world—

"This place is a money rake," George groaned as we stumbled along the wooden walkway.

"Yeah," I mumbled.

The Boardwalk was alive with giddy tourists and partiers, living large and racking debts on throwaway merchandise. Smiles graced each face passed, but I couldn't help but wonder what bizarre creatures were crawling under the endless stretch of wooden planks built up over the beach. Neon signs flashed in all directions, stabbing at your conscience, luring you to rationalize the purchase of a shirt that read: *My baby-sitter went to Ocean City and all I got was this lousy T-shirt.*

The sun had just completed its tour of duty, and the sky was lit like the blast of an explosion captured motionless, frozen momentarily in time at the mercy of the night's thaw. The moon shined high over the sea as the kites struggled against the gentle ocean breeze. The crashing waves sizzled over the giggling chatter of the carefree pedestrians. Kids scurried through the people—cotton candy in hand, glowing necklaces around their wrists and scrawny necks. Lovers wandered aimlessly as if they had walked right out of a Drifters song, or had secretly contemplated a quick horizontal dance under the wooden planks of the Boardwalk.

George and I stopped at a stand, checking out the inflated prices with empty pockets.

"There's nothing like eating bad food while on vacation," I said. "Makes you feel like you're really doing something fun and exciting. What's a day at the amusement park, ballpark, or beach without eating stale nachos or big, salty pretzels?"

"Yeah, someday when we have money we should come back here."

"Hey, pickledick!" Marty screamed over our shoulders to the guy at the stand.

"What's up, Marty?" the guy with frizzy, fiery hair groaned. He had horrible acne that covered his splotchy, freckled face. "Don't harass me while I'm working."

Marty stepped up and slapped his hands on the stainless steel. "Got these guys here from Kansas, they're a band called the Jerk Offs. Think you can spot them some food? They're broke...c'mon, man. Support the cause."

"I don't know. I got my boss coming back sometime—"

"Ah, you pussy," Marty scolded with sheer disappointment. "Listen to you, subservient to the man. Why don't you shove your tongue another inch up his—"

"All right, all right. What do you guys want?"

"No shit?" I asked excitedly. "Nachos, lots of jalapeños. And a Pepsi."

"No Pepsi, just Coke."

"Make it a Mr. Pibb, then," I requested. "George?"

"Yeah, nachos," George said with a smile. "A Coke, maybe?"

"How about one of those fat pretzels?" I asked him.

He shook his head with a menacing smirk as he poured our drinks. His face was turning a color that didn't quite match the shade of his tangerine hair. "You owe me, Marty."

"We'll give you a record or T-shirt or something," I said.

"I'll take that record at the party tomorrow," he told us quite seriously. "Don't forget." He passed the food over the stainless steel counter to our quickly receptive hands. "Now get the hell out of here before I get fired."

"Thanks, pickledick," Marty said. "You can keep your milk money next week."

We followed Marty through the crowds. He ended up wandering inside one of the tacky tourist traps. The most inane things caught his attention. He roamed through the shop, filling his hands and pockets with useless items. He dragged a handful to the counter, releasing it in a disturbing pile. "Can I have this stuff?"

"What, are you crazy?" the sexy employee asked with a quick flip of the hair. "Of course not."

"You're shitting me. C'mon! What's it worth to you?"

"Do I know you?" she asked irritably.

"No, but you should. Do you want my number?" He dug deep inside his pockets for a pen. He paused temporarily to dig the underwear from his ass as a crowd stared.

"God, no," she moaned. "Now leave before—"

He dropped the merchandise and walked out the door. "Man, some people..."

"Did you know her?" I asked before shoving a jalapeño into my mouth.

"No. Wouldn't want to, either. She needed to be annoyed. Most people do. Like doormen and bouncers. Some of the most boring and unimaginative people in the world hold those jobs. Tell you what, next time you guys go to a show, try to walk right past the doorman without showing ID or paying. They give you the whole: *Hey, get back here!* type thing. They live for that shit. Then you just lay down the whole: *Do you know who I am?* Nothing gets them more than that. Ask them the cover and then refuse to pay for such a sucky band like the one they booked. They really dig that, too."

I tossed the plastic nacho container in the trash as we followed him down the Boardwalk. He walked up to a pizza stand and waited patiently in line. A massive neon sign flashed over the counter, the word: PIZZA!

"Do you guys have pizza?!" he screamed ignorantly before his turn came up.

"Can you read?" an anonymous voice exclaimed.

"Oh, yeah...right there. *Pizza.* Cool. Is it free?"

"What do you think?" the worker sneered bitterly.

"Hmm," Marty said curiously. He waited in line until it was his turn. He made odd noises that loosened the space around him.

"Did you want a pizza?" the worker asked him.

Marty stood quietly, staring with a bright smile that enraged the worker. "No. Why?"

"Get lost, pal. You're slowing up my line."

"I see you're busy," Marty said, never removing the obnoxious smile from his relaxed face. "Your boss should be proud..."

We left slowly, continuing casually down the Boardwalk.

"That guy believes in his work. People like that make me proud to be an American," Marty said as we mixed further through the crowd. Catching the eye of a stocky man wearing a muscle shirt, he switched directions. "Hey, tough-guy, I like your ass!"

The man turned, caught eyes with Marty, and smiled.

"You little noodle!" the guy said as he slapped him firmly on the back. "Where you been?"

"Just hangin'. Check it, bro—these guys are playing at Victor's pad tomorrow night."

The man clutched a busty blond tightly against his chest. "Jerk Offs? Yeah, I'll be there."

"This is Frank and George," Marty said. "And this brute is Cunningham."

"How's it going?" Cunningham asked us with a chiseled, masculine grin. "Enjoying this place? I don't know how you couldn't with this clown. And I mean *clown*. Nice to meet you guys."

We smiled affirmatively as he walked on, dissolving into the crowd.

"Cunningham's a cool guy," Marty told us. "He does his own thing, and he doesn't let shit get to him. So, what cool places have you played on this tour?"

"Our best shows have been the smaller towns," George said.

"Isn't that always the case? It's where you least expect it. You can play CBGB's in New York, be on stage where the very style of music you're playing got its name, and no one cares. It's those little filler spots in no-name towns that make the difference. Check out the line at this stand," Marty said of a hotdog cart at the opposite corner. He walked over to it and stood at the end of the line. "Hey, Ricky, did you ever figure out why all those people were getting sick over these hot-dogs? I'm surprised you're still open."

"Get out of here, punk!" he growled furiously.

"Ah, okay, man," Marty said, discouraged. He shrugged his shoulders and stumbled away.

"You know everybody, don't you?" I asked.

"Almost, but I didn't know that guy," he admitted. "He looked like a Ricky, didn't he?"

"Do you ever get your ass kicked?" George asked.

"Never. I believe I'm a good judge of situations. I know just how far I can push it. For instance, that guy...what's he going to do? He's working too hard anyway. I'm just trying to make his life easier. He should respect me. Ever heard of a physics term called the principle of least action? Things will arrive at their own time, at their own proper pace. I see life as that, as a pre-determined route. It's not about distance or arrival, but how the trip was endured and enjoyed. Besides, everyone needs their limits pushed from time to time."

"Here comes Hazel and Harold," George said. "Case in point."

They came our direction, glanced at us, and kept walking. Marty watched them. "That's her name? I forgot. I'm going to show them around a bit. Down with that?"

I nodded.

"See you on the flipside, Kirk out." He ran to catch them.

"He's a character," I said to George as we stood on the edge of the Boardwalk looking to the amusement park.

"I like the way he slips in and out of the surfer-dude accent."

I laughed. "Kind of endearing, isn't it?"

The top of the main water slide towered in the distance. Its highest platform covered the bottom crest of the moon over a cloudless sky.

*   *   *

198

I looked down from the platform of the water slide upon the people walking along the Boardwalk. They looked like tiny insects. Life appears much more trivial at higher elevations. The wind tickled my dripping wet body, the unbridled element high over the resistance of buildings and trees.

I imagined myself as a giant—

"Come on, pal," the attendant with the sculpted body complained as he scratched the tip of his white nose with his pinkie finger. "Are you going down or not?"

I placed the foam mat on the slope of churning water. It splashed up against me, a nice contrast to the burn across my body. I pushed forward, sending myself on a wild frenzy to the pool below where Hazel and Specky waited.

"You're going to be fried if you don't come in out of the sun," Specky told me as I pulled the mat through the chlorinated water.

I meandered through the kids that wrestled to control all the mats. Finally, I found my way to the bank and took a seat alongside the two of them. I wadded my dreadlocks together and rung the water out.

"It's getting kind of late, isn't it?" Hazel asked as the three us climbed from the pool.

Specky rubbed his shaved head with a rough hand. "A little bit late." He banged the side of his head with his fist in an attempt to force some water from his ear. "George went to pawn our records at the local music stores."

"We could always donate plasma," Hazel said. She turned and walked into the women's bathroom.

I followed Specky out the exit door where we wandered with dripping wet clothes to the parking lot. The heat of the sun worked at me, threatening with convincing determination to break me down.

I waited in the blistering heat as Specky fumbled with his keys to unlock the van. The foul stench of a locker room smacked us in the face as the door slid open. Our duffle bags covered the floor, overflowing like shaken cans of soda. I reached for my own, pulling it to me by the handles as socks and underwear seeped out like an infected wound. Frustrated by the heat that feasted on my body, I grabbed a handful of socks and underwear and escorted them to the nearest trash deposit.

"I don't need this stuff on this tour," I rationalized. "The more possessions I have out here, the more of a nuisance. I'll buy more when I get back to Kansas."

I've yet to make that purchase again.

The summer sun seemed to sizzle on the pavement. I closed my eyes as I leaned in the van. The heat had its way with my body like a cheap floozy. The sound of waves crashing against the shore was a soothing distraction. I focused on the chirping of seagulls soaring through the parking lot. Other than the repressive heat, I was submerged in a very comfortable atmosphere, unlike any I had ever known. When I opened my eyes once again, Hazel stood over me, scowling.

"You're in my way," she told me as she stepped across.

George, Harold, and Marty came around the side of the van. George gripped a box of records in his tanned hands.

"Sold about five copies," he informed us. "Selling them without consignment, they really aren't interested. But we can put it in the gas tank to keep us going. Sucks, though. We're practically giving them away out of desperation."

"Chow?" Marty asked, his clean hair blowing across his peaceful expression. He squinted inside the van, his tanned skin soft and shiny. "Grub? Anyone?"

"Everyone," I said as I stepped up on solid blacktop. "Let's eat."

199

*   *   *

Very few people could be crammed inside the old tool shed where we delivered
our Ocean City performance. The backyard was full. Those who couldn't fit inside the
crumbling wooden structure peered through the windows at me with gleeful smiles.

"We're the Jerk Offs," I announced into the microphone. "From Lawrence,
Kansas."

The crowd cheered with ignorant laughter as they tipped their beers and smoked
their cigarettes, staring upon me with stoned and cloudy eyes.

I lowered the microphone and leaned toward the band. "Ready?"

"Ready," Specky confirmed.

"We need some cash to get to New York City," I said into the microphone once
again. "There'll be a tip jar going around. Specky here will suck all your dicks if you
donate just a little...and he does swallow for an extra buck."

I watched the jar float across the crowd like a lifeboat collecting loose change for
our survival.

It felt like an eternity since we had last performed. The little shed was too small
for the people to dance, but the enamor of their eyes was all the response I needed to
know they were enjoying themselves. Due to the small confines, the sound was quite
clear as opposed to the poor monitor mix often available in fancier clubs. As an added
treat for the party, and as a practice for ourselves, we went through every song we
knew, playing almost two full hours. It was a good opportunity to scratch away some
rust.

When the long set ended, I sat the microphone down gently and walked through
the crowd with heavy strides. Beer splashed on me every direction I wandered. A layer
of smoke lingered in the fresh ocean air. I felt a need to get away from it. I retreated to
the beach for the last time, staring into the distance where the night sky bled into the
sea a faint blend of blue. It smeared like tears through mascara.

"Let it hang, bro," Marty told me as the van awaited our departure the following
morning.

"Thanks for everything," I said as I strolled back to the van. "Have a good year
lifeguarding."

"We're still rockin' in the free world!" he exclaimed, causing silence to fall upon
the parking lot as he stroked his air guitar passionately.

I smiled and waved as I climbed through the open door. My stomach was full and
my body was clean. It had been a good break from the steady commotion. The beach
would soon be just a memory to savor. We were on our way to New York City.

Conversation was low when we crawled through the dense traffic into the city.
The sight of it was breathtaking to a smalltown boy from Kansas. The skyline was
everlasting through the thick shroud of pollution. People lined the streets in faceless
droves like so many trees. Their presence made no difference to the vast numbers that
walked the same walk, talked the same shit. The value of life in the city is but a
commodity easily replaced. In New York City, you're nothing, nobody. I liked that.

We stopped at a small Italian restaurant in East Orange, New Jersey to get better
directions to the radio station.

Artificial grapes hung from the restaurant's deep green walls. The artist formerly
known as Dino Martini swooned through *Innamorata* over a small radio that delivered
absolute ambiance. Ceiling fans loosened the otherwise stuffy air that reeked of garlic.

200

A flag of Italy covered the wall behind the bar. Red and black tiles criss-crossed the floor.

"Can I get ya sompun?" the thick Italian asked from behind the bar. His black, greasy hair was combed over to cover a shiny bald spot. His mustache was highlighted gray. He maintained a firm pose while polishing a set of wine glasses with a white linen. He stared at me with an even, condescending glare.

"Is this East Orange?" I asked.

"What the...what, are you crazy? Are you stupid or sompun?"

"Uh, I'm looking for a radio station, we're not from here."

"Yeah, well, no shit! Radio station, what the—what radio station? Hold on—" he paused as a group of young black kids rushed into the joint to play video games. "You lil' fucks! Get the shit out of here if you ain't payin' for nut'n! *Buono a nulla...*"

The kids quickly left, giggling innocently.

"What radio station, pal?" he demanded lightly. "Ain't got all day..."

"WFMU."

"Across the fuckin' street. Down a couple fuckin' blocks, now are you buying sompun?"

"No money. Thanks, though," I said, leaving in a hurry. The little kids sat on the edge of the corner, throwing rocks at passing cars. I walked to the van just in front of them where everyone sat quietly. "New England hospitality...we're close. He pointed this way, so I guess we head west."

Harold steered casually through the tight streets, trying desperately to adapt to the anarchistic driving style of New Yorkers. The neighborhoods we had been through were probably constructed at about the same time people considered venturing to a land that would someday be called Kansas. The air was rich with history and social decay.

His abstract directions were somehow helpful. Eventually, we arrived at our destination. Once there, we waited patiently in the lobby to perform for the largest audience of our musical career.

"Who's Frank?" a middle-aged man asked as we arrived at the studio.

"That's me."

"Ah, I'm Jules, I talked to you on the phone," he said before shaking my hand. He appeared to be the age of my father, based on a similar fashion sense. "I'm excited to have you guys."

"We're excited to be here," I told him.

"Ever heard of a band called Hunger Artist?" he asked impatiently without pausing for a response. "Well, they're playing with you at the Pipeline tonight. They're from Arizona. They'll be headlining. I'm expecting you guys will likely have a draw."

"That's good," I said.

"Well, hey, I'd like to talk, but I'm running late. It was nice meeting you."

The afternoon bled effortlessly into the evening, and my one meal that day had already nourished my weakening body. My sunburnt skin itched. I sat watching the clock, waiting. I had sickening memories of high school, staring at the clock with great anticipation. As the hour approached, further came the anxiety. I listened to Jules announce shows at the Ritz and CBGB's and at their very own, the Pipeline. Stiff Little Fingers at the Ritz, what a show. Too bad we'd be across the city...

As the music continued, Jules stepped out of the sound-room and motioned us over to him. "Are you guys ready to do a check? It's about that time."

"Sure," Specky said.

We opened the door to the small sound-room where our equipment awaited our arrival. I sat in the corner listening as each person in the group tampered with their gear, making small adjustments as the sound-man prepared the microphones. I could feel my heart race as the check finally found its way to me. I stood up to the microphone and put the headphones over my ears.

"Okay, Frank—that's your name, isn't it?" the sound-man asked.

I nodded.

"The band won't be able to hear you, and they can't hear me now," he told me. "You'll be the only person in the band that will be hearing the actual transmission. Can your band handle that?"

I nodded again.

"Okay, it'll be just like a practice for them, without the vocals. You'll hear Jules announce the show, and when I point, that means you're on the air."

"Got it," I said.

"Okay, it's down to a couple minutes, so if anyone needs to rush off to the bathroom, now's the time," he told me.

"Anybody got to use the bathroom?" I asked the band over my shoulder.

"No."

"You guys won't be able to hear my singing," I warned them.

"Good," Specky joked.

"You're down to a couple minutes," the sound-man warned. "After this song."

"Have you guys tuned?" I asked.

"Yes, I have," Specky answered quickly.

"George?" I asked.

"Yes."

"Are you sure it's in tune?" I repeated. "It sounded rather...funky...during the check."

"It's in tune," he insisted.

"That's not what I asked."

"What did I say?"

I stiffened my posture as I turned to face him directly. "It didn't sound right during the check."

"What's the deal?" he demanded. "You think I can't hear whether or not my bass is tuned?"

"Did I say that? I asked if you tuned the fucking thing! How hard is it to answer?"

He stared at me, angry and annoyed. "Fuck off."

"Listen, goddammit!" I snarled. "We're going to be playing for a hell of a lot of people right now. All I ask is you tune your fucking bass!"

He stood up and faced me, his bass slung over his shoulder. "Listen, I think I can handle my own instrument. Can you?"

The song ended in my headphones and Jules began to announce the Pipeline show. I raised my finger and tapped on the headphones. All eyes looked upon me as I stared at the sound-man with wide eyes, waiting for the cue.

"...and in the studio right now we have the Jerk Offs," Jules said over the air.

The sound-man pointed sharply at me and my heart felt as if it was about to leap through my chest. I closed my eyes and I could see the barren fields of Kansas with rows of wheat, perky and attentive.

"Good evening New York City. We're the Jerk Offs from Lawrence, Kansas," I said confidently into the mic. Turning to the band, I pointed a stiff finger. "Go!"

With four swift clicks, the momentum came through the headphones and the vision of a placid Kansas countryside faded to the wondrous spectacle of endless skylines. I visualized rush-hour traffic backed up over the bridges with people in cars adjusting the dials on their radios as they tuned in to the Jerk Offs. I could see kitchens in houses that understood no English, the dank city breeze blowing through open windows as the rhythms of the Jerk Offs poured through their living quarters. Couples making love as the radio played in the distant room, the songs of the Jerk Offs capturing a *Magic Moment*.

The passion of accomplishment severed me from the not-so-distant past. I was just a voice, yet a voice amplified through the airwaves of the *City of the World*. I recalled a promise made to me by a teacher whose name I struggled to forget. A promise of ill fate and failure. With the onslaught of one of my favorite bands as a youth to back me, I knew the world could not stop me. I could do no wrong while the music played. The music fed me, fed my ego, justified my ego. So long as I was a part of it all, I would never have a reason to come down, to become one of *them*.

"Thank you very much," I said calmly into the microphone with a scratchy voice as the program came to a close with our final song. "We'll be at the Pipeline in Newark in a few hours. Be there."

I stepped back and wiped the sweat from my sunburned forehead.

The Pipeline was tucked quietly away on a street opposite the tracks of prosperity.

I stepped down on the sidewalk cluttered with loose debris. The smell of urine was unavoidable. "This is it?" We walked together to the front door. Loud music blared from a massive stereo system inside. Broken bricks and trash leaned lazily against the stained wall. "Looks kind of dismal out here."

The doorman looked down his nose at us, waiting for us to forfeit the cover charge. Gold chains hung loosely over his wife-beater shirt. His body was as hairy as a Chia pet. The blue jeans he wore seemed painted on, revealing both his package and his religious background. The grease in his black hair kept it perfectly immobile.

"We're the band," I announced.

"You're the band, eh?" he asked. "Do I look like I give a fuck? What, you can't read the fucking sign? This is the front, you load in over there in the fucking alley."

We apprehensively retreated to the van.

"Hold on," George said, turning back to the doorman. "Mind if I go inside?"

"What the fuck do I care? And if you aren't in the band..."

"I'm in the band," he assured him with potent irritation.

"Let me stamp your hand, tough-guy," he said as a woman walked past with a purebred Boxer pulling firmly from the end of a leather leash. "Get that motherfucking dog outta here! What the fuck do you think dis is?"

"Hey, fuck you," she said as she paused to look up at the marquee. "What the fuck kind of a name is that—The Jerk Offs. Give me a fucking break. How you doing, by the way?"

"Not bad," the doorman responded coldly. "Yourself?"

"Just taking the dog for a fucking walk," she told him calmly as she continued down the street.

"Yeah, get the fuck outta here! You take it easy."

George put his palm out for the stamp of admittance. "Are drinks free? I could use a drink..."

"What the fuck?! Listen, tough-guy, drinks aren't even free for *me*. You can bet your sweet ass that you ain't getting a fucking drink in this hole. You're lucky you got a gig in the city, pal."

"Right."

"Hold it, Chief with the nappy-ass hair," he told me as I advanced behind George. "Where do you think you're going?"

"Inside."

"I suppose you think you're with the band, too."

"Yeah, I think that."

"So why should I?" he asked.

"Because I'll be on stage singing in a few hours."

"Give me your hand," he demanded as he patted the stamp into the ink.

"I need to use a phone, is it down the street?" I asked as he smeared my hand with a blur of red—a color that blended with the burn.

"Listen, pal, if you head down the street that way, you'll fucking die. I'm not shitting you. You don't even think about walking that way. Go down this way. How important is this call? There's a gas station down here. Just stay in the light, all right, tough-guy?"

I stared down the street with the glow of lampposts leading a path to an endless stretch of urban lives. In the distance existed a link back to a comfortable voice. I hadn't talked to Stanley in quite a while.

I made my trek, cautiously and quick. The gas station was slow with one employee safely behind a pane of bulletproof glass. I dialed the operator and made my collect call to its unknowing host.

"Hello?" a groggy voice asked.

"Collect call from Frank, will you accept the charges?" the tinny voice requested.

"Frank? What the...yeah, sure."

"Nice to hear your voice, Captain!" I said happily.

"Thanks for waking me up, you cocksucker."

"Yeah, well, I'm not in the nicest of areas, in fact if I get shot out here, it was because I felt some overwhelming desire to talk to you."

"Well, isn't that sweet?" he grumbled. "Where are you?"

"I'm in Newark, New Jersey. Where are you?"

"I'm in a soft comfortable bed sleeping next to a nekkid lady. Any contrast?"

I looked out over a landscape of harsh, artificial light giving a pale radiance to endless stretches of dilapidated asphalt. Wadded paper containing the news of the day lined the gutters. "A little bit."

"Coming home any time soon?" he asked.

"Not all that soon. We'll see what tomorrow brings."

"Are you playing tonight?"

"We did a spot on the radio a bit ago. And we're about to do a show now. We played on the radio for New York City."

"Sounds impressive," he said.

I peered down the street at pure desolation, hungering for the comfort in which he was immersed. "Don't heckle me about that whole soda thing..."

"No problem," he said. "How's the weather?"

"Nice. Stinks out here, but it's comfortable. They can give this city back to the Indians, as far as I'm concerned."

"Remember when we used to sit on the steps of the JuCo and talk our dreams?" he asked.

"Yeah," I said thinking back, bathing myself in its warm memory. "My Senior year of high school."

"Those times are gone, my friend, and I hadn't even taken the chance to say goodbye," he said. "The door shut behind us too quickly, and that's too bad."

"Whereas another one opened," I added optimistically.

"Did it? I guess I wasn't paying attention."

"I believe so."

"We'll never get the chance to live those times again," he conveyed with a deep sigh. "Are you living now?"

"I'm high on life right now, pal," I said as a section of newspaper flew around the telephone booth and down the street with the rest of the trash.

"Well, don't get too caught in it, it won't last. Nothing ever does. That's the way it is. Just need to accept the waves. Riding high in April, shot down in May. Things get good just as soon as they get worse. You'll never be at rock bottom, though. You have too many people in your life that really care."

I gazed into a neighborhood that lacked the same promise. "That's nice to hear."

"Just be happy for the time you have now. It'll all be gone someday, just as we will be."

"How's my town?" I asked.

"Iola?"

"Yeah, right," I groaned. "No, Lawrence, fool."

"Went there just last weekend," he said. "Saw fliers everywhere for your friends, the Media Whores. Those guys go all out on the promotion. I saw their name on every post, in every store window. They have a show with 7 Seconds at the Outhouse. Also heard one of their songs on KJHK."

"They aren't wasting any time," I said.

"How's the band getting along?"

"Depends on the day, and the situation."

He yawned briefly, giving me a second to check my surroundings for danger. "My new job is working out well, by the way."

"New job?" I asked. "What new job?"

"I've been working at Gates Rubber Company for about a month now. Did you forget?"

"Of course not. I just don't remember all that well. This tour has tunneled out my vision."

"Well, I got a new job, and it's going well. Kind of dull, but the money is really good. Hold on...okay. Claire has something to tell you..."

"...Hello, this is Claire of Iola. And you are?"

"Frank of Nowhere."

"Ah, Frank of Nowhere! I always wanted to go there...did that rhyme? That did," she said happily. "I'm more clever than I thought. Want me to bleed some paranoia into you?"

"Sure."

"Stanley and I were talking about this, and I think there's a big plot to take over our planet. We want you to be aware also. Also, you must promise to never allow this to be printed, okay?"

"Okay," I promised. "Thanks for making me part of your trusted circle, by the way."

"No problem. Okay, you know when that flying saucer went down?"

"Everything goes back to this, doesn't it?" I asked.

"Does it? Well, it just has so much potential for great stories, don't you think?"

"I do."

"Let's say this ship that crashed was a dummy with rigged technology," she proposed. "It was about that time that transistors replaced tubes, right?"

"Sure," I commented obliviously.

"Soonafter, at least that's what Stanley was saying. He was also saying that the technological leap from tube to transistor was a big one. Let's say that the occupants of the spacecraft want to take over this planet, right? Well, any smart person knows the best way to conquer anything is by corrupting the core. Let's say they placed that ship there so we'd find this technology and manufacture it on a large scale. Like velcro. You know, velcro was something that probably came from that crash site as well."

"I'll have to remember that," I said.

"Anyway, seriously...something we know about transistors is that when a nuclear bomb goes off, something knocks out all use of transistors. They just go dead. When UFO's are in the presence of transistors, they go haywire, too. Well, we've based our entire society on the use of a technology that goes bunk under certain unknown situations. Say there's some sub-atomic wave that is cast from an atomic explosion. If the aliens can create the sub-atomic wave without the explosion, there would likely be no physical destruction at all, but all our resources would be useless immediately. We'd be helpless."

"Wow, and the earth would just stand still. So you think we're going to be invaded soon?"

"Never know," she said. "Here's Stanley..."

"...Hey, man, I should be getting to sleep," he said. "Besides, this is at my expense, jackass!"

"Just wanted to reach out and touch someone that wasn't in the van."

"Glad I could help."

"Don't you always?" I asked.

"Do I?"

"Sure. Always quick with the advice."

"Exactly," he declared confidently. "Moral for the day: When the going is good, it's bound to sour. Never drop your guard."

"Point taken, padre. Now it's back down the street to play this show."

"Take it easy," he said.

"I miss you guys."

"You're missed, too."

I stared down the street at the quiet little bar in the distance. I took a deep breath—inhaling the putrid air—and began my walk back to the club. I walked slowly, despite the looming threat of danger. Dealing with the doorman was the only trouble I found.

"Wait a second, Chief," the doorman instructed me. "Where's the stamp?"

Raising a fist to his face to reveal the remnants of the ink, I passed cautiously through the door into the empty club.

"So, this is it?" I asked Specky who stood near the exit. He was buffing his Oxblood Docs with a cocktail napkin.

"This is it," he confirmed. "The band, the staff, and a few drunks. Oh, and some girl from Caroline records."

"Really?"

"She saw us in Pennsylvania at the Fire House," he said.

"No one was there."

"She was."

"So what's the deal?" I asked. "Is she here to sign us?"

"I don't think so," he said. "She just seems kind of curious about the band."

"These people aren't going to be *kind of curious*. They have better things to do than follow us around."

"Well, I don't know. Who cares?"

"It'd be nice to have an album put out at someone else's expense," I said.

"She's over by the bar. Let me introduce you."

I followed him through the club where everything seemed to glow some color of neon. He walked me to a stool where a petite woman sat over a bottle of imported beer. Her jet-black bob hairstyle seemed to devour light.

"Hello, Frank," she said, turning to me. Her thick red lips curved into a familiar smile. The freckles on her cheeks gave her a youthful flair.

I looked at her, confused. My expression was far from a pokerface because she read me like a card.

"It's only been a week or so, Frank, is your memory that bad? Or, is life *that* rough on the road?"

Then it hit me like a tire iron to the toe. "You talked to me after the show in Harrisburg. You were in the parking lot, and your name was..."

"Rebecca."

"Yeah, and you offered me a card, but said it was too tacky to offer."

"It is," she said casually before taking a short sip.

"So, you work for Caroline records."

"I do," she boasted proudly.

"What do you do?"

"A&R. I check out bands that pique my curiosity."

"In a city like this I'd think you'd have a lot of places to find bands," I said.

"My curiosity was piqued to be here for the evening. I enjoyed your last show, but I liked the radio show better. I look forward to seeing Hunger Artist, too. You guys are from Kansas, aren't you?"

I nodded.

"My friend goes to KU, and she's seen you guys several times. She recommended that I check you out. How long is your tour?"

"Too long," Specky answered quickly. "A little over two months."

"Straight?"

"Well, we started off straight," I said.

"No, two months straight?" she clarified.

"Yeah," Specky said. "Two *long* months."

"Good luck with it," she offered. "May you all be talking at the end of it."

We played a vigorous show for Rebecca. We would've played a vigorous show for anybody, had they shown. We had a pleasant but quick conversation with her before she left, never to be seen or heard from again.

We had hoped to earn enough money from the Pipeline show to pay for a much needed meal. The poor turn-out dictated the continuation of our hunger. We had only enough for gas. Nervous tension regarding our fate ensured the sleeplessness required to make the drive to Syracuse that night. Silence spoke for obsessive worrying. I could feel the cold surface of the wall closing in...Syracuse *had* to be a good show.

I heard George move through the darkness, saying not a word as he stuck his hand in front of my face. I reached out and grabbed it.

"For what it's worth," he whispered calmly as he clasped my hand. "My bass *was* in tune."

I smiled, feeling a slight sense of ease. "We haven't eaten in days. It makes for heavy tension. At least the radio show went well. Despite how shitty your bass sounded."

He laughed. "We won't get to Syracuse until tomorrow night if we stay somewhere. That'd be almost three days of not eating."

I shook my head with a belated grin. I leaned back and shut my eyes as the flickering lights of New York City set our course. At least the van was holding up.

I had a dream I was lying on a bed of rocks by the ocean as the tide slowly crept up to me like a black tar. I lay hungry and tired, unable to move as the waves thrust against the molten rocks, making them quake and tremble under the sheer force. When I awoke, I realized Specky's amplifier had become pillow. Its firm, boxed exterior shook with the tremoring determination of the van. A little too determined.

Everyone was awake, staring forward with washed-out expressions.

I sat up slowly, apprehensively. "What's happening?"

"Ah, you're awake," Specky said gravely.

Harold gripped tightly the steering wheel, dedicating briefly to me his attention. "The van's acting up again. We're pulling off at a gas station."

I gazed out at the vast rolling landscape. There was a strange blue luster to the sky, and I could only wonder how late, or rather how early it was. I dared not ask. "Where are we?"

"I don't know. Somewhere in upstate New York."

The van sluggishly climbed over a hill, revealing the lights of a gas station on the crest of a distant incline. We pulled into the quiet lot as the van sputtered to near death. We parked alongside the only car in the lot, an old station wagon that resembled Thik Toller's, my old drummer. Everyone piled out to examine the engine, or simply stretch tense muscles. Harold raised the hood to get a diagnosis on the crackling hack of our new motor. The engine seemed to have a desire to remove itself with a hostile convulsion. As far as it was concerned, it had had enough of the touring lifestyle.

I retreated inside the gas station.

"Car trouble?" the attendant asked as I requested the key to the lavatory.

The nametag read: *Roger*. His leathery skin was firm with muscle. He had the wiry gray hair of Hollywood's mad scientist, complete with the shiny crown. He glanced at me with squinty eyes, thoughtful and tired. He appeared thoroughly bored.

"The usual," I grumbled. "Trouble of some sort."

I wandered to the bathroom, turning on the light and finding myself pleasantly surprised at the cleanliness. Of all the bathrooms we'd experienced, this was surely the best kept. How easily amused when drowning in turmoil... I began to relieve myself, staring out an open window into the countryside of New England. The strangely faint glow still covered the sky. It carried with it a soft breeze that numbed my perception. I fell into a calm silence as I relaxed in the midst of a deep, murky rut.

208

Reluctantly, I stepped away from the window and returned to the greasy lot. Harold and George talked loosely with the gas station attendant who held tightly to a pair of pliers. He climbed up on the bumper and gazed at the engine. After a few brief seconds, he stepped back down with a cocked brow. He chewed the inside of his lip, thinking.

"Yeah, that's what it is," the attendant said, pointing to the driver side of the engine. "Motor mount."

"Shot, huh?" Harold verified. "What are we able to do about it right now? Nothing?"

"Well, not necessarily. We could rig something...possibly. I'll see what I have in the car."

He stepped away as the van's engine rumbled and shook mercilessly. The three of us gazed at one another as the stranger opened the back of his station wagon and tore through piles of tools and building accessories. After a few minutes of shuffling, he returned empty-handed.

"My name is Roger, by the way," he said to us calmly.

With a finger pointing to each person, Harold introduced us. "Specky, George, Frank, and I'm Harry."

"I like your shoes, Specky. Nice thick soles. Maybe too thick, anyway. Frank— that was your name, right?"

I nodded.

"Those canvas shoes you got, I used to own a pair when I played basketball in high school. Chuck Taylors. Are you really attached to them?"

"Why do you ask?"

"Well, we need a piece of rubber about this thick," he said, gesturing with his fingers an inch apart. "And the rubber soles of your shoes doubled over would be just about the exact size we need...could save you a lot of money."

"Money we don't have," Harold added.

I knelt down and untied my right shoe. Pulling it loose, I handed it to him, placing my bare foot firmly on the oily ground.

"Let me get my razor," he said, retreating to the station wagon once again. "This is the fun part."

"Do you have another pair with you?" George asked me.

"No."

"Okay, boys, here goes nothing," Roger said as he placed the shoe on the ground. "Lots of military training put to good work here."

"Did you serve time overseas?" Harold asked.

"Vietnam. Hard times, both during and after." He paused a moment to direct his attention to the duty at hand. "What brings you folks out here? I see the tags are from Kansas. Are you following the Grateful Dead?"

"Definitely not. We're following our own agenda," Specky said. "We're a band."

"This could've been a pretty sizable expense by a real mechanic. I usually work mornings, but the graveyard person just up and quit this afternoon. It's your lucky day. I would assume you're a rock band?"

"By how we look?" I asked with a smile. "Yes, we are...so did you see a lot of action in Vietnam?"

"I did, unfortunately. My legs are scratched up, I have numbness throughout most of my right arm, and my back isn't what it once was. The government gives me ten percent, which is about seventy-two dollars a month. Not much for rent, I would say.

So, yes, I have some problems with aspects of this country. Did you guys play in New York City?"

"Earlier this evening," George said proudly. "Now we're off to Syracuse."

"We played live on the radio earlier in the day," Specky added.

Roger had just made the final incision, and was ready to conduct the surgery. "Is that right?"

"I suppose you need some manpower here," Harold offered. "Just tell me what I need to do."

I stepped aside as they crowded to the van's engine. "What will we owe you for this?"

"You guys are playing in Syracuse, huh? Well, dedicate a song to the vets. That's all I would want. Your generation needs to know, because it could happen to you. When they come for you, be prepared. Own a gun."

"You got it," Specky said.

"I may sound paranoid, but I've seen quite a bit too much," he told us as he prepared his Rube Goldberg-styled creation. "Never trust the man with the gun. Have your own."

He ducked his head under the hood, informing Harold of the details of the operation. Harold would be the man hoisting the motor with a broomstick...I stepped away, allowing the men to do what men do. In the meantime, I watched. And waited.

An hour later, we were on the road once again. The strange blue coloration of the sky had slowly transformed into a lighter shade. I fell fast asleep within the first ten miles. When I awoke, we were stationary in a rest area baking under the summer sun. Harold was propped up on a wooden picnic bench, sleeping awkwardly in the shade of a row of trees. I could see the sweat saturating the white shirt under his black leather jacket.

Everyone else slept together in a moist coil with only a mutual layer of sweat separating one another. Flies swarmed over us as if we were one with them. I could feel them crawling on me, tickling my back. I wouldn't move. This is where I lived now. Amongst the flies, amongst the sweat and hunger.

I looked out the back window at the traffic that passed along the busy highway. I had no idea where we were, but I knew we were safe for the moment. That's all that mattered. I shut my eyes and returned to sleep.

By the time we arrived in Syracuse, the rain began to fall.

We stopped at a gas station to make the fateful call. I stepped across the soiled pavement with bare feet, splashing carefree through the downpour as I covered my valuable notebook with a dirty shirt. The rain intensified my odor. I reeked like a wet dog. I dialed the number slowly with bony, sunburnt fingers that dripped water from the tips.

No answer.

I tried again with similar results. The rain cascaded upon me, washing away the filth which I had become so equated. It covered me like a gritty film. I looked up at the sky, feeling the drizzle pelt my stubbly, oily face before sliding off. It felt good against the burn on my back, across my shoulders.

"So what's the deal?" Specky asked me as I returned.

"No answer."

"What?" Harold questioned out of paranoia and routine.

"She told me she works during the day," I said calmly. "Maybe she isn't home yet."

"It's raining," Hazel growled.

"I noticed. We can try again later."

"Do you have her home address?" she asked.

"Yes, I do. Somewhere in my notebook."

"Did we sell the notebook for food or gas money?" Specky joked. "Oh, here it is."

"I haven't eaten in days," I sighed.

"Me, neither," George added.

Harold laughed. "Well, aren't you guys the martyrs. You can steal food like the rest of us."

Specky thumbed through the notebook quickly, finding the current date. "Here we go."

"Maybe we should take it into this gas station and see if it's an easy street to find," Harold suggested.

Luckily for us, it was. The location was simple enough—an old two story house, white with black shudders and a wrought iron fence containing a lemon-colored lawn. We waited quietly for hours, watching the rain. My stomach ached to the point of sickness. I felt weak and irritated. Other times when I had skipped several meals, my perception became finer tuned. I had reached my threshold, eliminating any concentration whatsoever. All I knew was the pain and yearning of the most essential element of my existence.

Soon after five o'clock, a black Volvo pulled into the driveway. The motorist patiently adjusted a black umbrella inside the car as we watched in secretive silence. The umbrella extended from a hand garnished with black fishnet and silver rings. Her skin was pale and white, accented by the contrasting black coloration of long, pointed fingernails.

Specky jumped out the passenger door and ran through the mud to introduce himself. He appeared as a pitiful bum, dirty and unkept next to this high-maintenance work of Gothic art. He exchanged a few words and pointed our direction from under the web-like claw of the umbrella. She turned, smiling.

Her head was clean shaven with a thick, ratty mohawk much like my own. Small silver objects were dreaded into an intricate weave. Piercings covered her face.

She signaled us to join them in the rain, pulling her out-stretched arm at us as if to lure us into her lair. We wasted no time, making a quick dash to the porch like insects blindly rushing the web of a black widow. We collected under the dry shelter of the porch.

"Hello, everybody," she said pleasantly as she reached inside her black leather bag. Her long nails clawed and scratched for keys. "I'm Sunshine and I'll be your host for however long you'll need."

We introduced ourselves as she hesitated with the lock to pay close attention to catch the names. She smiled with each introduction, nodding homogeneously as the pieces of silver that pierced her nose, eyebrows, ears, lips, and neck rattled with each motion. Her upper arms were tattooed with ancient Celtic imagery. I recognized the logo of the band Psychic TV amongst the symbols. It was the freshest one. Her skirt seemed to be several different layers of thin, black fabric loosely stitched together like a peasant child, yet fashionably elegant. A black crystal hung from a silver chain around her pasty neck.

211

With a twist of the lock, the door slowly creaked open as lightening ripped across the sky. A staircase sat eerily in the darkness, leading to an upper floor. We followed her steps upward where mannequins were sprawled out in every corner, each dressed in leather bondage apparel. The walls were bare with the exception of one poster that displayed two men embracing with a kiss on a skyscraper overlooking New York City.

She ignited the lights in the main room. "My roommates should be home soon." She sauntered to a small table covered with candles, tarot cards, and rune stones. The candles were displayed in the shape of a pentagram, red, blue, and black. She slowly began lighting each. "I'm surprised they aren't here yet."

"Does it always rain in Syracuse like this?" I asked.

"No. Just lucky, I guess. A lot of bands that come through claim the rain seems to follow them. Have you guys noticed such a thing?"

"Not really," Harold recollected. "Only the luck that goes with it."

"Has it been bad?" she asked.

"It's been *hell*," he responded smugly.

She smiled, taking a seat by the window next to an armless mannequin. "It builds character."

"So do a lot of other things you can do at home," he said.

"Are you the promoter of our show?" Specky asked her.

"Yes."

"Have you done a lot of shows?"

"A few. Enough to feel comfortable with the turn-out tomorrow, if you have any doubt. I've been having some really successful shows at this hot gay bar off campus. It's called the Back Door. Usually no less than one hundred people attend the shows."

"Syracuse isn't all that big, is it?" Specky asked.

"Not really." She paused to look out the window. "Ah, here comes one of my roommates. Would any of you care for a drink? I didn't mean to be so rude as to not offer."

"No, thanks," George said.

She stood again and glided into the kitchen. "I'll be starting a meal soon. I assume you guys would accept food."

George turned quickly to respond. "Absolutely."

I visualized us gathering around a table, sharing a goblet filled with the sacrificial blood of virgins...

"Does pasta sound good?" she asked.

"Sounds *great*!"

The front door opened, followed by short, slow footsteps up the staircase. Through the army of mannequins where dark shadows seemed part of the decor, the top of a leather biker hat bobbed upward with each slow step. The shadows concealed the details, but it was clearly a woman. The mannequins stood sentry like a troupe of effeminate gargoyles, armed with whips, chains, and strap-ons. She paused in the shadows, aware that the living room was filled with unfamiliar faces. Staring for a moment under the protection of darkness like a skittish cat, she advanced into the light with hips thrusting side to side. Her face was expressionless and strong, yet stunningly beautiful with striking features. Her hair was dyed black, short and well managed. She was staring at Hazel's black shirt with a pink triangle when a smirk lightened her morose expression.

"Hello," she said in a sultry, yet purely male voice. Her gender bled into some foreign shade of gray with that one word, crossing lines that aren't crossed often enough. "I'm Ezmerelda Dear."

"Hey, Ray," Sunshine said as she returned to the room with a tall glass of water. "These people will be our visitors for a little while. Have you met them?"

"Somewhat," Ezmerelda responded slowly with pouty lips. "This is the band?"

"Yes. The Jerk Offs."

"Lovely," Ezmerelda said with a sassy smile as she walked up to Harold. "I like the name. As I always say, if you aren't doing it yourself, it isn't getting done right."

"Harry Saucerocket," Harold said, introducing himself.

"How saucy," she sang as she advanced to George and me on the couch.

"I'm George and this is Frank."

"Glad I can offer my home to such strapping young lads. Let me know what else I can offer," Ezmerelda informed, staring at each of us with piercing green eyes that glistened between thick, black lashes. "And you with the tattoos?"

"I'm Specky."

"Specky, huh? Exactly what does that describe, Mr. Specky?"

"Not much."

"That's too bad," she said before moving on to Hazel. "Good to have Family in the house."

"And you're such a member," Harold said snidely.

Hazel stared, comfortable in the environment of something a little more queer than the common punk rock boys from the suburbs. "It's good to be here."

"Sunshine, have you seen my whipping boy?" Ezmerelda asked as she advanced to a closed door opposite the array of flaming candles.

"No, he must be working."

Ezmerelda cracked the door slightly, listening for more. "How was work, by the way, dar-link?"

"It was what it is," Sunshine said before peeking around the kitchen door at us again. "By the way, houseguests, I work in a vegan bakery. If you want some things for the road after your show, I can set you up for a day or two. Fresh-baked bread doesn't have a long shelf life, you know."

"She's a hard worker," Ezmerelda told us. "She knows how to work it."

"And what do you do for money?" Harold asked.

Ezmerelda extended a yearning eye. "Are you about to offer something?"

Harold chuckled to himself.

"She doesn't work," Sunshine answered. "She's above working."

"I'm not above going to bed in the early evening," Ezmerelda said, stepping through the bedroom door. She threw a quick glance at Harold. "Hint, hint." The door closed behind her, followed only with silence.

"So, you guys played in Newark?" Sunshine asked.

"Yeah, at a place called the Pipeline," Specky answered politely.

"Was it a good show?"

"Not really," Specky admitted. "Hardly anyone there."

"Where are you heading after this?"

"Lancaster, Pennsylvania," I said. "We'll leave the day after tomorrow's show."

"You can stay here as long as you desire. Tonight, if you guys would want, we can go to the Back Door. Tonight is Industrial Night. It's kind of a tradition in this house."

213

"Sure," Hazel said.

"And if you guys would like to swim tomorrow, there's this great place where the Syracuse diving team practices."

"That sounds good," I said.

"Then, after the swim, we can eat and do the show." She finished with a long breath.

"What a plan," I commended. "Seems you got this all down."

"Entertaining the band is part of the experience, at least that's how I see it. Should I go ahead and start making the food?"

"Yes, please," George said. "Haven't eaten in a while."

"Well, you guys can feel free to roam, if you wish. Do whatever you want, just do it with comfort and style," she told us before retreating to the kitchen.

Specky followed her. "Do you mind if we take showers?"

"Together?" she asked. "Of course I don't mind, silly boy. In fact, *do* shower. For me."

"I'm first," Specky declared as he headed straight for the staircase to get his bag.

The rest of us followed, rushing down the rickety stairs thick with atmosphere. We stepped in a single file line onto the porch as each person ran through the rain to grab their bags from the van.

"Seems to be running fine now," Harold said to Hazel and me as the three of us stood on the edge of the steps, waiting. "See what the next problem will be."

"The tour is more than half over," Hazel said. "We've gone this long, we can make it."

Specky and George came running up on the porch as Hazel and Harold dashed through the rain. George handed me my bag.

"She's hot," Specky said of Sunshine. "I'm going to nail her before we leave."

"Does she have a boyfriend?" I asked.

"Who cares?"

A red Subaru wagon rushed down the street, parking behind the van. A robust man of medium build and firmly erect hair stepped into the rain. His skin was shaded chocolate mocha. He looked up at the porch and began walking casually and carefree through the downpour. His hair slowly fell limp.

He greeted us politely as he stepped on the porch. "You guys the band?"

"Part of it."

He stared with a friendly smile as his coarse hair clung to his masculine cheeks. His facial bone structure seemed chiseled by Michelangelo. He wore a security guard uniform awkwardly with his radically prickly hair.

"I live here," he said, reaching out to shake my hand. His grip was firm. "Is this the hand you use to masturbate?"

Looking down, noticing it to be my right, I replied affirmatively with a smile.

"I'm KiKi. KiKi Chiquita. The whipping boy."

"I'm Frank, and this is Specky."

"I'm George."

"Is there any reason you're standing out here on the porch in the rain?" he asked with a crooked grin.

"We're getting our bags so we can take a shower," I told him.

"Group shower? Am I invited? Nothing like a shower with grown men. If you know what I mean...I got this new job as a security guard," he told us with childish reserve. "What do you think? Do I look like I'm in the Village People?"

"Do you want to?" I asked.

"Well, of course."

"Then yeah, you *totally* do," I said.

"Ooh, thank you. Shall we go upstairs?" He led us up to the living room, skipping three steps at a time. "Don't you guys hate it when you get a video, and you're having an intimate moment with yourself, and it just isn't happening? It totally freaks me out. If I can't appreciate my own company, then whose can I? You know what's worse is when you're right there at the point of no return, and then it just goes blank. You may as well just start over, because it's totally uphill from there. Where's that woman?! In the kitchen...that sounds right."

"Hey, watch it, pal," Sunshine warned with a smile. "Weren't you in the Village People?"

"I was only in a couple of them. If you know what I mean..."

"You've met our guests?" she asked.

"I stood in the rain with them a while. Bonding as we men do."

"The food's almost done," Sunshine said as the remaining members of the band entered the kitchen. "Kiki, maybe you should awake the Queen."

"If the Queen sleeps, then the Queen misses out."

"The plates are up here," Sunshine said. "Help yourself. I don't want to get too planted in the kitchen."

"Doing woman's work," Kiki joked again, trying unsuccessfully to reduce her level of composure.

We formed a line, hustling for position to get the quickest fix of nourishment. The meal was devoured quicker than it was served.

"Have you ever noticed how much you can tell about a person by their eating habits?" Kiki asked.

I slurped up a string of pasta sloppily with sauce clinging to my stubbly chin, too impatient for tact or etiquette.

"There's more where that came from," Sunshine said. "There's always more at this house."

I was the last person in the shower, finding immediate satisfaction in the cold water that rained down upon me. The soap slipped between my fingers, lubricated with the water that dripped passively down my thin frame. I would smell of this soap a few days before returning to the grime of the road. For now, it was a pleasant change.

The door opened and in walked Specky with a toothbrush, quietly, just like old times at the old house. I felt a moment of peace in a memory painted by hindsight's vividly unnatural colors.

"I just got off the phone with an old friend of mine in Lawrence."

"What's happening back home?" I asked.

"Vernon's been arrested."

"For what? Possession?"

"Murder."

"What?" I asked as I shut off the water.

"He did a drive-by shooting the other night. He and his girlfriend broke up. After several beers, he resolved to kill her. There were some people on the porch visiting that night. He missed. He ended up accidentally shooting some young girl who had just moved to town."

"She's dead?" I asked.

215

"She's dead. Got her right in the spine."

"Man…" I murmured as I stepped out of the shower. "In Lawrence?"

"No, Topeka. I guess I never knew him all that well…like I thought I did."

"Sorry to hear that," I told him.

"He deserved it—"

"Not for him," I corrected. "For her. Did anyone know her?"

"No."

I took the time to dry off as he brushed his teeth and shaved. My bag was split wide with dirty clothes protruding from the opening. I quickly slipped into a pair of shorts that reeked of sweat. I pulled a dry shirt over my shoulders and opened the door. A chorus of gay laughter rang throughout the house.

I was ashamed that I shared even a loose association with Vernon. I had nothing more to say of it. I left the room, shutting the door behind me.

"Frank," Sunshine said cheerfully as I entered the room. "I have some people for you to meet. This is Jenny."

I nodded to the small girl, young and moderately attractive. She had a large nose, contrasting to her less visible self-respect. She returned the gesture, watching me with frail eyes.

"And this is my boyfriend, Jimmy."

"Hello," he said politely, eyeing me up and down. "You the singer?"

"Yes."

He didn't say anything, but kept a watchful eye. He was short, very small and thin. Handsome, yet simple. I could tell by his curious expression and attention to insignificant detail that he was young.

"Jimmy has only one week left in town before he joins the Navy," Sunshine told me.

I nodded briefly, politely.

Ezmerelda walked out of her room, dressed in a regal red sequin gown with gaudy gold hoop earrings dangling from petite earlobes. Her lips matched the gown, a flair of color to a pale and gaunt face. Her black, Cleopatra wig hugged stiffly to her head. She put her arms out to display the evening's fashion, and I couldn't help but notice rows of crisscrossing scars on each wrist.

Kiki followed her, still dressed in his security fatigues. He was dressed for the night.

The music of Throbbing Gristle surrounded my environment. It was a nice, yet bleak contrast to the staple of hardcore and punk rock. The shadows of the room sat motionless as if dusty.

"You look ravishing, you bitch," Kiki said to Ezmerelda.

"Thank you, sweetie."

"If I could eat you, I would."

"You already did," she whispered with a mischievous grin.

"Ooh, stop now, girl. You're making me perspire. And that's so unattractive."

Jimmy stood, straightening his Revolting Cocks T-shirt before moving into the kitchen for a beer.

"Where's the cocaine and Dutch boys?" Kiki asked, revealing a handful of pills. "Ecstasy, anyone?"

The room perked with uncharacteristic joy. Kiki passed a limited dosage to those with extended hands, saving the majority for himself. Life would be blissful, if ever so fleeting.

216

"Maybe we'll get the DeeJay to play your record tonight," Sunshine told us. She picked up Jenny's hand and placed it on her upper thigh.

"I think we're ready to go," Harold spoke on our behalf.

Everyone stood lazily with dour expressions.

"All these people could fit in our van," Hazel suggested.

"Okay," Ezmerelda said. "That could be fun."

With little effort, the crowd made its way slowly to the door. I followed the crew, falling behind everyone except Sunshine who stayed back to lock the fortress of solemnity.

"Having fun yet?" Sunshine asked me.

"Never ends."

Jenny paused in the middle of the cracked sidewalk and waited to fall back with us. She ran her bony fingers through her poorly managed, frizzy hair. Sunshine pushed her softly, caressing the small of her back.

"Kiss me," Sunshine instructed openly.

I turned to her, shocked at her request of me, just to find that Jenny had taken the initiative.

"Later tonight you'll need to stay over, Jenny," Sunshine demanded. "My back will be sore after dancing. You may need to rub my feet also. There's a lot of dishes. I expect them done by morning."

I smiled, ever the fan of sarcasm.

Jenny responded seriously, just in time to prevent my misinterpretation from being vocal. "Of course," she spoke timidly.

"And maybe the band has some laundry they need done," Sunshine suggested.

They both looked at me for a response.

"We have laundry, but we could manage..."

"I'll do it for you," Jenny offered desperately. She looked to Sunshine for affirmation.

I felt uneasy, and searched for a casual response, my typical stock answer: "That's okay. Thanks for the offer."

We climbed in through the side door of the van, sitting in the rear with equipment and Drag Queens. As the van pulled away from the curb, and the conversations filled the crowded space, Sunshine leaned close to whisper in my ear: "Do you want to fuck her?"

"What?! Who?"

"Jenny," she replied calmly.

"Why do you say?" I asked.

"She does what I tell her. If that's something you want, let me know. She's helped out a lot of bands that way. I can imagine how frustrating it gets on the road."

"Well," I said, trying to come up with an appropriate response. "It's nice of you to offer."

"Just let me know."

The bar was located on the edge of campus, a typical dive with a not-so-typical clientele. Gender took a backseat at this explicitly gay establishment. The bathrooms were marked accordingly—the *little boys room* displayed a stick figure wearing a dress.

Skinny Puppy and Front 242 were the flavors of the night as the young cross-dressers pretentiously wiggled their tight bottoms, empowered by the decadence of

217

their lifestyle and the X coursing through their bodies. Just before the night had come to a close, the DeeJay announced our show with an excerpt from our record to follow. After hours of throbbing industrial, our music was received as a foreign tongue. The dance floor cleared as we watched the youths patiently wait for the song to end. I had a good laugh of it, and I could see that George and Specky shared my humor. I had to admit, it was nice to be out of our environment for a change.

Following a healthy breakfast of scones and challah bread, we were off again with a van loaded to capacity. We were taken away from Syracuse into some nearby town called Manilus where all that we found of it was the Fire Station #2. We parked just off the road and wandered into an area clearly marked with *No Trespassing* signs. There was a thin path we followed through the trees. The sound of rushing water guided us beyond the thick foliage. Suddenly, we came to a massive waterfall, ending in a fall-off that was breathtaking. The giant rocks below appeared as tiny pebbles. We stood on the edge of the land embankment gazing down at the calm pool far below.

"Well," Sunshine said, stepping down into the rippling water on the edge of the enormous cliff. "This is it. Who's gonna jump first?"

Jimmy followed obediently. Together they walked along the edge of the waterfall where large stones protruded like the backs of suspended porpoises. We watched, stunned as they took a step into clear space. The sound of their impact came a bit too late for my comfort.

"I gotta do this," Kiki said. His blue jean cut-offs rode high up his ass as he strutted down the edge of the waterfall.

"Let's go," Specky instructed the rest of us. "We're on vacation."

Everyone followed except George and me.

"I'm not that crazy," I said to George in an attempt to gain reassurance with my fear of heights.

"I'm that crazy, but not today."

Everyone took their place on the edge of the cliff, and with little apprehension, thrusted themselves into the stagnant water far below us.

"Do you ever wonder what we're doing here?" George asked me as we sat alone on the grassy bank.

"In Syracuse?"

"No, here in general. Do you really feel much a part of all this?"

"All what?" I asked.

"I don't know. The band, the goal..."

"I do, or I wouldn't be here," I assured him.

"Maybe it's just me. Just before we left, I started writing something. I would like you to hear it."

"What is it?" I asked.

"Music. A piano piece. I tend to not show people unless I feel they can respect it."

"How many people have you shown?"

"At this point? No one," he said. "You can be the first. I trust your opinion."

"I'd love to hear it."

"I've been working on some ideas for the band," he confided. "I'm not sure you'll go for it, but when I get my student loan for the upcoming semester, I plan to buy an Ensoniq Mirage keyboard. It samples. What would you think of incorporating some of that into our music?"

"Samples? Samples of what?" I asked curiously.

"We could use it for anything. A lot of weird stuff, we can make samples ourselves, or we could use it for string sections, and other such instruments."

"String sections?" I pried with suspicion.

"We can try doing something different. In the studio, we could do so much with a sampler. Right now, we're a punk band. No more, no less, just like the rest. If we had that little something that separated us from the pack, then we'd have our ticket, our *own* ticket. I feel like we're reinventing the wheel, over and over."

"Would string sections make it any less intense?" I asked.

"No. I know enough about composition to pull it off. Classical instruments can be really powerful when used properly. I know I can do it."

I sat quietly a moment watching the others far below us, struggling to climb the cliff to reach us. They giggled merrily as they helped one another with each small step.

"What do you think?" he asked.

"I'm not against it."

"That's what I hoped you'd say. Good."

"Do you still hunger for this goal?" I asked.

"I choose my resources well," he said. "I'm here for a reason. Not to play games, but to play music."

Harold was the first to make it up the side of the steep, rocky incline. He stared at us with a blank expression that conveyed some sort of disappointment. "The water's down there."

"Come on," Sunshine beckoned as the line of them returned to the waterfall. "I'll show you guys some neat caves. See that big chunk of rock sticking out from the waterfall? It's actually a little cave. And it's perfectly safe...come on!"

I looked to George, who looked to me evenly.

"Go ahead, Frank," he said.

"You're staying?" I asked.

"Not much a spelunker myself. But go ahead..."

I looked over at Sunshine, who was smiling politely with a gesturing hand. "Come on."

I stood slowly. "All right, all right. Only to see the caves. I'm not getting near that damn cliff!"

"Whatever you want," she promised.

I followed her lead, paying close attention to each step as the waves brushed firmly against my ankles, threatening to knock me into the jagged rocks below.

"This looks dangerous," I said with a shaky voice.

"Well, you don't jump here. See the water down below in the middle? That's deep. Deeper than it appears."

"I'm still not jumping."

"I'm not asking you to jump," she said.

I couldn't imagine taking that step. Control is all I've ever possessed. I cherished it.

We stood behind the others as the water slammed against our calves, making tremendous grooves in the slick downpour. Sunshine pulled me back to the protruding black rock. She ducked underneath, disappearing through a veil of overpouring water. I followed her.

It was dark inside, cold and musty with an even wall of water shimmering from the external light. The space was not much larger than a tiny closet. We sat, staring into the water that seemed to be some type of energy field bending the visibility of the outside world. It was the type of hideout every child aspired to create with a blanket and an upturned card table at a slumber party. But this was real, or as real as such things get.

"Are you excited about the show?" she asked, her teeth chattering.

"This is what I live for."

"I love putting on the shows," she told me lightly.

I smiled politely, rigidly. "I think your boyfriend has a problem with me."

"A problem?"

"He has that jealous look in his eye," I said, laughing. "I guess he thinks you and I..."

"You and I..."

"You know what I mean."

"Do I? Are you trying to say he has this idea that I want to fuck you?"

I laughed aloud. "Well, something to that effect."

"I do."

"Huh?"

"I do want to fuck you. Simple as that. He doesn't have anything to say about it. It's not as if I haven't had sex with other people before. If you lived here, you'd be my boyfriend instead of him."

"I would?" I asked.

"Yes, you would. I get what I want. What man is capable of saying no to sex? Especially to a woman who gives head as good as I do...no man would refuse me."

I laughed.

She stared at me. "Let me guess...you're a Leo—no, you're not. You're an Aquarius, aren't you? When's your birthday?"

"February tenth," I told her.

"I'm right. I'm always right. So, what do you think?" she asked casually.

"About what?"

"About fucking me."

"Not here..."

"Why not?" she asked. "Wouldn't that be exciting?"

"It'd be exciting, all right, but this is crazy!"

"Why? Do you know what you're turning down?" She lifted her shirt, showing me her large, firm breasts with hard nipples—both pierced with silver barbells. She removed her shirt entirely, setting it in my lap. "Go ahead, touch."

I looked at her, at her breasts, at her face. I didn't move. "This is crazy..."

"You know you want it. My nipples are hard, don't you want to touch them? You can warm them up with your lips. Or do you want to feel this?" She unfastened the top button of her jeans. "You can see how turned on I am. I've shaved recently, are you into that?"

"Let me tell you," I began uncomfortably, "your scene here is like none we've experienced."

"That's nice...so do you want to fuck me now, or what?"

"Well, that's not really..."

"After the show," she suggested. "Singers make me so wet that I can barely keep my legs together. I can't wait to watch you. You give it all, don't you, Frank?"

I struggled to maintain my composure.

"How about Jenny?" she asked. "Have you ever had two girls? She does anything for me. I've trained her well. She has a magical tongue."

220

"She's pretty loyal to you, isn't she?" I asked.

"She'd die for me."

I laughed nervously.

"I'm serious," she said. "Touch me. I want to feel you inside me. Do you like to talk dirty? I do. Does it turn you on when a girl asks you to fuck her?"

The clouds began to seep through my ears. My thoughts were suffering hormonal distortion. The base instinct of my existence began to roar. The temptation rendered me close to paralysis. I swept all my reasoning into a measly pile to muster my attention. I had the will to resist, to quiet the yearning. I couldn't give in, not this easily. "I don't think this is really something we should—"

"You musicians can be difficult. You love your instruments, and you love your music. Nothing else." She stuck her hand down her loose pants. "Taste?"

I stared at her hand as she brought it closer. She stopped and placed it on my chest.

"Don't touch me...I've got to get out of here." I quickly leaned forward, handing her the wet shirt. "Maybe we'll talk after the show."

"We'll talk, trust me," she promised as she put her shirt back over her pale skin. "I'll do anything you ask. Anything. I'm kinky. There's no place I won't go, and I'll let you put it anywhere."

"That's a very generous offer. One could get really creative, I suppose. I'm leaving. It's cold in here."

"I thought it was getting kind of hot," she said.

"It's kind of *something*."

I stepped outside the little rock fortress where everyone was standing on the edge of the cliff once again. As they jumped off in a single file line, I cautiously waded through the ankle-deep current to George, who hadn't budged.

"How was the cave?" he asked.

"The cave...well, it's funny you should ask. I'm not the spelunker, either. The cave, well, I think I'll have another chance to return."

I needn't explain.

The sun was receding to the horizon, emblazing the street with a somber tranquillity. It actually felt like it was someone's home. Kiki and I lounged on the steps of the club, waiting for the sound-man to arrive.

A fire hydrant painted as a police officer stood at the edge of the curb. Someone had used a magic marker to give the hydrant a gender. It was male—quite hung, apparently. A signpost was placed alongside it, a point-of-reference should the winter snow ever cover it completely.

A group of young punks walked down the broken sidewalks through the old neighborhoods surrounding campus. Every house reminded me of the student ghettos in Lawrence.

I liked Syracuse.

"You guys are from where?" Kiki asked me again for the third time.

"Kansas. And you're from Rochester. We've been through this."

He took a moment to primp his porcupine-like hairdo. "I can't believe you don't drink."

"Why?"

"That's so square," he said.

"I've met very few people in my life who don't drink," I told him. "From my experience, straight is radical. Everyone drinks. There's nothing odd about it."

The front doors opened and Ezmerelda came strutting out, placing her rear between the two of us. A fiery bee-hive rested on her head, garnished with gladiolas. Her shimmering red dress was scratchy against my leg, and she smelled wonderful. My senses were ignited to life once again, having been so attuned to the stench of sweat and grime. It was nice to be in the presence of such extreme femininity.

"What are you two boys doing out here?" Ezmerelda asked.

"Gabbing," Kiki said. "Talking about lovemaking."

Ezmerelda quickly responded. "As I always say, there's nothing like lovemaking amongst men."

"I'm finding that Frank here is a lovemaker."

"I knew that the moment I laid my lusty eyes upon him," she dispelled with a rough voice that scratched like whiskers. She batted her lashes thick with mascara.

"What do you mean?" I asked.

"Some people fuck, and some people make love. You're a lovemaker, correct?"

"It's been a while since I checked."

They both laughed.

"Aw, come on, Frank!" Ezmerelda said. "Loosen up, girl. Like I always say, any ass you pass is an ass you'll never have another crack at."

Specky wandered aimlessly around the corner as if lured by the subject of loose morals.

"Specky is *not* a lovemaker," Kiki said.

"Not by any stretch of the imagination," I confirmed.

"What's your favorite thing about sex, Specky?" Kiki asked.

"The conquest."

"And your least favorite?"

"The aftermath," Specky admitted as he leaned against the stone wall. He struck a match against it while placing a cigarette between his firm lips.

"Have you ever loved anyone, Specky?" Ezmerelda asked.

"I would say so. Unfortunately. I don't believe being in love is necessarily a good thing. It is an addiction, isn't it? A state of codependence? I don't know if I ever *want* to love anyone or anything. I'd hate to be so subservient."

"Will you ever get married?" Kiki asked.

"Marriage just makes the inevitable separation more difficult. At best, I'll spend my life in relationships lasting no more than two years. Exactly two years. If you can make it that long, then you have the endurance for many more."

"Two years?" Ezmerelda questioned. "I would say five."

"So, how long have you been in drag, Ezzie?" Specky asked.

"Since about noon...oh, you mean my life—about three years."

"Why?" Specky inquired. "No offense, just curious."

"Why do you cover yourself with tattoos?" she asked. "Same answer."

"Because chicks think it's cool," he chuckled confidently.

"Well, chicks think I'm cool, honey," Ezmerelda boasted.

"What would you do if your girlfriend cheated on you, Specky?" Kiki asked.

"I'd have good reason to do the same then."

"You wouldn't break up?" Kiki asked.

"No. Why would I?"

"What would you do if you found pictures of your lover with another man, Specky?" Ezmerelda asked.

"I'd confront her about them."

"Would you masturbate to them first?" Kiki inquired with a smile.

Specky laughed as he tugged lightly on his red braces. "Yeah, I would."

"Being gay is the only way," Kiki said. "Women have so many hang-ups. They have no passion about anything other than socks and hairspray. Guys are passionate about what they do. We *love* football, we *love* science fiction, we *love* rock and roll...why can't women talk about midget pornos? Swap masturbation stories..."

"Specky, you'll be a happier man when you just admit you're gay," Ezmerelda confided.

Specky laughed.

"Everyone's gay," Ezmerelda added. "They just haven't figured it out yet."

"Hey, Specky," Kiki said. "What would you do if someone offered you ten dollars to piss all over them?"

"You ask everyone this question," Ezmerelda scolded with a girlish sigh.

"Why?" Specky asked.

"Because," Kiki began, "I just want to make sure I did the right thing. So what made you guys want to load up this van and take off across the country?"

"Because we believe in what we're doing," Specky answered swiftly. "Isn't that right, Frankie?"

I smiled proudly. "Indeed so."

The lights were bright. So much that I could scarcely see the audience. I knew they were there, I could hear them. I could feel their presence and their eagerness for us to begin. I could see their spit hurling up at me. I stared down at the floor, listening to the band make minor adjustments on third-rate equipment. Funny thing to be so plugged with adrenaline, yet completely attuned with the most insignificant sound. Damn near a predatorial state, and the prey stood curiously in front of me, ignorant of the attack that would soon befall them.

For every minute of the day spent aimlessly wandering through life, there was a place for me, right where I stood. A place where I was Nietzsche's *Overman*, incapable of failure and other less appealing human characteristics. There were no distractions. Nothing else could make any more difference.

I glanced at each member of the group, catching affirmative eye-contact to begin the onslaught. Each of them carried their instrument of empowerment. Myself armed only with conviction, as always.

I raised the microphone slowly to my lips. "Okay, I believe we're ready. First, a favor. I'd like to dedicate this set to all the veterans of war. We thank you, and our van thanks you. We're the Jerk Offs from Lawrence, Kansas, and I thank *you* for the applause you'll soon be giving." My words were submerged beneath a velvety curtain of audible strength and velocity.

The crowd churned before me. Fists flew through the air as the disco lights flashed wildly about the club, washing their invigorated faces together in a panoramic blur. No less than one hundred fifty of them surged every ounce of passion we poured from our souls.

There was nothing more than this.

After the show, I walked away from the stage alone. My eyes ached from the smoke that lingered in the dense air. Sweat stained my dirty clothes. I felt a strange

223

sense of contempt knowing I wouldn't return to the stage for another full day. I walked barefoot out the front doors, finding a nice curb to claim on a nearby corner.

The clean air was a wonderful contrast to the murky dive. I felt happy for the moment, proud to be there. So many miles from the place I called home, carried by the music as if a Kansas tornado's momentum had thrust us to a far corner of the nation. Left on our own to return, it was a challenge of our wits and will. After the night's show, our will was clearly reigning.

I looked down at the ground around my bare feet, concentrating on what little there was to see. A cigarette butt, a few chunks of gravel, and a shard of broken glass—all manufactured by man, discarded without thought. These are the conquests of my fellow humans, designing disposable objects made for trash. My plight for distinction, I was certain would outlive me.

"Frank," a woman screeched from across the street.

I glanced up to see Sunshine stumbling my direction. Her drunken, lazy gait immediately annoyed me.

"What are you doing out here?" she asked.

"Relaxing."

"You guys put on a really great show. I tried to find you afterwards, but you weren't anywhere to be found. There were so many people in there looking for you. *You*. They loved your show."

"So did I."

"You've got an attitude, don't you?" she snapped.

"Sorry, I don't mean to sound as arrogant as I am," I replied irritably, honestly. "Should I return to the club? Kiss some ass?"

"You can do what you want," she said, taking a seat next to me. "What do *you* want? Anything I can offer?"

"To not be harassed, maybe? Listen, I think you're a very nice person. I really do. But this whole sex thing, and all this shit about how I'd be your boyfriend…it's all funny and charming. But I don't think so, my dear. Not tonight. Not any night."

She sat quietly a moment, basking in the awkward silence before standing firmly on the rippled pavement. "Okay," she said, stepping forward to wander back across the street. "Whatever you want."

"That's what I want," I said as she returned to the club. "Thank you for the peace…"

The next morning, we ate a massive breakfast before leaving. Sunshine set us up with a bag of baked goods, and we were ready to be on our next adventure.

"Don't forget to write, everyone," Kiki said as he and Ezmerelda stood by the porch, arguing some mundane point of style.

"Enjoy the food, and thanks for the show," Sunshine said, ignoring me entirely. "See you guys next year?"

"Sure thing," Specky said. "Take care."

Just as we pulled away, Kiki and Ezmerelda had come to blows, wrestling one another to the ground with fists flying. Sunshine had to jump in, tugging on Kiki's hair as the punches continued.

"What an interesting place," George said as we casually drove down the quiet street.

"I had sex with *two* girls last night," Specky gloated. "That little girl Jenny will do anything you ask…"

The ride to Lancaster, Pennsylvania was an enjoyable trip filled with conversation and laughter. We had enough money to get where we needed to go, and even a bit to spare. With a couple more fruitful shows under our belt, we could finally come out ahead. Spirits were high, and plans of the future were tossed about like compliments in a single's bar.

It was evening by the time we had arrived in Lancaster. We stopped at a gas station, taking advantage of a slow cross-intersection. The sky had darkened with the cover of dense clouds, resulting in a premature nightfall. We opened the van door wide as Harold fueled the vehicle, allowing the misty warm air to ventilate our stuffy quarters. I could smell the impending rain.

"I'm going to call the promoter," I told everyone as I stepped out of the van. I propped my arm on a stack of cases of soda pop sitting on display between the pumps. I scratched my shoulder, feeling the sheets of dead skin pulling up under my nails. "Is there a phone inside?"

"I can't see around the van," Specky grumbled, giving no extra effort to look through the window to see the gas station attendant.

"I'll find it," I said, walking around the van to the little concrete building where a row of phones extended from the wall.

My legs were stiff, hardened from lack of use. I stretched with each step as if my body was suffering rigormortis. The grind of the road, the lack of movement...such extremity, from lifelessness to the center of all attention, then back to nothing. Strange living.

I picked up the phone, cool and wet to the touch as I turned the pages of my little notebook to find the promoter's number. I fought the desire to rub the cold plastic against my scalding hot body. My sunburnt skin had an uneven sheen of redness, peeling like rot.

I quickly dialed as Harold walked past me to pay for the gas. The operator came on, informing me that the number had been disconnected. I hung up and tried again with equal results.

Harold quickly returned, stuffing the change in the pocket of his leather jacket, glancing at me as he passed. I grabbed his arm to stop him. "The number is disconnected."

He delivered a disturbed guttural noise, rolling his eyes with a slow exhalation of breath. "What?"

"Maybe I wrote it down wrong."

"Is the show at a club?" he asked.

"According to the notes I took—and they are careful notes—the show was to be at a rented hall. The only thing I can think of is to call the radio station. He told me he'd have it announced on the college station. I've got the station's number here," I said, pausing to dial. I waited patiently as the phone rang several times. "Do you know anything about a show tonight with a band called the Jerk Offs?"

"Who?!" the woman from the station asked.

"The Jerk Offs from Kansas. It's supposed to be at some VFW hall, or something—"

"I don't know. We have nothing about that down here. I would say it isn't happening. Sorry, pal," she said, slamming the phone down.

I took a deep breath before revealing the show's fatal prognosis. "According to her, there's no show."

Harold said nothing as he returned to the van. I followed him slowly. By the time I arrived, the word had already infected our quarters. Silence fell hard, and we stood in a slumped huddle as the wind picked up a sudden chill. The rain was coming.

"It's Bill's fault," George told us, attempting to lift some pressure. "Just like Marty said."

"Fuck that," Hazel exclaimed with a deep sigh. "Now what?"

"Now what, Frank?" Harold asked. "You're the big planner. Got a good idea?"

"No," I said. "We play in Pittsburgh in two days at the Sonic Temple. How's the money?"

"After two days?" Harold asked. "It'll suck. We'll need all the money we have for food and gas to make it."

"We could stop eating to make sure we have enough money for gas," George suggested. "Every time we eat as a group, it's like throwing out a tank of gas. We can go without food for a day, the van can't."

"Maybe *you* can stop eating," Hazel countered, "not me."

I cut in quickly. "I'm with you, George." I turned to Specky, hoping to find that uneven number that would make our advantage. Specky was fixated on the wall of cases of soda behind me. "What do you think?"

"What do I think? Grab one of those cases, Harold," Specky said. "Hand it to me, that's what I think. The guy isn't looking, he's yacking on the phone. We'll be out of town before he even notices."

Harold looked over his shoulder where the station attendant was completely hidden from view. He quickly grabbed case after case, heaving them frantically into Specky's arms. Having no interest in being arrested in Pennsylvania, I stepped around the van and climbed into the driver's seat. I waited for them to get as much as they could, watching the traffic on the road. The attendant talked blindly on the phone, paying us no attention whatsoever.

"Let's go," Specky said as the side door of the van slammed tight.

I raced down the street, straight for the city limits.

George and I did as we suggested and fasted two more days. We arrived in Pittsburgh on a beautiful summer day, ideal for the hope needed to raise morale once again. As we pulled into the parking lot, the gas tank was just above empty. Our finances were depleted.

The club had a good reputation from what I had heard. We met with the promoter, a young punk rocker about our age, soft-spoken with the eyes of mirrors. He assured us we'd clear at least one hundred dollars by the end of the night. That'd be enough to get us to Delaware.

As our luck would have it, only four or five people showed. We played a quick set, giving the few stragglers their money's worth before calling it a rough night. The small audience was very thankful for our efforts, and even managed to help us carry our equipment. Specky snuck off into the bathroom with a homely, overweight girl as Harold searched frantically for the promoter. He was nowhere to be found, and as the doors were closed and locked by the sound-man, we were walking away without a penny of compensation.

Our bad situation just got worse.

We gathered around the van, standing in a semi-circle with two young punks from the show joining our silent meeting. The sky was clear and the air dry. It was a nice change, but our thoughts were centered elsewhere. No humor could save us here, and as each person looked at another, there were only enemies. Our group had dissolved into a subjugated mutiny. We needed someone or something to take the blame for our circumstances. Without a scapegoat, the only answer was a direct hit to our spiraling ego.

"Sorry, man," one of the young guys broke the treacherous silence. He gripped our record tenderly. "The club usually brings a lot of people. We saw Gang Green last year and it was great. Maybe everyone was at the Adrenaline OD show. I wish I could help, but I have no money at all."

"Sullivan," the other exclaimed brightly. "He's working down the street."

"Yeah, so?" the little hardcore boy asked, scratching his bald head. "Sullivan is a geek."

"Yeah, but maybe we can convince him to sacrifice some food."

His partner contemplated before turning to us. "Would that help?"

"Sure it'd help," Specky said. "*Anything* would help at this point."

"He works in a deli. We can walk there."

"I want to tear that promoter into pieces," Specky growled, his fists clenched as we joined the little punk boys down the street. "He knows what situation we're in, and he walked away like that."

"That's the punk spirit," George mumbled as we stomped together in a massive huddle. He leaned over to me, away from the others. "What are we going to do?"

"Well, we may be here a while," I said coldly.

"We can't stay here," he said as we lingered back. "We could sell our equipment, use the money for a bus ticket to get back home."

I shook my head in disbelief. "Man, this wasn't supposed to happen..."

The two punk boys walked into a little shop, holding the door for us to enter. The place was without a single customer. The trash had already been cleared and the floors were freshly mopped. It was ready to close for the night. I feared we'd be spending many hours at this place, washing dishes and cleaning toilets until we had earned enough cash to return to Kansas. I would promise to never step foot outside the city limits of Lawrence ever again.

The memory of Lawrence brought a flood of emotion. I stood behind everyone, feeling overwhelming guilt for sending us on this overzealous trek.

"Hey, Sullivan!" the kids exclaimed with contrived enthusiasm.

Sullivan glared up from his tedious cleaning duties. His blond hair was fashionably straight and well managed. His face was clean and shaven and impressively attractive. He was as studious in appearance as they described. "What's up?" he said with a scratchy voice.

"These guys are a band from Kansas. We just caught their show and they were really great, but they got stiffed out of some money and are totally broke. Can you spot them food?"

"You know I can't do that," he told them flatly, looking at each of us with his soft blue eyes. They seeped compassion, despite the monotone rasp in his voice.

"They need it," the little guy pleaded.

"We'll be fine," George inserted proudly.

Sullivan shook his head. "How long have you guys been touring?"

"Over a month now."

He smiled to himself. "That's a long time. How much longer you going to be on the road?"

"Well, it kind of depends now," Specky said. "We have another month of scheduled dates, for what that's worth. Do you need any employees here?"

He laughed. "Do you guys have any records out?"

We all nodded.

"I've never met a band with records before," he said wondrously. "I suppose I could make an exception. Would I be able to get a record in trade?"

"We'll give you a shirt, too," I assured him. "It's the least we could do."

He opened the stainless steel sandwich table. The food was already stored for closing. He pulled out a bag of French bread and lined up several loaves on a white cutting board. "It's going to take a few minutes. You owe me...don't forget this."

"We won't," I promised.

We took a seat in a corner booth by the window, waiting patiently, avoiding conversation. Thoughts raced through my head, such as how we'd manage to get to Delaware, or if it was worth the risk. Finding the money to make it to Kansas seemed to be much more logical. Logic and dreams never seem to mix...

Out the window was the street of an industrial city. I hoped we'd be leaving soon. The view was slightly obscured by the reflection of the interior lights. I looked at our reflection, hating the fact that I couldn't escape the sight of these people who had started as my traveling partners, now the burden of my guilt. I reverted my attention away from our reflection, noticing a colorful array of fliers taped to the glass. I studied each one, getting a feeling for a city that I had no interest. A pink one with crude print caught my attention. It advertised a show at a place called the Continental in Erie, Pennsylvania for two bands I had never heard of, My Three Scum and The Piss Ants. There was a number at the bottom, and the show date was for the following day.

"Look," I said to the others, pointing at the flier. I leaned over to the young punk boys and asked about the distance to Erie.

"Not very far. A few hours, maybe?"

"Do you think we could get on?" George asked me.

"I can try," I told them.

"We need everything we can get," Specky insisted. "Ask to use the phone."

I slowly advanced to the counter, hating to request yet another favor. "Mr. Sullivan, sir...can I use your phone to call Erie?"

He shook his head. "My boss would kill me. All right, go ahead...make it snappy."

"Thanks," I replied. I felt morbidly uncomfortable, and perfectly helpless as I dialed the number.

"Hello?" a gruff voice said over the phone.

"I hope I'm not waking you up."

"Who is this?"

"My name is Frank, and I sing for a band called the Jerk Offs. We're from Kansas. We're in Pittsburgh and we just played a bunk show. We're at a deli and your flier for tomorrow's show at the Continental is hanging up here. Is it still going on?"

"Of course it is. Why?"

"Well, we are desperate..."

"Sure, we'll put you on. Just call me tomorrow, I'll be around all day. You can come over and we'll have some beer before the show. Hell, if you guys are all the way from Kansas, we'll let you headline. I don't give a fuck."

"That's great!" I exclaimed. "I hope I didn't wake you."

"Wake me? I'm not even drunk yet. Who did you say you were again?"

"Frank—"

"No, the band, Frank."

"The Jerk Offs," I repeated.

"Cool."

"Hate to intrude, but we have no place to crash tonight," I said, despite the fact that we had no gas to get there.

"Come on in town, it's easy to find this place. Do you have a pen?"

I quickly grabbed one from the register and proceeded to write on my arm. The directions were very simple. It was nice to talk to someone we hadn't yet burdened. Sullivan took two trays of sandwiches to the table as I read back the directions.

"See you in a few," he said.

"Later on…"

I placed the phone down and returned to the table where my food awaited. "We have the show."

"Great!" George said, already into his sandwich.

"It doesn't mean shit," Harold corrected. "We're going further out of our way for a potential let-down. If you think we're screwed now, consider how tomorrow could leave us…"

"It probably won't be good," the little punk boy warned. "Erie is a small town, it's not like Pittsburgh."

"Our options are few right now," George said. "We need to take that risk, because we really have no better choice."

"I'm with you," I said, pausing to take a massive bite out of the sandwich, chewing it briefly before forcing it into my painfully empty stomach. "We'd be stupid to do anything other than play this show in Erie."

"You should've had me set this tour up," Harold growled as he stood with his sandwich in hand. "It wouldn't have been hard to do a better job. I'm going back to the van to get Sullivan his record and shirt."

He walked out the door, stomping slowly down the street.

"Don't worry about him," George said to me. "I wouldn't take it personally."

"No problem. I honestly couldn't care less…"

Hazel and Specky looked at me, saying nothing as they finished their sandwiches.

"Well," I told them. "I think it's the best thing to do."

"I'm with you," Specky agreed. "I'm just tired, and I want to find the promoter that stiffed us."

"It's not going to happen," George insisted. "Give it up, will you?"

Hazel ate the last bite of her sandwich and quickly sprang from her seat. She threw her trash away and walked outside, standing in front of the window, waiting for the van.

"Tension runs high," George said, leaning back in his chair with a smile.

"This is like a bad movie, you know?" Specky mused. "Emphasis on *bad*. This turned into a big piece of shit really quick. By the way, Frank, I know whose fault all this is…and when Bill gets back from DC, I'm going to have his ass."

"Fault," George said. "What a concept. It's what simple people need as a deference of guilt."

"Whatever, George," Specky said with a relaxed smile. "You're just saying that because this is *your* fault!"

George grinned, nodding his head as a release of stress.

229

"Do you guys fight a lot?" one of the little boys asked, voicing a great deal of concern.

"We're a band," I said. "Of course we do."

"I think your drummer seems really mad. And your driver guy…"

The van quickly rushed up the street, parking illegally alongside the deli. Harold threw open the driver door and briskly stomped through the deli to the counter. The rest of us joined him.

"Thanks a lot, Sullivan," he said, lying the record and shirt on the counter.

"I could get busted for this, you know. But for a band out there putting their hearts on the line, I'm a sucker. Here," he said, reaching into a tip jar filled with dollar bills. "This is a full day's worth of tips. Take it. Get some gas."

"We couldn't do that," I said.

"The hell," Specky exclaimed, reaching out for the wad of bills like a vulture. "We'll take it."

"I wouldn't offer if I didn't mean it," he said with conviction.

"Thanks, man," I praised. "You've made a bigger difference than you'll ever know."

"That's the way it always is, isn't it?" Sullivan responded proudly. "Thanks for the shirt. I'll listen to the record tonight."

Specky and George both gave their appreciative comments as Harold and I walked out to the van that idled partially in the street.

"You're driving," Harold demanded.

"That's fine."

He climbed through the side door, joining Hazel in the rear with the equipment and bags. I waited for the others, bidding the young boys farewell and a well-deserved thanks. I watched them wander down the street, submerging themselves in the dark little crevices of the gray city we'd soon be leaving.

"Ready?" Specky asked.

"I'm driving," I told him.

"Okay." He climbed inside, behind George.

Pausing momentarily to wave to Sullivan, we began our journey to Erie, Pennsylvania. I was happy to be leaving, temporarily killing the fear of being trapped. The van had become my cell, serving time with others guilty of the same crime. I could feel the wear that the road was putting on me, exhausting every aspect of my personality, drying up my motivation.

No more than thirty miles outside of Pittsburgh, the entire band had fallen asleep. Except me, of course. I watched the signs, finding myself bitterly impatient to arrive at this new destination where fate would deal its lethal hand. We were being dragged along by the fear of failure, and I couldn't stop thinking what exactly was at stake. Harold was right. A typically bad show would be devastating. Advancing on to Delaware could easily have been a more realistic option. Instead, we chose another direction, clinging desperately to hope.

The yellow lines seemed to pull me like a trout on a fishing line, the first step to either the frying pan or the fire itself. The landscape was hidden under a starless night sky with only the green traffic signs and road markings to satiate my yearning for stimulus.

Fifty-five miles-per-hour.

I felt lost in a bitter realm of nothingness, arriving at a destination where my whole life had been spent dreaming. I remembered sitting in school, fantasizing about the roads of far off lands such as Pennsylvania. Now I sat uncomfortably in the seat of the van, steering my dream to the last strand of hope before falling prey to defeat. My stomach ached as if the sandwich had already distributed its resources and nutrients to my thinning body.

My anxiety was getting the better of me. Even my sense of humor had dulled from circumstance. I was rendered defenseless and perfectly incapable of allying myself with anything concrete. We had discovered a variable on the road that we hadn't planned: reality.

The wind rushed through the open window, blowing cool air against my unshaven, dirty face. I could smell the life of the spacious countryside, the perfume of green grass, pollen, and mold. As a child, I was very close to these scents, having no more concern than simple happiness and being. Those times had lost out to vengeance and aggression, impassioned by a desire to be somebody special, to do something substantial.

My bladder ached from nervous anxiety. I pulled over at a rest area and quietly opened the door, leaving it cracked to avoid waking anyone. I stepped into the small building, poorly lit and empty. My sense of smell found the way. The walls were covered with graffiti, and I learned if I was to be there at seven in the morning, a man in a blue truck would give me something special. I hoped to be asleep at that time.

The van waited quietly under a street lamp, its occupants silently dreaming. I stood some distance away as the wind seemed to blow through my thin frame. Struck by a child's dream, I found my location under dirty feet. This was the countryside of Pennsylvania, and this van belonged to one of my favorite bands as an adolescent: The Jerk Offs. This was *my* band.

I stepped back, moving into the darkness of nature to a picnic table littered with fast-food packaging. The ground was dry and firm. I took a seat on the grass where the lawnmower had cut the line that separates the so-called real world from the vast open space of insignificant life and living. I stared into the dark unknown, visualizing green pastures of knee-length grass. Hell, while I was at it, I threw in a couple of black spotted cows and a big grain silo. Why not, this was my picture, wasn't it? A more perfect one than what really existed, I was certain.

The grass smelled wonderful, cut no more than two days earlier. It was a simple pleasure, but one that was gravely significant. I knew we'd get through this. Even if the Erie show went as horribly as expected, we'd find a way. We couldn't stop. If anything, we had to persist, simply for the sake of persistence.

My naked feet, dirty and cold, clung to the ground below me. Low clouds covered the moon like violet tapestry, and it felt that the night consumed everything. Darkness surrounded me, but as I returned to the van, I could sense a subtle glow that I hadn't noticed for quite a while.

When I awoke the next day, the room was empty with the bright glare of the mid-day sun high overhead. I sat up, scratching my face where the carpet had left an impression. The brisk summer wind tossed the old brown curtains like the pouring of chocolate milk. Voices talked outside. I could hear Harold giggling through a road story of ours, something about a guy with a shotgun in Oklahoma City.

Stretching stiff muscles, I stood. I must have slept most of the day because the afternoon barbecue was already being prepared. The band sat in the yard perched on cheap lawn chairs. A few residents of the Erie scene were with them, listening to stories, drinking beer, enjoying the company. They had similar tales about the house in which we were staying. Many bands had crashed at this place, baring the same carpet impressions on their face as I had. This place that they affectionately called The Scum House.

Down the street, the van came rolling with a wake of dust to follow. Taking another glance at the barbecue party with several cases of our Lancaster soda spread across the yard, I realized George was not amongst them. I walked through the house, feeling the weightless comfort of a beautiful day. The screen door creaked open and I found myself on an old porch, looking out at a shanty neighborhood. I took a deep breath. It was the kind of day where even breathing had a pleasurable feeling about it.

The van rolled through the uneven driveway, running over the tiny patches of vegetation and weeds that struggled to exist in such an unlikely place.

George stepped out of the van, holding up a small folded wad of dollar bills. He smiled comfortably at me. "Sold some records. Got ten bucks, which will get us somewhere."

I scratched my face, trying to get the rug's impression off. "That's good news."

"There's a laundromat down the street," he informed me. "We should wash our clothes. Have you taken a bath yet?"

"Obviously not. I look like a vagrant child."

Hazel walked around the corner, stepping up on the old porch with us.

"I need to take a shower," she said to us, her tone strangely pleasant.

"It's a bathtub here," George said. "Frank was about to step in there."

I rubbed my eyes as she looked up at me. I smiled with an awkward stretch, feeling my burnt skin wrinkle uncomfortably. "That's okay, I can wait."

"Come on, Frank," she said, pulling me inside by my arm. "We're all family here. Let's take a bath."

We walked into the house through the living room's musty odor. I hadn't noticed it before. We grabbed our bags and went to the bathroom, closing the door behind us.

She bent down and turned the water on full blast. There were no windows and I felt safely restricted in the small quarters. The walls were an outdated color of green, faded from years past. I figured that the paint itself was older than either of us.

She removed her bra and I couldn't make myself not watch.

"I'm getting a beard," I mumbled as I looked into the cracked mirror over the sink.

She removed her pants, feeling no awkwardness. "My pussy really stinks now," she confessed. "I wish we could take showers more often."

"Yeah, me too."

"You can't smell me, can you?" she asked, spreading her legs.

I shook my head.

"Good. I'm getting in the water. Are you joining me?" she requested innocently as she lowered herself into the tub.

I looked at her body, noticing the water sticking to her skin, glistening like a boiled bagel. "I'll wait until you're done." I peeled my clothes off slowly as I stood watching her, waiting for her to finish. I assumed it was a very liberating experience for her to bathe with a man in a platonic environment. It wasn't liberating to me. With our gender of interest being the same, I found it more of a frustrating reminder. "How's Harold?"

She lathered herself with the remaining sliver of soap. "He's better today. He likes these guys. He just thinks you've done a really bad job organizing this tour."

232

I grinned to myself. "If setting this tour up would've been anyone else's responsibility, we'd have never left Lawrence."

"I think you could've made the dates closer together," she told me.

"We're not exactly a large draw. No one knows who we are out here."

She stood, letting the water drip down her shapely body. "Maybe." She looked at me, concentrated on unfamiliar areas, then smiled indignantly. "You don't look very good."

I handed her a towel as I stood waiting. "That's nice."

"You're getting really skinny and you still look like a lobster. You don't look good at all."

"Are you done?"

She stepped out of the tub, dripping water on the tile floor as she stared at the mirror. "Do you think I'd look good with short hair? I think so." She stuck out her chest, fancying her perfect breasts, striking poses as if for the camera. She looked rather embarrassed when she realized I wasn't watching. "I think I'd look good with short hair. I'd look more butch."

"You're what, five foot five, and less than one hundred pounds? I don't think you'll look butch."

"People would notice me behind the drums more, I think."

"They notice you now."

"We should do our laundry," she suggested. She put her dirty clothes back on, exiting the room without another word.

I lowered my limp body into the water.

"I think we stumbled the right direction," I whispered to George as My Three Scum finished their last song.

The club was packed. The excitement generated for the opening bands made me boil with anticipation. We stepped up, eager to take the stage as the audience applauded loudly their local diplomats.

"Are you guys the Jerk Offs?" a young rocker with a tight crewcut asked as we prepared the stage.

I nodded.

"Wow, I got your record through Blacklist. You guys are great!"

"Thanks," I said, genuinely flattered. "I hope you like the show." I felt such an urge to release the uncomfortable tension that my senses danced dangerously close to a meltdown. I was ready to explode. I couldn't wait to do so.

In no time at all, we were set. I checked with the band before confronting the crowd. Their excitement rivaled only my own. We were living for this show. The recent consequences had challenged us against a checkmate. As we saw it, this was the show of all shows.

"Hello," I said firmly to the crowd as they spit at me and yelled vulgarities pertaining to female members of my family. "We're the Jerk Offs from Lawrence, Kansas. We played Pittsburgh last night. Pittsburgh is a fucking shithole."

The crowd cheered, to my surprise.

Hazel gave four clicks, ushering in the best performance of my life. Aggression ruled our playing as if our damaged spirits had collided in some strange sort of perverted orgasmic explosion after a lifetime of abstinence. We were there for the kill, and the audience was witnessing the Jerk Offs as no one had ever.

After three encores, we unwillingly broke from the stage.

233

My Three Scum generously sacrificed every dollar of profit so we could continue our plight. Combined with the merchandise sales, we left Erie with full pockets and toothy grins. We were on our way to the south, with the majority of the tour behind us.

When we made our first stop for gas, I called the promoter in Delaware only to learn that the show had been canceled. The promoter was friendly and apologetic, informing me that when the Knights of Columbus learned of our band's name, they refused the show. We had indeed stumbled the right direction.

We continued on to our next stop: Richmond, Virginia.

Finding the club was no problem. It was a well-known bar in town: Twisters. Just about everyone knew exactly how to direct us there. We parked out front, enjoying the warm weather before another night would fall upon us.

"Frank," George said, staring at several fliers taped inside the window of the bar. "Come over here."

"What?" I asked, casually stepping up beside him.

"Look at this," he instructed, pointing sharply at a flier for a Grateful Dead cover band. "This show is here. Tonight. There's nothing about us, and I know we aren't being billed with hippies."

We checked the other fliers. Nothing about our band anywhere.

"It'd be pointless to call the number I have," I said as Harold and the others wandered up, keen to our tension. "It must be for this club, and we won't know anything until someone shows up."

"I think there's more bad news," George informed them.

Harold shook his head. "You don't say? Well, isn't that odd..."

"It must be an error," Specky said optimistically.

"If it's an error," George began, "the show will be a dud regardless without the proper promotion."

"What is the money like now?" Specky asked.

"We have about fifty dollars left," I answered. "We filled the tank coming into town. We'll have enough money to get us to South Carolina."

"Why didn't you double-check these dates before we left?" Harold asked me shortly.

"You need to call these places the day before, at least," Hazel snapped at me.

"*You* can't make that call?" I asked.

She shook her head indignantly.

"This does nothing for us, all this yelping," Specky said. "We just need to hang out here and wait for someone to show up."

Harold retreated to the van in a furious huff. Hazel joined him. Specky wandered aimlessly down the street behind them.

"The fun never ends, doesn't it?" George asked me.

"Just a few weeks and we're back home," I responded from a daze.

"We don't have homes, what are you talking about?"

I pondered briefly, realizing that the street in which we stood was just as much home as anywhere.

"If Bill had just shown up when he was supposed to, these fliers would all be right," George joked lightly. "First thing to do when returning to Kansas—"

"Besides vow to never tour?" I asked.

"Right, but after that, we fire that bastard."

"Then we can go eat at Muncher's Bakery," I said.

"I wonder what's going on in Lawrence now," he pondered. "I wonder which cars are sitting at the intersection at 23rd and Iowa. Who are those people, and do they have any idea that some stranger in Richmond is thinking about them?" He smiled, scratching his chin. "I wonder who's eating at Yellow Sub right now. That's where I'd want to be if I was in Lawrence. I wonder who's standing at the counter."

"You only say that because we'll be fasting again soon, it seems."

"Yeah," he said with a chuckle. "Looks like it."

"It is pretty funny, I guess. Then again, what isn't funny from the right angle?"

"Maybe we should go inside the van and find out. I'm sure they know of some things. This tour, for starters," he said with a laugh.

"If they can't take a joke...who needs them."

He leaned against the pane glass of the club, shaking his head with a smile. "If you step outside all this, you suddenly see a street in front of us. We're in Virginia! It's so amazing that this tour could be viewed as anything other than successful. The fact that we're still out here makes it successful. We did this ourselves. And you, Frank, took all this on yourself. So we haven't had all that many great shows—we're lucky we were allowed to play."

A car pulled up and a lanky gentleman of poor style stepped out to unlock the doors of the club.

"Hello," he said to us, sensing our direct attention to him. "Can I help you guys?"

"I talked to someone named Phillip about a month ago, and he booked us here tonight," I said. "This flier says nothing about us."

He unlocked the door, releasing the musty scent of stale beer and cigarettes into the summer sky. "What band?"

"We're the Jerk Offs, all the way from Kansas."

"I know we didn't book a band with that name tonight. And if Phillip booked you, you may have stumbled across some bad luck. See, Phillip quit this place about a month ago. Moved to New Hampshire. There's a chance that maybe...all the way from Kansas, huh? I'm afraid I really can't do much to help you guys out. There's another band playing here tonight. Let me double-check the schedule." He walked through the club to a small office in the back.

We waited just inside, near the stage as he closed the office door for several minutes. The stage was directly to our right, against the front window of the club. Microphone stands leaned against the speakers, most of them new.

"Want one?" George asked. "We're obviously getting stiffed again. You don't have one, you know."

"Keep an eye," I said as I climbed up and grabbed one.

The office door remained shut as I proceeded to the van. I crept across the dry sidewalk with dirty bare feet, tip-toeing quickly to the street. I opened the side door, handed it to Harold, then slammed it shut without an explanation. I returned to the club, standing with George as we waited for the guy to return.

After a few long minutes, he swaggered out, taking his time to check the thermostat. "Sorry, guys, there's nothing I can do."

"That's it?" George asked. "Simple as that—no show?"

"Are you expecting some kind of hand-out?" he asked with a laugh. "Go on."

We walked off, saying nothing. I looked over at George, who looked straight to the ground.

"What a dick," I said.

"So, how's that stand? Think it'll work?" he asked casually as we climbed into the front seats of the van.

"Oh, yeah."

"It's probably worth more than we would've made tonight anyway," he said, turning the key of the ignition. "I'll drive us to the North Carolina border. Then someone else has to take over."

"No show, huh," Specky confirmed.

"I'm afraid not," George said, pulling the van into traffic.

"Harry and I decided that if we end up running as low on money as in Pittsburgh, that we'd call home and get money for bus tickets back," Hazel said.

"What's the point of that?" I asked. "We're almost done with this. We have five more shows to play, then we're back home."

"This is all getting really old," Hazel said.

"It's your summer vacation," George told her. "How many chances do you get to see the country like this?"

"Hindsight has a way of airbrushing things," Harold said. "I don't think I'll forget all the trouble this has been."

"I'm not going home," I said flatly without recourse. "Specky?"

He looked at me, then back down again. "I don't know. It does get old."

"Oh, come on, man. You're right. It gets old. My patience has died out here. I'm sick of looking at each one of you. But this is what I want to do. It's what *we* want to do," I emphasized. "Don't tell me *you* can't take it, tough-guy."

He looked up at me and smiled, shaking his head as he hesitated to respond. "Yeah, you're right. About the tough-guy part, that is. We've gone this far..."

"Hazel?" I asked.

"You've done a really shitty job setting this up," she told me bluntly before lying down.

"It just gets old," Harold added. "I'm sticking to my word. If the rest of the tour is as it has been, I'm going back."

"Okay," I said. "Whatever you guys want."

No more words were exchanged.

George and I shared a smile as we left Richmond. I stuck my hand out, grasping his. We needn't say anything.

My stomach was already churning from the desire of nourishment. Fate would decide the resolve. If the band would soon suffer for our determination, then at least we would have the dignity to have given it a good shot.

I scratched my face, noticing that my jawbone felt strangely large. I rubbed it, realizing that all the bones around my face were protruding more than usual. My skin felt tight around them.

I opened my eyes, unaware I had fallen asleep.

I lifted my head slowly. My neck was awkwardly wedged between stacks of soda cases. Everyone was asleep, and silence covered everything like a warm blanket. We were parked in the lot of a gas station, and the sun was just coming up over the horizon. I sat, rubbing my eyes.

I found that sleep was the best thing for fasting. It temporarily kills the pain of hunger, and for a few moments after waking, you almost feel no aching. I scratched my belly, happy to have that peace for however long it would last.

I was consumed by a sense of disorientation, wondering where we were and how long we had been there. I looked down at Hazel. She looked so peaceful sleeping. I smiled at her, savoring the rare tranquillity.

The countryside through the window wasn't the terrain of the north. A dense haze clung to the ground. The rising sun seemed to cast a strange luster with a pink glowing sheen. In fact, the entire morning sky was pink. The air was warm, especially considering the early hour. The sound of thousands of insects filled the sticky air outside in the surrounding fields.

I leaned over to open the side door, bumping Specky's freshly shaven head in the process.

"What the hell are you doing?" he asked in a groggy voice.

"Go back to sleep."

He rolled over, then quickly sprang forward. "Where are we?"

"I'm going to find out."

"Let me go with you," he said with a slow, determined stretch. "I've got some change in my pocket. Maybe I can buy something for under a dollar."

We climbed out the door, stepping through the dirt lot scattered with potholes. The gas station itself seemed ancient with a strange southern essence about it. An elderly man stood behind the counter, talking to another about the crops, or something to that effect.

"Ya'll in that van out thar?" he asked us as we entered.

I smiled, finding great relief in his southern accent. I nodded in compliance.

"Can't stay thar."

"We'll be leaving soon," I promised.

"Where ya'll from?"

"Kansas."

"Kansas, eh? All that ways. What brings ye?"

"I don't even know where we are," I told him.

"Florence is just down the road a ways. Two and three quarters a mile-mile. You're in South Carolina."

I smiled. So this was the south. I looked around at the gas station, at the construction that truly appeared to have existed since the Civil War. It looked like it specialized in chewing tobacco and Beef Jerky. All the machines inside were circa 1950. Even the old man seemed to have been the big-man of the "Sock Hop" catapulted into an age he didn't quite belong or comprehend.

"I reckon ya'll can stay out thar fer a while, if ye ain't fixin' to stay lawng. Ye ain't doing me no harm, seems. Let me know if ya'll need some help finding thangs."

I couldn't imagine a punk rock scene existing in such an environment, and I was really curious to discover it.

I wandered through the aisles, looking at jars of pig's feet and other strange specimens. The shelves contained no dust, and were quite clean. The paint on the metal racks had long since faded, nothing more than a protection from rust.

There was a soda machine, the old kind with the long-neck glass bottles you pull out of the rack after having inserted the coins. The machine would be in a museum in the north. In the south it was simply ambiance.

I followed Specky to the counter, watching the old man hammer away on the keys of the relic cash register. Life was simple, and the people kind and generous. It was as if time was made of molasses in the south, spilt into one slurred collage, connecting the past century into one moment of the perpetual present.

237

"Like I said, boys," the old man told us as we opened the door. "Don't stay lawng."

"Yes, sir," I told him before walking out into the strangely warm sunlight. "And thanks."

"That was weird," Specky said, sipping from a small container of orange juice. We walked through the dirt lot back to our compound. "It felt like we were in a movie."

"Still does."

"Why don't you have shoes, Frank? You look like a hippy child with your long-ass hair, bearded face, dirty feet..."

"My shoes are in the engine. I'm fine without them. They're just a nuisance anyway."

The sun was rising higher overhead, and the heat at such an hour was unbelievable.

"Maybe we should hunt crawdads," I said. "People eat crawdads here, you know."

"They eat pig guts, too. The prices in that store were unreal. I guess we've spent too much time in New England. A can of pop in New York was sixty cents! Outrageous..."

"Hell, I saw a can for one dollar in DC," I said.

"They were thirty-five cents in that store." He laughed as we stepped up to the van. "We can't afford one anyway. Can you believe that? We are so broke that we can't even afford a can of pop!"

His comment struck deep like a voice echoing from the past—a voice of naïve innocence. A voice that once declared the purchase of a can of pop would determine success. It was a voice that once resembled my own. I cringed at how far away I had found myself.

I lowered myself to the ground. The dirt was hard, but the van offered a nice envelope of shade to relax beneath. Specky joined me.

"So, now that this whole thing comes close to winding down, what are your thoughts?" I asked. "Any regrets?"

"I regret we didn't call ourselves the Beatles, or the Rolling Stones," he said with a throaty chuckle.

I laughed, happy to make casual small-talk with him. The simple things were becoming priceless.

"Why *not* use those names?" he thought aloud. "For one, there wouldn't be a lawsuit for a band that is just clubbing locally. Say a band uses one of those names. They'll get massive attention immediately. Not that anyone would be fooled, but people would have to wonder what they were possibly thinking. Hear that name once and it'll stick. So let's say this band builds the following they likely would, simply for having the name. They get big enough that the *real* Rolling Stones would notice and sue them. Well, think of all *that* attention! And by the time the band had made it that far that it would bring about a lawsuit, then they would be doing quite all right as it stood. They do a cover of a Rolling Stones song, have a hit just for the nerve of it, pay off the lawsuit, and retire a year or two later."

"You have interesting ideas," I told him. "Maybe you think too much."

"I've had plenty of time on this tour."

"Sounded like an idea Merle would have," I mumbled.

"Merle is kind of a businessman about music, isn't he?"

"That's *everything* he is," I said. "Music is secondary with him. He wears the suit that sells the product. I could easily see him as a successful businessman. In this business, I think he will be."

He laughed with a shake of his bald head. "That's all right. I hope the Media Whores make it huge. Honestly…"

"This tour will just broaden our scope," I declared optimistically. "No band from Lawrence has done a tour like this since the Micronotz. If anything, it'll make us all bond tighter…"

"Say that next year at this time," he mused as he lit up a cigarette.

"Okay," I assured him. I picked up a rock and threw it into the nearby field, hoping to quiet those angry insects. "You know what I want right now?"

"What's that?"

"I want a good bed. A nice, firm bed with clean blankets. Blankets that smell like detergent. I'm tired of sleeping on amplifiers and asphalt."

He took a deep drag on the cigarette, nodding firmly as if the thought was euphoric. "It's been a while since we've slept in beds. Park benches, sand on the beach, hardwood floors…they aren't the best places to sleep. Have you ever slept in a bed with a down pillow?"

"No."

"Nothing like it. I'll take one of those pillows for my bed."

"Funny," I said softly. "That sounds better than *anything* right now. Even better than sex. Better than this dirt lot."

"Yeah," he said before we both fell silent. "So, you wouldn't want a woman in that bed?"

"No."

He laughed. "I don't think I'll ever get you…so tell me, if you could have one night with any girl, who would that be?"

"Any girl?"

"*Any* girl. Famous, not famous. Alive or dead, someone past their prime…you'd have them at their best. All diseases aside, birth control not an issue, no chase—this would just be fantasy."

"It wouldn't be someone famous," I said, thinking. "I assume it'd probably be someone I know, but I can't think of anyone that really moves me enough to have sex. The thought of casual sex sounds like one of the most uncomfortable experiences. I don't know… How about you?"

"I would choose historical figures. Someone that made a huge difference in the world."

"Why? Do you have some fame-worship complex? That's so American, Specky…"

"Imagine sex with Cleopatra. That's a little more intense than someone like Madonna or Cyndi Lauper, you know?"

"But historical figures aren't necessarily attractive," I said. "I would think a fantasy would involve unparalleled beauty for starters. It is fantasy, after all."

"My list of desired women changes by the minute. It almost becomes redundant and pointless. I've had sex with attractive girls, and the experience was no better than with the least attractive. Besides, it's those pretty ones that let you down the hardest. I always make sure the scales are on my side."

I laughed before adding my own perspective. "I'm rarely moved by people. Something about the women I tend to meet almost always turns me off. Something

239

they wear, something they say, or the way they carry themselves. Everyone is so insecure and unmotivated. They collect dust, not accomplishments. I find people to be generally a let down. With women…something has to hit me. That punch just doesn't come all that often. I suppose I'll have a long and lonely life, waiting for someone to impress me."

"Yeah, I'd have to agree."

"What are you going to do when you get back to Kansas?" I asked.

"I'll probably get a new job. Work, hopefully get some new tattoos. I want matching swallows on both sides of my neck, as a pair."

"What does that mean?" I asked.

"It's a sailor thing."

"You aren't a sailor."

"So?" he asked defensively. "I'd like to get webs on my elbows, too. Maybe a *Man's Ruin* on my upper arm, if there's any more room. What about you? What are you going to do?"

"I'm going to cut my dreadlocks off," I revealed with deadpan seriousness.

"Why?" he asked.

"I'm through being cool," I told him as I tore a layer of skin off my forearm. "Look at me. I'm coming apart out here." I scanned the scenery, noticing how the crops in any field look the same. I found comfort in that. "Remember when we were talking about songs we could cover for our triumphant return?"

"Yeah."

"I don't think that's going to happen. I feel tired, worn down. I'm past the point of simply being hungry. I've fasted more days than I've eaten, it seems. My body itches so badly I think I'll be going insane soon. I doubt I'll talk to Hazel or Harold for the remainder of the tour." I shook my head as he absorbed my words.

"We could still do a cover song," he said.

"For what? For when? How about one for our last show on the road? Do you know *Nothing* by Negative Approach?"

"I could figure it out in the amount of time it takes to hear it."

"That's what I want to play," I told him. "That's what I feel."

He took a deep, long drag from the cigarette. "You know how Lank and Skeet went off to California?"

"Yeah," I said, wiping away the sweat clinging to my brow.

"They got caught up in some trouble out there. According to Lank, some Nazi skins caught them in a park. Lank got the shit kicked out of him. They broke a couple ribs. Skeet, not so lucky. He got his throat bashed in with a crowbar. The doctors told him he'd probably never speak again. He's lucky to have survived it."

I shook my head slowly, leaning back against the grill of the van. My skin stretched awkwardly as if it was ripping. I felt driven to insanity by the numbing irritation of it, wishing that a cure for such a thing existed. Reaching over my shoulder, I scratched firmly, shaving the dead skin with my lengthy, dirty fingernails. I shut my eyes, searching my mind for comfort.

In less than two hours, the heat had engulfed the van, waking each person from a sweaty slumber. We rolled into Florence soonafter.

The town was worn like an old shoe stretched across a simmering landscape. Despite the heat, which I had yet to accustom myself, it was a pleasant community.

We pulled up to a Piggly Wiggly grocery to make the fateful call. The parking lot was filled with automobiles of moderate income, waiting for working-class mothers to adhere to generations of gender conditioning as the family nurturer.

George and I stepped into the blistering sun, fishing for quarters in otherwise empty pockets.

"I'm famished," I said, my voice edged with irritation.

Two overweight people passed us, giggling as they held a paper plate of sandwiches and potato salad. I stared at them, resentful and angry. I wanted their food.

"Here...here's a quarter," George mumbled as he stuffed it in the pay phone.

I dialed the number and waited.

"Yello..." a voice said over the phone.

"I'm looking for Pete," I demanded.

"Got him."

"Pete? This is Frank. I'm with the Jerk Offs."

"Made it, did ye? Good, come on over," he offered generously.

His accent stirred an array of interesting mental images. I visualized a farmboy with a T-shirt tan chewing straw while lounging in the barn with pigs under each arm.

"We're at a Piggly Wiggly store," I said. "So, is the show still going on?"

"Hell, it better be! I'll be one unhappy troll if it ain't."

"How do we get to your place?" I asked.

"It's pretty easy, if you're at the nearby Piggly Wiggly..."

He gave the directions and we were quickly on another wild chase through trailer parks and low-income housing. We finally found the little beige trailer just on the edge of town where the deep grass seemed to threaten the existence of modernization. There was a breeze in the air, hot and sticky. The trees shook slowly, and I wondered how they'd taste if I was a giant. Like broccoli? Probably not...

We pulled up in the yard where the driveway ended to a cascade of tall, green grass. An old 1957 Chevy sat dormant in the yard with weeds consuming it from all sides. George shut down the engine and the doors seemed to explode in unison as each person rushed to exit the cell on wheels.

I was the first to advance to the door. I checked the address twice to make sure we had the right place. I pushed in on the doorbell and waited, glancing nervously at the van as footsteps slowly approached. The door creaked open with a child's head peeking around the edge of the door, knee-high at best. She stared, dirty and dressed as poorly as me. An innocent smile expressed blissful happiness. The world would wipe that smile away within a decade...

"Howdy!" she offered.

"Hi. We're hoping to find Pete."

"Daddy! The music boys are here!"

With those words, a tall man lurched over the little girl, picking her up as he opened the door for us to enter.

"I'm Pete," he said with a friendly drawl. "You Frank?"

"Yes," I replied, walking into the little old trailer.

The rest of the band followed, each making an introduction before passing through. Pete was a tall man with baggy overalls and no shirt. His arms were bony, his back red from the sun. He wore thick glasses, held to his face by a red strap around his head, kept up by the bags under his eyes. Faded tattoos covered his shoulders—his right, the bars of Black Flag—his left, the logo of LA's Wasted Youth.

"Sit down, make yerselves at home here," he offered.

241

We gathered on the floor in front of the television set. Several of the family photos that hung from the wall were slightly crooked. It annoyed the hell out of me.

"Do you expect a good turnout?" I asked, thinking of nothing more important.

"Hell, I hope so! Ye can never say, but the kids, they like it. How's the tour going? I can tell ye folks have been out a while now."

"We're into our second month," I said. "How can you tell?"

"The road has a way of haggering people. And ye folks have that haggard look about ya'll. Seen it before."

"I can't tell if I should consider that a compliment or not," I said. "I suppose it's just an accurate observation."

"No harm intended."

"None taken," I assured him.

"You wouldn't happen to have any food, would you?" Hazel asked.

"Well, my fiancé is on the way back from the store. She's gettin' some fixin's. Spaghetti sound decent?"

"Anything sounds decent," George said.

"We haven't been eating all that much," I told him.

"I know how these things go. I've booked a lot of bands in my day. Don't worry. I'll make sure that yer fed, and no matter what, you'll leave after tomorrow's show with at least gas money. Where's yer next gig?"

"We're playing in Columbia this weekend," I told him.

"Are you staying with Bedlam Hour?"

"I believe so. We're not playing with them, but we'll be staying over there," I said.

"Ya'll are playing with Bedlam Hour here. They're opening fer ya'll. They can draw a crowd. They were on Positive Force, I reckon ye know that."

"I didn't know that," I said, half-interested. "We could certainly use a draw for the show."

"Where do you work, Pete?" Harold asked.

"I don't. Can't find a job right yet. But when I do, I'll be gettin' hitched with my gal."

A white Volkswagen beetle pulled into the driveway behind our van, stirring a cloud of dust. The passenger door and hood were faded green with spots of primer.

"That's her. I know ya'll would like to just take it easy. Maybe watch *Tom & Jerry*. I think that Tom is pretty funny...hell, I don't know. Gilligan comes on after this, if ya'll like Gilligan. I personally don't..."

Everyone stood, except me. I felt strangely exhausted. I was ready to sleep again.

"Hello," his fiancé said, passing everyone on their way out. "I'm Pam."

"This is the band, honey," Pete introduced as we scattered inconsiderately. "These guys are the Jerk Offs."

She applied her best artificial smile. "Great."

"They're lookin' fer some food. Can ye work up some of that magic of yers?"

"Sure can. It'll be just a bit..." she replied graciously, heading straight into the kitchen with their little girl clawing at her tight Jordache jeans. She had the essence of a seventies pin-up, watered-down to the social caliber of the trailer park. "Just a minute, Sarah, I'm busy..."

The cicadas sounded like they were organizing a battlecry, unifying to conquer man's civilization, bringing it to ruins. I had never quite noticed the insects as I did in

South Carolina. As I sat up in the van, sipping a warm soda from our diminishing cases, I visualized that fantasy bed once again. I needed some time alone. For two months the five of us had been attached at the waist. To be in the open arms of quiet solitude, nothing else could compare.

"What are you going to do when we get back?" George asked.

"I thought you were asleep," I whispered.

"I'm not. Haven't been able to sleep lately."

"I don't know what I'm going to do," I admitted. "Maybe we all need to get on the phone and figure some things out."

He rolled over, facing me with alert attention. "I'll probably stay with my parents until school starts up again. We won't be forgetting this trip all too soon."

"Doesn't that suck worst of all?" I joked loosely.

He laughed, and it felt like a tremendous release for both of us.

"Maybe tomorrow I'll call my friend Stanley. He'll put me up until I can get back on my feet."

"Pete's wife makes good food," he said.

"I thought it was his fiancé?" I asked.

"Oh, really? Who cares? She makes good food."

"Any food is good food these days," I said. "I'm still hungry." I looked out the window, barely able to distinguish the trees against the night sky. The insects carried on, and I found myself lost in a van somewhere searching for life. Still searching...

"Jerk Offs!" someone screamed with a thick southern drawl from the rear of the venue. "Hell, yeah!"

We stepped up on stage, looking out at a landscape of eager faces. My dreadlocks hung low on my shoulders, crawling across my back. I clutched the microphone, staring into it bitterly as the spit splattered against my body. *This microphone is mine. There are many like it, but tonight this one is mine...*

"Ya'll the band?" some young guy asked me curiously.

I stared at him, shaking my head. "Are you an idiot?" He spit in my face. It dripped down my chin onto my sweat-stained shirt.

The crowd bobbed up and down, waiting for the music to floor them as I knew it would.

"We're the fucking Jerk Offs from Lawrence, Kansas," I recited from routine as a broken beer bottle flew inches from my head. I decided to add a new twist to my presentation. "Eat shit, you southern motherfuckers..."

The band slammed into a song and the crowd was feeding from our hands. The mix of the music was wretched. I couldn't hear the bass for anything. Luckily, I knew the songs intimately. The words had developed a new meaning. A deeper meaning. The passion of the lyrics had somehow gained depth, and I felt I only existed within them. Nowhere else. The person in the mirror was a facade. On stage I felt enormous, a massive iceberg in the polar regions of my own mind. In this region, I was alone. Nothing mattered. No one cared. And I, also, couldn't give a shit.

"Man, that thar was a great show!" Pete exclaimed as we loaded our equipment off the stage some time later.

"Thanks," I replied quietly, working around him to pack our gear as efficiently as possible.

"Here's yer share, pal. Two hundred dollars! Not a bad turn-out, I reckon."

"This was a good show," I mumbled, accepting the roll of bills with a quick hand. I worked to get around him as he stood before me, grasping for my attention.

"I hope everything goes well with the rest of the tour," he offered.

"Yeah, me, too." I turned to walk away.

"Wish we could've had more time to talk…"

I stopped dead in my barefoot tracks.

"Maybe next year," he said, looking at me.

"Yeah, maybe." I stared down at the ground, dry and torn from the southern heat. "It's been a rough couple weeks. No offense…please, I don't mean to be rude."

"I understand. It's that determination ye have that keeps me coming back fer more, Mr. Smith," he confessed excitedly. "That's what I love about this music."

I smiled, nodding my head. "Thanks for the show, man. Really, thank you."

"Thanks fer playing. See ye 'round."

That night we followed Bedlam Hour back to Columbia with Hazel riding in *their* van. I watched the road signs on the short trip, anxious to be able to sleep once again. The tour began as a wide open adventure, a quest for more. By the time we had arrived in the south, I felt as if we were lost, trying desperately to find our way—*any* way.

"Do you believe humans have a hive mind?" I asked George as the van rushed through the open landscape of South Carolina.

"Oh, definitely. Pathetic pieces-of-shit…I believe in the existence of *them*. The drones that do as they're told. They make this world very difficult with all their shortcuts, easy-way-outs, thirst for mediocrity, role-playing games…if someone has no idea of who *they* are, then they must be one of *them*. Most philosophers refer to these people. The flock, the masses, whatever…you've heard it through the ages."

"When one stands alone larger than the crowd, who cares when the crowd is against you?" I asked.

Specky placed a razor blade against his forearm. "Which do you suppose we crave more?" He began carving his initials into his arm, careful not to cut any of his expensive tattoos as the blood spilled down his elbow. "Pain…or love?"

I answered with little emotion. "Fuck off, Specky."

"That girl that lives with Bedlam Hour, she's going to get Positive Force going again," Hazel told me the next morning over a breakfast of leftover French bread. "She really liked our show in Florence. When she gets the label going again, she wants to put a record out by us. Isn't that exciting?"

"That's nice, Hazel," I said. "What other bullshit stories did she tell?"

"Why are you always such an asshole?"

"Because you're always such a bitch, maybe? I don't know, tell me…"

"Fuck off…" she said. Her words trailed into babbling profanity as she stomped out of the room.

"That would be cool," Specky told me from across the table. "A lot of great bands started on Positive Force."

"That label is defunct. What difference would it make to us? I can talk a lot of shit, too."

"How do you know it's bogus?" he asked me.

I chewed off another chunk of stale bread, taking my time to chew it. "Because everyone is full of shit. This person would qualify as a part of the group known as everyone."

"So would you," he said.

"Exactly. You want to know what's realistic? Going down to that record store and selling some of our records. That's real, that's tangible. Having this girl revive the Positive Force label successfully, that's not realistic. We'd be better off putting our own album out than messing with something like that."

"We're almost out of records. I think we're down to like ten more shirts. We'll be out of merchandise before the tour ends."

"That'd be fine," I said. "Beats returning with a full box."

Specky stood, stretching as he finished his glass of milk. "I'm taking off."

"Where?" I asked.

"Outside. I don't know...who are you? My mother?"

"Just making sure you aren't taking the van anywhere. And making sure I know where you are so I don't go there."

"Well," he said sharply, "I was going to take the van to the record store. Is that okay?"

"If you don't, you know I will. I'm the default man."

He walked out of the room, leaving me alone in private. Had I known it was that easy, I'd have lost my tact long ago...

The bar in Columbia was a typical rock and roll dive, supported by the Greek society and suave pseudo-sophisticates. It was the one show we ever gave where I was happy to have our music be a mere irritation to the audience. A couple of snotty punk kids had shown, but I didn't really care. We made our guarantee regardless, and besides, it's always a good thing to remember where your limits are—and how to get there. These people despised us, and I hadn't felt that successful at my goal in quite some time.

It was nice to be frothing like an animal on stage, my body covered with sweat and spit from audience members of the past five shows. Each corner of the stage carried the foul odor of each band member. I felt honored to have had the most putrid scent. I must have gone a whole week without taking a shower. There was no reason to care on the fringe.

The frat boys with their nice clothes and cologne seemed foreign to me. I was so much the other extreme, so dirty and unkept. I felt good about it. I wasn't like *them*, and that was all that really mattered.

As the show ended with no encore, we collected our money and were on our way to Augusta, Georgia that night. Each person had their few inches of space in the van, and no one talked for at least an hour. Tension was running its course...

"We only have two more dates after tomorrow night's show," Specky told us, looking at the schedule.

"I would like to offer a suggestion," Harold said from the driver's seat. "I don't mean this to sound negative, but I think we should play this show tomorrow, then cancel the rest."

"Why?" Specky asked.

"We have enough money to get home now. If we hang out in these other towns, we'll likely end up spending more money. If those shows aren't good, then we're in the same boat."

"No," I said swiftly.

"We're not going to cancel any dates we already have," George insisted.

"Harold has a point," Specky said, still looking at the schedule. "We'll have three days to wait before the show in Nashville. Then another day to sit before the Antenna Club in Memphis."

"We've gone this far," George said.

"We should feel proud we did, and go home," Specky suggested. "What's two more dates?"

"To you? Nothing. To me? It's giving up," George said.

I could feel the overwhelming urge to be rid of these people, but I had to continue.

"You guys are out-numbered," Harold said. "If you value this band, I wouldn't add any more friction. Insisting that we all stay out here isn't going to help in the long run. Look at your band, it's splitting at the seams. Are two shows worth it?"

There was a long silence that followed.

"All right," George confessed. "You've got a point. We've reached our goal. We lasted. What more can we do? I only have one request. And that's that Frank doesn't make the phone calls to cancel those shows. Everyone has bitched about every aspect of it that wasn't quite to their liking. There's a feeling of failure here, which is so wrong. We did what we set out to do. We accomplished the goal. Thank you, Frank. I'm proud to be in this band with you. I'll make those calls if these guys won't."

No one said anything. George ended up making the calls the following day.

"We'll meet again after a month," Specky said to the others. "When school starts, we'll pick it back up. We could use the time to rest."

"Augusta," I said into the microphone as I looked into a few hundred faces. I could tell when they looked at me, they looked at a gaunt and fucked-up individual. That's what they paid money for, and I was happy to be the spectacle that I had spent my young life perfecting. They honored me with indignant banter and a shower of aluminum cans and glass bottles. I preferred the spit over the glass. "I'd like to thank Anti-Schism for opening."

The crowd cheered as I backed away from the microphone, waiting for the band to bring everything together. It was one of the nicest and oddest venues we had yet played. It seemed to be a large lakehouse where Shriners would hold year-end barbecues. It was impeccably clean and massive. It could've housed at least one thousand people. Maybe someday—*definitely* someday.

"This is the last show of our tour," I told the crowd. "We've been out two months now." I turned to Hazel, waiting for the cue that would summon the attack. She looked at me and nodded, lifting her sticks strongly to give the countdown. "We're the Jerk Offs," I told the crowd quickly. "From Lawrence *fucking* Kansas...you worthless fuck-ups."

The show was a powerhouse of sorts, the kind we had grown accustomed to performing. The set went quickly, quicker than usual as we anticipated the finale of our first major tour. We left the stage, only to be beckoned back by the adrenalized ranting of the entire venue. We returned, reluctant to play another note together.

I picked up the microphone, tapping the end of it to make sure it was powered. The clicks of my long fingernails echoed through the lakehouse as if the walls were coming down.

"We're going to give you people a special little treat," I said to a ravenous roar of applause. "Don't get all excited, we're just going to play a cover. A cover of a Journey song...okay, really we're doing a little ditty by Negative Approach called *Nothing*."

246

Specky released the feedback, allowing it to shriek through the hall. I looked at the distant wall where bodies slovenly slouched, returning my gaze with distant and unreachable eyes.

The hostile attack of the guitar hit me from all directions. I looked at Specky with a short smile as I bathed in the piercing feedback. The words went through my head, and I felt ready to explode. Inside, I was as strong as ever. Outside, my body was weak, tired, and aching. The mixed proportion unnerved me. I resolved I would bridge the two, as soon as I regained control of my fate once again...

The song crept up with the bass, running into full steam with the drums. We were all lost within the limits and vastness of our own world. I could see through my eyes the vision of hate, of torment. The music aided this. So much desire, so many plans...

"Try to make things work and gain something—it's all no use. It's all worth nothing. Complete satisfaction is too impossible to believe. Nothing's ever fucking gonna work for me..."

"Will ye sign this?" a young boy mumbled as he stuck a copy of our record in my face.

"Sure," I said, grabbing the pen and scribbling *Ronald Reagan* on the cover.

"This was the last copy," he told me. "Ya'll ran out."

I nodded my head, looking at the boy with tired eyes until he walked away.

"Hey, man," a guy said, grabbing my shoulder and pulling me aside. His tall mohawk was leaning from too much motion and sweat. It was clear we gave him his money's worth. "Ya'll rocked, man! Rocked!"

I looked at him, thinking of the words that would describe exactly how I felt of his presence. "Fuck off..."

We woke early the next morning, each of us taking turns driving the distance back to Kansas. The van was silent, empty of conversation. That was fine with me...

The scenery changed slowly as we spent many grueling hours driving westward through the plain states so aptly named. I felt certain the familiarity would liven my spirits, bring me out of a lull. It didn't. I stared out the window numb, feeling nothing but fatigue. There was something different about the flatlands, something slightly altered, a different angle or coloration. Something I couldn't quite put my finger on. Then I realized it wasn't the fields that changed, it was the eyes that perceived them.

I suddenly recalled the moment when I overheard Billy Christ suggesting that Harry sabotage our tour. To the best of my knowledge, it didn't happen. Apparently, Harold had more respect than I had given him credit...

"We did it," George whispered to me as we approached the state line of Kansas. "We left here two months ago."

"We were different people when we left," I mumbled. I hadn't really spoken to anyone else in the band since the Columbia show. His words lay flat over my conscious, sinking into the depths of me like quicksand. As they splattered against the base of my comprehension, I felt an overwhelming stir of emotion. Tears were forming from an unexpected burst of pride.

I shut my eyes. I was low, desperately needing something to awaken my spirit as music once had. Time was the only answer. My impatience avenged me. I couldn't wait, I wanted life now. Fatigue, hunger...what are these if not new challenges to overcome? I fell quickly asleep, waking again as we passed through Kansas City, only a stone's throw from Lawrence.

Bad Brains' *I Against I* played over the stereo as we entered the city limits of Lawrence. I concentrated on the lyrics, unable to focus on anything else, repeating over and over in my head: *What are you gonna do? The truth is looking straight at you.*

The sun scorched the streets, making them seem liquid. Or maybe it was just me...

The van crawled into the parking lot of the Southern Hills Mall where Stanley stood alone. He perked up as the van crept next to him, smiling as our dusty old prison reached its final stop. I couldn't wait to be rid of this experience.

Specky thrust the side door open, allowing the sunlight to pour down upon our sickly bodies. Clean air rushed the van, forcing out the stench of two months of sweat and grime. He stared at us blankly, smiling with a curious look of concern.

"You made it," he said with reserve, approaching the van sheepishly. "I'm proud of you guys."

No one replied.

He grabbed my hand and squeezed it. "You don't look all that good."

I stared at him, unwilling to force a smile. The stretch of such an expression would likely tear my peeling skin anyway. "I need a vacation."

"Are you ready to go?" he asked.

"Fuck, am I ready to go..."

"Hop in the new ride," he said, pulling me to his new shiny white Honda Accord. "You must have some stories..."

I felt weak next to him, clinging to his shoulder more as a feeling of support than affection.

A hand gripped my elbow. I turned to see George staring with a powerful smile.

"I'll talk with you soon," he said to me. "We've opened a new door."

"Crossed a new barrier," I added. "Now let's get some sleep."

He turned and stumbled slowly down the street, alone and on his own once again.

"Where do you want to go?" Stanley asked me.

"I don't care," I sighed. "It really doesn't matter as long as it's away from here. I can't bare to be anywhere near this van for another fucking second. I need a bed. A *real* bed. With nice clean blankets, and a nice pillow. Have you got a down pillow?"

"No," he replied as he unlocked the door for me.

"That's okay, doesn't matter at this point," I said, sliding into the new car that smelt alien. The seats were soft, and the air-conditioner discharged an unfamiliar blast of cold air with the gentle turn of the key. It was as if I had entered the modern world once again, and the reality of it shocked my dulled senses.

"We could get some food," he said. "Or we could just go somewhere to relax."

"I don't care where we go. Just as long as we drive really fast to get there."

Feeding From An Empty Plate

The smooth landscape of Kansas passed outside the window in a golden blur. The heat of the day had reached its peak by early afternoon. My eyes ached from the glare of the road. Our destination lie beyond the reaches of my tolerance and patience. The hills of Douglas county drifted in the distance like scoops of fudge sundaes. It was the wrong season to appear with a whipped cream topping.

We would soon arrive in Lawrence where I'd be on my own once again.

Studying the controls on the dashboard, I found myself lost in a climate-controlled world of sterilized comfort. My week at Stanley's home went too quickly, yet it was the most time we had spent since our paths separated into different lives. We vowed to dedicate more time for one another. We laid down many promises, most of them we knew we couldn't keep. It was the sentiment that carried the largest voice.

The streets of Lawrence were quiet and under construction, waiting for the students to revitalize the economy.

"It was good having you down," Stanley said as we pulled up to Merle's house. "We need to see each other more often, now that you're back."

"We will." I had gotten used to the smell of his new car. The luxury of it had quickly faded into expectation, as expected.

"You look better," he said, rubbing my head. "I like your haircut."

I glanced into the mirror, smiling at the clean-cut hot-rodder with the eyes of fire. At least that's how I liked to see myself. "Your wife did a good job on it."

"Cutting your hair makes a new person of you. You'll notice people will approach you with a different attitude. Not necessarily better, just different. There's no better way to reinvent yourself than to change your image."

I opened the door, releasing the artificially cool air into the summer wind. I stepped down onto the ground with my new Chuck Taylors, stiff from lack of wear.

"I'll contact you soon," he promised. "We'll hang out sometime, maybe next weekend."

I looked inside the car, into the depth of his eyes. "It was good to see you."

"We'll meet again *soon*."

I slammed the door as he cautiously merged into the traffic through the student ghettos. He disappeared down the long concrete path, consumed by the impatient river of steel.

I was alone once again. Finally...

I bounded up the grassy hillside to the uneven sidewalk. I expected to hear the Media Whores plugging away in the basement as I walked up to the porch, but I was met only with silence. I pressed my finger on the doorbell as the traffic ran its course on the busy street below. The scent of roses surrounded me, yet there were none to be seen.

The door heaved open, and Merle faced me with a wide smile. His flat-top was stiff and tall, like his muscular frame. White streaks shined in his hair like brindle. He wore an old sleeveless T-shirt with horizontal stripes of red and black. It appeared to have been lifted from Bert and Ernie's collection. It fit as if it were, too. Cut-off military fatigues hung loosely around his waist. The padlock and chain around his neck bounced against his chest like a gong.

"Frankie!" he exclaimed. "Come on inside! Your hair, your lovely hair! What happened?"

"Cut it all off."

"You look so savvy," he told me as we walked into the immaculate living room. "Do you want something to eat? You look emaciated. It's good for the cameras, but you know how mothers are..."

"Food was scarce on tour," I told him as we sat at opposite ends of the couch. "I had a huge breakfast this morning. It's nice to finally be able to deny an offer of food."

He laughed, slapping his hand onto his bony knee as he leaned back in the deep couch. "So you need a place to crash until you get back on your feet? The couch is yours. Had some great, tender moments on this couch before. Sometimes with more than myself! And I offer it to you...may it serve the same purpose... So what about work?"

"I talked to my old boss at Pizza Shuttle. He has an opening for me during the day. I'll be making the pizzas now, not delivering."

"Do you still have the car?" he asked.

I nodded.

"We're opening the Pedal Jets at the Bottleneck," he told me. "This will be our first weekend gig there."

"A weekend night at the Bottleneck?" I stated with firm disbelief. "You're kidding..."

"We've been doing pretty well since you guys left. Got some good shows over the summer, good reviews. It was a busy season at the Outhouse. Had a lot of exposure. We also made a record. I've got a copy that I saved for you, it's in my room. KJHK is playing the hell out of it and we're rolling."

"That's really great," I said happily. "You can't get a better weekend gig in town than the Bottleneck. They usually turn their cheek to punk. I'm glad to see you guys are breaking tradition. Maybe you'll be able to pull some headlining shows there soon."

"That'd be nice," he said. "I bet that bands playing a weekend show at the Bottleneck are bringing in no less than a grand a show. That's not bad."

"Not bad at all. I think we never got much more than two hundred a night on the road."

He stood quickly, strutting awkwardly into the kitchen. "Do you want anything to drink?"

"No, thanks."

He poured a glass of water for himself, quickly returning to the couch. "Did you guys have some decent shows out there?" he asked, sipping from the cup with his pinkie finger extended gracefully. The cubes of ice knocked calmly inside the glass. Little waves brushed them in circles.

"Some," I told him. "We had a few really bad ones, too."

"You must've really made a name for yourselves out there."

The thought really hadn't occurred to me. I took a moment to consider. "It didn't seem like it, but if we were to consider how many people went to all the shows combined, we'd come up with a decent head count."

"You definitely reached people. If you toured again next summer, you'd see that."

250

"*Tour* is a four-lettered word."

He laughed politely, abruptly silenced by another sip of water. "When are you guys going to play a show here? I was expecting a big return at the Outhouse."

"It felt as if we crawled back into town, really. I haven't spoken to the band since we got off the road last week."

"Man, must've been rough," he speculated. "Honestly, I have to thank you guys for leaving. We got nearly every opening gig in your absence. Your tour helped us as much as it helped you."

"Nice that it worked out that way. About that record…I'd really like to hear it."

"Sure," he said, jumping swiftly to his feet. He paused briefly to place the glass on a corkboard coaster. "Let me get it." He rushed upstairs quickly, bounding back down no sooner than he had left. "Here it is." He reached the record to my receptive hands as he lifted the glass of water once again to his lips. He looked at me and smiled. "Your hair. I can't get over it. You look so…down-to-earth."

I studied the record, concentrating on the professional packaging and how nice the Media Whores name appeared in print. The cover art was a replica of the Coca-Cola logo with the band's name conspicuously replacing the old standard words. The lettering was a good match. It took a second glance to even notice. I pulled the black disk out of the sleeve. "Play it…"

He grabbed the edges, pampering it as his offspring, like an investment in his very future. He placed it on the record player and lowered the needle, watching it spin with one open eye. It cracked and popped—the sweetest introduction to any recording. Suddenly, the room was ablaze with happy havoc, controlled and delicate. The force of the rhythm jabbed me in the kidneys. I was lured by a masochistic impulse to submit myself to it.

Merle crossed his legs, sipping calmly on the water as he watched my reaction. He could hear it through my ears, judge its effectiveness in my reaction. As a musician, I was aware of this strange effect, what I called *hearing your music through other people's ears.*

When his vocals forced themselves through the sludgy riff, I could feel the hair on my upper arm become erect. The beat stomped slowly, slowly like the relief of constipation. The vocals caught me, grabbed me mercilessly by the throat. Merle was on top of the music, enslaving the lethargic rhythm like a chic dominatrix. So rarely does a singer sound so thoroughly in control. I looked up at him, taken aback by the fact that this cordial gentleman was the same voice growling over the speakers. As the chorus hit, I felt envy for its catchiness. My single complaint was that I had not been its creator, its owner. I leaned forward instinctively with an extended hand. Merle smiled as he reached out to shake it.

"Amazing," I said as I clutched his grip tightly. "Amazing."

The alarm screamed at me, yelping that strange digital bark. I rolled over to turn it off, appalled by the number on the face. *Six-thirty in the morning.*

I rubbed my eyes. This was absurd! I considered rolling over, going back to sleep…

I sat quickly to avoid temptation. I gazed out the window with foggy vision. The sun hadn't quite made it up over the roofs of the nearby houses. It was dim and hazy outside, and the world seemed to be glowing a tranquil shade of blue, much as I remembered of upstate New York. I leaned back, shutting my eyes. The room was quiet. All I could hear was the hum of the neighbor's air-conditioner. I stretched my

251

body, blissfully loose and relaxed. There was peace to be consumed. Intoxicating in its purity. I felt so alone, and it felt so *nice*...

I pulled myself off the couch, dragging my feet to the hardwood floor with a dull thud. The wood was cool and slick, a nice contrast for my warm, tender toes. Eventually I stood, finishing my stretch before quickly folding my thick blanket. Taking it and the pillow to my designated spot in the corner, I continued through the kitchen to the rear of the house where my shower awaited.

The water was warm, slipping down my body that wasn't really dirty. At least, not by my recently adjusted standards. I picked up the shampoo bottle, squeezing a bit of its contents into the cup of my hand. Running my fingers through my short hair was a feeling I hadn't quite gotten used to yet. One of those luxuries denied after several years of possessing dreadlocks. Washing my hair had become an exciting new hobby.

Reaching for the soap, I raised the temperature of the water. I have a tendency to get too used to the temperature and spend most of my showering experience raising the heat to an ungodly level. In the shower as in life, I suppose...

By the time I had made it to Pizza Shuttle, I was already six minutes late.

Kelly, the owner stood at the dough table over a lumpy mound of dough. She stared at me as I walked past. "You're late." She was short and lean with the arms of Popeye. An oversized ball cap sat loosely atop her small head. The cap concealed her short, dark hair. "Clock in...*now*."

I rushed to the time-clock, scratching my name on a card before sliding it into the machine. With the click that signified my time belonged to another, I rushed over to the dough table to adhere to her next command.

"Wash your hands. Did you wash your hands?" she asked, looking up at me curiously.

"Not yet," I replied indifferently, dashing effortlessly to the sink. I returned in a matter of seconds. "Okay..."

"Stand over here," she demanded. "What do you know of dough?"

"This is dough right here," I told her, pointing at the blob on the table. I had seen things like this kill people in the movies. I kept a watchful eye. "Is this thing from outer space?"

"Huh?" she grunted with exhausted eyes that seemed to peer through me.

"Never mind..."

"Have you ever stretched doughballs?" she asked, this time more pleasantly.

"No."

"Well, you're going to learn."

Armed with a shiny, stainless steel dough cutter, she chiseled away at the blob, slicing off pieces for the scale. At roughly ten ounces, the chunk went hurling onto the pans. She quickly snatched one up and did some impressive folding that instantly produced a perfect ball of dough.

I worked the strange putty as best I could.

"Takes a while to learn," she said, slashing at the dough like a butcher. "It's not as easy as it looks."

I desperately worked to keep pace. "I see that."

"You'll pick it up eventually," she said calmly. "You'll learn how to mix it, how to proof it...so how was your trip?"

"Glad to be back," I replied. "It's a bit early for me, if I seem a little distraught."

"I figured it must've been bad, or you wouldn't have cut your hair," she said. "Are you quitting the band?"

"No."

She shook her head as she slashed violently at the dough. "Damn. I hate having all these band people working here, wanting so many days off…"

I glanced out the front window, looking out at 23rd Street in the distance. The traffic was thick, slowly moving the people to the places where they would spend their lives. The sun was bright, and the day not quite yet alive. I could tell I would like the job.

"So this string walks into a bar, right?" Stanley hollered to me as we sat at a corner table in the smoky, dirty Bottleneck. The stereo system was deafening. The choice of music was equally annoying. "And the string goes up to the bartender—"

"Is it a gay bar?" I asked.

"No, it's a single's bar, I think…"

"Is the string Jewish?"

He shook his head.

"Is the string black?"

"No. It's just a string. A plain white string."

"Why is this string going into a bar?" I questioned. "And wouldn't the bartender find it odd that this string is walking around?"

"Okay, so this string is at the bar, and he tells the bartender that he wants a drink, and…and…shit! I forgot, hold on…"

"So the bartender tells this string he's a frayed knot…"

Stanley snapped his fingers. "Oh, yeah…wait, if you know this joke…"

"You know, when I was young," I told him, changing the subject tactlessly, "I wanted to invent a new color. I used to sit and wonder what it'd look like. Have you ever tried to imagine something inconceivable to the mind? I did, for many years. Then I got older, and I realized you can't just invent a new color. I regretted the wisdom that forced the disbandment of my goal. Nonetheless, life went on."

"I always wanted to build a Harley from the ground up," he confessed. "I still do."

"You're so practical."

"*Too* practical," he corrected.

"I'm ready to hit it hard again," I said strongly. "Look at this crowd…" I gestured to the stage. "This is where I belong."

"These guys have taken off. And fast," he told me as we concentrated on at least five hundred people taking their place before the shrine of the Media Whores. "They're hotter than a jacked-off tomcat."

"Yeah," I said softly, amazed at the anticipation of the crowd. "They're packing them in…I look forward to playing a crowd this size again."

"You guys had a good year," he said as the music over the speakers slowly died down.

"Hello, boys and goirls!" Merle chanted through the microphone, his voice tinny and small. His flat-top was stiff as nails. "We're the Media Whores."

The crowd applauded politely. Stanley and I delivered our attention to the stage. Four clicks crept through the speakers as all eyes fell upon James' drumsticks. Suddenly, the club condensed with a flood of power like molten shrapnel. Their music was simple and tight, easy to follow, easy to grip. The band writhed in their own style as if they were making a mockery of the genre itself. Merle grinded on the microphone, his face buried in the music with eyes shut tight. The group pulsated to the rhythm,

253

allowing it to possess them, to send their bodies in convulsions as the music grabbed the sternum of each person present, slapping them into agility.

By the demise of the first song, the considerate applause had transformed into a shower of screams and praise. I was one of them.

The new kid had arrived...

"Frank!" Tom screamed over the classic rock. It was four minutes to the hour of five. "The night-shift doughboys are here. Finish that tray and you're gone."

I picked up the scraper with stiff fingers and placed the metal edge under the blubbery hide of the dough. The thought of doing *another* tray was appalling. I glanced up to check out the rush-hour traffic on 23rd Street. Cars sat motionless on the street waiting for something to change, such as their miserable lives. They'd settle for another color of light—settling as they had their entire lives. Lying the tool on the metal tray, I quickly removed the individual doughballs with the skill of several weeks effort. I was becoming a skilled laborer, and the thought of that could always bring a smile. A smile based on the absurdity, not pride. Dying in ten years of white lung didn't sound all that attractive to me.

I picked up the roller and began mashing my previous morning's creations into flat saucers.

Tom stepped up next to me, watching. "Getting pretty good."

"This is my contribution to the world—rolling doughballs, saucing doughballs, rolling doughballs..." I removed my apron and wadded it up into a ball. My day was finished.

"Clock out," Tom demanded.

I wasted no time finding the time-clock, dropping the lever on my card in an action of defiance and freedom in my five o'clock world. *Such a wonderful sound*, I thought as I walked to the sinks. I dropped my apron in the linen basket and continued to remove a mask of flour that would otherwise burn my eyes hours later. "See you on the flipside, Tom."

"Later, Frank."

As I left that day, I noticed the faintest scent of fried food in the sweltering summer air. I inhaled deeply as I slowly opened the door of the Ranchero. The hinges creaked, and the interior had the scent of something ancient and lived-in. The old relic was probably maxing out at seventy on some open highway at the precise moment I was being born, I figured. It was likely ancient then, too.

I brought the car into Reverse, careful to avoid all the delivery drivers that swarmed the shop like bees. The steering wheel felt hard and uncomfortable, my forearms sore and stiff. If there's one thing about the shop's management that could be said, they certainly get their work out of the employees.

I raced down Naismith drive with the hot wind ripping through the cab.

As I drove to Hazel's new apartment, I felt immense relief. I hadn't expected her to be the first member of the band to reach me. The future of the Jerk Offs depended greatly upon the success of our meeting. I was anxious to get through with it.

I pulled up to the apartment on Louisiana Street, parking in a lot at the corner of 12th Street.

I strolled confidently to the address with a swagger of comfort and confidence. A porch light directed my attention to the little wooden numbers over the door, summoning me to make contact with a person whom I had little interest to ever meet again.

I knocked lightly on the door and waited with my hands stuffed limply in my pockets.

She threw open the door as if anticipating our meeting as well. "Come on in."

I walked through the small studio apartment, ending up on the love-seat against the opposite wall. The room was cloudy from the burning sticks of incense struggling against the odor of decay and cat urine.

"Your hair," she said, smiling at me like a mischievous child. "You look so gay!"

"So do you."

Her forthcoming expression exuded immense pride. Her brief smile faded into a straight and rigid glare. "How have you been?"

"Better since I haven't had to deal with the likes of you," I said with a light smile, though I meant every word.

"I spent a while at my parent's place," she told me. "Spent a lot of time playing the drums. I have some great new beats I'd like to try out. I'm tired of the same old songs. We need new ones. I've been playing these songs so *long* now."

"George has some ideas he's working on. He says—"

"George?" she threw out quickly. "Specky is the one who writes the songs."

"George wants to try out some other avenues, see if we can pull out a new thing. He's getting a sampler keyboard, and we'll be able to try some really innovative stuff for a change."

"A keyboard?" she said, laughing in a tone that somehow suggested curiosity. "That'd be an interesting twist. We'll see what Specky thinks..."

"It's worth a try. We can pump out hardcore songs dime a dozen. It's time we tried something that would actually challenge our creativity."

"That sounds good to me," she said, stepping closer to the couch. "My parents may be buying me a new drum set. I don't know for sure, but it seems. I need one. My old Rogers set is pretty tired."

"That'd be great."

"I really want this band to get back on its feet," she said quickly, passionately. "I want to begin practicing again. When we left town we had a lot of really good opportunities coming at us. I'd like to pursue those. It's time we come alive again, have that glamorous return show we neglected."

"I agree," I told her, feeling a strong sense of comfort in her words. I could feel the itch once again, and I was ready to go. "Have you talked to anyone else?"

"No, but I know Specky is working at Taco Johns on 6th Street. I could find him and get back with you."

"I can find George," I said.

"I was afraid the tour had killed everything we've worked toward," she said cautiously.

"No...not at all. Not at all. We're ready to come back, Hazel. I can totally feel it."

"Excuse me," I commented to a young girl toting a bulky cello case into Murphy Hall.

She turned to me, to a face in the crowd like any other. A face of no importance, much like her own.

"Yes?" she asked, pausing at the front door, giving me her absolute attention.

I pulled the door open for her. "I'm looking for the practice rooms. Do you know—"

"I'm a freshman. I don't know *anything*," she said blandly.

The long hallway was filled with students wandering aimlessly, looking appropriately confused. It was the first day of class and everyone was seeking their niche to fall into. The building was rich with the excitement of chaos and confusion.

I turned to the young freshman who stared up at me like a skittish cat.

"I know it's on the second floor somewhere," I said to her. "I guess I'll just find it myself."

"Sorry I wasn't much help. I'm new here," she said as I began to walk down the slickly polished hallway. "Are you a music major?"

"No, I'm meeting a friend," I told her. "He's a music composition major, and my bandmate."

"What band?"

I smiled, happy in the thought that my appearance gave no indication. "I sing for the Jerk Offs."

She absorbed the words with expansive eyes. Her attention quickly strayed. "Oh..." She turned away, walking blindly into the crowd as I continued forward to the courtyard.

People scurried like lost sheep, gazing curiously in notebooks, surveying class schedules and syllabuses. I weaved between the masses, searching for a flight of stairs. I finally resolved to stand still, scanning the long hallway, looking for some type of recognition.

Suddenly, my eyes were caught like wild game in a hunter's trap. My heart quaked inside my chest, sending a shockwave of numbing discomfort to my limbs. My eyes remained fixed across the full length of the hallway as people passed between like rush-hour traffic.

She was shrouded in what seemed a luminous glow of superhuman brilliance. Intensity radiated from her vibrant spirit, making dull machines of all who surrounded her. She could make a reasonable atheist reconsider rigid beliefs. It was already clear that she could make a hopeless idealist ponder similar issues of faith in humankind.

The lights dimmed and I found myself on a stage somehow fronting the Nelson Riddle orchestra. A white silk tuxedo hugged my body to a perfect fit. A yellow carnation was pinned to the breast of my smooth jacket—that perfect splash of color like candlelight. Jazzy tones poured like sweet chardonay. I threw a sassy, cocked brow at her as I raised the cumbersome microphone to my puckered lips. "Heaven, I'm in Heaven," I crooned with quixotic passion. "...and my heart beats so that I can hardly speak, and I seem to find the happiness I seek..."

She appeared to be the recipient of a flawless bloodline from India. Her skin was dark like chocolate mousse. Her frazzled, curly hair streamed over her bony shoulders like malted syrup. Her nose was as large as her chin was small. Thick, black eyebrows perked with each smile. Her dark almond eyes were sunken over high cheekbones. They absorbed light like blackholes. They absorbed my attention like the barrel of a gun. A loose shirt draped her docile frame with the words *Kansas* etched in bold letters across her flat chest. She glanced often at the gold watch wrapped loosely around her bony brown wrist.

Shiva...

Her eyes squinted as she smiled in response to a one-sided conversation with a chatty cohort. The corners of her mouth curved slightly upward...and her ears, so perfect. Her elbows were smooth and pointy, just how elbows are ideally supposed to look, I figured. I felt a quickening hunger I had never known. My lack of experience with such a famished yearning was maddening. I felt untamed, and it felt good.

256

She scratched her head with a slender finger, pulling her black hair into a bun like pumpernickel. She never once looked away from the speaker. That attentiveness was so very attractive.

She leaned down to open a duffel bag, pulling out a pair of slippers that she tossed over her scrawny shoulder. Not slippers, but toe-shoes. She was a dancer...

Watching her, I suddenly understood what all those songs, all those books, all those movies were about. *This girl*. And seeing her, I realized their failure in communicating the complete brilliance of this wondrous specimen. Before me stood the source of all man's passions, and strangely no one else seemed aware. It was this immortal beauty that made the artist seek the brush and canvas like a subservient slave, in turn to be owned by his own shortcomings, victimized by the inability to transcribe the true elegance of the subject. Never in my life will I be so successful as the genes that worked up this masterpiece. My definitions of beauty were drastically reinvented with a single glance.

Taking a moment to say a few closing words to her friend, she nodded with a bright smile before she continued down the hall. She was coming my direction, passing through the crowd like Jaws, unleashing certain death with each step. I had to move, I had to disappear...something. If those eyes were to pass at a casual glance, it could be messy...

Absorbing myself in a group of trombonists discussing warp drive, I watched her pass harmlessly, all the while staring at her thin legs, muscular with awkwardly knobby knees. She stared downward, having no interest in those who filled the space around her. She withheld herself naturally silent, yet too purely inward with contemplation to seem arrogant. Her intelligence burst from her eyes, her humble attitude written with every step, every quick and passing smile.

She floated past me like a ghost. I watched her retreat to the front door, heading the direction of Robinson Gym.

I liked her shoes. I knew Claire would ask, so I took a special note. Navy blue Vans.

As she walked out of my line of sight, I became aware of pointless chatter. I looked around, noticing a massive hall filled with people. Annoying, subpar people. I wandered with steps as light as the air in my head, eventually finding a set of double-doors in the far corner by the courtyard.

As I reached the top step of the second floor, George stood looking down at me.

"Did you get lost?" he asked impatiently.

My face was flushed, and I felt very disoriented. "I just saw the decline of the rest of my life..."

"What?"

"I saw the vision of a woman that will haunt me...forever...am I making any sense? I sound like I'm reading from some high school poetry book."

"Ah, you're just horny. There's a bathroom down the hall if you need to have a moment to yourself. Good to see you, by the way." He delivered me to a tiny little room with a shanty, upright piano. Shutting the door behind us, he sat down at the bench, extending his fingers gracefully over the keys. "This room has the best piano...so how have you been?"

I thought a moment, still thinking of her. "Okay..."

He grimaced with one brow cocked. "Man, she must've cast some spell on you."

257

"She was a honey. No, wait, she was more than just that..." I gazed blankly into the corner of the tiny room before I threw him a partial smile. "I didn't know they came like that."

He lowered his fingers onto the keys, allowing a dissonant chord to fill the little room. It carried a strange feeling that crawled under the skin like a rash. "I spent several weeks in Kansas City waiting for classes to begin. Glad it's here. I still need a place to live. Maybe we could find something later today?"

"That'd be good," I said. "Merle should be fairly sick of having me around by now."

"I assumed everyone has been commenting on your hair, so I didn't want to say something too quickly, but it looks really good. Much better, actually."

"Thanks..."

"Are you ready to hear my music?" he asked. "I'm curious what you will think. I've spent a lot of time working on these few songs. That's basically all I did in Kansas City."

"Okay."

"Well, here's the first one. A quick word—this will sound like neurotic drivel. It'll sound disconnected and whacked out. It'll sound like chaos. Strangely, it's constructed with a very rigid form called twelve-tone. There is order in chaos—at least *this* chaos. I've developed the basic idea for this first song on the Fibonacci series. Imagine that this first part will be played by a string section. This one is really odd...see, rock and roll hasn't fully explored a lot of techniques that have been used for centuries, such as counterpuntal music or non-temporalism. Let me try to explain, and then I'll get to the really *heavy* shit..."

"So, tell me," George slurred as we leaned against the pinball machine at the Bottleneck. He clutched tightly to a bottle of dark ale. "What do you think of the girl sitting at the table over there with the two burly rockers?"

I looked around the dimly lit crevices of the bar, squinting with burning, bloodshot eyes that had been subjected to too many hours of smoke in a poorly circulated bar. I scanned each table until I spotted the young blond sitting, talking excitedly with two rugged creeps. Her company seemed smothered under a blanket of pretense.

"I like her energy," I said. "I don't like her hair. Fake blond...insecure...all that makeup. You don't see me wearing all that. She seems too easily entertained by those guys, she's searching for something. No, that girl is way too insecure for me."

He smiled, shaking his head. "Over there, that girl sitting alone at the bar with the dark hair. Long dark hair—you've got to like that."

"She's been at the bar all night. I don't mind if someone drinks, but that girl has to be a lush. And look at her expression. It takes effort for her to smile. You spend a lifetime molding your face. If you smile a lot, the lines and muscles in your face will default with a consistent cheery disposition. When her face is without a definite expression, she looks pissed. She's worn that expression often. No, I don't need an attitude like that, especially from a lush."

"I've been pointing out girls all night, and every one of them has some problem. What the hell?"

"I read people well," I replied shamelessly.

"How do you know you're right, you bastard? I'm as cynical as you, but come on!"

"I'd be willing to bet money. You don't need to tell me my standards are unbearably high. I know that. Sucks being up here, let me tell you. How about you? What about these past two girls?"

"Hell, I'd take either home. I'd take them both home if they wanted! You're too picky, and for what? Maybe you overrate the whole experience."

"Too much is on the line during sex to rate it anything but vastly significant," I told him.

"I think I'm getting a good grip on what you're looking for, though," he revealed optimistically. "You like them short, like midgets—flat-chested, brunettes, fifth generation librarians with an edge..."

"Actually, I'd break through those preferences in a heartbeat if the person had the right attitude and intelligence," I said. "People *wear* their intelligence and ignorance. You'd be a fool not to judge the book by the cover when the pages have complete artistic control."

"We should be going soon," he said, glancing at the clock. "You're drunk by association. We both have to work tomorrow."

"I may have found a place for us to live, did I tell you that?" I asked.

"Where?"

"Off 25th and Redbud, on the corner. A few blocks from Pizza Shuttle. We could check it out tomorrow, move in next weekend, if you like it."

"Cool," he said as we stood slowly. "I bet you'll be glad to get out of that den of rock and roll depravity."

"They'll be glad to be rid of me."

"Why...do you masturbate in front of the television all day?"

"Not all day. Hell, I work all day..."

Later that night, I gazed uncomfortably at the clock. It was four-thirty. The thought of the stagnant band ate at me. I was swimming in the murkiest of waters, far from shore. I could feel myself becoming lost in the idle float of non-existence. These waters carried a warmth from the urine of countless others who happily shared the same immobility. Its emptiness tore at my innards, forcing me to seek a way to change the course. I knew change was an issue of time. And that was the hardest part, the waiting.

I sat up on the couch and looked around the room at all the darkened shapes. There is an atmosphere that exists only at night. Few moments are as peaceful. I rubbed my eyes, still burning from the smoky bar as I stepped firmly onto the cold hardwood. Careful not to make a noise that would wake Merle or James, I tiptoed to the front door, unlocking it slowly.

I was blasted by the cool breeze of late summer. The sound of the city had died to a quiet hum of streetlights and insects and air-conditioners. There was that fragrance of roses that I couldn't quite place. I inhaled, allowing myself to become a part of my surroundings as I retired to the steps, looking up at the sky. The moon was bright, yet only a few passes from being completely new. Low clouds blew quickly overhead, each one splashed with the blue shimmer of moonlight.

I considered George's music. I wondered how the others would feel about such an extreme change. My thoughts soon swayed to the girl from Murphy Hall. Where was she now? Was she sleeping at this precise moment? Or was she lying in someone's arms? How many times had she sat looking up at this same moon? Was she looking at it now? I wanted to meet her. I had to know more than I did, for which I knew nothing.

Except those shoes…she was a dancer, and that was as good a lead as any. I would have to pursue it somehow.

I leaned back, sliding down the wooden steps. The night seemed so open. Sitting there alone, resting between the change of days in a time mostly unknown to the world, I felt I had found a place for which to rest from the traffic of the world. I would return to this hour more often. If for any other reason than simply knowing just where I stood on my journey up the mountain of my endeavors, and how much more effort I would have to give in order to feel I had finally reached the peak of *something*.

Moving my possessions into our new place on 25th Street was easy. I had so few. George arrived later in the day, waking me from an afternoon slumber on my used mattress.

"Check this out," he said as he lugged a long box up the wooden stairs. He laid it down on the floor and opened it. "It's the Mirage. I finally got it. Even got a bunch of disks for it. If you'll help me get my amplifier up here, I'll play those songs again. This time the way they're *supposed* to sound."

My heart raced at the thought of creating music again. I rolled off the mattress, eagerly joining his dissent down the steps. Together we hauled the amplifier by its awkward handles, just as we had so many times over the summer.

"Have you talked to Specky yet?" he asked me.

"Not directly," I told him. "Hazel has. They plan to come by sometime today."

He plugged the keyboard into the wall, summoning yellow digital lights to dance lively on the face. It spoke with chirping noises like an insect. It was the closest I had ever been to a computer. I assembled his amplifier as he inserted a disk into the keyboard.

He placed his fingers over the keys. At once, the sound of violins filled the room tangled in a thick, intense chord. "How about that?"

I smiled.

"Here, listen. Remember how this sounded on piano? Check this out…"

He began playing a bizarre melody, somewhat quirky, entirely insane. The rhythm was odd, and I sought to understand it. It was every bit as maddening as the music of Schöenberg, but with the intensity and speed of hardcore punk rock. His theory was right—nothing in rock and roll's existence could be compared.

"That sounds really…different. I'm excited. You should give me a tape, so I can figure out some innovative approaches."

"I don't know how well people are going to handle this, but I like it."

"I do, too," I said. "That's all that matters."

Footsteps rumbled up the steps, shaking the rafters of the makeshift wooden staircase with each climb.

"Hey, men!" Specky said happily as he and Hazel peeked through the open door. "What's going on?" He stepped through the door, shifting his attention between the keyboard and my hair. "I heard you cut your hair. I was afraid you'd look stupid, but it looks good. Maybe you'll get laid now. So what the hell is this *thing*?"

"It's a fucking keyboard," George replied defensively.

"How are you, George?" Specky asked politely, placing a supportive hand on his shoulder.

"Not bad."

"I can *almost* say I missed you guys," Specky admitted. "Hazel tells me you want to use keyboards. It's a joke, right?"

"No," George said sternly, staring down at the keys. "I've got some ideas. I want to try something different."

"Can you believe how huge the Media Whores have gotten?" Specky asked with an odd subject change. "Everywhere I look, there they are. KJHK is playing the hell out of them."

"They know how to sell themselves," Hazel said. "Look around town at every street post, at every wall...you see their fliers. Everywhere you look, you see their name on some bulletin."

"Merle wants to succeed," I told them. "He knows what he's doing. If you see the name often enough, you assume they're good. Wouldn't you?"

"They are good," Specky said. "Good at what they do. They're constructing their music around a niche. They're playing to an audience, and the audience is responding."

"I want to try something different," George told Specky, continuing his train of thought. "We've been doing the same thing for years now. I want to take a new approach."

"What we're doing works," Specky said shortly. "That's why we had such a great year. Hell, we were packing the house! It's not broken, why fix it?"

"I'm bored, maybe?" George offered.

"Trying new ideas is one thing, but adding keyboards to this kind of music is ridiculous..."

"You haven't even heard what I'm doing," George said. "I don't have any interest in playing a certain *kind of music* anyway."

Specky shook his head. "George, why do you have to be such a pain in the ass?"

George laughed in a tone thick with contempt. "And you're not?"

"Well," Specky said, sitting next to George to get a better view. "Let's hear it."

"Keep in mind that this thing can sample...it can do lots of things. I have some song ideas..." Wasting no time, he hammered down on the keyboard, playing the same progression he had performed for me not five minutes earlier. After about thirty seconds, he stopped to look at Specky.

"I don't like it," Specky said with chilled irreverence.

"Why?" George asked defensively.

"It's not what I want to do."

"What do you want to do?" I asked.

"I want to play *rock* music. I mean, what the hell was that?"

"Something different?" George suggested snidely.

"No reason to change things that work just fine as they are," Specky said. "Is this some kind of a joke? We're a hardcore band. We're the Jerk Offs! When you hear a name like that, do you think of music like what you just played?"

No one answered.

"Frank, what's going on?" Specky asked. "We're a hardcore band, you know that. Shit, man, you believe in the music as much as I do."

"We're a good band, Specky," I told him. "We can't change that. We can grow, and I feel that doing these songs would be a challenge. I want to try them."

He looked at me with distant eyes. "I *also* have some new ideas. This is not something I want to do, George...and Frank. What do you think, Hazel?"

She smiled, looking down at the keyboard. "I kind of liked that little riff. What was the time signature? I'd like to try it. We could just do it in the studio, play the more rocking songs at the shows."

261

"Why bother with that?" George asked. "No, I want this to be the direction of the band."

"I don't," Specky countered. "I don't see any logic in changing our sound. It'll destroy our following."

"If no one comes out to our shows, then that's the way it goes," George said. "Have we ever really cared about the audience before? Have we ever written our songs *for* an audience? Well, maybe you have, Specky, but I never saw it as that."

"This is music, George," Specky said. "The creator of the art has to know its audience, to dance that political dance with the listener."

"Then let's have some integrity for a change," George said. "I know there can be more to rock music. We can pioneer something new. We can be the band that takes rock music to a new plateau, a higher level of academia."

Specky laughed. "You're kidding yourself if you think the common man gives a shit about your music education. The kids just want to rock…"

"What about the old record?" I asked. "I got a letter from one of our distributors asking for five hundred. We made a dent on the east coast, apparently."

"I don't want to play those songs ever again," George said quickly.

"What?!" Specky exclaimed. "Those are the songs that brought the massive crowds—"

"I don't want to play those songs, either," Hazel added. "I'm tired of the same old shit."

"Specky," I told him bluntly, "I don't know that I want to discontinue those songs, but I am burnt on them, too. We've played them hundreds of times—most of which over the past couple months. If we put them in the closet for a while, we'd be better off. In several months we'll be into them again."

I could feel Specky's anger as he sat shaking his head slowly. "They're still intense to me. I think we should press more records and continue at the pace we've been going. If people want to buy it, we should press more. That's obvious to me. Have you lost your minds?"

"You're the collector," I told him. "If we have a demand for more and we stop at this point having only pressed six hundred, think of the value. If we oversaturate the market, there won't be *any* value. If we stop now, it could become a collector's item. Those records are all over the country, all over the world…we could eventually release it again in a different format, different packaging."

He sat a moment, then nodded his shaved head submissively. "Yeah, I can see that."

"Okay," I said, trying to calm the situation. "Practice this weekend."

"We can use my place," Hazel offered. "I've already checked with the neighbors."

"Does that sound decent, Specky?" I asked.

He let out a long-winded sigh. "Sure."

"Okay, how about Sunday evening?" I asked. "At around seven?"

Everyone nodded quietly as the room buzzed from the sound of the live amplifier.

"All right," I said proudly. "We begin again."

Later that night I lay sprawled on the mattress, staring up at the ceiling. I felt I had been there before. I feared I would be there again, often.

I sat up, wondering how I had arrived at this point so readily. I picked up the telephone, looking at the glowing green numbers as the dial tone sang quietly in my hands. I pressed Stanley's combination of numbers and waited.

"Hello?"

"Claire, this is Frank."

"Hi, Frank. What's happening?"

"Not much...not much at all."

"Really? Sounds like *my* life. You know, when I was a little girl, I used to think my life was a book. When it was time to go to bed, I imagined that the reader had to go to bed, too. Now that I'm older, I feel it's all the more true. And the book is no bestseller, by any means. Here's Stanley."

"Nice talking to you, Claire."

The phone changed hands quickly as if he were close at her side.

"Frankie?" he asked.

"Stan, my man, how are you?" I said, collapsing to the pillow again.

"I'm okay, I suppose."

"Years ago I remember sitting in front of my stereo listening to the Jerk Offs. I dreamt big dreams. Now what?"

"Was this everything you ever wanted?" he asked.

I sat quietly a moment. "Not really."

"Why is that? You *got* what you wanted."

"Yes, I did."

"I admire you, Frank. You do what you set out to do. You accomplish things, you stop at nothing to get what you want. I envy that. I'm as broke as you are, I have a job that will likely take up the rest of my life. I know you think I sold myself short. Maybe I did. I could've been more. I could *still* be more. But I'm happy."

"You're happy?" I challenged in disbelief. "You still live in that town..."

"Home is where you find your passion. I guess you can hang your hat there if you wear one. I feel that your passion has a way of trampling all over the beautiful green grass to get you where you want to go. Once you've arrived at your destination, the only view you have is the ruts you carved along the way. You're a strong man, Frank. You strive to succeed and I'll forever be impressed with you. I feel you'll forever be disappointed with me. I have to say, though, your efforts to better skin the cat leaves you with a lot of scratches and heartache. I don't envy that."

"I'm not disappointed, Stanley. We've ventured down different paths. I respect you a great deal. Would we still be this close if I didn't?"

"I live my life at a different pace than you. At the end of the day, what does any of it really matter?"

"You think I should slow down and smell the flowers, is that your rhetorical advice?" I asked.

"No, not at all. You better not! *I* live for your accomplishments. At least *one of us* does...no, I think you should just learn to appreciate the strides you have taken in your young life. So, what did you call for? A lecture?"

"I was wondering why I'm sitting at home on a weekend night. Especially with my new hairdo and all..."

"Don't sit at home, go somewhere. Buy a pop, do it for me. Celebrate your life. It's time you bought that soda. It's time you realized your successes and stood amongst the living."

"Yeah..."

"Whatever, man. Now excuse me, pal. It's a weekend and I have this woman here just waiting for the man that will deliver the goods."

"Well, tell her I'm sorry I can't make it. Can you cover for me?"

"Just this one time," he grumbled sarcastically. "This adulthood thing, it's for the birds. If I had known what being an adult was all about, I wouldn't have signed up for it so young."

I smiled. "I'll see if maybe I can get out of the apartment."

"Go buy that pop. You owe it to yourself, and you owe it to *me*. Talk to you later..."

"Later on, Stan."

I sat the phone down and glared up at the ceiling. There were no cracks, nothing to concentrate on to lose myself within.

I thought about the people beyond my walls. The people that would be piling into the venue when the Jerk Offs would return. The people that would amount to the number of one thousand. In the meantime, there was only this room...

"Pizza Shuttle," I said into the phone. I grabbed a pen to take the order.

"I want to talk to someone about this pizza I got here a few hours ago..."

"Okay," I said. "What's the address?"

"Over here at 23rd and Iowa, just round the corner. This is Mr. Richards...you know, I was the auto mechanic..."

"Is there something wrong with the pizza?" I asked shortly.

"Well, it appears your pizza-maker masturbated on it. There's shredded condoms in it..."

"Hold on," I said, lowering the phone while turning to Kelly. I only had a few minutes before my shift was over, and this was the last thing I cared to handle. "This guy says there's a condom in his pizza."

"Is that Mr. Richards?" she asked. "Tell him there's no condom in the pizza."

I picked up the phone again. "The owner made your pizza, and she told me to assure you that she did not stick condoms in it or masturbate on it."

"Well, I know what I see...just the other day I saw my neighbors wearing my clothes. They wear my clothes around, you know. Now I only have these shorts to wear. Did you masturbate on my pizza?"

"Not that I'm aware of."

"Well, maybe you should talk to your drivers," he suggested with a disturbing monotone. "You can talk to that skinny guy that wears my shoes."

"The skinny one...okay, I'll give him a good talking to. I don't know what to tell you about your pizza, man. I'd go ahead and eat it if I were you."

"Well...I'll just pull all the little pieces of rubber out from under the cheese. I'd just appreciate it if you could show a decent man some respect...I am a decent man, you know."

"To say the *very* least," I said. "I'll see what I can do about it. Okay?"

"All righty...you talk to that skinny guy."

"Talk to him—hell, I'll probably just fire his ass when he gets back here. That dirty bastard..." I said, rushing the phone down.

Kelly stood behind me, passing the peel to Tom to end her shift. "He always has some problem with the pizzas," she told me. "He's a little out there."

"I pieced that much together...so am I off yet?"

"You're off, Frank," Tom confirmed. "Can you stick around a minute, though?"

"I suppose so," I said, looking at the booth in the small lobby.

"I'll be just a minute," he promised.

264

My apron was speckled with white dust. It sparked the curiosity of what amount of flour pasted the walls of my lungs. I removed the apron, tossing it in the linen sack before my ritualistic facial rinse.

Eddie, the husband of Kelly and part owner walked in through the rear door, swaggering loosely to the front. His loud, Hawaiian shirt demanded attention. As the signer of our paychecks, he got it.

"Hi, Frank," he said to me as he passed.

"Hey there, chief." I followed him.

"Frank just got off the phone with Mr. Richards," Kelly told him.

"Oh, yeah?" Eddie replied as he stood by the oven, studying the schedule. He pulled a couple of twenty-dollar bills from the drawer. "Did you cum on his pizza?"

"Guess so," I said. "Can't pull a fast one on him."

"So when is your band going to play again, Frank?" Eddie asked.

"No idea. I'll let you know when we do."

"You do that," he said, retreating to the back door once again. "I'll talk to you all later."

As everyone said goodbye, I smiled, watching him leave faster than he arrived. I respected Eddie. He was one of us, as I saw it. He was raised in the same class, worked for everything he had, and created a fast-food empire with conviction and knowledge. I could aspire to be like that man...

I wandered to the booth in the lobby where I watched an elderly couple circle the quiet interior of the mall. I couldn't guess what Tom wanted, but I could tell it was important by the way he expected me to wait. The minutes passed—as did my patience.

He eventually wandered up to me, peering down with a calm smile. "What's new?"

"Not much."

"Why do I never see you with women? A guy like you should have a different woman hanging off his arm each day. Always helps your image, having women hanging on you." He looked at me, waiting for a reply that didn't come. "Surely you've got your eye on someone..."

"Well," I mumbled reluctantly, "there's this dancer—"

"You've been out to the Dirty Bird without me, Frank?" He shot me a crooked smile. "You know I'd spot you a lap dance or two."

"Not a stripper..."

"You dated a stripper already, didn't you?" he asked.

"Yeah, but this girl isn't—"

"I understand, Frank. I get stuck in ruts, too. Hell, how long have I worked here? Anyway, I've talked with Eddie and we both feel you could handle more responsibility around the shop."

"That's very nice of you to say."

"We'd like to offer you the position of day-shift manager, Frank. Of course, you'd get a raise. You'd work a lot more hours..."

"More pay, huh?"

"You'll have to talk to Eddie about that. So what do you think?"

"Restaurant management? I don't know. The title sounds a little frightening."

"Well, consider, Frank...I dropped out of college. You never went. You should think long and hard about it. There's a decent living to be made in management."

His words seemed to ring like Deja Vu, and I could've sworn he said: *This is the rest of your life.*

"That's pretty heavy," I muttered. "I'm so young."

"Good time for you to start. Besides, what else are you going to do?"

I instinctively nodded my head. "Why not? If it sucks then I'll quit a week later."

"Good choice," he said. "Maybe someday in a few years you'll be running your own place."

I laughed briefly before falling back into a pokerface. We both stood quickly.

"Aren't all restaurant managers coke fiends?" I asked.

"Is that what the kids are saying these days? Hmm..."

"I could handle it," I assured him seriously.

"Glad to hear it, Frank," he said, shaking my hand with an unnaturally friendly smile. "Your hair looks so much better now. Maybe you should stop knocking off those strippers. You spend too much time at the titty bars."

"Yeah..."

"Get out of here. You're off now."

I headed straight for the door, feeling a sense of frustration as I left. He was probably right. This would be the rest of my life.

As each car raced down 25th Street, I wondered about the occupants and what story each life could tell. It was a Friday night. Summer would soon be fading into fall, the most beautiful season in Lawrence. I sat on the edge of the balcony with my feet dangling, watching the traffic rush by me.

Over my shoulder, I could see that George's bedroom light had come on again. His date with some employee from the nearby Food 4 Less grocery had never made it out of the apartment. In fact, it never left his bedroom. After about ten minutes of annoying shrieks and growls, I had retreated to the balcony for silence.

My peace was broken once again with what sounded like a shoe hitting the wall. "You don't even know me...how could you ask such a thing?!"

Suddenly a door slammed, followed by thunderous footsteps down the hallway. In a matter of seconds the screen door thrust open, and there stood the grocery checker, dressed only in a pair of wool socks and poorly fitted boxers. She stared angrily at George, shaking her finger at him as he stood in the doorway, watching.

"I can't believe you..." she cried, her breasts jiggling with each accented word. She threw her shirt over her head, struggling desperately to pull it down over her shoulders as George and I exchanged a quick and casual glance. "I'm leaving."

"Okay," George conceded, stepping slowly onto the balcony as she rushed down the steps. "I'll talk to you tomorrow."

"Yeah, right!" she challenged furiously.

"Does this mean we're off for next weekend?" he asked loudly as she lumbered across the lawn.

She didn't reply.

"So, Frank," he said, taking a seat next to me. "What's happening?"

"Just hanging out."

We waited, allowing his date to pull the car up over the curb, tearing up the edge of our lawn. With the maddening screech of tires on asphalt, the car zoomed around the corner.

"Women..." he said. "Are you pissed about the little write-up in the fanzine?"

"I'm used to it by now. It seems every interview I've ever given got printed with an incorrect slant. That's the way the media creates a story, I suppose, but to dismiss

266

our record because they thought it was a drum machine? That's absurd... I need you to make me a tape of your songs, George. I've got too much time on my hands."

"I need the whole band to play them for you to get the idea. It should be a pretty odd thing."

"And if no one gets it?" I asked.

"Life goes on, I guess. Then we form a Metal band like every other washed-up punk band."

I laughed.

"Come on, man, lighten up," he said. "What's your deal?"

"Bored of boredom. I want the band to get going again. I feel empty without it. It's like I only live when I have that microphone in my face, screaming my lungs out."

"That's not a bad way to live," he said.

"Maybe we should start working out. After winter."

"Seriously?" He took a moment to consider as a carload of screaming adolescents raced through the neighborhood. His face stiffened with the challenge of a new conquest for which to assert determination. He nodded his head. "Okay."

"I'm sorry," Specky said over the hum of the amplifiers. His tone was thick with insincerity. He tossed his pick on his amplifier head, dusting nervously a clean corner of it. "This is not the kind of music I'm wanting to do. These parts are way too intricate for people to grasp."

"If they can't handle it, then I prefer their distance," George said.

"The kids want to rock," Specky said. "Stupid as it sounds, that's what it's all about. Do you think we can't impress people with simple grooves that make sense? The ones that have worked since the inception of rock music?"

"The simple grooves have been done thousands of times," George said.

"Who are you trying to impress anyway, George?"

George shook his head, smiling in a way that demeaned every word Specky breathed.

"Do the rest of you guys want to do this complex shit?" Specky asked Hazel and I.

"I like the idea of pushing ourselves," I said. "We'd still do old songs."

"I want to do these songs," Hazel told him bluntly. "The rock beats just don't challenge my ability to play. I'm not just a girl that plays drums. I'm a damn good drummer."

"So this is all about what we can prove?" Specky asked.

There was only silence.

He took his guitar off his shoulder. "I don't know what to say to that. When's the next practice?"

"We just started fifteen minutes ago," I said.

"Well, I'm done for today."

"Are you quitting?" George asked.

"I'm asking when the next practice will be."

"What did we agree on?" I asked, prying for neutrality. "Next Wednesday at seven."

"Okay," he said, dusting off the top of his Ampeg cabinet again. "Give me time to think."

"For what it's worth," I said to the others as I passed a copy of the latest issue of *Maximum RockNRoll*. "Our interview finally got printed. I planned to show this earlier, but I was too interested in getting started. Now we're already finished…"

Specky reached out to grab it, staring at the folded page proudly. George dismantled his gear with vague interest.

"Frank," Specky said to me, placing a firm hand on my shoulder. "This is great!"

"Did they print a picture of me in there?" Hazel asked, rushing from her drums to check it out.

"Yeah, they printed pictures of each of us," Specky replied with a gravity-defying grin. "I have to show Skeet. This will cheer him up."

"See you guys on Wednesday night," George said quickly as he rushed to the door. "Ready to go, Frank?"

"Yeah. You can have that copy, Specky. I can get another one."

"Thanks, man," he mumbled, never letting his eyes leave the print.

I followed George out the door to the Ranchero. There was an unusually cool breeze in the air. It was perfumed with that faint smell of winter. Change was coming. The air breathed it.

"Specky isn't going to work with this band," George said flatly as I started the Ranchero's cold engine. "He's not right for it. Even his equipment sounds too…*punk* for this stuff. To make these songs work, the guitars will have to be a lot more distinguishable. He plays an Ampeg with cut speakers. Of course it's going to sound rough."

"Specky is such a great guitarist," I told him. "He's like a rhythm machine, very precise. And he plays with such intensity."

"We're moving into a different kind of intensity, Frank. He isn't going to work. He needs to know."

The cold wind seeped through the cracked window as we sped down the street. It was quite clear that nothing would ever be the same again.

"I don't know what to think, man," Specky told me the following night in the lobby of Taco Johns. "It seems the band has lost its mind. Trying to do these songs that may as well be played by some jazz band on psychedelics. This is crazy…"

"I like the ideas," I said.

"Do you like the ideas, or the songs?"

"Both."

"Oh, really? Conceptually, it's all great. But who's going to go out to see this? Tell me how many people will brave the cold to get to a club in the middle of nowhere to watch a band play in different times, none of it going together. But man, will it be impressive! *This sounds fucked up. Must be hard to play. Guess that makes them good.* Do you think they'll want to buy an album of this shit, to listen alone in the dark and feel something—anything?"

"Who knows."

"What happened to you, Frank? When you got to this town you were so high-spirited about all this. You put our band on the map. What changed in you?"

"I haven't changed at all. These people that comprise our audience—they don't care. They're weak, just as they want to be. No one stands up for anything because they don't believe in anything. When we play, and we're out there on the road…those people are there to get drunk, they don't give a fuck about us. The words, the music…it means nothing to them. Never did. What kind of respect is that?"

"That's the way it's always been. You know that."

"I now realize that," I told him. "I don't *like* that. I don't like the type of apathetic people that flock to our shows. I hate playing for a bunch of retreads and burn-outs."

"You don't pick and choose your crowd, Frank. You get what comes, and you be happy that they even come out in the first place. No one hands you anything in this world. Just because you want a certain something, doesn't mean you get it. I feel I've lost you. When Norm quit, *I* wanted you in this band. *I* was the one. I knew you were right for the job. I could feel your determination back then. It bled into *me*. I convinced George to keep with it long enough to see if you could work. It wasn't easy. He was ready to quit. George isn't easy to sway, but I did it. And I was right, it worked—*you* worked. We've achieved national recognition on a small, yet expansive scale. The doors are still opening. I don't understand all this..."

"You act as if I'm turning on you," I said.

"You are."

"I'm not. I'm no less true than I was a year ago."

"True to this goal? True to this music that made you what you are now?"

"True to myself," I said.

"You believe in our music, Frank. I ask you...reconsider."

I looked at him, staring at the pink and tender outline of skin around his new tattoo. It was covered with a sheen of moisturizer, as if pasted to the side of his neck with sticky glue. "I want to change the way we approach music. It's not a sell-out."

"Tell me about it...if we'll accomplish anything with playing these fucked-up ideas, it'd be to achieve pure inaccessibility. I don't want to do it."

"I guess that's it, Specky. What more is there to say?"

"I'm out of the band? Is that what you're saying, Frank?"

I looked at him, wanting desperately to challenge him to a taco-eating contest. Just like it used to be. I wanted to thank him for offering me the chance to be a part of his band, for introducing me to a world I had only once dreamt about. I wanted to thank him for believing in me.

I bowed my head. "Yes, Specky, that's it."

He stood quickly, shaking his head, staring at me with distant eyes. "Okay...then I guess that's all there is. Have a good life, Frank." He turned and walked away.

"Goodbye, Specky," I mumbled to myself as he rushed out the door.

As he bounded with rugged steps down the street, I watched him painfully. Is this what I wanted? There had to be no sacrifices for this dream. Nothing could stand in my way if I wanted it to be real. George was right, Specky would not work with this. It had to be done. The fraternity of punk had collapsed my ability to breathe, and I had no choice but to move away. Specky locked me to it like a ball and chain.

Time would repave the roads, I felt certain. In a year, Specky and I would probably be eating at the same restaurant, laughing about all the things we once held so sacred.

I never spoke with him again.

"No, man," Merle mumbled through the phone, his voice dim and partially present. I could hear Andy Griffith talking loudly in the room from the boxy television set. I had tactfully worked for ten minutes to retrieve Merle from Mayberry. It was an effort in vain. "I don't know any guitarists that don't have a band. Specky's out, huh? Man..."

"It's been so long since we have played a show," I told him, staring up at the ceiling, feeling deep anguish and absence of self. "I have no idea what we're going to do. We're in a vulnerable position."

"How's that?" he asked dully.

"Specky gave us a lot of *street credibility*, if you will."

Merle laughed. I was relieved to know he was actually paying attention. "Maybe so. But you guys sure as hell could bring the crowds. You'll get some good response. Who wouldn't want to play with the Jerk Offs? I mean, come on..."

"There's nothing I hate more than idle time."

"Are you going to our show this weekend?" he asked. "Friday night, finally got a headlining spot at the Bottleneck."

"You guys have really taken off," I told him, feeling a bit of grief over my uncontrolled jealousy.

"Tell me!" he exclaimed in disbelief, his voice suddenly bellowing excitedly. "We have some guy from the *Note* coming to our practice tomorrow. They're doing an article about the music scene in Lawrence. They believe really good things are around the corner for this area in music."

"Hmm...could be."

"So did Specky leave, or did you guys give him the boot? You don't mind me asking, do you?"

"No, not at all. I'm not really sure. I think Specky and I came to a crossroads together, and we've chosen different paths. His guitar was such a major part of the energy I felt. I'm paranoid that I've just circumcised the very thing that had inspired me."

"There's always been that guitar and singer connection in rock music," he said. "Not to turn the sprinklers on in the rain, but think of Page and Plant, Bono and The Edge—"

"Marr and Morrissey..."

"Richards and Jagger. Just be positive. Things will work out."

"Yeah," I mumbled, staring longingly into the loose wires of the lighting fixture overhead. "I just need to be patient."

"I think my sexy girlfriend just pulled up. Yes, I need to go. Got a dinner date."

"Okay," I said.

"Good luck, and remember to keep your head high. Otherwise, you'll miss the opportunities that pass."

"Talk to you later," I told him, feeling his attention stray to his surroundings once again before hanging up.

"Guitarist wanted...why *wanted*?" Stanley asked me as the two of us studied my flier hanging on the inside window of the Bottleneck.

I pulled my jacket tightly together as the wind pushed its way down New Hampshire Street. The air was cool and dry, a sort of parade to the coming freeze. "If I had said *needed*, then it would seem too desperate, and I didn't want it to be *that* honest."

We stood motionless on the sidewalk under the bright glow of the marquee. *TONITE: MEDIA WHORES*. The line wrapped around the front of the entrance like a scarf. Standing, shivering in the cold, under-dressed for the season, I watched a full game of pool through the window before advancing a single step.

"You didn't even print the name of the band," he said.

270

"The only response we've gotten are from punk guitarists. We had the best, there's no reason to go there."

"Specky played like an animal," he said.

"He brought the best out of me," I acknowledged with a smile. "Time to move on to new pastures."

"Greener, you mean."

"Well, newer, at least."

"Man, I feel like we're waiting to see Van Halen," he groaned. "Maybe we should go elsewhere."

"I can't do that, I told Merle I'd show up."

"Whatever..."

"Frank Smith?" a frail voice whispered from behind my shoulder. I turned to a pale, skinny man with passive green eyes. His narrow head was shaved with the exception of a thin, wiry mohawk. He stared at me, his eyes wide and confused, almost frightened. "The Jerk Offs are broken up?" When he spoke, his peach-fuzz blond mustache wrinkled like a crawling caterpillar.

"No."

The enormity of his Adam's apple diverted my attention to his awkward boyishness. It gave him the appearance of a buzzard. The wrinkles around his fluttery eyes hinted a further distance from youth than his demeanor suggested.

"A friend told me Specky is out, and that the band is now defunct."

"The band is *not* over," I told him. "We simply need a guitarist."

He suddenly perked, his eyes squinting with fleeting passion. "I play guitar. Well, I don't play like Specky, but I can play. I've been playing a few years now."

"Are you in a band?" I asked.

"I've never been in a band before," he admitted. "I can play all your songs, though. You guys are the best."

"We're doing a different kind of music now," I warned.

"I used to stand up at the front of the stage singing with you. Do you remember?"

I looked at him, finding no recollection. I had no desire to hide my poor memory, or his inability to make a lasting impression. I shook my head.

"Well, maybe you were as drunk as I was at all those shows," he said with a laugh that made his rosy cheeks glow with an unflattering splotchiness. "Man, I never missed you guys. I want to try out for the band. I can do it. I *know* I can."

"What kind of amplifier do you have?" I asked.

"My parents just bought me a new Gallien-Kruegger with built-in chorus. Has a really clean distortion. I have a great guitar, a Gibson SG. I plan on getting a digital effects rack to do some really weird sounds. I'm not as fixed on one thing as Specky. I like to experiment. I'm very into soundscapes and ambient tones."

"We should have you sit in on a rehearsal sometime," I said, feeding on the words I so wanted to hear. I took two steps forward, following the movement of the line. "My name is in the phone book, give me a call. Where do you work?"

"I don't. I take some classes and mow my parents' lawn in trade for room and board. So I'd have all the time in the world to play. Doing music is what I *really* want to do. I'll call you tomorrow—hell, I'll call you tonight! I just want to play in a band. To join the Jerk Offs...that'd be my dream."

"What was your name?" I asked.

"Alan. Alan Michaels," he said, reaching out to shake my hand.

271

I grasped it firmly, feeling it fall limp in my hand. It was warm and clammy. I looked down at his relaxed arm, drawn by innumerable scars that crawled up his entire forearm. "Give me a call tomorrow."

"This is Stiff Willy on your sound alternative, KJHK. We're only minutes away from talking with Frank Smith and George Esposito of the Jerk Offs. First a word from our sponsors...."

I stared at the dials, at all the tiny intimidating lights that ignited with each breath of the DeeJay. On the edge of the mixer sat the current issue of the *Note* with the Media Whores on the cover, ushering in the *new music revolution* in Lawrence. I had read the article several times, written by a young journalism major named Rex Howe. Referring to me as Frank Young was one of many errors, and certainly not the grandest.

"Ready?" Stiff Willy asked. His shaggy white hair crept over the collar of his jean jacket. "Five seconds. Four...three...two...one...joining me in the studio are two members from one of Lawrence's oldest existing punk bands, the Jerk Offs. Frank and George, glad to have you."

"Glad to be here," I responded politely.

"This article in the *Note* claims you guys broke up months ago. Apparently this is a misprint."

"Obviously," George replied. "We have nothing to say about the *Note*. I personally choose to not read it."

"Yet it has been quite a while since you guys played a show. Why the hiatus?"

"We've been working on new songs, and a new direction. Something more challenging to us as musicians," George replied quickly.

"We had a falling out with Specky, our original guitarist," I revealed.

"So you have a new guitarist?" Willy asked.

"Yes, a guy by the name of Alan Michaels," I said. "Everything is working out as we planned."

"Any plans for recording?" Stiff Willy asked.

"Eventually," George promised.

"For what it's worth," Willy recollected, "when I first arrived at KU a few years back, nothing could compare to a Jerk Offs show at the Outhouse. I have a record cued up here for the listeners. Here is *Crack In The Wall* by the Jerk Offs in their original line-up with Norm on vox. On KJHK."

We sat quietly, uncomfortably as the song played the vibrant passion of a time past. Specky's guitar ripped angrily like the tearing of flesh, bitter without remorse. Time had failed to dissolve its intensity. It sent a chill up my spine, as it always had.

"Good stuff," Willy mumbled to himself as the song closed. He leaned forward to the microphone, taking a breath, staring into the dials. "We're here with the Jerk Offs who will be playing at the Outhouse this Saturday, their first show in almost six months. We'll take any calls, our lines are open. So, Frank, tell me about last summer's tour."

"Well, it was long. A little over two months."

"Two months too long," George added sourly.

I laughed. "It was a good chance to see a lot of the country."

"Did you guys use a booking agency?" Willy asked.

"No, I set up the whole thing," I said evenly.

"You guys have had an impressive career for a local band."

George leaned into the microphone with a cocky grin. "Thanks. I would have to agree."

"Well, let's play another track, one from the second record...Mr. Frank Smith holding the mic. this time around," Willy said. "An intimate moment with the Jerk Offs here in the studio. We'll be back after a nice public announcement." He cued a tape resembling an eight-track. Flipping some knobs, he leaned away from the microphone. "Having the press refer to your band as defunct isn't a good thing."

George nodded indifferently. "Yeah, we know."

"As they say, rock journalists are just failed musicians," Willy said.

"Such is life," George told him, unaffected by doubt. "Our placement in life is based on our failures, not our successes. It's what we had to fall back onto after each dream dies."

Willy cocked his brow, shooting a hard glance at George. "I prefer to be a little more optimistic. Okay, ready to go...three...two...we're back in the studio now with some of the members of the Jerk Offs. This is *Persistence, Resistance.* Keep on getting on like you know what's going on..."

"The phones are dead," I mumbled.

"Are you going to be at our show?" George asked him.

"I have to work that night. Besides, I already made plans to go to a party afterwards."

"Any bands playing the party?"

He nodded apprehensively. "The American Pigs."

"Isn't that Specky's new band?" George asked.

Stiff Willy sat quietly, staring into the dials as his eyebrows slowly raised. "Yes."

"This is it," I said, feeling painfully distraught as I stood in a partially vacant lot. "No one is here."

"They'll come," Stanley insisted.

"It's already ten-thirty. If they aren't here, they aren't coming."

"Maybe the promoter didn't do the right kind of advertising," he suggested.

"Yeah, maybe," I mumbled softly. I felt suddenly defeated. My voice must've reflected it.

"Keep your head up," Stanley demanded. "Don't forget why you picked up that microphone in the first place, Frank. I know, I was there."

I shrugged my shoulders defensively. I didn't care to deal with his condescending judgment of my disappointment. "A lot has changed since then."

"The music was all that mattered. That's what brought you here. Who are you trying to impress now? It's all about how many people show up here. Then it'll be all about selling albums, but they don't call it *selling albums.* It's called selling units. Units. Your art, your songs, and it's called units. Let me tell you, Frank, when you head down that path, and all you care about are the units, the numbers...you can be successful. But let me tell you, I won't give a shit about that can of pop. Did I say *can of pop*? I meant units of carbonated liquid refreshment."

I laughed.

"Look at how many *did* give the time," he said. "I have seen hundreds of people give a night of their lives to watch you perform. Now *that*, my friend, is success. Your records are all over the country. Isn't that everything you wanted?"

"Frank!" Hazel screamed from the back door of the Outhouse, waving me to advance toward her. "We're almost ready to play!"

"Go play your show," Stanley said to me. "And Frank, don't play for the audience, play for yourself."

I stepped down onto the firm ground that contrasted my stance. Taking one small step forward, I ventured alone into the Outhouse to give my comeback performance. It was clear beyond any doubt, I had returned—to what I feared most.

The curtain went up and the sound of wonderful music filled Swarthout recital hall. The lights flooded the stage like water in a fishbowl, bringing to life a peaceful setting from the previous century. It was my first ballet experience, *The Nutcracker*.

I was taken aback by the care that went into each aspect of what was presented before me, from the music to the lighting to the choreography to the stage—the lifetime work of countless individuals. I was on the edge of my seat, astounded at the determination so overwhelmingly present in each motion, each sound, each visual. Tchaikovsky's reputation was well earned—he knew the corridors of the human heart very well. I envied his insight.

Suddenly, she appeared before me as if hurled from a dream. The Sugar Plum Fairy.

My eyes followed her tighter than the spotlights that made soup of the stage. Leggings the color of burgundy wine clung tightly to her firm muscles. The lights melted into her dark skin like a cup of café latté. It made me thirsty.

That blissful, fleeting feeling of hope grabbed me once again. Somehow, everything seemed less static than it did just minutes earlier.

Her movements were flawless and elegant. I couldn't help but wonder what determination brought her to that precise moment. Was she a slave to this, and if so, was it worth it? The question of her personality intrigued me. I wondered what motivated her to arise each morning, the fruits of her passion that beckoned like breakfast. I felt certain I was witnessing that answer, but I knew there had to be more. I wondered if she spoke the same language, shared the same vision on life. Did she grow up with roller skates on her feet like me? I imagined couple-skating next to her under the disco lights, asking her favorite color, her favorite flavor as if we could base the love of our lives on something so trivial…

I sighed, shaking my head as I watched her calculated movements. I wanted to know her. Yet at the same time, I felt somehow I already did. I could see a bright future with her, and I wanted that future more than anything. I wanted to grow old with this person. I cared nothing about what was in common. There was something there, something I knew worked like the matching of clothes after weekend's laundry. I wanted to wear those clothes.

I studied the expression buried under the disciplined control. A scene played itself in my head as my imagination ran wildly to a brighter tomorrow. In this vision I sat on the edge of a bed before an open window. The Sugar Plum Fairy was sitting next to me, as she had for years. It was night, and it was late. We sat silently looking down upon a yard covered with fallen leaves, sharing the intuitive thoughts that needn't be spoken. It was autumn, but on this night the weather was mildly cool. The wind drifted through the window at loose intervals to remind us of its presence. I was older, wiser. The yellow grass below had once been trampled by our young feet, years earlier. The grass was greener then, but our lives no less content. Suddenly, a large bush stirred and out sprang a child, running to homebase in a game of hide-and-seek. We had once done that, too.

I returned to the dark theater where she danced for me.

After the performance, I left the hall as the audience cheered the bowing performers. I returned to another lonely winter night. I feared the empty room where I would surrender myself.

George was sprawled on the couch, watching television when I walked in the door. I nodded politely as I passed.

"How was it?" he asked me.

"It was cool."

"Did you end up seeing that girl?" he asked.

"I did."

"Did you talk to her?"

"No," I told him.

"Well, she's probably some bitch from Johnson county anyway. Don't turn on me, Frank. They need to stay in Kansas City where the fake grass is always greener."

I smiled politely.

"If you really want to meet her, you should deliver a phony pizza to her dance class sometime."

"Do you ever see yourself with a family?" I asked him.

His eyebrows raised at the question he obviously didn't expect. "Probably someday. Why? What about you?"

"I don't know, really. That's so far from where I am now in life. The thought of marriage, it all sounds so...grandiose. I don't understand why marriage must be so gaudy. Materialism is *not* romantic. It'd be far more romantic to buy one of those big candy rings for a quarter in a gumball machine. Something so useless would suddenly become priceless. Instead of the ring proving the value of the love, the love would prove the value of the ring. That, to me, is romantic."

"Tattooing rings on your fingers would be cool. Then you know it's permanent."

"I would love to just wait outside, meet her now," I said. "Yet I know how women are about things like that. You can't just go up and talk to women like you do men. With guys, you can talk to them anywhere. Men will swap masturbation stories before they even catch each other's names. Women are so difficult."

"That's true," he resolved.

"Our society is not set up to approach people. We've created a fast world where everyone's in a hurry to get nowhere. And they're damn serious about it and everything else, too. I'm going to bed..."

My mind had wandered into the pleasant thoughts of having my voice amplified throughout the control room of a spiffy recording studio. In a few hours I would be there. I looked up at the clock covered with flour, hoping the telephone wouldn't ring again before my time was reclaimed. Outside, the wind whipped the snow in swirls of blinding white streaks under the streetlights. Cars were crammed down 23rd Street, sitting motionless as the world does when in motion. With every customer through the front door, the wind ransacked the lobby with a biting chill that stung the skin for a fleeting second. Life was not meant to survive under such conditions, I figured.

I tried desperately to appear task-free in representation of high labor needing to be sent home.

I had spent every night that week sitting in the lush control room of Lawrence's finest recording studio, Red House Studios. After several uneventful shows at the Outhouse, we decided the only way to regain our audience was to make another recording, our first full-length album of all new material. The sound quality would be impeccable. Throughout the week I had witnessed the slow birthing process of this recording, from the level adjustments of the drums to the placement of the sampled pizzicato strings. Tonight, my throne of the studio's couch would be turned over to the jury, my band. Tonight and the rest of the week was my turn to finish what we had started. I had spent months of quiet hours contemplating my approach. I was ready to give everything, and everything I would give.

"You can leave now, Frank," Tom told me.

I quickly pulled off my apron, already on my way to the time-clock.

I retreated to the back door, waving goodbye as I left. The bitterly cold wind knocked me stationary for a brief second. I stepped cautiously toward the mound of snow that contained the Ranchero. Clearing the windows with my arm, I chiseled the ice from the door handle with my key ring and slid inside, finding no resistance on the frozen seats. My breath immediately clung to the inside of the windshield in a strange crystal formation.

I turned on the headlights while digging under the seat for the plastic scraper. I would rather let the heater do the work, but I hadn't the time or the patience. The task took no more than three minutes at top speed, yet time enough to make my hands red and numb.

I turned on the radio to KJHK and listened patiently, sliding back into the stiff vinyl seat with my frozen hands stuffed deep inside my pockets. Bad Religion's *Yesterday* followed a commercial break. The recording was rough and unpolished, not at all like the songs we were currently constructing in the studio. The poor quality made me smile, like the haunt of a memory too pleasant to dwell upon. I turned it off to concentrate on how I would arrange my vocals to fit the bassoons.

The blinds in the recording studio trapped the intense light of the sun's reflection off the snow. It created a stronger source of light than the fixtures overhead. The week had been a grueling struggle for the most prominent audible dominance. All the clarity we had strived to develop was lost to a battle of self-importance. I felt the appropriate title of the album to be *Mud Pie*.

I held the bill in my hand, a total of one thousand, two hundred dollars. Surprisingly cheaper than we had guessed.

I reached in my pocket and pulled out a thin billfold. Inside were three one hundred dollar bills and two fifties. Many week's work went to achieve this goal. I laid the three larger bills down on the mixing board as the engineer, Ed Rose spliced the songs in the designated order for the master tape. George and Hazel stacked their money respectively without hesitation. Alan watched, looking a bit perplexed.

"Frank, can I talk to you?" he asked.

My brow sunk with caution. "Sure."

"Out here," he said with a gesture to the recording room.

I stood slowly, not feeling a good vibe from this.

He cornered me by the drums. I could tell by the glow of his cheeks that I would soon share his discomfort. Sweat accumulated on his fuzzy, blond mustache.

"I didn't know we were supposed to pay today," he whispered indiscreetly to an otherwise empty room.

"Well, we're finished today. Of course we're supposed to pay today."

"I thought they'd give us a bill—"

"To pay when we felt like it?" I asked. "No, they're a business. That's not the way things work."

276

"Yeah, well...I don't have it," he confessed lightly. "I didn't know it'd be done *this* way. I'll pay it," he sighed with deep resignation. "You just don't understand how hard it is to keep money. Especially without a job. I'll come up with the money, I'll talk to my parents."

"So what are we supposed to do right now?" I asked.

"If you can cover me for a week, I can come up with the money," he promised.

I shook my head, feeling not only annoyed with this, but still fuming over his inflexibility with his guitar level in the final mix.

I retreated to the control room and handed Ed one hundred more dollars. He allowed us to slide until the weekend.

We left the studio with a cassette tape of the final mix of the mud pie. Everyone bickered over who would get to listen first. Everyone except me.

The following week we had our first rehearsal since the recording. The first item on my agenda was to collect money from Alan. I waited by the front door until his parents dropped him off. He slowly stumbled up the steps, clutching a second guitar case in his hands.

"Hello," he told me as he opened the door. "My parents bought me a new Fender, check it out."

"Where's my money, Alan?" I demanded.

"Oh...yeah," he stammered. "I haven't had the chance to talk to my parents about it. It's all paid, right?"

I was immediately furious. "No, it's *not* paid. Not to *me!*"

"Shit, chill out, man," he said calmly, rubbing his arm. The flesh of his upper arm was covered with swirls of scars. "I'll talk to my parents tonight."

"I guess you can kiss your money goodbye," George told me several weeks later as he slouched to the side of the couch. A can of A&W Root Beer leaned in his relaxed hand. "Alan isn't going to pay you anything."

"I'll keep at him," I said dryly. "Now we have an album of material sitting on reels in my room. I'm too damn broke now to contribute any money to get it pressed."

"It's what we need to do, though. We can't get shows as long as the old records are falsely representing us."

"You know, speaking of Alan, what are all those scars?" I pondered. "Looks like his arms went through a meat grater."

"Let's call and find out," George said, leaning over to pick up the phone.

"Won't that be rude to ask?"

"Yeah, probably. Probably as rude as not paying you back," he said, dialing the number. "Yeah, is this Alan? Yes? Hey, Alan, this is George. What's happening? Not much...I just have a quick question. What the fuck are those disgusting scars on your arm? Yeah? No shit...did it hurt? Damn. Okay, that's all I wanted. I'll see you at practice tomorrow. Don't forget Frank's money. Oh...yeah, right. Well, when they get off work you should talk to them again. Okay, later."

I waited until he sat the phone down. "What did he say?"

"He had a bunch of bad tattoos a few years ago. His parents made him get them all scraped off by a doctor."

"You're shitting me..."

"Only if *he* was shitting *me*."

"What were they?" I asked. "A bunch of swastikas?"

"Knowing him, they were probably a bunch of naked ladies. Or a bunch of penises."

I laughed. "You know, those tattoos probably didn't look anywhere near as bad as the scars do."

"I think we've found the biggest loser possible to join our band," George said, laughing. "Maybe we should kick the fucker out. Demand that he pay up or take a hike."

"Guys..." Alan whined with uneasy wheezing between breaths. "I don't think it's fair. I don't even have a job. You don't know how hard it is for me."

"Maybe not," George said, trying to talk over Alan's unnerving pattern of spastic breaths. "You can't pay, you can't play."

He sighed uneasily with a whimper. "You guys don't know how hard I have it."

No one replied.

"Okay, Frank," he muttered heavily with defeat. "I'll bring you some money tomorrow night."

"You're going to come by my place?" I asked.

He exhaled painfully. "Yes."

"I'll be waiting for you."

Wait for him I did. It was an unseasonably nice night. I spent the majority of it on our balcony looking up at the stars that had been hidden under the gray winter sky for months.

A car pulled up, and sure enough, Alan had arrived as promised.

"What's happening?" I asked quietly from atop the balcony. My soft speaking voice carried easily through the motionless air.

He climbed the steps, each like thunder, like an adult child facing disapproval. He stood over me, shaking his head, breathing in that odd fashion again. I could assume by his convulsive breathing that this was something stressful for him.

"What's up?" I asked again.

"I'll give you all the money I have in the world," he cried with great sacrifice.

I held my hand out, unaffected by the difficulty he felt from this. He reached into his pocket and placed in my hand three rolls of pennies. The total amount—if counted and packaged correctly—one dollar and fifty cents.

"Are you kidding?"

"This is *all* I can give right now," he pleaded. "Maybe when I get a job...you guys just don't understand me."   "I guess not."

He stared for a second with weak, insecure eyes. "I've got to go home now." He winced with a deliberate cough as if parting from the coins would deliver his death.

I shook my head as he stumbled down the steps grudgingly. It was almost too unbelievable to stir animosity. As he rushed into his car, I laughed. I laughed quite a while. I couldn't wait to tell George. He was going to love this.

"Pizza?" the gentleman at the door asked me. "Did someone order pizza?"

"I guess so. Someone named Lippschitz in the Dance department. This is the Dance department, isn't it?" I asked, looking around at all the ballerinas stretching.

"Yeah, but there isn't a Lippschitz here. Do you have a first name?"

"Uh...no, I don't," I said quickly. "So what's going on in here?"

"Rehearsal," the guy told me as the dancers took their place in front of the instructor.

278

"For what?"

"*Coppélia*."

"I don't know much about it," I admitted as my eyes caught the woman of my dreams. I stood silently as the bottom of the pizza box burned my tender hands.

"See that guy there?" the man said, pointing to one of the male dancers. "His character makes dolls. And this girl here likes this guy over here."

I watched as he pointed, never fully leaving the sight of the most beautiful person in the world.

"But he doesn't like her because he's in love with one of the old man's dolls, so she pretends to be a doll to catch his interest."

"She is a doll," I said. "That's happened to me before. Then I popped a hole in her...can't get too rough with those things. Here, have the pizza," I forced it into his hands as I stared uncontrollably at her. The distance of twenty feet suddenly became a chasm that separated me from the rest of my life. "Who's that girl?"

"I don't know any of these people, but thanks for the pizza."

"She's beautiful," I said.

"Yes, she's kind of cute."

I nodded.

The water of Lone Star Lake lapped up against the dock, murky and gray like the sky overhead. I pulled my shirt off, feeling the material rub unevenly over my skin, coarse with goosebumps.

"It's pretty damn cold," I chattered. "Are you sure we should do this? That water must be freezing."

George dipped his toes, balancing on the edge of the old wooden dock. "No, it's not bad." He quickly pulled his shirt off and placed it next to his folded jacket.

I stood with my arms wrapped around my shivering body. "I can see my breath."

Without hesitation, he dove into the gray water, releasing a ring of waves around the point of impact. I waited for his limp body to float up. Ten feet away, his head surfaced with a gasp of breath.

"Cold?" I asked.

"Get in, hurry up," he demanded with a frightfully choppy tone.

I shook my head. At least I knew we wouldn't die of hypothermia. Not immediately. I dove outward into the icy waters that instantly shocked my body into severe tension. As I surfaced, I painfully choked down a breath. The water stung mercilessly like a swarm of wasps.

"Across and back," George gasped with stuttering breath. "That's probably about one-quarter mile. When it gets warmer, we'll head that way, over to the buoy."

My body still hadn't lost the feeling of shock. In fact, the sting of it was getting worse.

Together we swam silently to the other side amongst the grass and rocks and mud. The chill made me feel frantic to get out, but I knew that climbing up on the rocks would only perpetuate the cold. I stepped down, feeling the firmness of mud that gave no resistance. It was the texture of clay, solid from the winter.

Suddenly, it began to rain. It sizzled against the water that appeared as liquid mercury. The cold pellets smacked against my head. They felt partially frozen and hard, or maybe my senses were weakening.

The peaceful landscape offered adequate distraction as we slowly made our return. I spotted a small section of trees that had once been mangled by the violent grip of a Kansas tornado. I concentrated on them to occupy my mind.

Pulling my freezing body out of the water was as difficult as jumping in it. My limbs ached and my skin stung red as if sunburned. My breathing was choppy and irregular, but I felt worked, and it was a good feeling. The towel felt like sandpaper against my skin. The freezing rain belittled my efforts.

By the time we stumbled into our apartment, it was already dark outside. George resigned to the couch for the evening news as I made my way to the bathroom. A warm shower awaited me.

Just as I grabbed the door handle, the phone rang. I hesitated, allowing another ring to echo through our small apartment before I tiptoed to answer it.

"Hello."

"Is this Frank or George?"

"This is Frank. What's up Merle?"

"Good news. We've had a couple A&R reps from Sony Records check out our last show."

"Really?" I said, dumbfounded. "Are they going to sign you guys?"

"Doubt it. They just want us to make some demos to develop our sound. That doesn't mean they'd sign us, they'd just have custody of the recording of those songs until they would decide to *not* sign us. It's not a bad request, but we'll sit tight. Better offers are yet to come. If they're really interested, they'll propose a better offer."

I smiled at his earnestness. He knew what he was doing as he had all along. His approach wasn't for me, but if that's what music meant to him, then I respected his choice.

"Were you guys going to tour again this year?" he asked.

"Not if I can help it."

"Why not? You made a name for yourselves out there. I was hoping the Media Whores could join you. I'm only talking about a few weeks. Come on, man. You guys need to get out there again. You haven't played a show in months."

"We haven't been able to get a show!" I reminded him.

"Bullshit."

"Our audience is now comprised of a few nerdy musicians who spend too much time in guitar shops reading about Jimi Hendrix's picking style or Getty Lee's tone. That's hardly flattering to me."

"Maybe you should play more accessible music," he suggested. "I like what you're doing, don't get me wrong. You've carved your own little niche, and I'm impressed, but don't forget I'm one of those nerdy musicians from the guitar shops...if you want an audience, write music for one. It's all business, and it all begins with customers. The most successful bands in history were no more than sociologists with a good eye on trends. Specky knew. He created punk music for punk people. Make it simple, package it to your target audience, and watch the crowds flock. That's how you make it. Call it a sell-out if you want. I'll call it my art."

"I'm not sure all that really matters to me," I told him.

"I'm not sure I believe you," he protested. "To each his own. So what about the tour?"

"I'll think about it, Merle."

"You really should toss it around a while. Stay in the game, Frank."

I always hated hearing him refer to it as a game, despite the truth in it. "Well, I'll give it some thought, just for you."

"Okay. Talk to you later."

"Later on." I sat the phone down, thinking about the black stain in my memory: *Summer Tour.*

"What did he want?" George asked.

"He wanted to tour with us this summer."

"Look at this newscaster," he said, slouching on the couch. "I think she should share my bed. Do you want to drive me to the television station? By the time we'd arrive, it'd be over and she'd be leaving. What do you think?"

"Right now?"

"Well, only if you'll take me. I can't walk. Come on, it'd be fun."

I thought about it a second. "I need to take a shower. Here, you can borrow the Ranchero. The keys are on the counter."

"Okay," he said, standing eagerly. "I'll see you later." He left in a hurry, leaving the television running as background noise.

The grass felt cold against my legs. Itchy, but pleasant. My left arm had lost its feeling several minutes ago from supporting the weight of my head. It was a breezy spring evening, and George and I decided to turn our front lawn into an outdoor theater with the television set propped on the balcony.

As *The Green Slime* came to a close, I wondered what kind of fear I would have if a latex monster was chasing me. A monster with a poorly fitted head and rubber eyes that didn't move. Would this frighten me? I guess to some extent it could be more fearsome than a more imaginative monster.

"It's getting colder," George said. "Are we still going to swim? I think it will rain soon."

"It's almost midnight, we better leave now, then."

We both stood, stretching stiff limbs before hustling upstairs to shut down the television set.

"Do you think the people who made these films still aspire to create more?" I asked as we walked to the Ranchero.

"Probably. Unless they've seen just how bad their work actually turns out."

"Wouldn't the simple desire to grow in one's art outweigh the quality of the work?"

"Yeah, but a bad artist is still a bad artist," he said.

"Do you feel the Jerk Offs are a better band now than we were a year ago?"

"Definitely."

"Why?" I asked.

"We're more complex."

"If a band becomes more, then they become something different altogether, wouldn't you say?"

"Maybe the evolution of pop music is about to change," he said. "Maybe we're the ones to change it."

"Yeah, maybe. Then again, maybe not. I mean, that is our hunch, isn't it? That's the sole reasoning behind our band's existence at this point. We're not playing shows, we're not doing anything with this costly recording...what are we in it for these days? Our own ego's sake?"

"We got a show next week, what do you mean?" he said.

"Yeah, we're opening a local show at the Outhouse."

"Well, it's a show," he said.

"You know, I've been thinking about what Merle had said about another tour. Maybe it isn't such a bad idea. After all, we'd have better luck getting a show out there than we would in Lawrence."

"That last tour practically destroyed us. Kind of makes you wonder what would've happened if we hadn't toured," he contemplated. "If we had stayed here and kept playing shows, would we have control of this town right now? We were on a roll before we left."

"I sometimes wonder if me joining this band was the last decent idea I've had."

He flipped on the car's radio. A song played, one of highly produced, poor writing quality you hear on all commercial stations at all times. "Music really sucks these days."

"Something's about to break," I said. "You can always tell when the water gets this calm. There's no direction. Somewhere out there is a band that no one knows. A band with a dream, and that dream is about to change everything. Within three years, they'll redefine rock music."

"Maybe it's us," he said.

"Maybe."

"Hello, Lawrence," I said sarcastically into the microphone as five or six people sat at the far end of the Outhouse. I couldn't bare to be on the stage where my presence was the admission of failure. I wanted to walk away and pretend I never had anything to do with it. I looked over at Alan and felt an urge to slap him. There was no better time to start the show than preceding such a thought. "We're the Jerk Offs, you may remember us from last year. Or you may not. This is a new song: *Bounty the Cretin*."

Hazel delivered four powerful clicks and the band ignited with the most contorted and bent music available anywhere. The musicianship had transformed from raw angst to mechanical precision. I still hadn't assimilated to the rigidness of it.

Performing the set was hell. I desperately wanted to cut it short to remove myself from humiliation, but I dare not suggest it. Instead, I swallowed my pride and worked through each song with difficulty, all the while lying to myself and the few members of the audience about how much I really didn't mind.

Walking off the stage after the last song felt orgasmic. I had a secret wish to never have to walk back on it again. I wanted to end it then and there, but this was my life. This was my ambition from years ago, and the rut was carved with great time and passion of several challenging years. Walking out would be like walking out on myself.

"Hey, Frank," someone slurred at the edge of the backstage door. "Come on out here."

I stared into the darkness, lured by mere curiosity. A firm blow struck my shoulder, knocking me back as a stiff forearm pinned my neck hard against the wall. I stood face to face with Billy Christ.

He gazed into my eyes with unabridged hatred, clutching a bottle as he stumbled back and forth off the wall. "I was right about you. The Jerk Offs were a great band before you fucked it up. You killed that band. I wouldn't give two shits to wear your shoes. Without Specky, it's clear who *really* made the difference. You guys suck now. Look at how pathetic you are, pretty-boy! Gave you some shit and you went and cut your hair and changed your band's music. You're a joke, Frank. You never belonged out here, pretty-boy, Johnny-come-skately."

He stumbled away, spilling his bottle of malt liquor as he walked into the quiet parking lot. He climbed inside the passenger door of a waiting car that sped away into the night. I never saw Billy after that night.

I stood at the edge of the field looking up at the sky, at the clouds that seemed to glow a pale violet. My body ached from the impact of the fall. I had hit the bottom, it seemed.

"Frank," a timid voice requested from over my shoulder.

I turned quickly to a small girl, dressed appropriately goth for such a dismal night. I stared at her with distant eyes, waiting for her to introduce herself.

"Do you *not* remember me?" she asked.

For a split second I saw stormclouds consuming an evening sky as a small girl pushed a bike up a hill. The sound of the Fluorescent Condoms...then the vision faded into the face of this attractive young goth rocker standing before me, bridging many years to the present. I felt foolish for not knowing.

"It's me, Kimberly Powers. From Iola."

"I tried to wipe out all my Iola memories," I reasoned. "Looks like I've succeeded, huh? Sorry."

"I like your hair. You look good these days."

"That's nice to hear. And you look so...grown. You even have breasts. Where'd you get those?"

"Where'd I get them?" she asked casually, making it clear I couldn't offend her. "It happens to the best of us eventually."

"I'm still waiting for it to happen. So how is Iola?"

"Don't know," she said. "Maybe I should ask my parents. I live here now. I'm going to KU next semester."

"Are you following me?"

"I haven't stopped following you since I first met you."

I laughed. She didn't.

"Did you see our show?" I asked.

"I did. You guys changed. Why?"

"Seemed like a good idea at the time."

"Quite a drastic change."

"Apparently not for the better," I sighed. "We haven't had a good show since last year."

"Yeah, I remember. Last year at this time I saw you guys open Mad Parade. I couldn't even get to the stage. You guys were *huge*. So how was your tour?"

"It changed my life." I delivered a partial smile. "So, was growing up in Iola as ghastly for you as it was for me?"

"I think it was easier for us than it was for you," she admitted.

"Us? You mean, more than you?"

"More than *me*?" she asked. "Are you kidding? My class had more punks than your class."

"I didn't know that. Stanley never told me," I mumbled, feeling at once amazed and perplexed. "How was it easier? Let me guess...we diminished the shock value."

"Well, there could be that, but that's not what I meant."

"What did you mean?" I asked.

"On weekends we would travel to Lawrence just like you guys used to. We'd stand in line like the rest, waiting for those inspiring shows. Those crowded Jerk Offs shows at the Outhouse made us believe."

I felt I had swallowed my tongue. My eyes tensed. "So...how many punk kids are there in Iola?"

"Let's put it this way—If Iola hated you a few years ago, they *really* hate you now for what you started. My ride's leaving, Frank, I need to go."

I nodded with a smile.

"I'll see you around," she promised as she turned to leave.

My heart raced as I stood in silence. I felt powerful and suddenly alive. I bounded through the rear door of the Outhouse once again where George slumbered against the drum riser sipping casually from a can of A&W Root Beer.

"George," I said. "We're touring this summer."

The refrigerator was stocked for the nuclear fallout. A stack of corn purchased off the bed of a farmer's truck filled the bottom shelf. We had dined heavily on it throughout the week. I grabbed the pitcher of lemonade as the messages poured from the answering machine.

The bittersweet aftertaste of lemonade contains more memories than the most meticulous photo album. I drink it for the memories.

"George, this is Holly...the newscaster...um, you gave me your number and I'm calling you! Surprise! If this isn't a fraternity hazing initiation, I'd like to meet for coffee. You can call me at..."

"Mr. Esposito, this is Hastings video. We're calling about a couple overdue titles..."

"Frank, what's the word? This is Merle. Got your message, so you want to tour after all! That's the man I fell in love with...give me the details, give me a call! Sorry I missed your show the other night. Mandatory practice, then my girlfriend ate my homework, and...and...I'll just talk to you later..."

"Frank Smith, I was given your number by a promoter in Manhattan, Kansas," spoke an unfamiliar womanly voice. "He told me I should call you about setting up a date in Lawrence. I'm booking for a band out of California right now and have no contacts in Lawrence. If you could be so kind as to call me back and help me, I'd really appreciate it. Oh, the band is Cringer. Here's my number..."

I picked up the phone and dialed the number as she recited it over the machine.

"Hello?" asked an edgy voice—more irritated than the tone on my machine.

"I believe I got a call from you today. My name is Frank and I'm from Lawrence, Kansas."

"Ah, yes! What can you tell me about the Outhouse?"

"Well, that's the place you'd want to get a show booked for Cringer. It's one of the older punk rock venues in the country, and it can really pack a crowd with good promotion. Would it be summer?"

"Early in the summer. Next month. Actually, I have the tour almost entirely laid out. I'm filling in the gaps right now. There's some space between Boulder and St. Louis, a space of a couple days. It's been a pain in the ass."

"Is this the first tour you've booked?" I asked.

"No, in fact I'm booking another one for a band I know. They're going out to the east coast and I have most all the dates ready for them, too."

"Who are they?" I asked.

"Neurosis."

"When does their tour begin?"

"Starts in the middle of June and goes about three weeks."

Perfect, I thought. Just enough time, just long enough. "Tell you what, I'll trade you all the information you would need to get shows in Lawrence and Kansas City for the phone numbers and dates of all the clubs you have booked for Neurosis."

"That's reasonable," she said. "Why would you want their dates?"

"Because I'm in a band called the Jerk Offs and we plan to tour this summer, too."

"So you're thinking about trying to get on some of their shows?"

"I'd like to open *all* their shows if the venues would let me!" I told her. "Got a pen?"

"That's it," I said enthusiastically, gently setting the phone down. "We've got our second tour completely booked."

George stared blankly at the television set, watching the color radar track the day's tornadoes. His work clothes were folded neatly in his lap. A lime green beach towel wrapped his lean waist like a kilt. He was already late for work. "Three weeks, huh?"

"Two weeks with the Media Whores and a band called Neurosis," I specified. "The first week with just the Media Whores."

"So our guarantee is one hundred dollars split between us and the Media Whores. Fifty dollars a night, then."

"Well, for what that's worth. You know a guarantee is rarely kept up. Besides, we'll be playing with two other bands every night. I didn't want to jack the price too much to kill our chances at getting the dates."

"Fifty dollars would be adequate if we really got that money. Three weeks would be nothing. What next?" he asked.

"When we get *Mud Pie* back from the pressing plant we'll send it out. If the copies arrive on time, the radio stations will have them about two weeks before we play their town. Plenty of time."

"Cool," George said, smiling proudly. "We're back again."

"We've got eleven shows booked, that's about ten more than we've had this entire year."

The phone rang, vibrating in my hand. I picked it up and pressed its cold surface against my face. "Hello."

"Frank?"

"Yeah?"

"This is Norm!"

"Where are you?" I asked.

"I'm down here at the Shuttle. I have about an hour before I leave, come on down here. We can mosey over to Taco Johns to get some food. Just you and me."

"I'll be there in a moment," I told him before hanging up.

When I skidded up to the back door of Pizza Shuttle, I found him lounging against a brick wall. His long black hair tickled the wind as he smiled like a child with each step I advanced.

"Long time..." he said, throwing a firm arm around my neck. The sleeve of his red flannel was soft against my skin. "Nice haircut."

"Where have you been?" I asked happily.

"Man," he said, lighting up a cigarette as we began walking across the parking lot. "I've been everywhere." He stood motionless a moment, flicking the lighter against the wind as I took a few quick and excited steps toward our destination. "Why the hurry?" he asked as he cupped his hand around the cigarette. "Do you know how to mosey?"

"I assume you walk really slow," I said sarcastically.

"Ah, it's more than that!" he told me gingerly with a grin as he sucked on his lit cigarette. He peered at me with squinty, thoughtful eyes. "I've moseyed across this country twice now. It's like this..." He took one calm step slowly after another, advancing at a pace that would annoy a retirement community. "See, this way you miss *nothing*."

I slowed to pace myself. He was right. There was something magical in it, something strangely therapeutic. The art of moseying...

"It's nice to step out of the traffic for a change. It makes you realize the speed everyone chooses to live their lives. So the band, how are things?" he asked calmly with a smooth drag from the cigarette.

"Things have been better. We've booked our second tour in an effort to regain ourselves."

"Everything went downhill after Specky went his way, eh?"

"Well, pretty much," I confessed. "We just became something different altogether. The audiences don't seem to be as into it as we are."

"In pop culture, you become branded by your own reputation. Any changes are never accepted when there's a new face coming at the consumer every day. Rock and roll is nothing but commercialism, and there's always someone out there planning on taking your place. It's the way of the world, I hate to say. So why did you change the music?"

"We just wanted to evolve it more thoroughly."

"That's George's reasoning. What is *your* reasoning?"

"My reasoning," I mumbled, feeling my feet rush ahead a moment before falling back. I stared at my destination, at the taco joint across the bustling intersection. "It's not what I thought it was. I expected a lot more."

"I'm not surprised to hear you say that. No offense, but I always figured your faith would eventually outweigh the potential of your dreams. Not that you aren't an amazing vocalist, because your stage-presence reduces me to envy. It's just a small pond with little room to expand. Is the work more than you bargained for?"

We stopped to wait for traffic to pass before crossing the busy street, slowly.

"Actually, I love the work. It's the response of my efforts that bothers me."

I opened the door for him, feeling the cool blanket of air rest itself on my pale shoulders. We placed our orders and took our food to a booth in the far corner.

"How do you feel about the songs themselves?" he asked. "Do you like the new style?"

"Oh, yes," I responded quickly, confidently. "George, I feel, is a musical genius. What he has created is so far ahead of the times. I'm very honored to be a part of it. Really."

"Do you still enjoy performing?"

"Not always. It's more a job now."

"Maybe it's time for a new job, then. Here, I have something for you. Something you can take on tour. It's for luck," he said, reaching into his bag. His long black hair fell loosely over his solid cheekbones. He presented me with a wreath, a small wrapping of graying leaves. "It's sage. Burn it for good luck."

I grabbed it, holding it in my hands like a coiled snake. "Thanks."

"Don't mention it. I had to lighten my load anyway. See this bag? This is everything I own. The less I have, the more free I become."

"So now you're above possessions, you cocky bastard?" I asked snidely.

He laughed with loose comfort. "Absolutely not. Every possession can tell the story of a lifetime if you take the time to listen. That Government Issue shirt, when did you get it? How and why?"

"You want an answer?" I asked.

"Sure!"

"I've had this for years. I got it when I was in high school. It was in August at the Outhouse, I remember. My friend Stanley and I both got shirts because we had some spare cash from our parents. That was a good night. The shirts cost eight dollars each."

"How was the show?" he asked.

"Good. I was happy just to be away for the weekend."

"I thought that show was awful, or maybe I was just too drunk at the time. I think I got my ass kicked that night." He took a minute to reflect on the dark clouds that lingered over his blind-side, the clouds that served to power his belief. I knew the feeling. They powered mine, too. "Everything has a story. *Everyone* has a story…"

"So where are you heading next?" I asked.

"I may go up north. Never been to Canada."

"When?"

"As soon as I leave this restaurant."

"That's soon… Anything you want me to tell the others?"

"No," he replied quickly. "Don't even tell them you saw me."

We rose together, staring hard into each other's eyes as we prepared our farewells. We smiled in unison where words would've cluttered our otherwise perfect communication. We walked to the door in silence.

As I stepped out into the sun, I smiled upon the memory of his voice snarling passionately to me in my youth. He had been a friend long before I had ever met him.

"I've always looked up to you, Norm," I confided. "Thank you for everything."

He smiled, standing in the glare of the setting sun. I squinted, trying desperately to see him through the radiance of the blinding light cast from the distant horizon. It was calling him home.

"This is your life, live it," he said before turning.

I stood silently, watching him mosey around the corner following the blind lead of his heart. He would wander forever down the trails of my warmer memories. That was my final visit with Norman Malley. His trip through Canada would be cut short by an accidental collision with a semi-truck, abruptly ending his young life.

"This is Pizza Shuttle, you're on the air," I announced into the phone.

"I'm what?" a confused voice asked. She hesitated briefly before continuing. "I need to get some pizzas."

"That's what we do."

"Well," she said firmly, her voice edgy and annoying. "I need to pick up ten pizzas for my boyfriend's fraternity."

How subservient, I thought. "Okay."

"Just make them all pepperoni."

"No vegetarian?"

"A couple cheese, I guess," she told me with a high-pitched, nasally voice. I could almost hear the silver spoon clicking against her teeth as she spoke down to me. "They can deal with it."

"Fifteen minutes."

"I'll be there. My name is Rahan Sankar."

"Okay, then, bring thirty dollars. Bye-bye," I said, neglecting her response as I hung up the phone.

I only had a half hour left of my shift before the tour would officially begin. After I finished making the ten-pie order, I rushed into the back walk-in cooler.

The contrasting temperatures within the cramped icy quarters felt good against my warm body. In a matter of seconds I stood completely exposed, staring down at my clothing on a stack of cheese boxes. I lifted the dusty apron and put it over my head. Its coarse fabric was rough against my firm nipples. It felt as if I was wearing a red party dress with my ass perfectly revealed.

I strutted to the front once again, more than adequately aware of the flopping motion of my penis beneath the apron. I had always fancied the idea of working in such loose quarters.

I was anxious for Tom to arrive. He was either going to love this stunt or absolutely hate it. It was my last day, what was he going to do—fire me?

The phone rang just as I cut the last of the ten pizzas. I bounced to the front counter, feeling loose and comfortable. Public nudity is so underrated.

"Pizza Shuttle, how can I best serve you?" I said into the phone.

"Do you guys have pizza?"

"Yes, that's correct," I said as the front door flew open. I didn't look, but I smiled at the thought of their reception to the partially naked man behind the counter. I'd try to play it off casually. I continued with the call as I ignored the counter entirely until I had completed the order.

When I glanced up, I was shocked to find myself staring into the poisonously intimidating eyes of my dreamy dancer. I took a step back—one of defensive measures as I gazed into those powerfully hypnotic eyes for the very first time.

"Is there a dress code here?" she asked irritably.

I nodded with a fixated glare.

She stood uncomfortably, watching me stare like a savant. "I'm here for the ten pizzas. I'm Rahan."

I nodded again, or still.

"Here's my money," she told me, reaching across the counter with three ten-dollar bills. She seemed careful to avoid physical contact. I couldn't help but notice the gaudy engagement ring on her finger. I hadn't noticed it before. "I'm kind of in a *hurry*, please."

I retreated backward to avoid flashing her my ass. I picked up the stack of pizzas and slid them across the counter. "Thanks."

"Maybe you should get some clothes on," she snapped as she walked to the front door—out of my life and out of my dreams.

I turned just in time to see Tom swaggering through the back door.

"What the hell is going on here?!" he demanded with a smile. "Good Lord... I need to get my camera."

"Tom," I said softly, feeling the cold wind of reality trample the fun of my jovial prank. "I need to go. I'm not feeling well."

"You're looking worse," he said. "Maybe you should shave your ass. Or at least comb and part it."

I stared at him with a straight face.

"Get out of here," he grunted. "Have a good vacation."

I wasted no time dressing myself and finding the exit. I opened the door of the Ranchero and slipped inside it comfortably like an old sock. I stomped firmly on the accelerator, releasing my tension with breakneck speed as I raced through the parking lot. My car was all I had. It was my home. The Ranchero was family.

I rounded the corner just as an old beat-up butterscotch 1967 Valiant Scamp made the same turn the opposite direction. We collided hard with the sound of an explosion. The Ranchero's gray metal hood folded like a deck of cards. My heart felt much the same.

I stepped out of the wreckage, looking down at the frightful mess as steam hissed from both engines. I shook my head, furious in disbelief. Although I somehow evaded injury, the Ranchero was history.

The driver of the shabby Scamp jumped out of her own heaping mess. "I'm so sorry. I guess I was going fast..."

"Yeah, well...no shit."

"I'm sorry, really, I am!" she offered with limited persuasion.

I threw her a hard glance before giving a more detailed examination of my poor Ranchero. It had lived a fruitful life. I would miss it.

I glanced down at the Scamp's tags with their elite Johnson county sticker. Figures. "You've totaled my car."

"Yeah, mine, too. I love this car," she said pensively. "I've been through so much with this boat...I'm afraid a flat tire would've totaled the value of these cars just as effectively. Excuse the humor... I'm really sorry about this."

"Yeah, well..."

"My dad's a mechanic," she offered politely. "Maybe he can fix them. Hell, I may as well just get a bike, or some roller skates."

I looked down upon her with a firm glare. When I caught the stream of her eyesight pouring from her calm puppy dog eyes, I felt very little of anything. Her soft brown hair was pulled tightly into a ponytail. Her nose fit enormously on her heart-shaped, mousy face.

"I'm going to be late for work," she said. "In fact, if you don't mind, maybe tomorrow we can deal with all this?"

"I won't be around tomorrow," I told her flatly. "I'm leaving for two weeks, early in the morning."

"Vacation?"

"Tour."

"You're in a band?" she asked curiously.

I nodded shortly with squinting eyes that advertised my irritation.

"What band?"

"You wouldn't know," I told her abruptly.

"Okay, tough-guy, what fucking band are you in?"

I shot a hard glance that she returned effortlessly. "The Jerk Offs."

She busted into laughter. "I'll have to tell my mother that, she'll love it! How exciting! I just love music. What do you play?"

"I scream."

"That is *so* cool. I haven't got a creative bone in my body," she confessed as I examined the Ranchero's tires to see if it could still be driven. I edged her out of my way as best I could to better concentrate. Her style-less jogging shoes were as loud as the steam hissing from both engines, and equally annoying. "I think that'd be such a wonderful way to live, playing music. What kind of music is your band? Gospel?"

"Punk."

"Yeah, I would've thought that. You know, you seem kind of agitated, and I understand," she said. "We're both screwed. I'm sorry about this."

"I'm sorry, too."

She sighed heavily. "I don't know where I'll get the money to get another car."

"Same with me."

"Maybe you'll make enough money on your tour," she considered.

"Yeah, right." I knelt before the Ranchero, running my fingertips across the mangled fender.

"Well, you never know," she told me optimistically.

I hadn't the desire to discuss such a thing with this stranger, but the words came without regard. "The odds of making a living in the arts is slim to none. For every success story out there, there's about ten thousand people aspiring for the same goal. It's a *very* saturated business. You're better off playing the lottery. Besides, punk music will *never* top the charts or fill concert arenas. The day a band like...Bad Religion makes it big, I'll fucking pack my bags and move to...Texas. That's the way it is, and that's why I love it."

"I really wouldn't know much about it," she admitted. "But I think it's cool!"

"Yeah," I said bitterly, shaking my head.

"Should we call the cops about this?"

"I'd prefer not," I told her. "I don't like cops."

"Yeah, I don't either, really. We could exchange numbers and see if I can get my dad to fix them for us. Here, let me get a pen."

I bent down and looked at the hood of the Ranchero. Steam rose like the smoke of a last cigarette.

"Here," she said as she scribbled on a piece of scrap paper. "When you get back from your tour, call me and we'll take care of all this. You'll have to tell me about your trip, too. I never get to go anywhere like that...never take any trips. I could vacation vicariously through your second-hand dissertation. This is a shitty way to begin your tour, I realize."

I stood and grabbed the slip of paper. "I'll call you." I looked down at the name. "Jill Johnson."

Little did I know the happiness this person would bring in the years that followed.

The band had endured several major fights by the time we had reached Reading, Pennsylvania. Luckily, sides were quickly taken in the first week and our subsequent silence temporarily eliminated further quarrels. I hadn't spoken a word to Hazel or Alan for the past three shows, which was how I wanted it.

The venue in Reading was the nicest hall we had yet played—an old theater converted into a club called the Silo.

The first band of the evening was a regional group named Leather Rose. They seemed to have achieved immortal fame without anyone else realizing. They sported the image of the Ramones, but their music represented nothing of the same quality.

Their bodyguards out-numbered the band members two to one. The band out-numbered their fans four to zero.

George and I sat at the back of the hall drinking heartily the complimentary pop as their "roadie" walked onto an empty stage to introduce the self-appointed rock icons to a silent, small crowd.

"Hello, Reading...are you ready to *rock and roll*?!" he exclaimed quite seriously to the crowd.

Silence.

"I'm talking about Leather Rose! These guys have just completed a full-scale, major tour of Pennsylvania," he declared enthusiastically. *"Are you ready to rock...and...roll!?"* he repeated.

This time George and I laughed loud enough for him to realize there actually were people in attendance. Our heckling roused the steady drinkers at the bar into a toast. The band took the stage, unaffected by the lack of response, living safely inside a bubble of false hope.

"This, Frank," George said over the annoying music, "is what I hate about rock and roll."

"I understand perfectly."

He tapped the sweaty glass of soda with a stiff finger. "The odd thing is if we were to achieve our ultimate goal, we'd be playing for a bunch of fucking idiots like these guys. It makes me really reconsider my ambitions."

"What do you suppose goes through their heads?" I asked. "Maybe they just need it to justify their existence."

"I'll believe in *myself*," he replied pompously. "People are so weak. I know everyone has had their shit to deal with—I'm certainly no exception. So why do the experiences that made others so weak make me so strong?" He smiled with calm enthusiasm. He took the time to finish his beverage before commenting. "And when those tanks roll down the street with my face plastered on them, I'll remember you, Frank."

"Thanks, man."

"Did I ever tell you about the time I played at the high school talent show?" he asked.

"No," I said. "Do tell."

"I was a guitarist back then. We were playing *Stairway to Heaven*, which is quite a stretch for a high school cover band, huh? We had two guitarists, but on this song, I had the solo. Halfway through, I stepped on my cord, pulling it out without realizing it. I stepped up like a total cock-rocker to take the stand in front of everyone to show them my licks, unaware the guitar I could hear was his, not mine. I was practiced. I was prepared for this. Finally, the girls would see what I was made of. As I struck that first note, there was nothing! I stood like a lame idiot—a novice guitarist unable to find my way back in the song. I fumbled on the floor, crawling on my hands and knees to find my missing cord. I stared into the crowd like a fool, totally frozen. Needless to say, I didn't get laid that night."

"Look how far you've come," I said, pointing at the small crowd scattered throughout the large club.

"Yeah, we're moving...nowhere fast."

"Alan has his parent's credit card. Did you notice that?" I asked.

"I noticed he's been eating very well. My parents never gave me anything, and if they had offered, I would've declined. Although when my grandmother died, my mother got a little bit of inheritance. I think I got twenty dollars, which is twenty more than I expected. My mother spent all her inheritance on furniture. She did buy a piano, which was nice. I was glad when my granny finally died. She had Alzheimer's. We used to have to get all dressed up to go visit her every Sunday afternoon at the nursing home. Every time I'd walk up to hug her as my mother insisted, my grandmother would stiffen up and say in this gruff voice: *Kiss me on the neck, boy. Don't look at my titties. Kiss me on the pussy, boy!* This was my grandmother! The thought of that could've easily made me abstinent for life...all that emotional scarring and no inheritance. Too bad because the odds of us making a living off music is very unlikely," he decided quickly. "We love music too much to make it in this industry. All the better...I couldn't live with myself if I was to play crap like this."

"There's still the lottery, I suppose."

A young punk boy tapped my shoulder. His stubby blond mohawk was gelled into a crisp fin.

"Yes?" I asked, leaning to face him.

"Sullivan!" George exclaimed.

My face lit with a smile. It was Sullivan, the boy who saved us in Pittsburgh with food and tip money the previous year. He looked entirely different. He looked entirely punk.

"How are you guys?" he asked.

"Better."

He threw a scowl to the stage. "Who are these jokers?"

"Who cares?" George replied. "Sorry we didn't play Pittsburgh again."

"I saw your tour dates in *Maximum RockNRoll*," he said. "I took the day off to road trip here. I'm excited to see you guys. Will you be playing any songs like *Persistence, Resistance*?"

I shook my head.

"I know this sounds cheesy," he said. "But that song changed my life."

His new punk image had already given that away.

"I'm going to get a Coke," he told us. "I'll be back."

As he turned, we were struck by our band name spray-painted with enormous green letters on the back of his leather biker jacket.

"...collect call from...Frank...will you accept charges?" the operator asked Stanley.

"Sure," he complained with a deep and exhausted sigh.

"What's up, Stanley-boy?" I exclaimed.

"Just you, jackass. What's with the collect call?"

"Had to hear your lovely voice...how are things?" I asked.

"Where are you?"

"I'm outside this club called Populous Pudding in Willimantic, Connecticut. We just played."

"Did you get paid?" he asked.

"Kind of. The people here are very accommodating. We're staying with this tax attorney, actually. His name is Charlie, and he's a great guy. He loves hardcore for some reason. Has a great house, very friendly. Fed us tons of food, and there's lots of space to sleep."

"That's cool."

"Yeah, it is, for a change. We played our first show with Neurosis tonight. They really dug the keyboard sampler. They asked George a lot of questions about it. They're a good band, very intense."

"How's everyone getting along?" he asked.

"Horribly," I told him. "I've spent a lot of time riding with the Media Whores. I only talk to George."

"That's too bad."

"Really? I think that's great! Saves my sanity."

"Have you cleaned the van lately?" he asked.

"Of course not."

"Remember when I was at your place a couple weeks back?"

"Yeah," I said.

"Well, I left you a gift under the mattress. I knew no one would be cleaning, so I hid it there."

"What is it?"

"Something I felt you should have," he said.

"Now I'm curious...any hints?"

"No."

"I'll have to do some digging tonight," I told him.

"Feeling like things may be picking up for the band?" he asked.

"Not really. The audiences generally don't know what to think of our music. The serious punk kids hate it since we don't play by formula. They laugh at us. No one is buying *Mud Pie*, either."

"That must be hard," he said.

"It is."

"How are things with the Media Whores? Are you ready to kill them?"

"Not at all. There's been a representative from Empire records meeting them at shows here and there. They're supposed to have several reps come up from New York City tomorrow night. We're playing at a restaurant in Storrs, Connecticut."

"Good for them," he said.

"I need to go check the van to see what's there."

"You do that," he said. "I'll talk down to you later."

"All right, pal. Me and you..."

"...against the world," he concluded. "Goodbye."

I sat the phone down and took a deep breath of the cool New England air. A thousand scents filled my mind with memories scattered throughout my life. It was a good place to be.

I waited to check the van until everyone had retired to the comforts of Charlie's house. Sitting on the edge of the floorboard with the door wide open, I propped a flashlight overhead against a pile of clothes. I crept my hand under the musty mattress. It felt cool, slightly damp. Suddenly, my fingers slipped across a stiff folder. I pulled it gently into the dim light. I recognized it immediately. It was the short essay I had written for my Psychology class in high school. It was about positive role models, the Jerk Offs. The title brought forth a flood of memories: *The Day I Will Know Success*.

I reached inside my small bag to locate the sage Norm had given for the trip. I couldn't think of a better time than this. Planning ahead, I stashed a lighter in my bag just for this occasion. I ignited the dry stems and watched as it crackled a glowing orange that quickly withered into a blackened char.

293

I looked down at the essay and flipped the page. My eyes fell immediately upon a line from which I always remembered Norm telling the crowd. "This is a night of your life. Live it accordingly."

Smoke rose from the sage, filling my senses with a familiar scent, marijuana. There was a difference, though ever-so-slight. Suddenly the van vibrated with flashes of blue and red that spun like unearthly spirits. I looked up to see a police car across the street with its lights ablaze. I scurried to put out the sage, rubbing it against the interior wall of the van as the glowing stems cracked and flaked into a smoking mess on the floor.

"What's going on in here?" the officer asked me.

"Just hanging out," I said casually.

"This your van?"

"It is."

"From Kansas?" he asked.

"That's right."

"What's that smell?"

"This," I told him, handing the smoldering sage.

He looked at it without touching it. "What is it?"

"It's a gift from a friend. It's sage. It's a spiritual thing, I suppose. At least that's what he'd say."

The cop stared at me with a brisk, cold expression. I returned it.

"You been drinking?" he asked.

"No, not for a few years."

"What are you doing out here?" he asked.

"I'm a houseguest of Charlie's." I gestured to the enormous house lumbering at the top of the hill.

He stared directly into my eyes. I stared directly back with underlying contempt masked with a pleasant demeanor.

"You keeping firearms?" he asked.

"No."

"I don't want you staying out here late, keeping up the neighbors."

"I won't."

"Well," he mumbled, taking another quick and cautious glance at Charlie's quiet house. "Get on with your business, but do it inside."

"Okay," I said as I gathered my things.

I spent the night sleeping on the porch with Neurosis.

"This is it," I told George as we drove through the streets of Storrs, Connecticut. "Taco Tyrone's."

We pulled into the parking lot where a massive plaster taco was perched high atop a signpost. The paint had long since faded on the taco, giving it a rather unsavory appearance. I would imagine that the plaster taco was as bad for business as it was good. Being wedged between a tattoo parlor and a taxidermist wasn't all that helpful, either.

Inside, there seemed barely enough room for our equipment, let alone an audience. Dull blue walls reflected light from open windows. The wall next to each table was stained with the splatter of salsa. Flies buzzed around the room like a miniature airport. Stiff, wooden seats occupied few patrons. The food, it was said, was amazing.

We designated a stage area next to the jukebox, right beside the velvet painting of the store owner, Tyrone. In the portrait he stared longingly into the distance with passionate and contemplative eyes. A thick white turtleneck covered his dark neck. His ethnicity wasn't clear in the painting. Come to think of it, it wasn't clear in real life, either. Tight curls of dark hair were gelled and parted down the middle. It appeared as oozing motor oil. The painter had captured this effect quite well. Too well...

The food was free for the bands, and we took full liberty on Tyrone's generosity. After I had eaten all I could, I ate a bit more before retreating to the van. As I sat alone, enjoying the quiet, Alan came out to ruin my peace.

"Frank, I can't handle this," he seethed with hostile resentment as his hands twitched annoyingly. Verde sauce hid sloppily in the corner of his mouth, clinging to his fuzzy mustache.

"Can't handle what?" I asked.

"This type of living. We're barely eating out here. I haven't had a good night's sleep in two days."

I laughed.

"This isn't for me," he threatened gravely. "I may need to take a bus home."

"Listen—*deal with it*," I said firmly, feeling no more desire to even discuss such a thing. I looked down at my essay, which I clutched in my hands. "Did you ever learn *Persistence, Resistance?*"

"I know it flawlessly," he stated proudly.

"Okay," I told him as I stood to leave. "That's all I need to know."

I stepped outside the van, feeling the joy of having him out of my space. I would walk until I kept it that way. As I wandered down the ragged sidewalk cracked like dry skin, I spied a couple of young kids sneaking through the alley. When they saw me, they hastily went about their crime with a mad dash to the parking lot of Taco Tyrone's. They grabbed hold of the signpost and began desperately climbing the shaft to reach the plaster taco.

Tyrone burst out the kitchen door, clutching his apron with thick hands. He clenched a forceful fist firm in the air. "You kids get down off that taco!"

I walked to the tattoo parlor, clutching my essay.

The odor of cigarette smoke lingered in the joint's stale air, foul like death. The faded white walls were stained from the smoke, plastered with rows of pictures of standard tattoo art clichés.

"What can I do for you?" the old man leaning against the counter asked with a tattered voice, deep and rough.

"I want a tattoo," I told him. "Will you take an out-of-state check?"

"Where from?"

"Kansas. I'm in a band that's playing at Taco Tyrone's."

"Will it bounce?" he asked.

"Doubt it."

"All right, then. What would you like?"

"Something simple, all black. Let me show you." I took a pen and paper from the poorly kept desk. I began to draw the simple logo of 7 Seconds, along with the title of one of their songs.

"That's it, huh?" he asked.

"That's it."

"Committed for life..." he mumbled.

"Yes, sir."

He nodded his fat head, slowly eyeing me up and down as he scratched his scraggly gray beard. "Let's do it," he resolved, leading me to a nearby chair.

The lights burnt a vibrant red onto my scrawny frame. The bright illumination hid the audience before me—an audience of underaged, suburban kids who had paid a lofty door charge at this dive of a Metal club in New Haven, Connecticut. How I despised Metal music...and such unresponsive crowds.

"This is our last song," I announced to the lethargic crowd. I'm sure they were happy to hear. I looked over at George, who looked right at me. "We have made a lot of changes in the past year. I just want to state—for the record—that at least we never went Metal. I'd like to dedicate this song to the few people who always believed. This song is called *Persistence, Resistance*."

George's eyes widened, and I could feel the discomfort surround me. He grabbed my shoulder and edged me over to the drums. "What?" he demanded.

"For old time's sake," I told him. "Can you remember how to play it?"

"Of course, but..."

"Well, let's do it, then," I said.

Hazel nodded at me with a belligerent smile.

"We've got nothing more to prove, George," I told him. "Nothing we haven't proven already."

I turned once again to the crowd, staring into the bright, wondrous lights of the center of all attention. Somehow, I could feel the tension of the final curtain over my shoulder. It would have to wait for one last song.

"Remember, kids," I said to the crowd. "This is a night of your life."

George slammed against the bass with his pick, igniting the song into life that surfaced an intense and wild passion from within. I jumped forward, clutching the microphone, feeling the predatorial drive of the music that had always moved my life with great ferocity. Once there was nothing that mattered more. I would never forget that time. The power of my belief had somehow made me vulnerable to the voices that breathe down my neck daily by the faceless pedestrians. The thickest of shells, the toughest of souls—all the burdens that would haunt my world at night—sharing my bed only with endurance.

No, I would never forget those days.

For those in the crowd, they were watching the memory of something wonderful, a band truly worthy of legendary caliber—the band that existed before I ever wandered upon a stage. A time when I was just another face in the crowd, fueled by passion and faith, committed for life.

It was an overcast day in Burlington, Vermont when we arrived that fateful day. The show had a typically poor turn-out. After we had loaded our equipment back into the van, I wandered around the block aimlessly. It was quiet and strangely cold. I could tell I was far north, far from home. I didn't belong there.

As I returned, Alan pulled me aside by my arm, squeezing tightly to my fresh tattoo. I knocked him back forcefully.

"I'm leaving in the morning," he threatened.

"We're down to our last two shows," I scoffed. "What the hell?"

"I can't take this. It's been almost two weeks. We haven't even made a profit."

I shook my head as George and Hazel wandered up to us.

"That was the worst show we've played in a long time," George said.

"Yeah," I agreed as Alan peered away from all of us. "Alan here wants to take off."

"Without you guys," Alan snarled fiercely. "I'm sleeping in the van—"

"What's new?" George growled.

"And in the morning I'm taking a bus back to Lawrence," he finished.

Everyone stood in a circle, seething as the Media Whores exited the club with several well-dressed executives from Empire records. Merle gave me a quick thumbs up. I smiled. I knew immediately what he meant.

"I think it's time we ended this whole thing," Hazel said. "There's no point."

"What do you mean?" I asked.

"It's time we break up the band," she said.

I was speechless. What would I do? How would I live? What would motivate me to rise each morning? "I don't know if agree."

"I do," George said to my surprise. "We've over-stayed our welcome."

"Glad to hear it," Alan asserted. "Because I quit anyway."

"Then that's it," George said flatly. "The Jerk Offs are over."

I breathed deeply. The guillotine had dropped. I searched to find my head, to force it to speak out against such irrational behavior. Words would not follow. I didn't have a case.

"I'm going to sleep," Hazel said. "We should just let the Media Whores finish without us. They could have our part of the guarantee." She stumbled to the van as Alan rushed to challenge her for the better sleeping quarters.

"That's it," George said evenly as we stood alone.

I nodded slowly as a strange sense of fear gripped me.

We eventually wandered in a meandering style to a nearby grassy embankment by Main Street. I collapsed on the cold ground to face the stars overhead. My environment suddenly seemed immense.

"We traveled a long way with this band, Frank," he said. "How many Lawrence bands have reached such a large audience as we did in our prime?"

"Very few," I mumbled coldly.

"It's been a very successful venture. Don't worry, Frank. We'll survive. That's what people like you and I do."

"This isn't how I figured it would all end," I told him. "We never got our return show…I don't know what I'm going to do now."

"Maybe you should write about all this," he suggested. "You'd have to exaggerate everything in it, of course, to make yourself seem like a real warrior. It could be written so it seemed we really roughed it out and got *nothing* in return. Nothing except the babe! You could end it with you meeting a woman."

I dug in my pockets, feeling a scrap of paper wadded amongst the lint. I pulled it out and examined it. "I forgot about this," I said as I handed it to him. "My car is destroyed…"

"Jill, huh?" he said as he read it with a crooked smile. "There you go!"

When I had awaken the next day, Alan was standing tall over the two of us. Another one of those pedestrians…

"See you at the top, motherfuckers," he told the two of us as he dragged his gear down the quiet street.

I sat up, feeling cold and sickly. The Media Whores' van was already running. Several empty wine bottles were scattered throughout the parking lot. It was the first step of many for the Media Whores. They would finish the tour alone, returning to Lawrence as heroes with a record contract. Their first and second albums would be smothered under the grunge explosion, lost in the herd of every record company's quest for the next Pearl Jam. For the Media Whores' third album, Merle took a risk and returned to the sound of his roots, punk rock. He speculated that the trend in popular music would sway that direction. They spent over two years writing the material for what easily could've been their last Empire records release. They recorded a version of *Persistence, Resistance,* the song Stanley and I had written together years earlier. It was the B-side to their first smash hit single. They were the rock and roll sensation of 1994—the year that the critics affectionately called: *The Year That Punk Broke.* Their name would remain on the tongue of the world for many years to come.

George Esposito continued in music only through academics. Neither of us returned to rock and roll.

I fell back asleep, only to be stirred hours later by cold pellets of rain. The Media Whores had already left us behind. Our van sat alone, shrouded in anonymity. Our history would soon follow.

The rain fell hard on my face. It felt painfully cold, and absolutely nourishing to my stiff body. I sat alone, staring up at the gray sky.

The Jerk Offs were one of the most successful hardcore punk bands ever to hail from Kansas. I was certain we would always be remembered, although our past had already faded in the public's eye. The basis of my certainty lie within the reaches of my own eyes. I would be the one remembering, and that's all that really matters.

That's all that ever matters.

We Had Run Miles, While Others Walked

The fragrance of her body teased my better judgment. I had grown accustomed to the scent of her, more so than my own. Sweet, like vanilla. The light reflecting from the pool danced across the silky dress that caressed her body. I felt jealous of its intimacy with her. What I craved couldn't happen here...unless we were to sneak under the properly trimmed hedges that withheld the party.

A jazz quartet supplied the mood as waiters with spicy red bow ties served crackers and cheese and wine. Evening gowns twisted in the breeze like ornate tapestry, bridged by the stiff suits of perfect gentlemen balancing stiff cocktails. Somehow, I was mixed among this crew, if only on her arm. Her natural beauty seeped through her pores like sweat, yanking at my throat with a curiously gentle touch. So elegant, yet so much more. I will always remember...

"Care to dance one last time?" I found myself pleading as the memory slowly disintegrated to the cold corridor of the Kansas City International airport. "Just *one* more time?"

"Guess this is it," the kid tells me as he yanks on my jacket sleeve to consume my attention once again.

I almost forgot he was there.

"Guess so." It occurred to me that I should ask his name, but it made little difference to me. I prefer the anonymity. "Hope you enjoy Kansas."

"Same to you," he tells me gravely. "So...what was the name of your friend that died?"

"His name was Stanley Stockton."

Silence follows. We walk together quietly, absorbing the stale atmosphere. The airport is cold and drab, much as I remember. The landscape outside is a perfect match, suited in gray as always.

"I'm supposed to meet my dad here," he informs me. We slowed to the pace of the pedestrians, waiting for each to acquire their possessions at the baggage claim. The weight over my shoulders contains my life...

"I'm supposed to meet my friend George," I mention.

"Does he live here?"

"No, he's a music theory professor in Colorado."

We stroll down the hallway, slowly, quietly. In the reflection of the window, I watch his clumsy gait next to my rigid stature. He studies every crack on the ground like they were the trenches of alien soil. Every blemish in the walkway captures his attention. His awkward interest in the world reminds me of another time when my path had yet been tread. Maybe room remains for curious wandering... I smile, never allowing my eyes to fall from his haphazard strut.

"Did you buy flowers for Stanley?" he asks.

"No. I felt I should've, but I knew him too well for something so contrived." The thought of it concerns me. I edge closer to my destination empty-handed.

"So was your band very successful?" the young guy asks me.

"Successful?" We approach a row of vending machines. "Depends on how you define such a thing."

"How would *you* define such a thing?" he asks, pausing at the water fountain for a quick sip as the duffle bag tugs desperately on his thin neck.

I glance up at the vending machines. "Success is living with your eyes open." I nod my head and smirk as the memory of my life radiates before me like a spotlight. History has erased its luster, but I remember. I always will. I dig deep into my pocket to retrieve my life's savings. "Here, have one," I tell him as I slide my money into the vending machine's orange slot. The thought of having to skip a meal for this sends a warm chill throughout my rigid body.

"What's this for?" he asks as he slams his fist against the big plastic button. The can plummets through the machine into his bony fingers. The surface of it is cold and sweaty, much like my own. He pops the top carelessly with great finesse. "Are you sure you don't want it? Last chance…"

"I've never been so sure in my life," I respond lightly. "Enjoy it."

"Thanks."

"No problem." We continue down the corridor to the front doors. "Was I successful? *Definitely.*"

He slurps on the soda, squishing it through his cheeks.

"How is it?"

"The taste is pretty consistent," he tells me with snide sarcasm. "Have you ever had a Pepsi?!"

I laugh as we step through the doors. "Never."

The fierce wind knocks us back a step as it howls through the concrete world beyond. Cars rest against the curb, waiting for loved-ones to return with open arms. The amber taillights glisten in the sparkling downpour of frosty condensation.

"There's my dad," he says as he flaps his free hand in the air. He quickly turns to me with a cheery smile. "Thanks for the soda."

"With that pop is a message that I want you to hear, and remember forever."

"Okay," he says. He leans in closer as he takes a quick swig of Pepsi.

"Tonight is a night of your life," I whisper. "Live it while you can."

He nods his head curiously, confused. "Okay."

"Take it easy."

He steps off the curb, clutching the can with a shivering hand. "Don't forget the flowers," he reminds me. "Well, goodbye." He turns and walks across the icy street where an ivory Buick awaits with blazing flashers.

The snow tumbles from the sky in thick clumps, dying upon impact, upon arrival. Yes, it's all about the journey.

He slips inside the Buick and waves happily as the car blends with the traffic. I stand motionless, watching the future move forward around me. It suddenly occurs to me, as the relentless winter wind tosses my clothes like a flag in wartime, that tonight, also is a night of *my* life.

I will live it accordingly.

Coming Summer / Autumn 2001

Details available:
www.flash.net/~layman

Charles Romalotti, wit and writer (pictured here
with the full beard and distinguished brow) has
no awards or education for which to impress you.
He is an avid collector of useless paper. He currently
lives in Austin, Texas and is working on his
second novel, *Rash*.